THE INFINITE ONION

ALICE ARCHER

SHINE

EVEN IF

The Infinite Onion
Alice Archer
www.alicearcher.com
alice@alicearcher.com

Published 2020 by Shine Even If
www.shineevenif.com
publishing@shineevenif.com
1430 Willamette Street, Box 224
Eugene, OR 97401-4049

Cover design: Tracy Kopsachilis Art & Design
Front cover book photograph copyright © iStock.com/ranplett
Front cover circles illustration copyright © iStock.com/Svetlana Kachurovskaia Lanpochka
Back cover and interior blackberries illustration copyright © iStock.com/Liliya Shlapak
Interior circles illustration copyright © Colleen Sheehan
Font Nothing for You copyright © Dafont.com/Agustian Eko Saputro
Font Le Sofia copyright © Dafont.com/Nenny Septiana

Excerpt from *Sex, Lies and Creativity* by Julia Roberts used with permission of the author.
Excerpt from *Part Wild* by Deb Norton used with permission of the author.

First Edition
Library of Congress Control Number: 2020900389

ISBN 978-1-7342493-5-4 (print)
ISBN 978-1-7342493-4-7 (e-book)

Join the

READER LIST

Alice Archer's reader list members get free stories, free peeks behind the scenes, and unique items to accompany the books.

Members are always the first to hear about Alice's new books and giveaways. See the back of the book for details about how to sign up.

For Vashon Island

and the creative clan I was privileged to belong to
there for several years in the 1990s.
I love you yet and forever.

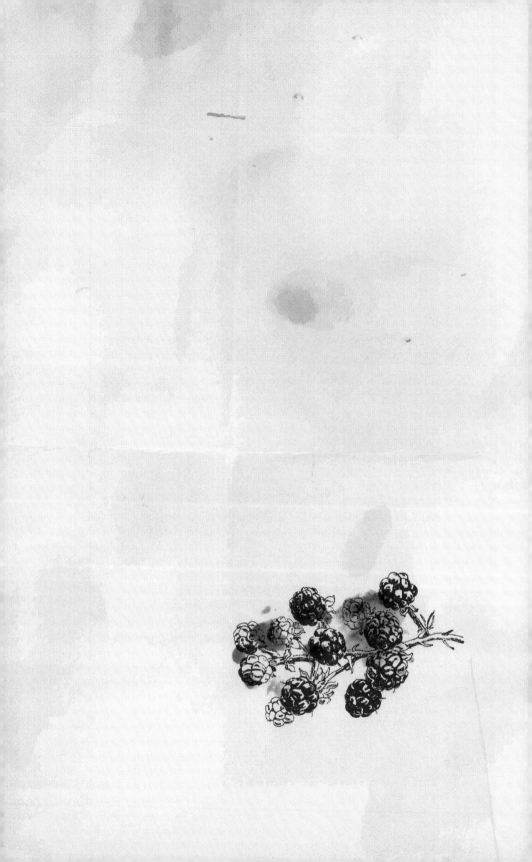

Feeling shame is the exact opposite of feeling creative.

Julia Roberts
Sex, Lies & Creativity

Chapter 1

GRANT

It began with an impulse buy at a gas station grocery store.

I paid for a muffin as big as a baby's head and glared at the two quarters I received as change. Not enough for breakfast from the fast-food counter, but, God, the bacon and eggs smelled good.

The guy behind me in line tapped me on the shoulder. "You done, mister?"

I scanned the crowded countertop. Instead of the beef jerky I was looking for, I found a box of tiny scrolls inviting me to *Start Your Day the Zodiac Way*.

Why the hell not? It would be utter bullshit, but if I couldn't get the food I wanted, I might as well pay fifty cents for a laugh. I dug through the box to find a Cancer scroll for the month of June, paid for it, and went out into the dreary Seattle chill to stand under the awning and read it.

Don't get too attached to your job. The planets picked you to mess with this month. Your best bet for getting through is to get creative.

Maybe I could get my money back, because I sure as hell wasn't laughing. Without my job at the copy center, crap though it was, life would get bleak in a hurry. The planets had better back off. I shoved the scroll into the front pocket of my jeans, pulled up the hood of my jacket, and walked the rest of the way to work.

At random moments that day, I'd find the tight scroll in my pocket and be surprised I hadn't thrown it away. I *did* chuck it once—tossed it into the trash can under one of the cash registers. An hour later, I pawed through the crumpled papers to get it back.

Most of the university students we catered to had fled the scene after commencement over the weekend, leaving me restocking paper behind the counter on a dead Monday, courting The Zone, a state of mind I strived for. No one and nothing could touch me in The Zone. I became a robotic drone, a walking copy center instruction manual, the big guy people called over to reach a high shelf or lift a heavy box. When I wasn't in The Zone, I tended to ask myself why I gravitated to jobs that required so little of me.

Nothing good ever came from asking questions like that.

Five hours into my shift, I ticked off two more items on my to-do list, waved to Marcy, and tapped my watch to let her know I was taking my dinner break. When I dipped into my pocket for the keys to open the door to the staff area, my fingers touched the scroll again.

When was the last time I was creative on purpose?

In February, the store manager had praised me when I'd come up with a solution for a woman who needed a print on a nonstandard canvas size, but I hadn't *felt* creative. I'd barely felt human. I'd been motivated to come up with a solution for the same reason a serf was motivated to over deliver—out of hope for a holiday ham from the bastards in the castle. *Food on the table, baby.*

"Peeved prick on register two." Marcy's voice came through my headset, which I hadn't yet taken off.

"Can't you handle it?" I asked into my mouthpiece. But she had her hands full fitting a new roll onto the spindle of the banner printer. Noah, the new kid, stood at register two, which meant I'd have to deal with it.

"It's a simple print job, for fuck's sake." A middle-aged man in a classy suit leaned across the counter and waved a sheet of paper in Noah's face. "Ten resumes I can be proud to pass around. How difficult is that?" He seemed one curse away from getting physical. *Fix this,* I imagined him saying, *or I will cover your sorry face with paper cuts.* I chuckled at the thought and the man transferred his attention to me.

Noah, frozen with his mouth open, kept his eyes on the threat.

"I've got this." I gently moved Noah aside. With a blink, he closed his mouth and hauled in a breath.

Suit Guy peered at my name tag, which included the words *Assistant Manager,* as did all name tags once an employee passed the three-month mark. "Finally," he said, "someone who's not a fucking idiot."

The zodiac scroll chose that moment to emit a *hey, remember me?* pulse against my thigh. I straightened, curious about my options.

"How about this, *mister*?" I got a bit sarcastic with the *mister*, which was new for me, but Noah looked like he was about to faint, and Suit Guy's attitude pissed me off. "You tell me what the problem is, minus curses and insults, and we'll fix it." I picked up a cream-colored resume from the stack on the counter and scanned it. Lawyer looking for work. Could be tricky. Might even require a bit of creativity. The idea of using creativity to get things back to boring and normal made me release an amused snort I managed to convert to a sniff.

The lawyer's gaze sharpened. "I asked for your nicest resume paper. *This* is shit." He sneered, his curse a glove thrown at my feet. "Flimsy, subpar, loser *shit*."

I set the resume down and withdrew my hands beneath the counter to mime cracking my knuckles like a fighter prepping for a brawl. *Stop it.* I needed the job more than I needed to pretend to be creative. "This is our top-quality stock, sir. What would you like us to do? I'd be glad to give you a full refund."

I thought of all the picky customers I'd placated over my years of working in copy centers—jerks I'd bent over backward to serve when they'd complained and bitched.

The zodiac scroll emitted another pulse.

"Or," I said with a fake smile, "we could redo the job on fetching sunny-yellow card stock. Won't be flimsy. That particular yellow really makes the black ink *pop*. Might get you more action." My snark was inadvisable. So was my wink.

The lawyer's voice hardened. "Show some respect here."

For the first time since long before the divorce, I felt alive. I widened my smile. "I will if you will."

"Grant, what are you doing?" Marcy said through my headset.

The lawyer pointed at Noah. "If you don't fire that incompetent *infant* right now so he doesn't screw up anyone else's career, I will make your life hurt."

I put my hands flat on the counter. "Watch yourself, or I'll ban you from the store."

The Zone was long gone, replaced by a heady, unfamiliar feeling, a surge of power an emperor might lean into as he shook up his realm to sift out the riffraff.

The lawyer poked his finger at me, almost close enough to make contact with my sternum. "Go fuck yourself with a printer cartridge."

"Nice one." I granted him a cool chuckle and adjusted my mouthpiece. "Hey, Marcy, I need you to bring me a printer cartridge and then call the cops." When I played the scene forward in my mind, the threat of cops made Suit Guy back off and turn complacent, and I got to be a hero for a change. In reality, the law-yer's face flushed and his eyes turned mean.

"Wow," I said with a suave detachment I wasn't totally feeling anymore. "That particular color of red doesn't look healthy."

He reached over the counter to grab the front of my company polo shirt. His other hand balled into a fist he aimed at my face. His wild eyes told me he needed an outlet—*any* outlet—for his life's current misery.

Not wishing to be laid up in the hospital without health insurance, which I hadn't had since the divorce, I wrapped a hand around his arm holding my shirt and yanked him forward to pull him off balance. It didn't stop his fist from con-necting with my face, but it deflected the blow.

Nose intact. Left temple not so great.

The physical contact seemed to drain the lawyer's energy all at once. I rushed around the counter to support him. As the victor, I felt I could spare him the indignity of a collapse to the floor from career distress.

Suit Guy was still crying when the cops arrived.

On my delayed dinner break, I sat in the back office and chewed tasteless bites of peanut butter sandwich while I wrote up the incident report required by company policy. I kept having to go back and edit out the swagger.

It felt good to have done something positive. In the six months since Laura had surprised me with the divorce, I'd slogged through a swamp of apathy. I was still waiting for the shock to wear off.

"It's not about you making so little money," Laura had said that day. "If you're not even going to reach for your potential, I don't want to be married to you anymore." She'd had a valid point. It had been easier to leave than come up with a counterargument.

The day after the Suit Guy incident, I was ready to forget all about it, unlike Noah, whose sappy gazes and moony eyes were getting on my nerves. In response, I revised the July work schedule so Noah and I shared only a few shifts. To cel-ebrate, I splurged on a small bag of potato chips from the vending machine in the break room to eat with my peanut butter sandwich.

Partway through my meal, Noah walked in and said in a reverent voice, "There's someone here to see you." He tacked on a belated "sir," which he'd never done before. With my back to the door, Noah didn't see me roll my eyes.

"Thanks," I said without turning around. "I'll be right out."

At first, like a fool, I thought someone had come from headquarters to deliver a commendation. "With gratitude for your courageous protection of a fellow worker," the regional manager might have said as she presented me with a certificate I could tape to the splotchy wall of my motel room.

Someone *had* come from headquarters, but not to deliver the message I'd imagined. Suit Guy had filed a complaint. I was suspended, effective immediately, pending review.

I swiveled in the desk chair to face the wall and hide my expression—a pained squint familiar from testicular exams, back when I'd had annual checkups. And a doctor. And a car to drive to his office.

Ten minutes later, I stood on the sidewalk with a plastic bag of junk from my locker. I couldn't even say I was surprised. Deep down, I'd known my attempt to get creative would end in disaster. What *had* surprised me was my choice to quit instead of wait for the review. The result was no job and no income, compounded by no savings and no prospects.

I turned toward home, such as it wasn't, plodding along in the drizzle. To conserve money, I skipped the bus and walked all the way to the Easy Night Motel, the shabbiest in a series of way-below-average motels I'd called home since I'd moved back to Washington State.

Laura remained in California with her successful life-coaching business and high expectations. I could have retreated to Eastern Washington, where my parents and siblings lived, but those expectations would have been even harder to manage than Laura's.

I walked faster to escape that train of thought, which hurt my chest and made my sore temple throb. What would I do without the comforting void of The Zone? By the time I inserted the key in the doorknob at the motel in the awful end of downtown, I couldn't breathe.

Barricaded behind the closed door, I toppled on the bed in the room's inky darkness. The anvil of rejection pressed me into the mattress. Fear tried to elbow in, but I looked the other way. I could wonder where I'd be in a week, but I wouldn't relive rejections from long ago.

The anxiety attack woke me from a dream of dark shapes and heavy silence into a world not much different. I turned on the TV and got up to take off my boots. I drank cup after cup of water from the bathroom tap, but I couldn't get my lungs to inflate. I pulled the expired health insurance card from my wallet and stared down at it as I sat on the edge of the bed and wheezed.

When Laura had dropped me at the Greyhound station in Santa Barbara, she'd said, "I deserve someone better than you." I was tempted to call her a bitch for that, but I really couldn't, since I agreed with her.

In the motel's cramped bathroom, I took a shower so hot my back seared, but my breathing slowed and my mind finally blanked. I left the TV on and crawled into bed, grateful for another night in the haven of the tiny room.

The next morning, warm and cozy under the covers, I made a new resolution. I'd given creativity a chance and bombed. Going forward, I'd stick to steely logic. Furthermore, I'd stay in bed until I had an actual plan for getting my shit together.

During a mental review of people who might let me couch surf until my next job kicked in with a paycheck, I considered Laura's brother, Mitch, who lived in Seattle, then quickly rejected him. He hadn't liked me even before his sister divorced me. The few times Laura and I had visited Mitch, he'd chatted with her and turned a cold face to me, like it was my fault Laura had made the bad decision to marry me.

I shook my head to dislodge Mitch's judgment and challenged myself to stay in bed until I had a viable plan. But I *really* had to pee. An image came to me of peeing outside. I sat up and put my legs over the edge of the bed. Maybe Mitch *could* help. Best of all, he wouldn't have to know.

I leapt up, did my business in the bathroom, then grabbed my phone and dove back under the covers to find the old email from Laura in which she'd shared news of Mitch and his wife, Sonya, buying a cabin on Vashon Island. We'd visited them not long afterward. They'd taken us to Vashon for lunch and a quick tour of the island. So quick Mitch had only pointed to the driveway of their new property, and then rushed us to catch the next ferry back to Seattle.

Using Google Maps on my phone, I pieced together our route around the island to see if I could pinpoint the location of Mitch's driveway. It had been on the west side. *There.* Off Southwest Huckleberry Lane. Sonya had told us they'd bought the Vashon property so they could spend summers on the island with easy access for Mitch to his downtown law firm.

The Washington State Ferries website informed me of a passenger-only water taxi from downtown. I had a plan. I'd go to Vashon, find Mitch's cabin, try to get in without having to break in, and stay just long enough to clear my mind, breathe some fresh air, and minimize expenses. Also, I could pee outside.

I didn't expect a sojourn to Vashon to help me "reach my potential," as Laura liked to put it. Laura and I both knew me reaching my potential was unlikely if it hadn't happened yet. But if I could slow my downward spiral, I might find another job before my money ran out. Otherwise, my next stop would be a homeless shelter.

I spent one more night in the motel, then hoisted my backpack full of everything I owned and walked down the hill to the dock, where I boarded the 7:40 a.m. water taxi.

The small boat motored southwest toward Vashon, a land mass eight miles wide by thirteen miles long tucked into the southern reach of Puget Sound. We would dock at the north end of the island. At the south end, another ferry ran to the city of Tacoma. I learned all of that from the big map on the wall inside the passenger cabin of the boat.

There were plenty of empty seats, but I didn't feel like sitting. After I read everything on the bulletin board, including the business cards and flyers, the slap of water against the bow and the scent of sea enticed me out to the open-air deck.

The clouds and rain of the previous few days had given way to bright blue water and sky. As we bobbed closer, I picked out a few houses high above us, atop the island's steep sides, amid the greens of springtime. Cool air blew through my hair and filled my lungs.

I couldn't decide what I felt. I was either brilliant or doomed for concocting a plan to squat at Mitch's cabin. More trees clicked into view and excitement won out over anxiety.

Twenty minutes after we'd left the dock in Seattle, a deckhand secured the water taxi to the Vashon dock. A small waiting room building crouched at the end of the dock. Past the building and a row of parking spaces, the main road from the dock curved up and away to the left. Straight ahead, a smaller road ran uphill to a large parking lot and beyond. The Vashon map I'd picked up on the water taxi showed that either road would take me to the town five miles south of the dock.

When the deckhand gestured me forward, I disembarked onto Vashon Island and walked toward the wall of trees.

Chapter 2

OLIVER

I'd almost reached Violetta Road when my phone blared with Talia's ringtone. I accepted the call with one hand and stopped pedaling to coast along.

"Talia? I'm biking home from town with groceries for the freezer. Can I call you later?"

"If that's all you have to say, why did you answer?"

"It's you. I always answer when you call."

"Aw. How sweet. Freddie just boarded as a walk-on."

I fumbled the phone, almost dropped it. Freddie, globe-trotting journalist, my friend-with-benefits, only returned to Vashon to write and repair between long trips abroad. "How does he look?"

"He looks like shit. With a double helping of stinky crap." Talia's nosy nature and her job as a deckhand on the car ferry between West Seattle and Vashon made her a stellar source of gossip. "Where's he back from this time?" she asked.

I didn't answer because I didn't know. "Did you talk to him?" I asked.

"No. I looked for him on my break on the crossing, but didn't find him."

"He probably fell asleep under a table." I stopped at the turn onto Violetta. I'd need both hands on the handlebars on the gravel road. "I have to hang up now."

"Later," Talia said.

I tucked the phone in my pocket and made the turn. As I bumped along I couldn't help lapsing into a preview. Freddie didn't return to Vashon often, but our arrangement had begun right after high school, so I had a lot of good material to draw on.

I followed Freddie's progress in my mind.

He shuffles up to his mother's house on the hill above the north end dock and crashes hard for a few days before he shows up at my place. He arrives at my door well rested, well fed, and too tan for late June in the Pacific Northwest, his curly brown hair freshly cut by his mother, a bag of trinkets for me in his hand. I don't care. Booty call trumps terrible gifts.

Freddie's gift bag drops to the bench by my front door. He sets his hands on my hips to push me back into the house, too busy with me too fast to bother closing the door. I lead him toward the bedroom, strip before we get through the bedroom door. Forget the bed. I lean into him as he hugs me close, kisses me for the first time in months, until I—

Hit a fucking pothole. *Ow.*

The bike seat crowded my swollen happy parts. As a safety precaution, I put my fantasy on hold and stood to pedal faster. As soon as I got home I'd hurl the bike under the carport and retreat to my bedroom to continue the fantasy.

Freddie is back.

Chapter 3

GRANT

"Thanks for the ride," I said to the young man in the old Chevy. He chatted on as I hauled my backpack and the plastic bags of groceries off the back seat.

From the ferry dock, I'd hiked uphill past the big parking lot until I reached the main road, then stuck out my thumb to catch a ride. No one had obliged. I'd walked to town, stashed my pack at the customer service desk in the grocery store, and roamed the aisles to conduct a careful price study.

Grocery bags thumping against my calves, I'd trudged half a mile down Southwest Bank Road before I got a ride from the young guy, who took me all the way to Mitch's driveway.

"Best of luck," he said before he drove off.

Finally. *Silence.*

Well, not exactly *silence.* Birds twittered. A breeze sang through the hemlock and pine trees. My feet crunched on the gravel.

It was a long driveway.

My shoulders hurt from all the hauling. I prayed the cabin had a bathtub. A soak and a meal would go a long way toward rebooting my brain. I'd spend what remained of the afternoon in contemplation of my situation. If my crap cell phone could pick up a signal, and if I had enough credit left on my pay-as-you-go phone plan, I'd start a job search. I didn't expect it to take long to find a new job. All I required was The Zone and enough money to keep my ass out of a homeless shelter. On the other hand, I was a thirty-eight-year-old underachiever who'd been suspended from a menial job and then quit, so maybe the ship of employability had sailed without me.

The driveway ended at a small parking area in front of... I groaned and closed my eyes.

When Mitch had referred to the structure on their property as a *cabin*, I'd pictured a house, cute and complete. It was only a lean-to with nothing to lean against—a pathetic, shabby, off-kilter shack. No way it included a bathtub. Or plumbing.

My concern about how to get inside without breaking anything had been unnecessary. The flimsy plywood door opened with a nudge of my foot to reveal a grungy pallet of blankets, a child-size table with two milk crates for chairs, and a plastic ice chest. My mold meter pinged at *call an ambulance*, and the shack smelled like rat.

With a sigh and a sneeze, I dropped my pack on the stoop and rummaged through the grocery bags. All the food not in a jar or a can went into the ice chest. Instead of taking a long bath, I would fill my afternoon with a trip to town for bags of ice—a fool's errand, since I'd return with bags of water if I didn't get a ride back.

It was naive of me to look for a job in Seattle from Vashon. My phone had limited everything, including limited coverage on the island. No signal and no electricity at the shack meant daily trips to town for ice and to use a computer at the public library.

I arrived on Vashon on a Thursday. By Saturday, I'd contacted a dozen copy shops in Seattle to see if they were hiring, filled out eight online applications, and made zero progress. A few places had openings, but my lack of references and my refusal to say why I'd left my previous job made me a hard sell. I couldn't persuade my phone voice to project enthusiasm.

I also couldn't persuade myself to leave Vashon. Since I got an instant sinus headache whenever I stepped into the shack, I spent most of my time outside walking around. I discovered a view of the Olympic Mountains to the west, out beyond a bright green field. I remembered the names of birds and trees. The rhythm of my footfalls along trails and country roads made me feel like I was going somewhere, like at any moment I might have a thought I'd never had before—and it would be *good*.

Early Sunday afternoon, I moseyed toward the shack after my daily walk-and-hitch for ice and internet, anticipating a lunch of a can of garbanzo beans and a carrot. I came around the last bend of the driveway, lifted my head, and froze.

Mitch leaned against his BMW with his arms folded. I tried to think of a reason for being there that didn't make me seem as pathetic as I was.

"Uncle Grant!"

"Kai. Hey." I dropped the grocery bags to squat and open my arms to Mitch's son. *God, he smelled good*—like innocent child and sweet sweat. I kept the hug short. I'd only managed to bathe with a washrag dipped in water that had once been ice.

"Sorry." I pulled back. "I smell."

"I don't care," Kai said.

I hadn't seen Mitch's youngest son in a few years. The dark circles under his eyes surprised me. I kept my hands on his thin shoulders to study his face.

"Are you trying to figure out how old I am?" Kai held steady under my grip, but his shoulders felt sharp, like he hadn't been eating enough. "I'm already eleven."

"Really?"

The grin Kai graced me with relieved the stress on his pinched face for a moment. The fact that he remembered me and seemed to like me made me feel bad for not keeping in touch with him. "Um. Listen, buddy. I'm sorry I didn't write to you, or call."

"It's okay." Kai shrugged and hugged me again, which made me laugh. When he let go, I stood and looked at Mitch, who pointed up at the trees behind me.

"Security camera," he said. "To keep an eye on the supplies when we start to build."

I turned and saw the camera, high on a wooden pole that blended with the surrounding trees. A flush of embarrassment made me wait a few heartbeats before I faced him again. "I swear I didn't hurt anything. I only came for a quick break, before I head back to the city to... uh."

Mitch cocked his head to the side. "You lost your job? Again?"

"I'm on it, okay? Give me some credit. I'm not trying to mooch off you and Sonya. I just needed a change of scenery to come up with a new game plan, get some breathing room."

"Getting fired is how you take a break?"

Kai put his hand in mine and gave it a squeeze, which I appreciated, even though it made me feel like one of Mitch's sons who'd been a bad boy.

I knew Mitch to be a good man and a good father, although he tended toward seriousness. Whatever was going on with Kai, I couldn't believe it was because of Mitch or Sonya being inappropriate with him. I took the opportunity of my staring match with Mitch to take a closer look at him too. His handsome face seemed to have settled on the worried side of serious.

"Kai." I bent and took Kai's chin in my hand to examine his face again. He let me, watched me with his sad eyes and open face. "Why don't you go ahead down the driveway. I'll join you in a few minutes and we'll take a walk together." I looked up at Mitch. His brow furrowed, but he nodded approval.

Kai whooped and took off.

"Is he sick?" I asked Mitch. "What's going on with him?"

With a shrug Mitch said, "We don't know. The doctor says he's fine physically. Sonya and I decided to move our Vashon plans forward. Maybe a summer on the island and spending more time outside will help him. Sonya can run most of her business from here while she oversees the build. I'll come over as often as I can."

Laura had told me before we divorced that Mitch and Sonya's plans for their summer house on Vashon had stalled because they couldn't agree on a design. Sonya, a white-blond Valkyrie, CEO of her own construction company, had many strong opinions she wasn't shy about sharing. She and Mitch argued constantly—two alphas vying for dominance—but I'd seen the way they regarded each other, the unmistakable banked heat. "They *reach*, as individuals and as a couple," Laura had told me. *Well, life is easier when you're a god*, I'd thought at the time, jealous of their success.

Maybe Kai was waking up to the fact that he was the oddball introvert in a type-A family, which included Kai's sports prodigy older brother, Joel. During my visits with Laura to see Mitch, I'd noticed Kai's reserve while his noisy parents and brother took up all the space.

"Might do Kai good to take a walk with you." Mitch uncrossed his arms. "He talks about you sometimes."

I nodded, pleased. "When do you break ground?"

"In a couple of days. That's why I came over. The crew's coming early tomorrow to prep the site for the trailer."

Another nod was all I could manage.

"They'll raze the shed," Mitch said. "Do you have somewhere else to go?"

When Mitch referred to my current home as a shed, a wave of shame flooded me. The shame made me lie. "Yeah. Sure. Of course. I'll get out of your hair this afternoon."

"Once we're set up in the trailer, maybe you could come over from Seattle for the day."

It wasn't an enthusiastic invitation. It wasn't an offer of a patch of land to camp on or a job as Sonya's gopher. It wasn't even an offer to let me stay overnight in the trailer with them when I visited. And I wasn't Mitch's relative anymore.

"Right, then," I said. "I'll pack my stuff when Kai and I get back." I glanced at the security camera. "Thanks for not kicking me out sooner. You must have known I was here."

Mitch nodded and opened his car door. "Be back in half an hour. We can give you a ride to Seattle." He had his laptop out before I'd turned away.

Chapter 4

OLIVER

The storm rolling in threatened to take away the pleasure of sunlight through trees. I inched along Bast Road, steadied by the bike trailer I'd left on after the morning's yard work. Sun and shadow played over my eyelids like flickers in a bygone cinema. I kept my eyes closed, captivated by the movie's plot. *Dark. Light. Dark. Light.*

I was ten minutes from home when the wind picked up, rushing in from the west over the peninsula. I opened my eyes and pushed harder on the pedals to get home before the rain began.

As I turned onto an overgrown driveway for a house never built, another gust flew down my throat. I coughed it back out, sealed my lips, and made the next turn, a hard left onto a trail to Violetta Road through the shelter of deep woods.

At the edge of the woods, a sunbeam picked out a fern—the cinema's final flicker. I slammed on the brakes and became only thirsty eyes, drunk on the light show starring a sword fern and a boulder.

I snapped a few photos, but they weren't going to be enough. I dug through the pockets of my cargo pants. Pencil. No. Black Sharpie marker. Yes. I took off my sweater and tied it around my waist so I could push up the left sleeve of my T-shirt. The sunbeam flickered and strengthened. I drew fast. Ran out of left arm, started on the thighs of my pants.

The sunbeam shut off.

My heart thudded with the thrill of the gift. I blinked and let the moment go, clipped the Sharpie into my pocket, then fought the wind to redo my hair and get it out of my face.

Two days after Freddie's arrival on Vashon was too soon to expect him, but maybe he'd show up early. I leaned over the handlebars and shot down the Violetta Road hill toward home, spurred on by the mass of dark clouds on the western horizon. The bike trailer chased me with a clatter.

I almost missed it.

With one eye on the clouds, the other on the gravel road, and sweat in both eyes, I almost didn't see the pile of rags in the ditch. It took me a while to stop on the gravel. I rolled back to take a closer look.

In spite of the urgency of the storm, I stood there for a minute to try to make sense of what I saw. And then I spaced out to memorize the vision.

A man slept on his back in the shallow ditch. A boy slept on the man's chest.

Tall grasses curved and bobbed over their heads in the wind. The man's greasy hair was too short to spread over the flattened grass around his head, but the contrast of his black hair and the greens struck me as worth remembering. Black eyelashes touched cheeks pale enough to make me wonder if he was healthy. Dark scruff spread over his jaw. Dark circles curved under his eyes. His pale lips turned down in a frown.

But the way he held the boy made me think *comfort.*

The boy was maybe eight or nine. He flopped face down, arms and legs splayed, like he trusted the man completely. A fall of blond hair hid most of the boy's face. His round baby chin rested on the cobalt blue of the man's T-shirt. The circles under the boy's eyes matched the man's and made the hairs on my arms stand up. They looked abandoned. Castaways holding tight to each other in a tempest.

My breath slowed until it matched theirs, long and even.

I took pictures with my phone, then stared at the castaways again. The photos didn't capture enough. I stared and opened my mind's eye wider to mentally record the scene in more detail. I'd begin with dark pastels on gray paper, draw quick and loose, then switch to charcoal sketches to figure out the composition before I painted. I could explore an alternate vision of Ophelia, the tragic girl from Shakespeare's *Hamlet*, do a riff on John Everett Millais's painting of Ophelia on her back in the water, singing before she drowns, surrounded by nature rendered in lush detail.

As the first drops of rain fell, I took the measure of the black sky and made a decision.

Chapter 5

GRANT

"**Ophelia. Hey**, now. Rise and shine."

I heard the words in my sleep, tried to turn onto my side to make the dream shift, but couldn't breathe. I often couldn't breathe, but in the dream it was different, like a horse had parked on my chest. I opened my mouth to suck in a better breath. When my chest didn't move, I opened my eyes.

That's when the dream got really weird.

"Oh, good," the voice from my dream said. "You stopped playing coy and pretending I'm not here."

"Uh." A shallow cough caught me by surprise and woke me more. I lay on the ground with Kai's head on my chest, the sky a menace above us. I suddenly remembered my life and closed my eyes again, hoping to escape back into the dream.

We'd walked too far. It had been obvious Kai wanted to tell me something, but he wasn't finding the words and I hadn't wanted to let him go.

I was going to deliver Kai late and rain-soaked. Mitch would be angry. I groaned at my ineptitude.

"Nope," said the voice above me. "Wrong answer."

"What was the question?" My first attempt to sit, to get Kai off my chest so I could take a better breath, failed because I needed the breath to make the move.

"I asked if you wanted to get wet," the voice said.

"You did not ask me that," I snapped.

"Feisty, even while being rescued. Intriguing."

I looked up at the voice for the first time and discovered my vision had gone monochromatic while I slept. Amused copper eyes in a tanned face surrounded by a reddish-brown beard and moustache. Auburn hair, tendrils fallen from a messy topknot. All against a backdrop of gray clouds.

The man's mischievous expression pulled me toward something I hadn't wanted in a long while, not since before I met Laura. He made me want to hold my breath and make a wish.

"Cozy ditch?" The man's eyes twinkled.

"Ditch?"

"Activate more brain cells, Ophelia. It's going to pour in two minutes, and we have a bit of a ride. Hop to it."

A fat plop of rain landed between my eyebrows.

"Oh, that landed right on your third eye. You've been anointed. Arise!"

"Do we *know* each other?" I grumbled, too annoyed to be polite.

The man didn't answer except to hold out a long arm covered with black tattoos of ferns. I didn't know what to call the tattoo style—tribal art, prehistoric cave painting, and Renaissance masterpiece, all rolled into one. I couldn't tear my eyes away.

"Drug hangover?" The man asked. "Lost your meds? Escaped a cult? Whatever it is, your first step to a solution is to get vertical."

It bothered me that the host of the strange reality I'd woken to seemed to think I needed to be rescued, even if I did. I ignored his hand, kept one arm around Kai, and rolled to my side. *Poor little fellow.* Whatever bothered Kai must have kept him from getting enough sleep.

Without Kai's heavy weight on my lungs, it was easier to think about what to say. I set Kai on his unsteady feet on the road and straightened up. It pleased me to find out I was taller than the auburn-haired man by a good five inches.

He squatted in front of Kai and said, "Hey, soldier. Want to hop in?"

I moved to stop the man from sucking up to Kai, but my brain blanked when I saw his leg tattoos. *His tattoos bled through his pants.* Wait. Probably not tattoos, then. A Sharpie hung in a side pocket of his pants. *Creative guy.* The realization dampened my attraction.

Kai mumbled and turned his head into my stomach, my comrade in crankiness.

I looked around to see how far we'd walked from Mitch's place. The gravel road extended to the horizon in both directions. Hell, no wonder Kai had needed a nap. He sagged harder against my legs.

Before I could stop him, Copper Man scooped up Kai and set him in a trailer attached to a bicycle.

"*This* is the ride? In a bike trailer?" I felt too weary to suppress my disdain.

"Yep. Climb in, unless you want to walk in the rain to wherever you're headed, which can't be close, 'cause there's no one out this way but me."

More rain splatted onto my head. I looked around for any option other than the humiliation of climbing into a tiny trailer to be hauled away like a load of garbage by an artistic hippie, but there was nothing except fresh, damp nature as far as the eye could see. A field of tall grass sloped down to a wall of evergreens. Though I felt weary to the bone, the beauty gave me a jolt of hope. I drew in a slow breath and wondered what bargain I'd have to make with what god to be a king in the country instead of a serf in the city.

I met Copper Man's amused gaze. He stood beside the trailer with his arms folded, waiting for me to get my act together.

"Uncle Grant." Kai curled into a ball in the trailer. "I'm cold."

I shed my leather jacket before Copper Man could untie his sweater from his waist. "Sit up," I told Kai. When he did, I draped the jacket around his shoulders.

"It's not far," Copper Man said. He put a leg over the bike. "Then I can give you a ride in my van to wherever you need to go."

I squeezed into the trailer, only because my humiliation, like the cold rain, threatened to turn pervasive and bitchy. I just wanted it to be over. Kai huddled between my knees and I hugged him close to warm him up.

"All set?" Copper Man asked.

"I guess." I knew I sounded like an ungrateful ass, but I was too disappointed in myself and worried about the impending lecture from Mitch to care what a stranger thought of me. As soon as we got out of the rain I'd call Mitch. I patted my jacket pocket, to make sure I hadn't left my phone in the ditch.

The bike wobbled and slid in the gravel for a few yards. We bounced along at a sharp clip that rattled my vertebrae, heading farther from Mitch's property. A lone driveway came into view on the right. *24281 Violetta Road*, according to a fancy sign hung from a big mailbox. A red flag flapped on a pole beside the mailbox. We stopped long enough for Copper Man to unclip the red flag, stuff it into the mailbox, pull out a green flag, and clip it on.

The creative vibe emanating from the dude exhausted me.

"Almost there," he said in his clear voice. "You okay back there?"

No. Rain began to seal the shoulders of my T-shirt to my skin. My butt bones hurt more with each bump of the trailer. The driveway went on forever, around curves, up and down hills.

I stared up at Copper Man's back. He didn't seem winded in the least. His wet T-shirt hugged the moving planes of his back. I hated him for a moment for knowing how to get things done.

The crunch of gravel, the racket of the trailer, the rush of wind and rain made raising my voice to answer his question seem like too much effort.

As we started up a short rise, the irksome man began to whistle a tune so bright with unwarranted cheeriness it made my skin crawl.

Chapter 6

OLIVER

We didn't beat the rain. I ushered the big grouch and the sad boy into my house, where they dripped on my doormat.

"Hang on. Let me grab us some towels." I shucked off my boots and trotted across the great room to the linen closet to grab a hand towel for myself and two of my biggest, fluffiest bath towels for my guests. I tried to hand one to the man with the anxious face—who hadn't stayed on the mat by the door.

"That's not necessary." He waved away the towel, as though he suspected it to be disease-infested, then frowned at his cell phone and dripped all over the rug my grandmother had brought over from Italy.

The boy, on the other hand, entered my home fully present and accounted for. He took off the man's leather coat and handed it to me in trade for the towel, which he draped around his shoulders like a cape, as I'd done with my towel. Mouth open, he turned in a circle to examine the great room's combined living room, kitchen, and art corner.

While the boy gawked, I hung the coat on a hook by the front door and took my first good look at him. Scrawny. Shoulders slumped under the weight of the world, too much weight for his age. His gape landed on me and bloomed into a grin.

I smiled back and flopped onto the couch.

The boy sprinted to me with no hesitation and sat right next to me, as if all it had taken was one good look at my home for him to know that *of course* we were friends.

And so we were.

"Hi," I said. "I'm Oliver."

"My name is Kai. It's very nice to meet you."

His earnest formality almost made me laugh. I wrapped his towel around him tighter, indulging my impulse to turn him into a burrito. "Well, what do you think?" I asked.

Kai wiggled deeper into the couch cushions. "I think you have a lot of really interesting things."

"What else do you think?"

With a happy sigh, maybe from being asked what he thought, Kai said, "You must have a lot of fun in here."

"That I do. Want to ask me about anything in particular?"

"Yes, please. Tell me about *that*." He pointed to the corner of the room. "That's the *first* thing I want to know about." He squirmed sideways and studied my face as he waited for my answer.

His haircut and clothes—button-up shirt, chinos with pleats, and leather lace-up boots—told me he wasn't neglected, at least not in that regard. But his pallor and the melancholy in his soulful eyes suggested there was more to the story.

Kai offered me a shy smile with a lot of love in it, which hurt my heart and made me wish I could keep him and his uncle around a bit longer to figure them out. Maybe to help.

"It's a stage," I said with a nod toward the corner Kai had pointed to.

"Like for doing a play?"

I nodded. "My dad and my granddad and I built it when I was ten."

Kai up straighter. "Really? I'm eleven already."

That surprised me, and made me wonder how Kai fared at school. Eleven could be brutal for small, serious types.

"Could you show me how to build a stage?" Kai asked.

"I would love to."

"Okay. But I have to ask my mom." The joy vanished from his face. "She builds things. She might want to do it a certain way."

"Well, there are lots of different ways to build a stage."

"I guess." Kai pulled himself together. "What do you do on it?"

"Whatever I want to."

That made the smile bloom again. "Like... make up stories? Then do them on the stage?"

"Yep. Or make things up right when I'm doing them."

"Oh." Kai's cheeks flushed, like that was the best idea he'd ever heard.

I looked again at his clothes. Golf at the country club might not be Kai's choice for a future. Someone had aimed him toward an adulthood too far off to be that predictable.

"Does it make you feel better? When you make things up on the stage?" Kai asked.

"Indeed."

With a glance at his uncle, Kai said, "Even if you feel sad?"

Together we watched Ophelia drip on the carpet and mutter into his phone.

"Even if you feel sad?" Kai prompted, since I hadn't answered.

"Yep. Do you want to do something on the stage now? Do you feel sad?" I was sure the answer would be yes, but Kai surprised me.

"No." He shook his head and slumped against me a little. "I mean... I do want to play on the stage, but Uncle Grant *needs* to. Mom and Dad let him stay on our property for a while, but..." The crease in Kai's pants suddenly needed to be finger-ironed. "I don't think Uncle Grant has anywhere else to go."

Grant must've heard Kai say his name. "What?" He lifted his head and scowled. "Kai," he said in a sharp voice. "Get up from there. Right this instant."

Kai turned to look at me with his brows furrowed.

With a shrug, I said, "I don't get it either, kid. But you'd better get up. We wouldn't want Uncle Grant to have a brain seizure because you're sitting on my couch and we're having a conversation, would we?" I stood up.

Kai tittered, but stood with me. We faced Grant as if awaiting further orders. I couldn't help myself.

"Private Kid and Petty Officer Oliver reporting for duty, sir, yes, sir!" I barked out with a salute. Kai got into the act, straightening up to snap off his own crisp salute.

The disapproval on Grant's face shifted to something more like loneliness. He huffed. "Oh, for Pete's sake." To Kai, he said, "Your dad's coming to pick us up."

I tried to catch Grant's eyes. Big, dark eyes, but not Bambi-big, and not inno-cent. I watched him examine my home with a frown and a protective hunch of his shoulders. His greasy black hair stood up in the back. Bits of bright grass hung from the backs of his pant legs. Between his eyes, a worried crease pointed down to an assertive statement of a nose, straight except for a slight bump near the top. He was taller than my six feet by quite a bit, with *long* legs, and muscles that made me think he did a lot of walking. Dark eyebrows scrunched with concern. His untrusting gaze landed on me.

Whatever Grant had seen as he looked around my home had a different effect on him than it had on Kai.

"What the hell is this place?" The question almost sounded rhetorical, like Grant didn't need me to respond in order to know the answer, and the answer was that I was a nutjob.

Kai slapped a hand over his mouth and said from behind it, "Uncle Grant, you said *hell*."

I nudged Kai's shoulder with my elbow and whispered, "So did you," which made him giggle.

To Grant, I said, "You must have put on the wrong pair of glasses this morning, Ophelia, if you can't recognize heaven when you're standing right in the middle of it."

"Stop calling me that."

"I might," I said. "Or I might not." It had been a long time—*years*—since I'd gotten on anyone's nerves. Or enjoyed it so much. For some reason, Grant didn't like me, and that *thrilled* me. Strangers didn't often stumble into my corner of Vashon Island. Especially not ill-tempered specimens I yearned to paint pictures of. I hoped Grant and Kai lived on Vashon at least part of the year. Maybe then I could persuade them to visit again.

"Do you want something hot to drink?" I asked.

Grant shook his head, his face hardened in a staunch *no*.

Ah, well. Maybe it was for the best. The man would be a prickly project for sure.

"Suit yourself," I said. "But if you hadn't wanted me to give you a ride, why didn't you call Kai's dad from the ditch? You'd be the same amount of wet."

Grant was almost out the front door by then, his hand on Kai's shoulder blades to rush him. Without turning, he grabbed his coat from the hook and muttered, "Took me a while to wake up."

"Keep working on it," I called out.

The front door closed with a bang, leaving a whirlwind of barbs in the air.

I smiled, satisfied with my work.

Too hungry to change out of my damp clothes just yet, I started in on the baking project I'd planned, humming around the kitchen as I gathered what I'd need.

All the while, ferns in a rogue ray of sunlight shifted along my arms. In my imagination, I overlaid colors and tweaked shadows and lines to pose the ferns over a weary man and a mournful boy asleep in a stream.

Sadness and sunshine.

Dark. Light. Dark. Light.

Chapter 7

GRANT

I shut the door with more of a slam than I should have, considering the guy had tried to help us. I paused, but decided it didn't matter. *That guy*, for all his helpfulness and interesting looks, rubbed me the wrong way. So what if he thought I was a brute. I'd be on a ferry within the hour, getting up my nerve to ask Mitch to ask Sonya if she needed help at the construction site.

A review of my nonexistent construction site skills gave me a stomachache.

Kai stood on the covered porch and stared out over the driveway. He must have heard the faint clatter from inside the house, because he dashed over to peer into one of the windows facing the porch. After a moment, he smiled and waved.

When I'd looked up after talking with Mitch and seen Kai smile as he cuddled beside the weirdo, I'd felt... *stuff*. Suspicion. Jealousy. Attraction. Humiliation.

I was a mess.

I'd been too focused on assuring Mitch we were okay to take in the room until I got off the phone. *Eccentric artist* summed up the decor, with an addendum of *bulldoze it*.

Outside, I felt safer and less overwhelmed. Until I realized the eccentric artist decor extended outdoors. Sculptures studded the driveway and the yard. If Copper Man's home was the result of being creative, it was good he lived in the country on an island. In the real world, where I had to earn a living, he would stand out to a dangerous degree. I tried to imagine him in downtown Seattle on a weekday, with his excess of hair and his Sharpie tattoos. If he walked into the copy shop—probably to ask us for something so unusual and complex we'd have to... I didn't know what. Send him away unsatisfied. Or get creative ourselves.

The circular nature of my internal rant whirled me into thin air and I turned to look at Kai, who'd put my coat back on. I dug through the coat pockets to find my wool cap and tugged it down over Kai's head.

His grateful smile drew me down to squat with my back against the house between two of the windows. I drew him close and put my arms around him. The cautious breath I drew against Kai's frail back didn't make me cough. In spite of the pile of steaming crap the day had delivered, and more crap to come when Mitch arrived, air flowed in and out of my lungs nice and easy. My exhales bled tension from my shoulders.

For a few minutes of silence, I studied the sculpture of a giant wooden chainsaw in the middle of the driveway roundabout. Perhaps the sculpture was ironic. The sorry state of the high hedge beyond the roundabout made me wonder if it had been trimmed in Kai's lifetime. The combination of untamed yard, well-cared-for house exterior, and in-your-face art made my brain whimper.

Kai shuffled his feet. "You didn't have to be mean to Mr. Oliver."

"I wasn't mean." I reviewed my interactions with Copper Man, whose name was apparently Oliver, with more attention. "Okay, so I wasn't as nice as I could have been. But he was mean too."

"He wasn't."

"Sure he was. He kept calling me Ophelia."

"He was teasing. He was *nice*. You were *mean*. And I *liked* him." Kai must have had enough of my attitude, because he took a small step forward, turned to face me, and folded his arms over his skinny chest. The arms of my coat flapped like seal flippers.

I wasn't mean. Even the voice in my head sounded defensive. I tried harder to find traction for my stance, but spun out, which left me right where Kai already knew me to be.

"You're right," I said. "I was mean to him."

"You should go and apologize."

I narrowed my eyes at him. "Who raised you?" I teased.

"*Duh.* Mom and Dad."

"Right. That explains it." For all their opinions and argumentativeness, Mitch and Sonya were sticklers for manners and appearances. I wondered if Kai's troubles had to do with the strain of *appearing* correct while *feeling* incorrect.

Kai took my hand and pulled to get me to stand, then pushed me to the door.

I gave a perfunctory knock, opened the door, and stuck my head inside. At first, I couldn't locate Oliver amid the wall-to-wall mayhem. My gaze blew past enormous potted trees, overlapped rugs, three thousand pillows, and a driftwood floor lamp. The orange upholstery of the gigantic couch burned my retinas. Framed photos and artwork covered every inch of the walls. Built-in bookshelves in the far left corner held what looked like art supplies, stereo components, musical instruments, and... I tore my eyes away from a row of animal skulls.

The room only had four walls, but that one look around felt like an endless day at a craft fair with Laura. *After* the divorce.

French doors to my left led to a covered side porch. In the near left corner of the room, a stage extruded into the living room area. *For Christ's sake.* I rolled my eyes, saw more crap hanging from the rafters, and called it quits. Instead of looking for Oliver in the melee, I closed my eyes to listen. When I heard a cabinet door shut, I opened them. The sound had come from straight in front of me.

Oliver crouched in the open kitchen area, in the aisle between two long counters ending at a back door.

My determined march across the living room to get my apology over with faltered when I noticed the wet spot on the carpet where I'd stood to talk with Mitch. I grabbed the folded towel I'd refused off the back of the couch and paused to pat it over the wet spot. A glance at Kai told me he was checking up on me.

"Hey again," Oliver said. He sent over a wry grin from where he rummaged through a low cabinet jammed with pots and pans. "Change your mind about the ride?"

"No."

"Then why don't you wait inside? I'm making hot chocolate."

Kai appeared at my elbow. "Yes, please."

"No," I said again, then remembered my manners. "But... thank you for the offer. I only wanted to... er, apologize for being... a bit gruff before."

"No problem," Oliver said.

Kai scowled up at me. It made him look like a scary Mitch doll. That look meant my apology had been subpar. I shrugged him off. A moment later, when Kai spoke up on my behalf, I wished I'd done a better job.

"Uncle Grant is going through a rough patch," Kai told Oliver, "because Aunt Laura refused to budge an inch."

Oliver's burst of laughter rattled the pots in his hands.

"Who told you that?" I asked Kai.

After a deeper reach into the cabinet and a final clatter, Oliver straightened with a stack of muffin tins and grinned at us.

"Dad said it to Mom," Kai said.

"Christ." I turned away toward the door. "Come on, Kai. We're done here." Not wanting to chance Kai running any more of the show, I lifted him into my arms and hastened out to the porch so I could close the door—firmly but quietly—on my embarrassment.

Oliver's smile followed me, wreathed as it had been in hair and beard and eyes the color of sunlit pennies.

I spent the next ten minutes teasing Kai to get back in his good graces.

Kai spent those same ten minutes with his nose against the window. According to his reports, Oliver made the hot chocolate—"He dropped a *whole bar of chocolate* right in the pot!"—and moved on to doing stuff with flour and butter and "more muffin tins than even Mom has."

By the time Mitch pulled up, the peace I'd found in my days alone on Vashon had degraded to a memory of a vacation in a previous lifetime.

Kai turned away from the window. His smile as he took my hand and looked up at me brought me a small relief. Adding Kai to the list of people disappointed in me was not an option.

Chapter 8

OLIVER

When I heard a car splash along the driveway and stop, then voices, I crossed the room to crouch behind Matilde, matriarch of the ficus trees, and watch the show outside. Maybe Grant would display more of his entertaining defensiveness. He'd wanted me to see *tough* and *badass*, but I only saw *hurt* and *desperate*. Defeat percolated through the man's every word and gesture.

Kai's dad left the fancy car's motor running and didn't get out. I shifted my focus to Grant and Kai on the porch. Neither of them made a move to go down the steps.

Kai looked up at Grant and took his hand, as if to offer reassurance.

After another minute of stasis, the car went quiet. My first reaction to the man who emerged was that I didn't like him. He opened the rear door of the car and pulled out a green-and-white golf umbrella. It was obvious he was Kai's dad, because Kai was dressed like a carbon copy of him. Maybe a child's set of golf clubs lay in the trunk alongside Dad's. Though I'd only talked with Kai a few minutes, I suspected a disconnect between Dad's view of Kai and Kai's view of Kai.

Through the inch of open window at my nose, I heard Dad say, "Let's go." He waved a hand at the car and frowned to let us all know how serious he was. "Come on. We missed one ferry. If we hustle, we can make the next one. I need to stop at the office before dinner."

No movement from the porch.

Dad didn't seem angry. More like concerned, with a side helping of impatience. A man with a plan, and no fan of deviations. He finally got the message that compliance would not be automatic.

"What's going on?" Dad's gaze lowered, perhaps to Grant and Kai's joined hands.

I wished I could see Kai and Grant's faces.

Dad gestured at the car. "I packed up your stuff, Grant. We can drive straight to the ferry."

Grant shook his head.

"Let's discuss it in the car," Dad said. "I'll help you with a job plan."

Fuck. Grant's life *sucked.* No wife, no home, no job. I sprang up and made my way to the door, unwilling to let them go before I got some answers.

With a bright, "Hey there," I stepped onto the porch and put my hands on my hips. "You must be Kai's dad. I'm Oliver Rossi." Instead of going down the porch steps to offer my hand to shake, I stayed put. I wanted to maintain the high ground as the drama played out.

Dad nodded but didn't offer his own name. *Quick thinker.* I needed a name so I could find out where his property was on Vashon. I hoped it wasn't far. I liked Kai. I knew some kids his age he might enjoy being friends with—kids interested in things like art and theater. Kids who dressed like kids.

"Do you live on Vashon?" I asked Dad.

He gave me a look of disapproval, like I'd asked him for access to his trust fund.

I smiled and held his gaze.

For the first time, Dad seemed to really see me. His scrutiny paused on my arms, moved up to my long hair and beard with palpable dismissal. It made me feel perversely happy.

Perceptive Kai spoke into the cold void, in a rush of words, maybe because he knew his Dad would shut him down. "My dad's name is Mitch Martensen. Our Vashon property is on Southwest Huckleberry Lane. Mom's building us a house there this sum—"

"*Kai,*" Dad interrupted. "We do not share our personal business with strangers."

I folded my arms to put my drawings front and center for Dad and waggled my eyebrows at Kai. "And I'm more strange than the average stranger, right?"

A laugh burst out of Kai's mouth. He let go of Grant's hand and came to me with his right hand held out. "Mr. Oliver, thank you very much for rescuing us and for letting me see your house and your stage. I'm really sorry I didn't get to have any chocolate-bar hot chocolate, but it's been a pleasure anyway."

Sheesh. This kid. I shook Kai's hand, but he lunged in for a hug. When I leaned to wrap him up for a moment, Dad's worried frown turned stony with disapproval. I let go of Kai and took a step toward the stairs down to the driveway so I could get a look at Grant's face.

So much going on there.

I resisted the urge to dash inside for a sketchbook.

With defeat in his eyes, Grant met Kai with a hug and a whispered, "I hope I'll see you again soon, buddy."

"But you're coming with us." Kai removed Grant's cap and coat and handed them to him. "Didn't you hear Dad?"

"Get in the car now, Kai. I won't ask again." Dad used a tone that made Kai scoot out of Grant's embrace, shoot past me, and run through the rain to the car. Dad held a palm out sideways for Kai to slap on his way past. No hint of anything amiss in their interaction. No sense there would be a beating later if Kai didn't comply. Only the firm rule of a respected father.

"I'm not going with you," Grant said. He squeezed the knit cap in his hands and then yanked it down over his head.

Mitch shrugged and turned back to the car. He held the umbrella over the trunk and started hauling stuff out one-handed. First out was a backpack. *Fuck,* it was big. Grant rushed off the porch to fetch it and bring it back to the porch. Meanwhile, Mitch pulled out plastic bags of what looked like cans of food and set them on the driveway. Next out were cloth shopping bags with what looked like clothing sticking out of them. Grant hustled to take the cloth bags before they hit the wet gravel.

Mitch closed the trunk, got in the car, and drove away.

Kai waved through the back window.

And I was alone with Grant and his mountain of belongings.

Chapter 9

GRANT

Relieved I didn't have to leave Vashon yet, I began to pull things out of my backpack to repack so I'd be able to carry everything.

On the walk from the ferry, I'd passed a motel with a for-sale sign tacked onto the vacancy sign. Maybe they needed me as much as I needed them. If I'd asked Mitch to drop me there, he would have blown past it, intent on doing what he thought best for me.

I glanced up and saw Oliver studying me. "What?" I snapped.

"Nothing."

"Liar. You're looking at me like you want to scold me."

"Am not." Oliver's glower deepened. He folded his arms.

"You look at me like I'm a bad man, which I may be, but you're a baby," I sneered up at him. "You live in a beautiful house your parents probably gave you. Believe me, my life bears no resemblance to yours, so don't think you can *relate*."

Oliver narrowed his eyes. His eyebrows were the *exact* color of his eyes. Russet. Like dried leaves. "You're wrong," he said. "And you're rude."

I didn't need arguments. I needed *peace*. Before Mitch kicked me off his property, I'd walked every day through the trees and felt so much better. *Nature doesn't judge.*

"I haven't figured out my life," I told Oliver, "but I don't care enough about your opinion to have a conversation with you about it."

Oliver didn't like that. I could tell by the way he shoved his hands into his pockets and stared down the driveway. "Where will you go?"

"I have a date with a tree."

"Well. That sounds... kinky."

I folded and rolled the clothing Mitch had stuffed into his fancy cloth shopping bags, then stuffed the clothes and the bags into the pack. "Go inside and leave me alone."

"But... you need help."

Shame threatened to overspill the careful banks I'd constructed to keep it from flooding my life. I stood and took a few steps to get into Oliver's space. "We met a few minutes ago. Remember?"

Oliver swallowed and looked down. "I remember."

I leaned in and waited, noted the subtle freckles scattered across the sharp ridge of his nose.

When Oliver looked up at me again, I said, "Leave. Me. Alone."

The curiosity and concern on Oliver's face shifted to hurt. He nodded, lips tight within the glint of facial hair. He turned away and went inside.

By the time I'd emptied all the bags, the backpack bulged at maximum capacity. I stood to take the measure of the weather. The rain had picked up to a steady drum of white noise.

Late afternoon's dull light under the thick clouds weighed on me as I watched from the top of the porch steps. I wanted to leave, to be alone, to hike to a paved road and hitch to town, but I hadn't eaten since breakfast, the motel was miles away, and I was so damn tired.

I sat on the top step with my knees in the rain. The longer I sat, the heavier I felt, and the more energy I wasted trying to deny the obvious.

I needed Oliver's help after all.

Chapter 10

OLIVER

He called me a liar.

I didn't know Grant, but he didn't know me either.

When I went inside, I locked the front door. The doors hadn't been locked in years. It made me feel like a prisoner. I went back and unlocked it.

I vowed to have forgotten Grant by the time I put my afternoon snack on the table. Forget the way his anger veiled a mystery. Forget his fumbling navigation through a world that, I guessed, had rejected him for a long time. Forget the way he hid in plain sight and expected so little. I *wanted* to forget him. I could do it. I didn't even know his last name.

Grant and his life were none of my business.

After long minutes hunched over the kitchen sink staring at blueberries in the colander, sifting them through my fingers, watching light from the window play over the water and the dusky blues, I figured we were all—the berries and I—clean enough.

I decided to set the table with grandeur.

A grand table for one, please.

Chapter 11

GRANT

Oliver blinked a few times when he opened the door. "What now?" he asked in a tight voice. He nodded at my backpack. "You're probably an okay person beneath all the grouch, but we haven't known each other long enough to move in together."

I ignored his comment and downed the bitter pill of asking for help. "I'll take you up on that offer of a ride now."

"No, thanks," Oliver said, and closed the door in my face.

I blanked for a few seconds, then lowered my pack to the porch and opened the door to follow him inside. My request hadn't been wreathed in pretty bows, but his brusque response still surprised me. "Excuse me?"

"You're excused."

I tromped around the edge of the carpet to get to the kitchen area where Oliver stood at the counter.

He dumped a bowl of blueberries into a bigger bowl with goop already in it. Distracted by wondering how many people he planned to feed, I didn't say anything. I got distracted again when he dumped an obscene amount of what looked like white candy on top of the blueberries and started to stir everything together with slow strokes. When he was done with that, he set paper bowls into the cups of eight muffin tins lined up beside the mixing bowl and started to scoop the glop into them.

He acted like I wasn't even there.

My mouth watered.

Jesus. I needed to *immediately* dig out my can opener and a can of beans from my pack and *eat.* "Why won't you give me a ride? You offered."

I could tell by the tight set of Oliver's shoulders that I'd strained his hospitality.

"I'm sorry," I said. "Again. For being rude. I'm not having a very good day."

"I'll give you a ride after we eat."

I wasn't up for making stilted conversation with someone who had the leisure time to spend an afternoon baking candy cupcakes, but the warmth of the room tempted me. I took off my cap and peered out the window over the sink. Murky light seeped through the rain and thick cloud cover. "Is this a late lunch or an early dinner?" Whatever it was, I decided I was going to take it. *Beggars can't be choosers.*

Oliver shrugged and continued to use a measuring cup to transfer batter into the muffin tins. He was patient and neat about it. I calmed as I followed his careful movements. Neither of us said anything until he'd used a spatula to scrape the last of the batter into the last paper cup.

Four tins went into the oven. I expected Oliver to start washing up, but he picked up another muffin tin and walked it to... another oven.

"You have two ovens?"

"Nope."

My interlude of calm ended with a spike of irritation. "For Christ's sake. I know you don't want me here, but you don't have to be a dick about it."

"I don't have two ovens, I have three," Oliver said in a steady voice. He pointed toward the far end of the kitchen counter.

The fire-engine red of the oven hurt my eyes. "How did I miss that?" For retinal relief, I glanced up and saw a dartboard on the back door, past the end of the kitchen area. "That's really unsafe. What if someone walked in after you'd already thrown the dart?"

"Like who?" Oliver asked.

I walked over to get a better look at the paper pinned to dartboard. It was a crude drawing of a hairy spider. "What's this about?"

"Beast of the month," Oliver said.

"Man, you have got too much time on your hands if you... What in the ever-loving *hell* is that?" In the corner by the back door, a wire cage higher than me kept a pile of junk in check. "Why not go ahead and take out your trash?"

Oliver's bark of laughter came from right behind me. I turned to see him set a handful of cutlery on a small table beneath the window at the end of the kitchen counter.

"It's not garbage." Oliver bent to straighten the placemats. The mass of his hair in its bun glittered gold in the dull light coming through the window.

I took a step back, and then another. The first step brought Oliver's whole body into view. The word *svelte* popped into my head, along with *sleek* and *sturdy*. And then *annoying*, which brought me back to reality. A third step back made the ends of the darts poke me between the shoulder blades. *Wake-up call.*

"Ouch," I said, but I stayed where I was.

The last time I'd been attracted enough to a man to want to do something about it, I'd been in my early twenties. The fact that I didn't even *like* Oliver didn't keep my body from trying to sway toward him.

With practiced movements, Oliver grabbed stuff from drawers and cabinets without needing to look. He moved with a grace that made my words dry up, and he didn't rush to fill the space with conversation, which was good. My internal argument required my full attention.

Oliver the entitled busybody repelled me. But his tanned ears lay flat against his head, and I really wanted to touch his hair. Toned arms. Hips loose as he moved. Small, firm ass. Was I mistaken, or had I sensed a hint of interest in his gaze, back at the ditch, before I'd gotten rude?

I closed my eyes to confront the thought. If I got up the nerve, I could toss a rope, see if Oliver caught it, see if he was interested. He lived way the hell out in the woods. Maybe he was desperate for a little something physical. *I can help with that.*

"That's Happy Hollow," Oliver said.

It took me a few seconds to figure out Oliver's statement wasn't a lewd response to my train of thought. "You *named* your indoor garbage heap?"

"Not garbage. Safe haven for hollow things—gourds, piñatas, papier mâché creations."

I took a closer look at the crap in the wire container. "Also," I pointed out, "a wasp's nest."

Oliver shrugged. The memory of Kai's insistence that I'd been mean gave me pause. I took a deep breath and tried to nudge my ridicule toward curiosity.

"Do other areas of your house have names?" I asked. "I promise I won't make fun of you if you tell me."

"I don't care if you make fun of me." Oliver nodded over his shoulder toward the red stove—a beauty with six burners, a grill top, and two ovens.

"Stoviet Union," Oliver said.

My laugh exploded into the air. The vast room absorbed it to silence.

I pulled out a chair at the table and sat, so I wouldn't keel over from hunger or burgeoning lust. As I watched Oliver transfer most of the fridge's contents to the kitchen counter, I wondered what it would be like to be him, to have so many things, and a house and enough income to keep it all.

When Laura and I married, she'd offered to support me until my career got off the ground. I'd pondered the conundrum of a career for myself while her coaching business grew. She bought a house, then a bigger house. My name wasn't on the paperwork, but that wasn't why those houses never felt like mine. From the beginning, I'd suspected Laura and I wouldn't be in it for the long haul. We married anyway, stayed married until she excised me with a surgical cut. I couldn't blame her for taking a stand.

Envy of Oliver and humiliation about the years Laura wasted on me put starch in my voice. "Why is your place like this?"

"Like what?"

"You live in..." I struggled for something polite to say. "A freak show." And failed.

"Excellent." The gleam in Oliver's eyes seemed genuine.

"You *like* it when I insult your home?"

"I don't give a damn what you think of my home. I like it when you're honest."

"You don't know when I'm being honest," I said.

Oliver paused to watch me with his intent gaze. It *almost* made me squirm.

"What are you?" I asked. "Some type of multimedia artist?"

"Sometimes. Mostly oil painting. I also teach and consult."

"Consult to help people do what?"

One of Oliver's straight eyebrows lifted in amusement. "Unclench."

I snorted. "Right. What's on your business card? Oliver What's-His-Name, Senior Ass-Stick Remover?"

Oliver set two plates—one red and one purple—on the green placemats. I took my elbows off the table and sat back, but Oliver kept his hands on the plate in front of me and turned his face toward me. We were eye to eye when he said in a low voice, "Hey, if the stick fits."

I did my best to ignore the fact that every single muscle in my body was, in that moment, clenched—from my sore feet to my sore shoulders and neck, and everything in between, including my asshole.

"You know what?" I said. "If you don't want to have a conversation, I can wait on the porch until you're done eating."

Oliver straightened and moved away.

Whatever creative shit Oliver did for a living, if his lifestyle was the result, I wanted the opposite of creativity. I wanted streamlined and spare. Minimalist and austere. Nature and peace. Not a chaos of stoves, throw pillows that mated and multiplied, indecipherable lawn sculptures, and nowhere easy for the eye to land. No matter how attractive I found Oliver physically, I needed to leave as soon as I'd eaten a few bites, even if it meant a long walk in the rain.

I could find my own solutions.

I tapped the zodiac scroll in my pocket and vowed to get rid of it once and for all, to throw it into the woods to rot. To prove I was serious about rejecting creativity, I turned away from Oliver and his home to stare out the window. The leaves of a cherry tree fluttered in the pelting rain.

"I consult about innovation," Oliver said. "And I teach art. Sometimes to kids."

I kept my eyes on the cherry tree. "Kai sure had an immediate thing for you."

"The feeling was mutual."

"So, the consultations you do—are they like... art lessons for grown-ups?" I asked.

"More like how to think around corners. How to stop fighting nature and enjoy the mess."

I had zero interest in fighting nature. I *loved* nature. And I didn't want to learn to enjoy chaos. The relief of realizing Oliver had nothing to teach that I wanted to learn calmed me and I let the subject drop.

The table filled as Oliver brought more to it. And then more. Butter dish with a painted cover shaped like a corn cob. Six jam jars in a metal caddy. Ceramic honey pot with a bee on the lid. Cow and farmer salt and pepper shakers. *Another* honey pot. Yellow platter of cut kiwis, strawberries, and mangoes.

"Overkill much?" I said. "My forehead hurts from raising my eyebrows at the ridiculous crap you're piling up here."

Oliver nudged one of the honey pots to make room for a bowl of candied ginger. "I'm setting the table."

"You're making a spectacle out of setting the stage for a muffin to enter the scene."

It shouldn't have, but it pleased me to see Oliver's lips twitch with amusement.

"Listen," I said. "The muffins smell great. Let's grab a couple and go. You can drop me off and come back to snack until dinnertime. Meanwhile, I'll check in at the motel, demolish a can of beans, and flop onto a creepy bed in a small room for a fifteen-hour nap."

"If you think you'll stop after one muffin, you're more out of touch than I think you are. So... no. I prefer not to underappreciate the food." Oliver pulled out the chair across the table from me and sat down.

"Wow." I faked a stunned look. "There must be a lot happening in your head."

"You have no idea," Oliver whispered, softly enough that I almost didn't hear him.

"Also, you're wrong," I said. "I'm not out of touch. I'm a realist."

"We're all out of touch," he said.

"Prove it."

"Okay." Oliver sat back and folded his arms. "Do you know why you don't have a job? I'd bet my house you have no idea why your life is in shambles."

That sounded suspiciously like the questions Laura used to ask me. Questions that led to her crying and leaving the room, even though she was a life coach, because that was how far beyond coachable I was.

"I don't want your dung heap of a house," I said. "No deal."

A timer dinged. Oliver took his private smile to the stove across the aisle from the sink. When he opened the oven door, a cloud of sweetness wreathed my head and made my stomach tighten.

"Maybe you want to wash your hands before we eat?" Oliver set an enormous bowl of muffins on the wide windowsill, and I declared my crap day worth all the trouble.

Before I'd finished chewing the first bite of hot muffin, I took a second bite. *Mmm. White chocolate chips.* Without pause, I inhaled two more muffins, one right after the other—and they weren't small. I didn't lift my head or pause for butter or jam or honey. I burnt my mouth. I also might have groaned. When I came out of my muffin trance to an awareness of how greedy I must seem, I forced myself to lean back and take a breath.

"Or not." Oliver snorted and made a show of lifting the cloth napkin from his plate, unfolding it in his lap, and slowly reaching for his first muffin.

"Er," I said. "Sorry?"

He grinned. "Not a problem."

"I just haven't eaten in a while." Embarrassed, I looked around at the food crowded onto the table. "Haven't you ever heard of protein?"

"Lunch was only a couple of hours ago," Oliver said. But he got up and went to the fridge, returned with a plate of crumbly cheddar cheese under a glass dome, which he managed to shove onto a corner of the table. "Don't stop on my account. Have at it."

"If this isn't lunch or dinner, what is it?" I asked.

"Afternoon tea. It's all about decadence."

"There isn't any tea on the table."

"Tea is the second course." Oliver didn't look up from the serious work of splitting a muffin with a butter knife. With his head bent, his trim mustache almost hid his lips. If I hadn't been staring at his face, I would have missed the quirk of his smile.

My unwashed thumb required a severe scrub against my filthy jeans to keep from reaching across the table to stroke Oliver's lips.

I sighed and reached instead for a fourth muffin.

Chapter 12

GRANT

Tipsy as I was on muffins, I barely heard the knock at the front door.

Oliver shoved a strawberry into his mouth and went to answer it. A brown-skinned pixie with an edge—spiky, dyed blond hair, pierced eyebrow—stomped in on a wave of words, saw me, and interrupted herself. "Oh. I saw the backpack on the porch and thought you'd be Freddie." She looked at Oliver. "Why isn't he Freddie?"

"Who's Freddie?" I asked.

"He's Oliver's..." She caught Oliver's hard stare and finished with, "Never mind. Hi. I'm Talia."

"You here for business or pleasure?" Oliver asked her.

Talia hung up her coat and made a beeline for the table where I sat. She gave Oliver a sheepish look. "Business," she said. "Aren't we having tea with this?"

"Tell me," Oliver said.

"Edward is in the slammer again." I couldn't tell if her sniffle was real. I wondered if I should excuse myself to give them privacy.

"What did they nab him for this time?" Oliver asked.

Talia shrugged and stared out the window. "Reckless endangerment? Oh, and thievery." Her chuckle seemed inappropriate for those serious charges.

"Isn't this his third offense?" Oliver fetched a chair for Talia from the dining table on the other side of the kitchen area, and then a placemat and plate.

Talia nodded. "He raced a Porsche down Bank Road. The lady pulled over and opened the car door to scold him. He shoved in and grabbed her purse. Ran off with it."

"Well, that wasn't too bright of her," Oliver said.

I almost interrupted at that point to defend the woman in the Porsche.

"I know." Talia nodded. "That's what I told the cop. He didn't agree." Talia's attitude seemed harsh, considering what her—son? husband?—had done.

"At least Edward didn't bite her," Talia said.

I couldn't keep quiet anymore. "What the hell?"

"In Edward's defense," Talia said, "the woman had a bacon sandwich in her purse."

"Oh, fuck." Oliver seemed to surprise himself with his peal of laughter.

His laugh stilled me. The skin at the outer edges of his eyes folded. His shoulders shook. He scooted his chair back and turned to the side to bend over, like what Talia had said was so funny it made him weak. "She did *not*."

The proud look on Talia's face made me say, "This doesn't seem like a laughing matter." I set down muffin six on my plate and wiped my fingers. "I can't believe your... son, or whoever, who sounds like he has some real problems, did all that, and you guys are laughing about it. Edward must be—"

"A dog." Oliver doubled over again with laughter. "Talia's delinquent Swiss Mountain *dog*."

"Whom I *love*," Talia huffed. "Even though my particular Swissy has issues."

"He means well," Oliver said, and they both snickered. "How did he escape your backyard this time?"

Talia gave Oliver a guilty glance.

"For heaven's sake, Talia. It's not Edward who needs the training. You're too soft. It doesn't help either of you."

She bowed her head. "He just wanted to go running with me. I even put him on the leash."

"Edward weighs more than you do, honey, so who walks whom?" A thoughtful look came over Oliver's face. "What about what's-his-name, down the street from you? Brian?"

"Brian Osborn. Yeah. So?"

"He's a runner, and he likes dogs. When we were in high school, he volunteered at an animal shelter in Seattle. Invite him to join your new running club and hand him Edward's leash."

"Uh-huh." Talia's eyes glazed. "Brian. Strong. Yeah, I could do that."

With another laugh, Oliver said, "Go easy on the guy," and offered Talia the bowl of muffins. "What did you bring me for payment?"

I'd had enough at that point. "Are you kidding?" I said to Oliver. "She's your friend. Why should she have to pay you for a chat about her dog?"

"The green flag is up at the mailbox," Talia said. "That means visitors with problems are welcome. Payment appreciated."

"Payment for what, exactly? Drop-in creativity consultations?"

Talia snorted. "Okay. Sure. I'll bet that's what Freddie calls it." She shook with silent laughter.

That made Freddie sound like Oliver's boyfriend. My irritation rose another notch.

"Oliver's like a country doctor," Talia told me. "He accepts payment in piglets and jam, but doesn't require it." She dismissed Oliver with a flick of her fingers. "He doesn't need more money anyway."

"Must be nice," I grumbled. A deep pang of envy pushed up from where I'd hidden it behind my disapproval of Oliver and his lifestyle. "How do you know what to pay him?"

"That's the fun part. Today he gets cleaning products." She turned to Oliver. "That eco brand you like was on sale."

"Talia's all about the variety," Oliver said. "Last week it was mangos, kiwis, and strawberries."

"Depends on the season," Talia mused. "In winter, I mostly pay in driveway maintenance, filling potholes, which helps me blow off steam, because of the—"

"Because of the ferry," Oliver said.

Talia's eyes narrowed and her shoulders squared. "The *assholes* who *know* how to drive, but the moment they board the ferry in the rain they become murderous—"

"Down, girl." Oliver patted the air in front of Talia then pointed a finger at the floor, which made Talia blink and snort.

"Dickhead," she said to Oliver. "Also, kudos for using dog commands to remind me I'm human."

Talia and Oliver's easy banter and friendship spotlighted yet another lack in my life. Before my internal pity party turned the air black, I needed to leave. "Excuse me. I need to go now," I said.

"Talia can give you a ride in a few minutes," Oliver said.

"Sure," Talia said. "If he pedals my bicycle with his backpack on, I can drape over the top like a princess."

Oliver hadn't even finished his first muffin, but I couldn't wait any longer. I'd hike through the lull in the rain, fueled by muffins and cheese, until I got to a busier road. I'd sweat out my confused feelings, find comfort in the rhythm of one foot in the front of the other.

I stood from the table and pushed in my chair. "I'll hitch to town, or take a long walk. It'll do me good. Um... thanks for the food."

"Are you sure?" Oliver asked.

Oliver and Talia wished me good luck but didn't try to stop me, which was a relief, as was putting a closed door between us. The effort required to lift my pack and put it on almost made me reconsider. I shuffled down the porch steps. When I passed the first curve of the driveway and could look back without seeing the neat blue house with white trim, I heaved a deep sigh.

The music of rain on leaves was all I needed. I tried to minimize the sound of my footsteps, to hear more of the swish and swell of leaves in the breeze.

At the end of Oliver's driveway, I turned left onto the gravel road, one more turn away from creativity's inexplicable, unpredictable mayhem and excess. I wanted *less*, not more.

Laura had wondered about my lack of big dreams. I never told her that at the beginning of my senior year in high school the guidance counselor had literally yawned over my aptitude test results. *Manual laborer or gardener.* I'd been more upset by the counselor's lack of interest than my test results. I'd snatched the paper and fled the room. After graduation, I'd fled my hometown and my parents' relentless work ethic. In Seattle, I'd tried working at a gardening center, but hated bossing around the plants and so I'd fled that too.

Trees don't have the option to flee.

If I'd been born a tree, I'd *have to* deal with whatever came my way—strong winds, lightning, bark disease. I ran my eyes up a towering fir tree and peace rose inside me.

For the first time in my life, I had a hero to look up to.

I walked on, head tilted back to commune with the stoic trees. Stable but not static. Grounded but flexible.

That bored school counselor almost got it right. What she missed was that I didn't want to *tend* plants; I wanted to *be* one. I suddenly couldn't believe I'd spent my life indoors helping people put ink onto dead trees.

That was never really me.

I was made for something else. I was made to breathe fresh air and move heavy objects from one place to another.

Simple work in nature.

Maybe I could build a new life on that.

Chapter 13

GRANT

Talia didn't pass me on her bicycle. She'd either turned right at the end of Oliver's driveway or she hadn't left until after I was out of sight. I saw no one as I plodded along.

In my motel room in Seattle, I'd done some internet research about Vashon. The island was part of King County, which included Seattle, so the bus system on Vashon was pretty good. On my walk with Kai, I'd seen a bus stop on Westside Highway, but that was a long way off from Oliver's.

The candy-muffin sugar crash slayed me without warning. I sat at the edge of the road and closed my eyes, using the pack I hadn't removed as a recliner.

Some time later, light rain and a poke from a can at the small of my back woke me to a workable idea, one I wished I'd thought of sooner. My pack was heavy because it held everything I owned—including food and camping gear.

As I walked on, I scanned the vegetation at the edge of the road until I found a hint of a path through the thick woods on my left. I dropped the pack into a riot of tall grass and took the narrow path at a jog, airborne without the pack's weight, hands out to high-five the leaves of my brethren as I floated past.

Before long, I came to a clearing. No, that was too optimistic. Where the path skirted a scatter of rocks, a touch more light from the sky pushed through the branches above. I bent to feel the sparse grass, dug into the dirt with my fingers. Damp under the thick forest canopy, but not wet. I sprinted back to the road to retrieve my pack and lugged it to my makeshift camping spot.

It took me five minutes to set up my one-person tent. I shoved the pack into the tent, rolled out my foam pad and sleeping bag. The pack took up most of the space, but it would have to do. I sat in the tent doorway to remove my boots, wedged them between the door and the bottom of the pack, and sat cross-legged on the foot of my sleeping bag to watch the rain.

Not a soul on earth knows where I am.

If no one knew where I was, no one could kick me out.

I zipped the door flap and scooted back to sacrifice that bastard can of beans for dinner. In the cramped space, my elbow whacked the pack every time I lifted the can, but I didn't mind. Cocooned in the tent, rustic as it was, I felt better than I had in any of the horrible motel rooms I'd lived in, or in Mitch's sorry shack.

A final scrape around the can, a swallow of rinse water, and I was done. I tied the empty can and the unwashed spoon into a couple of plastic bags and buried them in my pack to keep the critters at bay, then stretched out, lulled by the sounds of nature.

My thoughts spiraled up and away, and I slept.

Chapter 14

OLIVER

Grant would return to ask me for a ride. I knew he would. He'd slink back within the hour, exuding stink and bad attitude. I made a mental note to keep my smugness to a minimum when he did.

But he didn't.

For a long time after Talia left, I stood on the front porch.

Day became night, and my driveway remained empty.

That night, I woke in the darkness to an image of Grant crushed beneath the heavy weight he carried, broken at the side of a lonely road.

The big sketchbook I kept under the bed took the vision from me. I filled a page with Grant tumbling to his knees. Then another. Brought down by a stack of flat stones. Then asleep in the ditch with Kai. I drew ferns in sunlight, using the drawings on my arms as reference. I drew leaves and grass and closed eyes. I drew relaxed hands and faces, arms that comforted, until sleep took me away again.

The next morning the sky rang with blue. I pulled on a pair of overalls over a long-sleeved T-shirt and sat on the bench inside the front door to lace up my boots. On the way through the kitchen to the back door, I grabbed a muffin and my phone.

Worry about Grant evaporated in the dew-dazzled light of day. I leapt off the back porch and whistled across the lawn.

Face averted, I felt around on the cement floor of the toolshed to find the tool belt I'd left there, grabbed the mallets too, and slid the heavy door closed.

I'd taken a few steps toward the woods before I remembered the green flag was up at the mailbox. I needed to switch it if I didn't want to be interrupted until Clementine arrived. She would ignore the red flag since we had a session scheduled.

I dropped the mallets in the grass and ate the muffin as I walked down the driveway. Red flag up, I retraced my steps to retrieve the mallets and continue across the lawn to the woods.

I'd begun the carving project in April with a chainsaw. Buzzed an eight-foot stump into the rough shape of a throne with a roof, then started carving designs into the wood. It was a tongue-in-cheek project, a response to Freddie teasing me about being the ruler of my backwoods domain.

Before the first mallet strike of the day, I tucked in my earbuds and cued up the folk rhythms of the Les Charbonniers de l'enfer. The Quebec group's *Chansons a cappella* album focused my mallet strikes and urged me to an altered state where designs bypassed my mind, flowed through my hands into the wood.

As I worked, I reviewed my plan for the session with Clementine, a strong woman with a deep cavern of guilt. We used her love of theater to chip at the walls, to unearth her. I'd encouraged her to see a therapist, worried I'd inadvertently make things worse for her, but she insisted she wanted to work with me, and I couldn't say no. She kept coming back for more. I kept hoping she wouldn't need to come back.

I tapped the end of the chisel to finish a rabbit balanced on a leaf and moved around to the last uncarved area of the throne's exterior. As the carving and the music emptied my mind, all thoughts faded and I gave myself over to joy and the suspension of time.

At some point, Les Charbonniers irritated me and intruded—the other reason I listened to them. Time reasserted itself, delivered me to the world at my feet, the ache in my arms, my empty belly.

With my palm, I swept curls of shaved wood from the ferns I'd carved. Blank wood beckoned. I held the chisel like a paintbrush and used the tip to scratch in my next moves. One line led to another and I got lost again, until I heard Clementine's car in the driveway.

I grabbed the mallets and jogged to the toolshed to toss them and the work belt inside. If I hurried, I could fix us something to eat before we began.

Chapter 15

GRANT

My stench cloud developed its own microclimate.

I woke early the morning after I set up camp, eager to break free of the cramped tent. In a token gesture, I changed my shirt, then paused with a foot half inside a boot to do the math. I hadn't showered in five days of hard exercise—not since the motel in Seattle after I'd been fired. Suspended. Quit. Fled. *Whatever.*

I was alive and I'd slept well. I'd count that as a win.

When I stuck my head out the tent door, I couldn't help but laugh. Sunlight slanted in to sparkle on drops of water. I felt the earth breathe and filled my lungs to join in.

During my high-protein breakfast of a can of pinto beans, I decided to explore the neighborhood, so to speak, to see if I'd set up camp too close to someone's backyard.

An hour of bushwhacking in concentric circles revealed an expanse of woods, a wider patch of ground for a better campsite, and a backyard water spigot at a vacation home.

I moved everything to the new campsite then took my empty water bottles on the twenty-minute walk to the water spigot. The home appeared to be unoccupied, but they hadn't turned off the water. With caution, and apologies to whoever paid the bills, I filled my bottles. I yearned to strip and crouch to wash my body, but didn't want to steal that much water, or get naked in a stranger's backyard, even if they weren't around.

My next need was a food resupply. If my phone hadn't died, I could have checked a bus schedule. Instead, I'd have to walk and hitch to town. I assessed my funds and decided I could spend one night in the motel. I'd check in, shower and shave, park at the library for the afternoon, overnight at the motel. The next morning, I'd grocery shop. Maybe I'd buy a plastic ice chest—not to keep things cool, since I didn't have a feasible source of ice, but as a cache to thwart woodland critters.

I thought about motel check-in times and decided to head out around noon. Which meant I had hours to kill.

I did a slow spin to review my entertainment options at the campsite. I could retie the tarp that sagged over the kitchen log. Or read one of my paperback novels I'd read six times. Or memorize more of the Vashon map.

I needed a hobby, a leisure activity to distract my forebrain while I did the deeper mental work of persuading myself to look for a job. Walking was my first choice for a hobby, but I wasn't eating enough to be able to hike all day.

I could check on Oliver. That might be entertaining.

The barely visible track I'd camped on headed in the general direction of Oliver's house. I followed it and about ten minutes later caught sight of the house's blue siding through the foliage. I stopped to lift the small pair of binoculars I'd hung around my neck.

Wait. I lowered the binoculars for an emergency ethics check. Did I condone spying on Oliver? *It's a passing whim*, I reasoned. After paying for groceries and the motel, I'd be down to my last few dollars and I'd have to leave Vashon. Even a crap job on Vashon to keep me supplied with beans and weekly overnights at the motel to shower wouldn't be enough when summer ended and the rain settled in. Plus, I did want something bigger for my life. Rusted-out gears began to turn deep inside at the idea of *simple work in nature*. The sturdy tree at my back gave me a nudge. I could explore tree planting on the peninsula, or trail maintenance in a national park.

"Thanks, buddy." I patted the tree and crept closer to Oliver's house.

A cautious crab-walk took me to Oliver's orange Volkswagen van, parked under a freestanding carport with a bicycle.

Perhaps Oliver wasn't awake yet. I turned to lean back against the van in a crouch and examined the tangled greenery I'd emerged from.

For half an hour or so, whenever I heard a rustle in the vegetation, I played *find the source*. Birds mostly, chickadees and warblers, busy with their morning tasks. I couldn't identify an energetic bird foraging low in a bush. I'd look him up in a bird book when I went to the library.

A metallic scrape and clang startled me enough to make me drop the binoculars and slap a hand over my mouth, I guess to keep myself from crying out, which was considerate of me. I shifted to the edge of the van and raised the binoculars.

Oliver stood at the door of an outbuilding tucked against the wall of woods across the yard from the back of the house.

My new hobby had paid off.

He reached into the outbuilding and pulled out a leather tool belt—by feel, apparently, since he found it without looking. It wasn't until he bent his head to buckle it on that I registered what he was wearing. Denim overalls. Black work boots. *Christ on a crutch*, the man was beautiful no matter what he wore. I had a stellar view of lean shoulders and arm muscles as they bunched and shifted under the tight T-shirt. I swallowed hard and adjusted the focus on the binoculars.

I'd only ever seen Oliver in the gray of a rainy day or by lamplight inside his house. In bright morning sunshine, Oliver *glittered*. The high gloss of his burnished hair slayed me. Escaped strands from the fat topknot curved around the classic features of his face. I sent out a wish that he would let his hair down, but he didn't. He swiped at the loose strands to tuck them behind his ears. They came free again when he bent to pick up a couple of mallets.

At some point, I took a belated breath and asked myself what the *hell* I thought I was doing. My spying was indefensible. I knew that. But when Oliver walked away from me, I slunk to the edge of the van to prepare for a dash to the cover of the house so I could shadow him.

My new hobby almost came to an abrupt halt.

Oliver dropped the mallets and spun toward me.

I jerked back behind the van. My unprincipled heart banged inside my chest.

He didn't seem to have seen me. He passed the carport and continued down the driveway.

I stayed put, focusing the binoculars on Oliver's graceful lope and the fit of his overalls. He hadn't gone for one-size-bigger comfort. His delectable ass under the heavy tool belt made me wonder if he'd found a Vashon tailor who specialized in bespoke overalls. Various chisels hung from loops in his tool belt. They swayed and tapped each other as he walked.

Quite a while later—it was a *long* driveway—Oliver loped back and headed straight for the mallets. It wouldn't have surprised me to discover he had access to a rock quarry and was off to free a block of granite to start a new sculpture.

I followed and berated myself and continued to watch.

By the time Oliver was in full swing at the tall tree stump—earbuds in, tools in motion—I no longer cared if I was a bad man who spied. My new hobby had become a vice.

It was a full ten minutes before I tore my gaze from Oliver's body to take a look at what he was working on. A high stump had been shaped into a chair. The upper part of the stump remained as a roof over the hollowed-out seat.

I stole through the underbrush to get a better view of the back of the stump where Oliver worked. From a perch on a low rock behind a rhododendron, I focused the binoculars on what Oliver had carved. The hairs on my arms stood up. *Jesus.* Elaborate designs of vines, birds, and animals spread over the wood.

What in God's name was Oliver doing living on Vashon? He belonged in New York City, or in Italy, fending off paparazzi and knocking the glitterati on their asses. I couldn't believe my own eyes. As I watched, Oliver's confident movements with the chisel and mallet transformed a flat expanse of wood into a squirrel so alive I swear its tail twitched.

When Oliver set down the tools to strip off his T-shirt, I almost passed out from enthralled overstimulation, from the sight of Oliver's bare shoulders and arms, rendered in pure marble by a master sculptor.

I lowered the binoculars to hyperventilate, couldn't bear to miss the show, raised them again.

A ray of sunlight emerged in the wood. *What the serious fuck?* From the sharp end of the chisel, Oliver rendered a *sunray* in brown wood. I felt like I'd stumbled on a peephole to the rarified realm Oliver inhabited, a far-off land where leisure and creativity brought wealth instead of destitution. *Must be nice to believe in magic.*

I stared through the binoculars for a long time, watched and wondered and wrestled with myself about the spying.

I didn't know what to do with the fact that I wasn't going to stop.

At some point, a car door slammed in the distance. Oliver lifted his head and yanked out his earbuds. In a flurry, he gathered his tools and ran to the outbuilding to shove them inside.

I followed, hid myself behind a salmonberry bush, barely breathed.

The T-shirt tucked in the back pocket of Oliver's overalls swung from side to side as he hurried across the lawn to the back porch. He banged through the door and out of sight.

I remained where I was.

On my knees in the fragrant dirt.

Chapter 16

OLIVER

The ham-and-cheese sandwich Clementine ate at my kitchen table didn't erase the tightness from her face or soften her tense posture.

She came to me when she got stuck wishing for a different past, when she needed help to reunite with the present. I wondered if we would touch the core of her pain in our session. She didn't often allow herself to go there, but she'd said that when she did, she experienced the most healing. The session wouldn't be fun—for either of us—but it might be better than fun if Clementine could put another chunk of old pain to rest.

After she ate, Clementine excused herself to go to the bathroom. When she came out, she walked across the great room, stepped up the two wide steps onto the stage, and turned her impassive gaze to me.

I studied her for signs of hesitation. "Are you sure, Clemmy?"

She unclasped her hands to let them hang at her sides. "Yes. I'm sure."

I wished I'd stopped carving sooner, showered off the shavings, changed clothes. I didn't want Clementine to think I wasn't ready. I draped a towel over the end of the couch closest to the stage and sat on it.

Clementine waited, followed my movements.

"Aza?" I asked, to confirm she wanted to go there.

Her eyes filled with tears, but she nodded.

I gave Clementine my deepest focus, to be ready for whatever happened. "We're going to do two scenes today. Is that okay?" I wanted to try something new—a double whammy.

Clementine nodded again.

"The first scene is opening night for Aza's show in Seattle. You've put a lot of thought into your outfit." I pointed at the freestanding wardrobe by the stage, knowing Clementine would want to dress for the part.

"The scene begins at the door of the gallery," I said. "Show me what happens. You'll play both parts, yours and Aza's, so grab Aza's hat for when you need to switch roles."

Silence fell as Clementine stared into the wardrobe. The dress she chose—a classy wrap dress cut for an hourglass figure—didn't surprise me. She put the dress on over her slacks and blouse, toed off her flat sandals, and stepped into a pair of stylish heels from the bottom of the wardrobe.

I could feel Clementine trying to get up the nerve to touch Aza's hat on the top shelf. She stared at it for a motionless minute, until I cleared my throat.

Clementine snatched the hat.

"You're stronger than you think you are," I told her. "You come here and do this because you know I know the whole story, because you trust me to hold this safe space for you. I won't judge you, no matter what happens, and I won't stop you, not unless you say your safeword. Tell me what it is."

"Do-over."

"If you say your safeword, if you even whisper it, I'll be on stage to help you." Her nod was barely perceptible.

"Please say out loud that you understand."

"I understand." Her voice was quiet, but I heard her determination.

"Good." I took a deep breath and let it out slowly. "Our focus is on the change that's possible, on you. We can't change your past or Aza's past, but *you* can change *you*. Are you okay with those parameters?" I gave Clementine a variation on the same speech every time.

"I am."

"Action," I said, even though it wasn't a movie.

Clementine blinked, rolled her shoulders, and entered the gallery. I'd used my contacts to help Aza land that show. I'd walked him through the preparations, helped him hang his eerie paintings. In my mind, as I watched Clementine on the stage, I added her to my memory, wove her actions and the words she spoke into the events I'd experienced that evening.

The most painful moments of her performance were when she took on the role of Aza, straightened to mimic his taller frame, pretended to sweep his long hair over her shoulders, bounced on her feet.

Clementine peered at every painting and made thoughtful comments to Aza, who kept a hand on her arm as he told her about his work. Aza smiled with his whole body to have her there with him. When Clementine spoke to Aza about his paintings, she borrowed my words, words remembered from when I'd told her about the show she'd missed.

Throughout her performance, Clementine cried. By the time she left the gallery and waved goodbye to Aza, who smiled from the doorway, her tears seemed cleansing.

When she'd finished, she sat on the edge of the stage.

I got up to sit next to her and pass her tissues until she'd gathered herself enough to reach up and remove Aza's hat from her head and hand it to me. More than once, I'd tried to give it to her. She always refused. I knew it was because she didn't believe she deserved it. Someday I hoped she would. Until then, I would keep it for her.

On a protracted exhale, Clementine said, "You're really going to make me do another one?"

"No. I can't make you do anything. But I hope you'll try. It's a matched set."

Her sigh was heavy, but her steady gaze told me the grief had retracted its claws, so she was willing.

"You can safeword out," I said.

"No. I'm tired, but I'll do it." She stood to take off the dress and shoes.

"You'll only need one prop," I said. "This scene is cleaning up after Aza's eleventh birthday party, the one here with only the four of us. Remember what Dad gave Aza that year?" I handed her the prop.

Clementine took what I handed to her and shook it out. When she realized what it was, she laughed. "You're an ass, Oliver."

"Yes. Yes, I am." I went back to sit on my towel on the couch. "You'll play the role of Aza. This scene is not a what-if, but a reenactment of what happened that night."

Clementine set the whoopee cushion I'd handed her on the stage and bent to roll up her slacks. With a practiced movement, she unclipped the barrette to let her hair fall free, and mussed it with both hands to imitate Aza's wild mop. Her final adjustment was to tuck in her blouse and button it all the way up to her chin, a nod to Aza's hippie-artist-engineer style, which he'd settled into by age eleven, God help him.

For the life of me, I couldn't figure out how Clemmy did it. If I hadn't seen her performance with my own eyes, I wouldn't have believed she could evoke Aza's spirit as he'd been that night with such accuracy. The stage wasn't big enough for Aza's energy or the way he'd tricked us to get us to sit on the inflated whoopee cushion. Clementine-as-Aza roamed the room, embodied a boy with a wicked sense of humor and a desperate need to be liked.

Her performance made me remember too.

I remembered Dad's booms of laughter that night. I remembered Aza finally running out of steam and coming to me where I lay on the couch. I'd been fifteen. The sharp ache of Granddad's passing the year before had finally shifted into something bearable, into enough open space for the occasional return of joy.

That was the night Aza told me he'd chosen me to be his big brother. He told me and then fell asleep half on top of me on the couch. I'd wrapped arms around him, worried he and his problems wouldn't fare well in the world.

Aza had draped over me that night the way Kai draped over Grant in the ditch—with enough trust to escape his problems for a while.

I remembered how I'd held on, helpless and afraid.

Chapter 17

GRANT

Oliver disappeared through the back door. After I'd caught my breath, I got up off my knees and scurried through the woods until I could see the front of the house. A tall woman with brown hair and nice clothes stood beside a Volvo. She looked beaten down, like she might need a transfusion to get through the day.

Oliver met her on the front porch with his shirt back on.

"What have you been up to today?" the woman asked Oliver. "Something fun, by the looks of it." Her voice held a note of false cheer.

Oliver put his hands up. "Don't hug me. I'm covered in shavings. I was in town early this morning and then lost track of—"

"In *that* outfit?"

"No, Miss Vogue. I got a new chisel at the hardware store. When I got home, I wanted to use it." Oliver ushered her inside and closed the door.

Their voices carried out through the open windows. I needed to be closer. I crossed the front of the house in a crouched run below the high porch, to keep out of their line of sight. Around the corner, a cluster of bushes provided cover for a peek into an open window.

What I witnessed took me a while to decipher. With a few sentences of instruction, Oliver prompted the woman—Clemmy—through a process that transformed her from a sad caterpillar into a calm butterfly.

By the time it was over and Clemmy had emerged from the bathroom smoothed and polished, I'd morphed too. Huddled there in the bushes, I admitted to myself—with a crash of internal cymbals—that I had a crush. An unwelcome crush on someone who awed and annoyed me.

Damn it.

I pushed farther into the shelter of untended bushes and pressed my back against the house. I heard Clemmy leave, heard Oliver putter around inside the house, heard the front door open and close. A long minute of silence, then the sound of bike tires on gravel.

Oliver whistled as he rode away. The deep notes of his dirge faded into the distance.

I saw the bounty of Oliver's life, but I *felt* the dirge. Felt it inside the house against my back, in the neglected bushes, in the way Oliver had tossed his tools into the outbuilding without looking, in the sorrow he and Clemmy shared about Aza.

I wanted to not care.

I couldn't afford the distraction of someone else's drama—*private* drama I hadn't been invited to witness or comment on. I had no business mooning over glints in Oliver's hair or the sexy fit of his overalls or his freckled skin and shapely arms. I didn't want to wonder about the fate of Talia's dog or Clemmy's Aza or Oliver's Freddie.

None of that mattered as much as *food*.

The seriousness of my situation found and seized me, gave me a wake-up shake that made my teeth chatter.

Enough.

I'd put off answering the big questions long enough.

I crawled out of the bushes and slunk into the woods, resolved to refocus, to fade from Oliver's life.

That evening, under the disco light of the headlamp I'd hung from the ceiling of the tent, I sat with a notepad on my knees. My penance for spying on Oliver was a delay of my trip to town, to give myself more time to plan.

A pall of canned-beans-induced gas spread over my little campground. Even if I decided I couldn't afford an overnight at the motel, a menu revision and a trip to the grocery store were top priorities, or I was going to rupture something.

1) Get better food, I wrote on the notepad. I had a small camp stove. A bag of rice only cost a few cents. More vegetables would be nice. Carrots would keep for a while in the ice chest, even without ice. I started a grocery list in the margin of the page.

My biggest issue was income. I set the notepad aside and conducted a scrupulous search for assets. *Ninety-seven dollars and fourteen cents.* Once up on a time, I'd had bank accounts, though they'd never amounted to much. I'd relied on my parents and then on Laura to handle the finances. *And look where that got you.*

I admitted that if I didn't have a source of income, it didn't make sense to prioritize a night at a motel over food. When I landed a job interview, I'd splurge on a motel for a shower.

2) No motel. I tapped the notepad with the pen. I could manage camping. *Probably.* I enjoyed lying on the sleeping bag in the buzz-twitter-rustle of the forest where no one could find me. But I still needed a job.

3) Get newspapers. When I hitched to town for groceries, I'd pick up the Seattle papers for the classified job listings. Online listings would be easier and cheaper to scan, but I doubted I'd be welcome in the library to use their computers before I'd had a shower. Maybe I could hike around to find a signal for my phone.

4) Take cord to town and charge phone.

5) Make stealth grocery list. If I planned ahead, I could speed shop to minimize customer complaints about the homeless guy stinking up the joint.

6) Check bulletin boards. I'd noticed a big one near the grocery store, layered with local flyers and want ads.

So far, I'd only listed the obvious stuff.

I wanted to stretch beyond the obvious, to point myself in a new direction. I closed my eyes and tried to think.

7) Ask Mitch and Sonya for suggestions.

No. I couldn't face Mitch from the bottom rung. It was too humiliating. I added a question mark to indicate I'd think about it.

Cool air blew through the open tent windows. I leaned back and attempted to generate ideas for how to stretch in a new direction. An hour later, I'd come up with exactly nothing.

The breeze shifted from cool to cold. I stuck my hands in my pants pockets to warm them, not ready to get in the sleeping bag. I'd be asleep in two seconds once I did that, and I wasn't ready to give up on my list. My cold hand in my pocket closed around the zodiac scroll.

I woke many hours later, frozen and bleary, and fumbled my way into the sleeping bag in the wan light of dawn.

8) Buy headlamp batteries.

Two days later, I roamed the small town of Vashon and resolutely ticked items off the lists I'd made. My first task in the grocery store was to locate an electrical outlet. When no one was looking, I plugged in the charger at the florist desk and tucked my phone behind a display of greeting cards. After I'd finished shopping, I went back to get it.

Outside with my groceries, I watched people leave the store, to see who headed for the pickup trucks in the parking lot. I wanted to hitch a ride, but I didn't want to gross anyone out.

A city dude with an overkill truck and a full grocery cart trusted me enough to let me ride in the truck bed with his party supplies. My gratitude for a ride that didn't include an awkward chat made it easier to resist the temptation to swipe a roll or twelve of smoked ham from the nearest plastic-covered deli platter. Contemplation of the box of lube packets I'd chucked into my cart provided a nice distraction. I might not have a wife, and I might have a crush on someone I'd probably never see again, but if I rationed the packets, I could get myself off in comfort once a week for a few months. *Something to look forward to.*

I returned to my campsite with a small plastic ice chest, a pile of cheap food, lube, a charged phone, and newspapers—all for under twenty dollars. Operation Camping had begun.

Over the next thirty-six hours, I accidently started two fires—inexcusable on an island with limited freshwater supply. Mold appeared on the inside roof of the tent, brought on by my body heat and the dampness of the constant light rain. I tried to be careful when I cleaned up after meals, and kept all the uncanned food in the ice chest, but mice found enough scraps to be a nuisance.

All my clothing, except for the one set of clean clothes I'd double-bagged and stashed in my pack, smelled foul and looked like filthy rags. I tried to wash a T-shirt under the spigot at the unoccupied house. The experiment ended in failure. I hung the semi-clean T-shirt over the tarp line at my campsite, watched it mold in the damp air, gave up and shoved it into the trash bag.

I spent a lot of time growing my biceps as I hauled stolen water from the spigot at the vacation house to my campsite.

What I *didn't* do was go back to spy on Oliver. But I thought about him. Mostly I thought about his contradictions: well-tended house by an untended hedge, beautiful hair in a messy bun.

Who was I to talk about contradictions? I was an able-bodied man who resisted work, a guy who loved the woods but worked indoors, an uncle who wanted to spend time with his nephew but couldn't manage to clean himself up enough or gather enough courage to attempt it.

On the afternoon of my fifth day in the woods, I sat on one of the fallen tree limbs I'd hauled into the campsite, spaced out in the bright sunshine. My sleeping bag, unzipped and draped over a rope tied between two trees, wafted in the breeze. Spots of light danced across the fabric.

In those quiet moments, I found what I'd been missing for so long—*peace.*

I blinked and sat up.

I didn't need *money.* Not really. Not yet. What I needed was the way my mind unfurled beneath the forest canopy. If I could sink into the quiet for another week, I knew my mind would show me more options for the next stage of my life.

My actual needs were so simple: food and drinking water, plus occasional use of a shower, a washing machine, and an electrical outlet.

I needed amenities.

Oliver's yard needed help.

Maybe I didn't have to wait to find simple work in nature.

Chapter 18

OLIVER

After days at home without seeing anyone, even though I kept the green flag up, everyone visited at once. Clementine arrived with a carload of food as payment for our last session, Talia biked over with Edward, and Freddie finally appeared.

Clementine helped me put away the groceries, hugged me, and left. Talia and I sat on the front porch steps and talked while Edward dug holes in the driveway. When Freddie pulled up in his mother's minivan, Talia and I fell silent.

Freddie got out of the van and winked at me.

Talia snorted and said to me, "Take this however you like, but I'm going to go get a shovel." She called Edward and they disappeared around the house.

Freddie wore what I called his *I have an important flight to catch* outfit: dark blue blazer, lighter blue button-down shirt, khaki chinos. For the full look, he'd need a leather travel bag over his shoulder, a cell phone at his ear, and a backward glance. That was Freddie in a nutshell: thrilled to hurry off to somewhere else, preferably somewhere in Japan.

His appearance at my place meant he'd recuperated from his most recent trip enough to begin writing, but hadn't yet fallen down the rabbit hole of planning for his next long trip.

Freddie set a shopping bag at my feet and sat beside me. "Hi, honey, I'm home," he said with a wry grin.

"Welcome back, you." I let him kiss my cheek and stroke my beard for a moment before I pulled away to look at him. His clever face and close-cropped hair looked the same as always.

"Brought your loot." He nudged the shopping bag with his foot.

I knew I wouldn't want whatever he'd brought. Freddie persisted in thinking my sense of humor was cruder than it actually was. After he left for his next trip, I'd donate whatever was in the bag to a charity shop in Tacoma.

Edward's barks announced Talia's return with the shovel. It felt nice to be around people after days of being alone, even though I'd spent the days enjoyably. I'd carved on the throne, taken a few bike rides, and sketched variations of a man and a boy asleep in a ditch.

"I'm almost finished with the throne," I said.

"Show me." Freddie stood and held out his hand.

Talia paused in her repair work to salute us. "I'll show myself out when I'm done."

As Freddie and I strolled across the lawn and through the woods, he told me about the articles he was working on—something about Japanese cultural perspectives around career development. He didn't try to get handsy with me until we'd reached the throne. I gently fended him off. It sometimes took me a while to mesh my memory of Freddie with Freddie in real life. I tended to embellish while he was away.

"Why do I always forget this part?" Freddie gave me a fond smile. "I'll need to talk my way into your pants all over again, won't I?"

At least he was good-natured about it. I could tell from the look in his eye that he yearned for me. I yearned for him too, in a way. If he didn't travel so much, or if I liked to travel, we probably could have had a nice life together. Instead, we were friends and opportunistic lovers. I was the guy he sent strange postcards to and bought foreign oddities for. He was the guy who told me tales of the world and wrecked my bedding now and then. Our arrangement had worked well for seventeen years.

For the first time, I wondered if I might want to change it.

Freddie ran his hands over the carved designs in the wood. "Oliver. Hey, this is really something."

"Thank you. How long are you on Vashon this time?"

"I fly back to Tokyo in late August. Mom's fussing will send me around the bend before then, so I'm thinking I'll do some short trips up the coast over the summer. I got a lead on a Japanese prison warden who retired on Whidbey Island." Freddie hadn't seen the back of the throne yet, but he took my hand and pulled me toward the house. "Let's go inside."

The arm he wrapped around my shoulder felt nice, so I went along.

Freddie winked as he opened the back door. "I put up the red flag for us."

"I knew you would."

What I liked about Freddie was his predictability. We never surprised each other. He knew I felt happiest at home on Vashon, and he knew persuasion would be required to thaw me after a long separation. I knew Freddie's familiarity would bring me comfort. I also knew he felt most at home in Japan. Someday, I predicted, Freddie would bring a nice Japanese boy to Vashon to meet his mother. Until then, I remained his option for easy sex on Vashon.

Over the long months Freddie was away, I tended to forget I was a placeholder. I used my imagination to satisfy myself and lost track of reality, despite the photo I kept on my fridge as a reminder. In the photo, Freddie wore a tuxedo and a smile I'd never seen in person. Beside him, at a gala event in Tokyo, stood a handsome young Japanese man in a blue-on-blue embroidered tuxedo. The cool, acquisitive look the man gave Freddie made it clear they'd be all over each other in a back room within thirty seconds. *That* was Freddie's reality—hobnobbing with politicos and socialites, winning journalism prizes for insightful coverage of controversial issues, immersed in his best life in Japan.

I tended to ignore the photo.

The version of Freddie I reverted to when he was away was the longhaired teen who'd excelled in English, Japanese, world history, and soccer, but almost failed every other subject. Nostalgia replayed a young Freddie who pushed me into dark corners at parties or into the back seat of his car and used his mouth and hands and cock to distract me.

Freddie used me to remember our good times.

I used Freddie to forget.

I caught sight of that photo when Freddie hauled me past the fridge on the way to my bedroom, and wondered how my life might change if I was willing to remember more. The thought slid away, too impenetrable to stick. I pulled against Freddie's hand to steer him away from the bedroom.

His frown told me he wasn't pleased.

"I'm not trying to be a tease," I said. My nostalgia had to be dealt with before I got physical. I didn't want to have sad sex that made me long for a previous version of Freddie.

"I know," Freddie said, but his heavy sigh and plop onto the couch said he didn't believe me.

What I wanted to do was retreat alone to my bedroom, lie down with the curtains closed, and ask myself a few tough questions, but I couldn't do that to Freddie.

"Tell me something about your trip while I look at what you brought me," I said.

By the time I'd unwrapped a disturbing monkey mask, a plastic sword, and a sign I suspected Freddie stole from a bathroom, his smile had almost recovered. He sat close with his hand high on my thigh.

I almost didn't mind.

Chapter 19

GRANT

I took the back way to Oliver's through the woods, instead of using the driveway like a normal person. I didn't want to know if the red flag was up.

I'd done what little primping I could, aided by a dingy washrag and the reflective bottom of my metal camping plate. The result was a signature style I dubbed *rough-hewn hopeful*.

As I neared the house for the first time since I'd spied on Oliver carving the stump, I focused my thoughts on *peace*. Get the asking over with, work out the details, and then I could get back to fresh vegetables and the makings of a cheese sandwich at my campsite. I'd spend the afternoon chewing slowly and planning the next phase of my recovery.

I charged onto the lawn with my head down like a determined bull, which meant I was already out in the open when I noticed the ancient minivan in the driveway. And heard a man's laugh that wasn't Oliver's coming from inside the house.

I thought about turning around.

No. I would interrupt, but I'd be quick about it. I stomped up the porch steps, to give Oliver and his guest notice, and knocked, my eyes on the doormat to keep my focus. *Peace.*

When Oliver opened the door, his bare, freckled feet were almost enough to blow my concentration to hell.

"Grant. Hey," Oliver said in a bright voice. "I thought you'd gone back to Seattle." He opened the door wider. "Come on in."

"No, thanks." I cleared my throat. "Sorry to bother you, but I'd like to ask you something."

Oliver leaned against the doorjamb and nodded.

"Could we do a trade?" I asked. "I can do odd jobs around the property. In exchange maybe you'd be willing to—"

A second pair of feet and legs appeared behind Oliver's. *Close* behind. Brown shoes. Nice slacks. "Willing to what?" said the voice that wasn't Oliver's.

I took a step back and lifted my head. The man gave me a wary look and slid an arm around Oliver's waist. *Freddie.*

Oliver shifted sideways and turned to look over his shoulder. "Give us a minute?"

Freddie didn't like it, but he stepped back.

Oliver came outside and closed the door. "Sorry about that," he said to me. "Old friend just back from a long trip. What were you saying?"

I should have bought myself a goddamned cheesecake to reward myself for offering Oliver a deal, instead of a bag of baby carrots. I swore to myself if I made it through the next five minutes, I'd treat myself to two cheese sandwiches and require nothing of myself for the remainder of the day. Maybe tomorrow as well.

Aware of the open windows, I lowered my voice. "I want to trade odd jobs, preferably outdoor jobs, for occasional use of your amenities."

"Which amenities?"

"Er... shower, washing machine, water from an outside spigot. Maybe drop off a bag of garbage now and then. I'm on a vacation. Of sorts. Between jobs." I closed my mouth with a snap, to keep from exposing more of my pathetic self to a man who had so much. I didn't want to resent him—especially since I needed his charity—but I did.

I expected Oliver to ask me where I was staying, or to lecture me about campfires, but he only stared at me with his rust-red eyebrows drawn together.

I stared back and waited. He seemed older than I'd first assumed. The fine lines at the outer corners of his eyes deepened as he frowned. His straight nose made me think again of marble. Fucking Michelangelo had spent a year sculpting Oliver's nose to get it *just right.*

Stop it.

It seemed inappropriate of me to enjoy the way Oliver looked but disapprove of his creative lifestyle and resent him for having money and property. I was the first one to look away.

"I'll consider it," Oliver said, "if you come back tomorrow for a job interview." He looked distracted, as if he'd suddenly remembered a crucial item to add to his shopping list.

I thought maybe I'd missed part of the conversation while I studied his nose. "I don't understand."

"No interview, no deal."

I took a step back. "Are you kidding me?"

"No."

My worst glare, the one that made frat boys settle down at the copy shop, only made one side of Oliver's mouth quirk up.

Again, I was the one who broke first. "Fine." I turned away, clattered down the porch steps, built up speed when I hit the lawn.

"Be here at ten tomorrow morning," Oliver shouted after me.

I heard, but didn't respond. I was at the edge of the woods by then, wishing I'd been born a tree instead of a foolish human with more feelings than I could handle.

Chapter 20

OLIVER

Grant accepted my interview stipulation.

Freddie didn't.

As soon as I stepped inside, Freddie confronted me. "You're dating a homeless man now?"

"Really? That's quite a leap."

"Whoever he was, he looked awful. And dangerous."

"I don't think so." I flattened my shoulders against the closed front door. Grant's pale skin, dark hair, and the menacing expressions he came up with gave me all sorts of artistic inspiration, but he didn't seem *dangerous*. More like a cranky, scared, hurt baby animal. A size XXL baby animal. That made me smile.

"See?" Freddie threw up his hands. "You like him. He's a rogue, and you like him. He looks at you like you're—"

"He looks at me like he likes the way I look. Nothing wrong with that."

Freddie glared harder.

"I think he really needs help," I said. "He seems to be at the end of his rope."

"Great. Take in a stray right when I get back on Vashon—a stray who wants to pet you all over."

I felt a spike of irritation at that. "You seem to have forgotten we have an open relationship."

"So you *do* want to get with him."

"No, Freddie. I want to *help* him. But even if I *did* want to get with him, it wouldn't be reasonable of you to get on my case about it."

I'd known Freddie a long time. I'd studied, drawn, painted, and touched his face and body as we'd aged. His expression of possessive outrage was one I'd never seen before. Then again, the last time anyone besides Freddie had shown interest in me, we'd been in high school.

"What's up with you?" I asked.

Freddie didn't answer.

I patted him on the shoulder and walked around him into the living room. "I know what's going on. You, my friend, are having a sudden attack of hypocrisy."

His answer was to leave.

Poor Freddie. He'd shown up ready to bed the man he assumed had pined for his return. In truth, I had pined, but more for my imagined version of Freddie's return than the actual one.

I wandered around the house, lost to my thoughts.

By the time I went to bed, I'd clarified a few things.

I needed to update my fantasies.

Freddie needed to update his assumptions.

And if Grant needed a push, even if that wasn't what he'd asked for, I was the man for the job.

Chapter 21

GRANT

With any luck, Oliver's farce of an interview would be brief. I felt like a wimp to go along with it. He probably only wanted to yank my chain. As if I hadn't been humiliated enough when I'd asked for his help.

During my hike along the trail to Oliver's house the next morning, I told myself the adult choice would be to pack up my stuff, return to Seattle, and get a job—*any* job. But every time I played out that scenario in my mind, it ended in a long walk down a dark street to a homeless shelter, where I'd unroll my sleeping bag on a cot, trapped in a cramped room with a dozen other defeated men. No fresh breeze. No chitter of birds all around. No sunlight filtering through a canopy of leaves. No room to move. No sky. No stars.

No air.

Until I couldn't breathe.

Before I stepped onto Oliver's lawn, I touched the bark of an aspen tree and sucked in a lungful of the oxygen the trees around me breathed out. Compared to the hell of trying to breathe in the city, an "interview" with Oliver seemed like a minor inconvenience. If Oliver agreed to my proposal and I *still* failed—died in my tent from hunger and fart fumes—at least I would have lived my last days outdoors in peace instead of destitute in Seattle. I might *be* destitute on Vashon, but I didn't *feel* destitute. Not quite yet.

I climbed the porch stairs and knocked. The door opened right away.

A man with a superior air frowned at me from the doorway. He looked like Oliver. Sort of. Tortoiseshell glasses covered half his face. His tweed jacket sported suede patches on the elbows. He wore pleated corduroy pants, polished oxfords, and a button-down dress shirt, all of which were the color of...

"Interesting shirt." I leaned closer. "What color is that? Baby-puke beige?"

Oliver's brows furrowed. He shifted to look past me. "My mistake," he said in a sharp voice. "I thought you were the new applicant." He lifted his arm to check the ugly watch buckled around his wrist. His haughty dismissal seemed so genuine I couldn't help but respect his acting skills.

Then he closed the door in my face.

I expected him to open it again, with a smile and a joke, but he didn't.

Well, damn.

Oliver may have put on a costume, but he wasn't kidding around. I took a minute to get my mental shit together before I knocked again.

Professor Oliver answered with a raised eyebrow and a push of his glasses farther up his nose. His stare reminded me of the offended look Mr. Hawkins used to give me in seventh grade on days I'd had to work before school and arrived late to homeroom.

"Please come in," Oliver said. With a stiff gait, he led me past the couch and its profusion of pillows to the dining table. Two leaves had been added to the table, making it long enough to fill a corporate boardroom. Oliver pointed me to the left end of the table, where a tray of writing utensils, a pitcher of water, and a glass were arranged around a legal pad.

"Overkill much?" I muttered.

From my seat, I had a view of the kitchen side of the room. Between the kitchen and the front door were a closed door and a half-open bathroom door, through which I could see the shower stall. I wondered if Oliver had seated me strategically.

At the opposite end of the table, Oliver sat with a posture so rigid it made me tired. He bestowed upon me an officious smile and said, "Welcome, Mr. Grant. I'm delighted you're interested in applying to the program. You'll find an application under the legal pad. Please take a moment to fill it out."

I rolled my eyes and yanked out the sheet of paper. A pompous font prompted me for *Full Name*, *Phone Number*, *Age*, and *Emergency Contact*. I shook my head, but filled it out, writing *Mitch Martensen* and his phone number for my emergency contact.

When I'd finished, Oliver walked the length of the table to retrieve the paper. He studied it as he returned to his chair.

"Mr. Eastbrook, tell me about your work history."

I stared at him. "Are you serious?" I detected no sign of the Oliver I'd crushed on.

The set of Professor Uppity's mouth conveyed disapproval of my disbelief. "Your career, please? I'm waiting." Oliver picked up a pen with a floaty green feather attached.

I made an effort not to roll my eyes again. "No. Career." To annoy him, I spoke like a robot with a one-word maximum per sentence. "Only. Dull. Jobs."

"What was your most recent job?"

"Copy center in the University District."

Oliver's hoot of laughter surprised me enough to straighten me out of my slouch. "What's funny about that?"

"A *copy* center?"

"Hey. That job gave me food and a roof over my head." I wanted to make a point. "I didn't laze around. I worked hard."

"At *making copies*." That set Oliver off again, his laughter poking fun at my life. I shook my head and stood.

"Not seeing it?" Oliver's fit of laughter seemed to have banished the uptight bureaucrat. He assumed the louche posture of a 1960s poetry professor at a downscale community college. I almost expected him to whip out a doobie and offer me a hit.

I'd made up my mind to play along, but Oliver's whole attitude felt wrong to me. I could feel myself swinging out into the open—and I hated it.

"I'm not like you," I said. "Your games aren't *fun* for me. *This* isn't fun. I don't appreciate you using my low point to entertain yourself. That's... It's cruel, and I don't have time for it. I need a few basic things. You, for some reason, feel the need to be a pretentious jerk about sharing what you have so much of, which I've already told you I'm willing to work for."

My speech had no noticeable effect on Oliver. He watched me but didn't say anything. His message seemed to be that I could indulge in all the outbursts I wanted, but whatever I got from him would be on his terms.

We stared at each other over the length of the table until I managed to force my frustration down and remember I needed a job more than I needed my pride.

I sat down and braced myself.

Chapter 22

OLIVER

Grant behaved like a stump who dreamed of being a footstool.

I wanted him to realize he could be a throne.

It was fine for me to get creative with wood and a chisel, or to fill a sketch-book with drawings, but did I want to take on a creative project of a person, especially since Grant's hurt seemed as big as Aza's?

Clementine would tell me to do it.

I didn't know what Aza would tell me.

If Grant were as lost as he seemed to be, the challenge would be the timeline. I needed him out of my hair before my August break. I also needed him to stay outdoors so he wouldn't interrupt my painting process.

I decided to offer Grant five weeks of my attention, plus the use of the court-yard, but only if he earned it. He wouldn't like my terms any more than he liked the interview. He wouldn't like *me*. Well, so what? Grant would play by my rules or he'd leave. Either way, by the end of July he'd be gone and I'd have August all to myself before fall stormed in with after-school art lessons.

I counted on Grant's desperation to close the deal. He seemed one bit of bad news away from vibrating himself into a puddle of grubby outrage. Or coming down with a terminal disease.

My first goal for the interview was to get a rise out of Grant, to see what he reverted to when pushed. A five-week program wouldn't have a lasting effect unless I could gain access to Grant's psyche beyond his bluster. While he barked out his "pretentious jerk" speech, I lined up my next push.

After he'd had his say, Grant sat down and shot me a blood-tipped dagger of a glare.

I pointed over my shoulder to the bathroom. "Want to freshen up before we continue? Smooth your hair? Stuff wads of toilet paper under your armpits to staunch the anxiety sweat?"

"What would *you* know about anxiety?"

"I'll take that as a no. Let's continue, shall we?"

"Goddamned jerk."

I ignored the insult. "Before I make a decision about your application, I require you to answer a few more crucial questions. Your honesty will be the deciding factor in this interview. Do you understand?"

"Go to hell, Professor Bureaucrap. *Yes*, I understand the unnecessary and condescending requirements you impose for your own entertainment."

"Excellent." I picked up my pen and doodled a quick impression of Grant's disapproving mouth. When fearful, his default response seemed to be *hothead*. I needed to know if that was the only response to discomfort in his repertoire.

"First question," I said. "Why were you sleeping in that ditch?"

The circles under Grant's eyes seemed to darken as he sagged.

I flipped the page and began a sketch of Grant's shoulders curved around his heart. His physical fragility concerned me. He seemed too skinny for his broad frame. The man desperately needed to be rescued from himself.

Meanwhile, Grant seethed at me from the other end of the table.

I waited him out.

"Kai and I went for a walk," Grant said with a croak. He swallowed. When he spoke again, his voice had moved into a deeper register. "I hadn't seen Kai in years. He'd grown six inches, but he looked... not good."

Grant's pause lengthened.

"Go on," I prompted. "Get to the point."

"Fuck off. I lost my job in Seattle. Came to Vashon to squat on Mitch's Vashon property. Didn't notice the security camera. Mitch didn't have my phone number, so he had to come over from Seattle to evict me. He brought Kai. Kai and I went for a walk."

Grant's staccato burst of sentences faltered.

"It was just us, me and Kai, on the walk. I thought he was working up to telling me something. I didn't know how to help him get it out. Then the sun came out, right in front of us. Kai stared at that bolt of sunshine with... I don't know what. Longing, maybe? On impulse, I picked him up and hugged him. Poor kid started to cry, wrapped his arms around my neck, and held on tight. My back hurt after a while, but he wasn't done crying, so I sat, then lay down. It didn't *seem* like a ditch. I rubbed Kai's back, tried to let him know I was there for him."

I sketched without looking down at the notepad. I didn't want to take my eyes off Grant and miss anything. I drew the concern on his face, flipped the page. I couldn't fucking draw fast enough.

"The sunlight made Kai's hair shine." Grant's voice took on a flat tone, as if he'd lost himself in the memory. "He has the same hair as my ex-wife, that cornflower yellow. I put my hand on his head to try to settle him, and he fell asleep." He shrugged. "Seemed like a good idea to let him rest. I closed my eyes against the light—"

"And the next thing you knew, some stranger was waking you up," I said.

"I never did find out what was bothering him."

"You want to be there for him."

Grant nodded.

"But not in the state you're in."

"Correct." The hothead made a comeback in Grant's furrowed brow and tight lips. Of course he was angry. From his perspective, my "games" kept him from getting his act together sooner, so he could help Kai sooner.

Grant waved a hand at me. "Hurry up. Next question."

"Thank you for your answer," I said.

"I still think you're a cruel dickwad."

"I'm sure you do. Now tell me the top three worries that keep you up at night. First thoughts. Don't edit. *Go.*"

With a pained sigh, Grant gave me the finger, picked up a pen, and bent over his legal pad. When he'd written for a few minutes, he made three circles with his pen, lifted his eyes, and said, "I'm not telling you those."

"Answer the question or no deal."

Grant's sharp jaw firmed up, as if he was grinding his teeth.

I started another drawing. "And be honest."

We both paused for another stare-off.

I wasn't going to budge. There was too much at stake for Grant. "I'll know if you're not being honest."

The three circles on Grant's pad took some abuse from the pen after that, until the paper ripped and Grant threw down the pen. He folded his arms and said, "One. No matter how hard I try, I don't ever succeed. Two. Even if I started succeeding today, I'd never catch up."

"Catch up on what?"

"Like..." Grant looked around the room. "Owning a home. Being able to retire at some point. I turned thirty-nine last week. The future is barreling down on me and I can't... *move*." He rubbed his forehead and his voice descended to that lower register again. "I really, *really* hate you right now."

"That's fine. What's number three?"

"Three is the complaint I've heard from people all my life—that I'm afraid to try anything new. I'm not impressed with where that trait has gotten me. And that's the *only* reason I'm doing this, doing your absurd interview—to try something new."

"How's it going for you so far?" I couldn't help my snide tone.

Grant's lifted eyebrows and facial expression clearly conveyed *You suck, so it's going like crap.*

I doodled and considered, sketching a picture of a forlorn Kai curled inside Grant's chest.

A hard knock on the wood of the table startled me and I looked up.

"What are you waiting for?" Grant asked. "Don't stop at a partial evisceration. Come on, man. Kill me all the way. Lob another one. I can take it." He pulled a tissue from his front pocket to wipe his nose and his eyes, jammed it back in, held my gaze.

The fact that Grant had owned up to getting teary while he answered my questions made up my mind for me. "You're in," I said with a nod.

Grant's cheeks pinked and his forehead relaxed.

The stark hope in his eyes made my heart hurt.

Chapter 23

GRANT

It was silly of me to feel proud when Oliver told me I'd passed his interview, but I did. I expected him to move on to the officious details. Instead, he said, "Now it's your turn to interview me."

I sighed. "Listen, Professor Doobie, I appreciate the offer, but you really don't get it. I'm unemployed, broke, and camping somewhere I shouldn't. All I want is a little time to think about my trajectory, so please, *please* get to the point here. What does 'You're in' mean? I'm guessing it's more than a simple trade. Spell it out for me. What can I count on and what do I have to do to get it?"

The whole time we talked, Oliver took notes. *Nothing* I said was *that* interesting. I suspected his note-taking was a ruse to keep himself in character. He glanced up at me and wrote some more, and I became aware again of the man behind the role. The rust threads of his jacket brought out the rust in his coloring. Oliver's beard and moustache, glossy and neat, caused a surge of physical desire that clashed with my irritation.

"I require a five-week commitment," Oliver said.

My disbelief erupted in a laugh. "Get real. I can't afford to goof off in the woods for a *week*, much less five."

"Then no deal." The shrewd look Oliver sent me didn't bode well. "Also, you'll have to earn each amenity. I won't give them to you all at once."

"That's... *Jesus*. Why would you do that? You think since I'm homeless and jobless I should be taught a lesson, or cured, or something? I'm not asking for that."

Oliver leaned back in his chair. "Well, you're under no obligation to accept."

I felt messed up. My crush on Oliver and my hatred of him scrambled my brain, which imploded with a whimper of overwhelm and indecision.

Help.

Chapter 24

OLIVER

Grant would accept my offer. I knew he would.

"As soon as you sign the contract," I told him, "you're welcome to take water from the outdoor faucets. I'll give you one new amenity per week, in exchange for a few hours of labor and doing some assignments."

With a blink of confusion, Grant said, "Assignments?"

"One big assignment per week, plus two assignments you'll do for the duration: examine the rules you live by, and write in a journal every day."

Grant surged to his feet. "The *hell* I will. I didn't sit through this freak show to become an experiment, you goddamned busybody." His face turned a lovely shade of pink. "This is my *life* you're talking about. I'm trying to... I'm just trying to..."

To my surprise, Grant seemed on the verge of crying. I could tell from his scowl that he blamed me for his misery.

"You're trying to what?" I asked.

Grant's eyes went blank. If he'd had a straight shot to the front door, he might have sprinted out of the house, but he had to navigate around all the furniture.

I hurried after him. "Hey. Wait. You're just trying to what? What are you trying to do? Tell me."

By the time I reached the door, Grant was crossing the yard, and he wasn't slowing down.

"Please," I called out.

Beyond the stomp of Grant's footsteps, I located a gust of soft words. "I'm just trying to stay alive." Like a telepathic thought we shared.

I want to help you. I sent the thought out into the woods, then stood on my porch and watched the shadows, alone again in my tiny world.

Night came and went. And then another day and another night.

While I waited for Grant to change his mind, I passed the time with preparations for the Ophelia painting. The dining table with its added leaves gave me the idea of doing the painting as a mural. I spent hours drawing on white butcher paper unrolled across the table—my attempt to replace the images that came to me at night, of Grant dying of hunger in the woods because I'd refused to give him what he thought he wanted.

Absorbed as I was in a clump of top-heavy sedges over Kai's back, the knock on the door startled me. I yelped, threw the pencil into the air, and rushed to the door, expecting to see Grant.

It took me a moment to bring Freddie into focus. I watched him shake out his umbrella and stomp water off his shoes onto the mat. "It's raining?" I asked.

With a chuckle, Freddie closed the door and put his arm around me. "Yes, Oliver, it's raining. You must be working on something big if you haven't noticed. What is it?"

I glanced back at the dining table. Before I could stop him, Freddie steered me toward it. I was tempted to tell him to leave so I could keep working, but as I emerged from hyper-focus and registered Freddie's familiar smell, time scooted forward and I decided I could use a break.

Freddie must have sensed my decision. "That's it," he said and moved in to kiss me on the mouth. He didn't pick up where we'd left off the last time he visited me, with my accusation of hypocrisy and his outrage about Grant. That wasn't Freddie's way.

I put a hand on his chest. "Hold up, Casanova."

"Not there yet, huh?" He moved behind me, wound his arms around my waist, and rested his chin on my shoulder. "So, let's see what you've been up to."

A shrug was all the comment I had. Freddie could see for himself, and I didn't have words enough to explain.

"*Whoa.* Ollie," Freddie exhaled.

"Don't call me that."

"Well, then, *whoa*, Oliver. This is stunning." Freddie let me go to walk around the table.

I picked up the pencil and rolled it between my fingers, itching to finish that clump of sedges. "It's for a mural."

With his hands clasped behind his back, Freddie leaned in for a closer look at the roughed-in faces. "Who's the guy? He almost looks like..." He shook his head. "It's not me. Is it?"

"I haven't decided." I *had* decided, but Freddie didn't need to know that. Not yet.

I could tell from his tight mouth that he didn't like my answer, but he didn't push.

"It's a riff on Ophelia," I told him.

In high school, Freddie and I had sat beside each other in English class. I gave him a moment to remember the paper I'd written about Ophelia, Shakespeare's forlorn noblewoman who died in a brook.

"*Hamlet*?" Freddie asked.

I nodded.

"Ugh. I hated the tragedies. If you're going to paint something huge and in your face, why not do one of the comedies?"

Freddie's discomfort probably had more to do with the unspecified face of the man in the drawing than my choice of Ophelia for the subject matter. I didn't call him on it, since I wasn't being completely honest either. "I've always had a thing for Ophelia."

We stared at each other across the table, neither of us willing to be the first to veer into new territory and expose the stalemate of our relationship.

"Okay," Freddie said, like he agreed not to acknowledge the deeper issues.

But his gaze wandered back to the placeholder face, and the whiff of jealousy coming off him was new. It made me wonder if Freddie had reached a point of readiness for the committed relationship he'd once told me he eventually wanted.

I mentally stepped back to feed myself a dose of reality. *Freddie always leaves. He likes me, but he sleeps with other men when he's away on his trips. He's more at home in Japan.*

I hadn't conceived of the mural to shove the impasse of our situation in Freddie's face, but I could see how he might have interpreted it that way. I scanned my drawing as I tried to think of something to say. The pencil in my hand moved to the paper before I'd made a conscious decision to bend over. I blurred and extended the shadow under Kai's wrist, which rested on Grant's hip near a bunchberry.

Freddie came around the table and took the pencil out of my hand. "Come here." He pulled me close and squeezed me tight. "I'm sorry. I'm being weird. Your drawings are phenomenal. It's going to be breathtaking as a painting."

The timeless space I'd languished in all morning faded under a wave of relief, the hollow feeling in my abdomen sorting itself into simple hunger. "I'm starving." That made me think of Grant, who was maybe *literally* starving. It occurred to me I could try to find his campsite, to make sure he was okay. "I'm hungry," I revised, which felt more true.

Even with Freddie in the house, my thoughts returned to Grant and how gaunt he'd looked. My curiosity had deepened as I'd explored him with my pencil. I wasn't attracted to Grant, not really, not even as a potential friend—his hair-trigger judgments and lack of self-awareness were deal-breakers for me— but I was concerned and intrigued. My mind kept playing out different options for solving the problem of his broken life.

"What wall will you paint it on?" Freddie shuffled to turn us in a circle. "Not much free space."

"There." I pointed to the wall between the stage and the French doors to the side porch, a wall covered with framed art by my students.

"Really?" Freddie asked. "You want a dead guy front and center in your living room?"

"He's not dead."

"He *looks* dead. With a dead kid lying on top of him."

"They're not dead." My stomach growled again. I extracted myself from Freddie's embrace and headed to the kitchen. "Are you hungry?"

He followed me and gave me a speculative look. "Most definitely."

I took a deep breath, considered what Freddie had wordlessly asked, and realized I was willing, though I might need an assist. I remembered a fantasy I'd concocted over a long February evening and reeled out the scene in my imagination.

We're two strangers.

Freddie kissed my neck. "Mmm."

We meet at the buffet table at a gallery opening.

Freddie peeled off my shirt off. He ran his hands over my skin and pressed me against the kitchen counter.

The stranger presses me against the wall in the back hallway, where we've gone to escape the crowd. He opens the bathroom door, hustles me into darkness and privacy...

My fantasy spun out into mental nothingness. The tasteful charcoal gray of the bathroom walls in my mind's eye interested me more than the stranger's touch. Too bad. That fantasy usually worked. I tried again.

He pulls me toward the bathroom.

My hand lands on the emergency exit bar.

Alarms ring in my ears as I flee into the night.

It wasn't going to happen.

Freddie tried again to kiss me on the lips, but I couldn't get into it. He resorted to kissing my jaw and beard, until I tensed.

"Now you're being weird," he said. "What's up?"

"Uh." My mind felt too full. "I must be... I think I just need food, and I'm... distracted. Like, by the interruption."

Freddie disengaged and stepped back. "The green flag was up. Did you think you'd changed it?"

I hadn't thought about the flags at all, but I nodded.

"Damn it, Oliver. I wanted to get sexy with you before I head to Whidbey for that interview."

"When?"

"Now," Freddie said.

"You're going to Whidbey Island today?"

"Yeah."

"But... Why didn't you call first?" I asked. "You didn't drive all the way down here on a whim for a quickie before you hit the road, did you?"

Freddie's leer was answer enough.

"Um. Huh." It hadn't bothered me before how much Freddie assumed about our arrangement. He didn't call ahead or give me details about his travel plans. He just... showed up, assumed I'd be ready and willing. To be fair, I always had been, after an initial period of getting used to him again in the flesh, which usually took an *hour*, not *days*.

"Hey. Oliver, don't worry about it. I can wait. You're always reluctant when I get back. Not usually *this* reluctant, but it's not a total surprise."

"Yeah, well, I'm surprised too." But if Freddie wasn't worried, I wouldn't worry either. "How long will you be gone?"

"Week or two maybe."

"That's a long time for an interview."

Freddie shrugged. "I like Whidbey."

"Well, when you get back to Vashon, come over. I'll make dinner. You can tell me trip stories and stay the night."

After a quick peck on my cheek and a stroke down the front of my shorts, Freddie smiled and left.

Apparently, if booty was off the menu, he didn't want to hang around. I'd wanted to make him a nice lunch. We could have eaten and talked. I couldn't figure out why Freddie's visit disturbed me. He hadn't done anything out of the ordinary.

The edge of the kitchen counter dug into my back. I put my shirt on and closed my eyes to try my fantasy again.

The gallery set out a generous buffet. Canapés filled with mushrooms and gruyere. I reach for another just as someone else reaches for the same one. Our fingers touch. The jolt of sensation makes me yank my hand back and look up. The scruffy man who tried to nab my canapé wears too many layers of clothing for the mild weather. He looks a bit... desperate, like maybe he crashed the opening to swipe some free food.

He turns his back on me and hunches over the table. With his big hand, he grabs half the bacon-wrapped dates and makes a hasty retreat.

I pluck a few napkins from the holder and follow, drawn by the man's daring and the look he'd given me. Dark eyes, black hair, skin as stark white as Ophelia's neck in Millais's painting.

The opening night crowd fills the rooms between the food table and the front door. He veers toward the back hallway, eats as he walks, with jerks of his elbow, spitting a trail of discarded toothpicks.

At the emergency door at the end of the hall, the man whirls, snatches the front of my shirt, and turns us in a half circle until my shoulders hit the door. Huffs of angry breath and his hard look contradict the uncertainty I detect in the furrow between his brows.

We stare until I lift my arm and say, "I thought you might need a napkin."

In a move too fast for me to avoid, the man slams my hand against the door by my head, trapping the wad of napkins between our palms. I expect harsh words, but he leans into me with his full weight. I have to thrust my hips toward him to keep from pressing the emergency bar on the door.

"It's okay," I say. I want him to know I don't think he's doing anything wrong and I won't tell anyone he crashed the party.

In a blur of motion, he unfastens my pants with unmistakable intent. His mouth, when he kisses me, tastes of bacon and sweet richness. I smell dust and sun-warmed skin, like he's been outside too long. My hands around his upper arms grip muscles too spare on a frame built for heft.

He takes my cock in his palm slick from the greasy food he'd stolen, and yanks me in a tight, busy grip. His desperation makes me imagine ways I can make his life better.

When he bites my tongue, I blast my climax between us, cover his hand and the edges of my suit jacket with cum.

The man doesn't stop. He grabs at my kisses, rubs at his cock through his thin jeans, finishes with a grunt, mauls me with his mouth from start to finish—one long, angry, unbroken kiss.

I clawed my way out of the fantasy, snapped hard back into reality to find myself doubled over the kitchen counter, my hand and my dick covered in spunk. I shivered from overstimulation, tried to catch my breath.

Grant Eastbrook was officially messing with my life—a life that had worked fine without him for a long time. I hadn't invited him into my fantasy, but he'd barged in anyway.

I don't want him.

He was broken and furious. He'd cast himself in the role of victim. I had no business being attracted to *that*, to *him*, despite my imagination's rude betrayal.

I straightened and rinsed my *business* into the kitchen sink. When I failed to also rinse away the awareness of my physical attraction to Grant, I escaped the scene of the crime.

For hours that afternoon, I tried to lose myself in the motion of the mallet. Curls of wood dropped around me to the rhythm of Les Charbonniers on infinite replay. A forest of leaves, freed from the dead wood, grew from the tip of the chisel. I pushed beyond the ache in my arms, into the shadow of twilight, on a search for *one* leaf, *one* curve of *one* line, that didn't evoke the scene I'd drawn on the papers spread across my dining table, or the infuriating man who'd invaded my sanctuary.

Chapter 25

GRANT

After I rejected Oliver's terms and retreated to my campsite, I had ample time to note that I was still right where I'd been since I quit my job—flat on my ass.

To conserve energy and reduce my food intake, I didn't take a walk to burn off my anger. The reduced caloric intake impaired my ability to think.

I stopped doing much of anything.

I watched sunlight spray across the roof of the tent.

The second day after my interview with Oliver started with rain. I spent half an hour in a spot of forest near my campsite trying and failing to use rainwater to bathe, then lay on the sleeping bag and willed myself not to scratch my arms. Not bathing thoroughly for so long had made my skin splotched and itchy.

For the hundredth time, I tried to pinpoint the internal moment when my life had veered off track. I remembered what Oliver had said during the interview, right before I called him a *goddamned busybody*. Something about the rules I live by. Doing anything Oliver suggested didn't sit well, but as I stared up at tent fabric bouncing in the rain, outrage retreated enough to allow me to wonder about my rules.

People suck seemed more like a belief than a rule. *Rules* made me think of my parents. I tried to put into words the rules I'd grown up with. *Don't steal. Say please and thank you. Take out the trash when it's full.* Other rules shoved their way up into my consciousness, rules I heard in my father's voice with Mom as backup singer. *Beggars can't be choosers. No playing until the work is done. There's always more work to be done. School is play.*

I hadn't seen it when I was growing up, but as an adult, I understood how ridiculous some of their rules were. I'd never once questioned them. I squeezed my eyes shut, wishing I could close my mind to keep it from searching for more rules.

I also didn't want to look at the rules I'd made up on my own, but one of them nabbed my attention anyway.

If I don't like it, I leave.

My undernourished brain turned *leave* into *leaf.*

If I were a tree, I couldn't leave.

Due to the lousy job I'd done with the tarp, it didn't cover the entire tent. The single layer of tent fabric saturated and raindrops began to fall on me. When drops hit my face, I wiped them away. It made me feel like I was crying, but I wasn't. I rolled onto my side and put a sock on my head to keep the drops out of my ear, pressed my face into the side of the pack. I curled in so my back wouldn't touch the tent wall and pull in more rain.

For about twenty seconds, I achieved a state of perfect mental vacuousness—a trick my mind played to empty the arena before another rule stepped into the spotlight.

Creativity is play.

For the first time in days, I thought of the zodiac scroll. I could no longer totally hate it, because it had led me to Vashon and the idea of *simple work in nature.* Even when damp and hungry, I felt better on Vashon than I'd felt in Seattle, better than I'd felt during my marriage or when I was a kid.

With some urgency, I scrambled up to locate the pants I'd worn the last day I remembered feeling the scroll in my pocket. I'd returned to the campsite after a long hike, taken off my sweat-drenched jeans, turned them inside out, and draped them over the line by the cooking area to air overnight.

Too impatient to put on my rain poncho, I balled the sleeping bag into the middle of the tent, shoved my feet into my boots, and sloshed out to yank the jeans off the line—the jeans that had kept the tarp line taut.

With sadistic timing, I pulled the mass of soaked paper that used to be the scroll out of the pocket right when the loosened tarp dumped its load of collected rainwater onto the tent. The wet tent walls plastered against the sleeping bag and my pack, letting in more rain.

"Goddamn it straight to *motherfucking hell.*"

Someone laughed.

It was a child's laugh, and it didn't compute, not until a girl in a green rain-coat with a hood, flip-flops, and shorts walked into my outdoor installation of mishaps.

She smiled at me with a mouthful of metal braces.

"You should *not* be here," I told her. "Run away right now from the creepy man you stumbled upon in the woods."

Her grin remained fixed in place. She looked eleven or twelve.

"Seriously, honey," I said. "You don't know me. You can't just walk up to a... a stranger in the woods who's..." I looked around at the disaster of my current home. "Who's...?"

"Who's having a really bad day?" She *kept* smiling at me.

"I mean it." I made my voice stern.

The girl laughed and took a step toward me. "Don't worry. If you were scary, you wouldn't be so terrible at camping."

The incongruous vision of a kid splashing around the clearing in flip-flops adorned with plastic flowers made my brain grind to a halt.

The girl untied one of the tarp ropes and gave it a hard tug. Water flew into the air. With efficient movements, she retied that line to a different tree, then moved on to retie all the other lines, full metal smile in evidence the entire time. By the time she'd redecorated my campsite, the tarp covered the tent *and* the cooking area. She'd slanted the tarp to shed water onto the low side of the slope, which meant rainwater wouldn't run under my tent anymore.

"There." She put her hands on her hips and looked around.

The pail I'd been using to steal water from the spigot at the unoccupied home caught her attention. She set it under the steady drip from the tarp. And I had washing-up water on tap.

"I almost thought of that," I said.

I thought the girl was done blowing my mind, but she spotted the clothes-line. The clothesline I had not hung my pants on. After she retied the clothes-line, it ran along under the edge of the tarp, so whatever I hung on it would be out of the rain.

I must have looked as gobsmacked as I felt. The brutal efficiency with which she'd revamped my world stunned me.

"Are you okay?" she asked.

"Who are you? My fairy camping godmother?"

"You're funny." Her laugh shook her shoulders. "A small tweak of perspective can make a big difference. And my family camps a lot." She held out her hand. "I'm Penelope."

Her hand hung there for a long moment before I rallied and shook it. "Grant. And thank you. I'd be embarrassed about my ineptitude, but I'm too grateful to care how much of a dork you must think I am."

She shrugged, smiled wider yet, and headed off on the track I'd used to get to Oliver's.

"Are you going to visit Oliver?" I called out.

With a nod and a glance back over her shoulder, she said, "Last drawing lesson before art camp starts." As an apparent afterthought, she called out, "Supposed to be sunny this afternoon. Good luck."

I'd set up camp on Penelope's trail.

I clutched my drenched pants to my chest and stared down the path at her. Before I lost sight of her, I shouted, "I'm sorry I cussed."

I froze to listen better and heard a faint "No problem" float back through the patter of raindrops.

The thick forest swallowed Penelope, and I was on my own again.

For the duration of her campsite makeover, I'd kept the former zodiac scroll clutched in my fist. I decided if a change of perspective could do *that*, give me a renovated home in five minutes, I might be willing to push past my discomfort and try to see things differently.

I uncurled my fingers and dumped the handful of pulp onto the mud of rock bottom.

Chapter 26

GRANT

I sat at Oliver's dining table in the same chair as before, determined to do whatever he required so I could leave with a bucket of water I hadn't stolen.

Oliver slid a sheet of paper toward me before he took his seat at the other end of the table. It was a neat, one-page contract written in clear language. No posturing or ornate fonts, which surprised me.

When I got to the bottom of the contract, I saw Oliver's signature. "That's presumptuous of you." I set the paper down but didn't pick up a pen.

"Do you have any questions?"

Oliver seemed smaller. He sat with his body drawn in, no costume, no hint of the professor in his manner. I wondered if I was seeing the Oliver beneath the roles he played to entertain himself.

"As soon as I sign, I can take water from an outdoor spigot?" I asked.

Oliver nodded.

"And I get one additional amenity per week, in trade for three hours of labor plus the week's assignments."

Oliver nodded again.

I folded my arms and leaned back. "Why aren't the assignments specified?"

"I haven't decided what they are."

"That's messed up."

"I can help you," Oliver said.

"You assume you know how to do that?" I could feel myself yearning to take a chance, even though it scared me, but I wanted Oliver to convince me.

Beggars can't be choosers.

No playing until your work is done.

Creativity is play.

I rubbed my face to focus my thoughts. "Hard no on examining my rules. If you scratch out that part, I'll sign."

"Really?" Oliver sat forward in his chair. "Why?"

"Because I feel sure you'd require me to tell you about them. I'll try the journaling, but I won't share it with you."

"What are you more afraid of—sharing your rules with me or being homeless and jobless?"

"Jesus," I said. "What scares me the most is your presumption that you can wave a magic wand and resuscitate my life."

"But you need help," Oliver said. He was right, but his attitude rubbed me the wrong way.

"I don't like you," I said.

"I don't care if you like me or not. I can still help you. It might be easier if you don't like me." A hint of Professor Snooty Pants reappeared in Oliver's gaze.

"Right," I said. "We've established that I'm a loser and you're an arrogant prick, so can we move on?"

Oliver watched me with his steady gaze. He remained tight and distracted, like he had just enough energy to negotiate the deal, but couldn't wait for me to leave.

Whatever. I picked up the pen. "What are your fucking journal stipulations?"

"One page minimum per day, and if you won't do the rules, you have to do one self-portrait a week, which I get to see."

"Did you get some bad news today, or something?" I asked. "You seem... clenched."

Oliver snorted though his nose. "Don't worry about it."

"Gotcha. You're tense enough to crack granite with your asshole, but it's none of my business. Memo received."

"Leave my asshole out of this. Sign or don't, but hurry it up."

"Why? Do you have a hot date with—"

"Do you have any more questions?" Oliver butted in to ask.

"I was in the middle of asking a question when you interrupted."

"About the contract. Stop procrastinating. I have things to do."

"Let's cut it to three weeks," I said.

Oliver shrugged. "Five weeks. Take it or leave it."

"No negotiation about the timeline?"

"You're in a tough spot," Oliver said.

"You're an imperious dickhead."

We stared at each other.

Oliver didn't blink. I studied his face for signs of life. His skin seemed to have lost most of its blood supply.

"What happened to Professor Chatty Pants?" I asked.

"Sign it."

I huffed my way through an eye-roll and bent to read the contract one more time. I crossed out *examine the rules you live by* and wrote above it *do and share one self-portrait a week*, then initialed my edit and signed on the bottom line. What did it matter? It was all bullshit anyway, a figment of Oliver's imagination.

Oliver appeared by my side to swipe the paper. "I'll make you a copy. Your assignments for this week are to start journaling, do the self-portrait, and do three hours of labor, but you'll also do another self-portrait now, as part of the signing process."

"The fuck I will. I already signed."

"Start the self-portrait within the next five minutes, and I'll give you a signing bonus of a bag of muffins."

"Deal." I grabbed the pen and flipped to a new page on the legal pad.

Chapter 27

OLIVER

Grant smelled like a compost heap. I caught a deeper whiff of his stink when I picked up the signed contract. The way he scrubbed his hands over his arms tempted me to offer a shower as the signing bonus, but I figured he'd need motivation to get through the first week. If he did everything he'd agreed to, I'd give him shower access for a reward. I hoped he'd figure out how to take a bucket bath at his campsite before then.

"Not on the notepad." I set the contract on my desk and slid an easel toward the living room, to give Grant a view out the French doors. I'd already clamped a backing board and a pad of paper onto the easel.

"What medium do you prefer?" I scanned the art supplies in the shelving Dad and I had designed and built over a long winter.

"How about ballpoint pen on a legal pad?"

I decided to treat Grant as a kid. I grabbed a few paintbrushes, a tempera paint set with six colors, and a paint smock.

"Here. Put this on." I handed the smock to Grant.

He frowned. "What the hell is that?"

"It's an artist's smock."

"No way am I wearing an apron. This is already humiliating enough."

"At some point, if you stop resisting, you might have a breakthrough."

"Cease with the condescension, Snooty Boots. Just tell me what I have to do."

"I'm guessing what you really want is more than access to a shower and a washing machine. If anything's going to change, you'll have to shift your—"

"You piss me off so much." Grant snatched the smock from my hand and tied it around his gaunt waist with a sharp tug. His angry look reminded me of the look he'd given me in my gallery fantasy. No. The look an *imaginary* guy who'd looked like Grant had given me during a few minutes of confusion that resulted in jizz on the kitchen cabinet.

I took a deep breath and refocused.

"Go ahead and be pissed off," I said. At the utility sink in the art corner, I filled a cup with water, then set it in the cup holder on the easel. "Let me ask you something. If I gave you all the amenities now, would you do the assignments?"

"Hell to the fuck no."

"Well, then. There you go," I said.

The challenge in Grant's expression didn't bode well.

I stood my ground and lifted my chin.

"You act like you rule a kingdom," Grant said, "but you're way out here in the boonies." He took a step toward me. "People stop by to swoon over your pronouncements and that makes you think you have all the answers, but look around. It's a *tiny* kingdom. Out in the real world, shit happens that you couldn't imagine, not if *this* is how you've spent your life." He waved his hand to include me and everything around us.

My first impulse was to throw the cup of water in Grant's face. Not to cool him off, but to *hurt* him. His words had hurt me, though I didn't think he'd meant them to hurt as much as they did. I took a breath to say something, but Grant beat me to it.

"No amount of King Oliver's creative techniques are going to remove the type of shit I'm up to my third eye in. I'm not like you and your friends. Creativity is a luxury I can't afford, and I don't want you using it to poke around in my psyche. But, hey, if I have to jump through your hoops to *survive*, to get *basic resources* so I can *think*, I'll do what you're asking. I won't be creative about it, but I'll *do* it."

I took a step back and a deeper breath, forced my voice to sound calm. "You're right. It's a tiny kingdom, but it's all *mine*. Judge me if you want, but you're the one fighting reality if you think doing more of what you've been doing is going to change anything about your situation. I think you're ready to take a chance and learn something different."

"Maybe so, but not from a smug jerk of a backwoods dictator of a teacher."

"A teacher trying to help a reluctant student," I said.

Grant's angry glare held frustration and distress. His desperation showed in his painful thinness, yet he'd signed the contract and tied on the smock. He stood straight and looked me in the eye. *Pride.* I suddenly saw Grant's anger as a struggle to manage the hits to his pride.

I softened my stance, took my hands out of my pockets, and sat in a slouch on the edge of the dining table, to give Grant a chance to loom over me. "Look at it this way—what do you have to lose?" I asked. "Maybe this contest isn't between you and me, but between you and you."

After a final glare, Grant's gaze shifted toward the French doors and the view of the side yard.

I pushed off from the table and left him to it.

With my back to Grant and the easel, I busied myself in the kitchen. I heard no activity, even when I paused to listen. No tap of brush on water cup. No shuffle of feet. No sound of any kind.

I turned to see Grant facing the blank page, paintbrush in hand. With his back to me, I couldn't see his expression.

"Everything okay over there?" I asked.

In a rough voice, he said, "What if I'm already done?"

Chapter 28

GRANT

I heard a distinctive *tick-tick-tick* behind me. Oliver had set a kitchen timer.

"You have ten minutes to finish your self-portrait," he said. "Or no muffins."

With a brush full of black paint I slapped a stick figure of a man onto the paper. That took three seconds. The paint dripped. Over the next few minutes I used a smaller brush to add black details to my head, legs, and arms.

I looked like a nasty bug.

When I'd finished, I chucked the brush into the cup. A plop of gray water sloshed onto the wood floor. I considered smearing it with my boot, thought better of it, and walked to the art sink for a paper towel. *I can clean up my own mess.*

Even if Oliver *could* help me, the way he went about it made me feel angry and mortified, and what was the point of that? But, *okay.* If the next step up out of the mud and fart fumes of rock bottom required me to grovel for a few weeks, I could do it. I would consider Oliver's ridiculous assignments a menial job. *Labor* was something I understood.

"'A small tweak of perspective can make a big difference.'" I turned to look at Oliver. "You said that, didn't you?"

"That's something I say to my students. Where did you hear it?"

"Penelope said it to me."

"Oh. Are you camping out toward her house?"

"I have no idea. And I'm done answering your questions. It's my turn to ask you stuff."

Oliver dried his hands on a dishtowel, returned to his end of the dining table, and sat with his arms folded. I salivated over his shapely arms for a few seconds, stalled on the urge to ask how long his hair would be if he let it down. Would it drape over his biceps? I closed my eyes and shivered, irritated by my lust. Discomfort sharpened my next words.

"You told Kai you and your dad built that." I gestured toward the stage to my right but didn't take my eyes off Oliver. "Where are your parents now?"

Oliver frowned and hugged himself around the waist. "My dad and granddad built this house. I... inherited it."

It gave me a thrill to get a reaction from the guy other than amused omnipotence.

"Er. I'm sorry for your loss," I said. "Losses. Are both your parents dead?"

Oliver looked away. "My mother is... not in the picture."

"And yet you inherited the house."

"It wasn't... She never owned it."

"Your parents divorced?"

After a pause long enough to be rude, Oliver said, "Yes."

Weary of Oliver's hesitations and reluctance, I decided I wasn't curious enough about him to stick around, not if I could be noshing a muffin under the trees at my campsite instead.

"Final question," I said. "Do you have a couple of buckets with lids I could borrow to carry water?"

Chapter 29

GRANT

Oliver led me out the French doors, presented me two buckets from a storage closet at the end of the side porch, then taunted me with a tour of his outdoor shower.

We traipsed through the grass and skirted an offshoot of the one-story house until we arrived at a courtyard I'd never noticed. Birch and maple trees, wild roses, and smaller shrubs blocked the entryway.

Oliver held a tree branch aside and waved me through. "There." He pointed to a walk-around wooden shower stall in the near right corner. "I control the water valve from inside. Do this week's assignments and I'll turn it on."

And that was all it took to double my resolve.

I had to channel my inner brute to haul both five-gallon buckets of water at the same time. By the time I arrived at the campsite, I'd devolved into a panting mess of underfed muscles.

I flopped onto my back in the dirt and devoured one of Oliver's muffins. Bran with cherries and bits of dried ginger. The decadent treat reminded me I'd missed my own birthday, lost it somewhere between Mitch's shed and Oliver's contract. I took another bite. *Happy birthday to me.*

To resist immediate consumption of the remaining six muffins, I stashed them in the cooler, gathered my toiletries bag and clean change of clothes, and left camp. It hurt my arm to carry one of the full buckets as I bushwhacked into the thick underbrush, but I wanted to be far out of sight. It wasn't Penelope's fault I'd plonked my campsite on her trail.

The thorough shave and scrubbing I gave myself with the abundance of water felt so good I dawdled afterward. Also, I had to wait to air dry. I'd draped my only towel over a log to sit on while I bathed, which meant the towel was soaked by the time I was clean. To fling water off my hair, I shook my head until my brain rattled. Didn't help much. Water dripped over me while I lounged. Bits of sunlight moved across my closed eyelids.

I thought of Oliver at the dining table with his arms crossed, the rounded muscles of his shoulders and arms pushing against his T-shirt. I wondered again what his sparkling copper hair would look like freed from its sloppy topknot and spread over his shoulders. My fingers scrunched the towel as I gripped Oliver's hair in my imagination.

If he kept his hair up all the time to get it out of the way, why didn't he just cut it off? I was glad he hadn't, but it bugged me that I never got to see it down. I was half convinced Oliver only got under my skin because I couldn't think clearly around his glorious hair.

I'd never had a type—a collection of qualities I could count on to crank my motor. But I'd never seen anyone who looked like Oliver. So maybe I did have a type. *Ruddy, clear skin. Perfect, regal nose. Full beard. Biceps galore. Miles of glinty hair.*

If Oliver sat next to me on the towel and let his hair down, freed it to flow over his freckled shoulders in the dappled sunlight...

Jesus.

I opened my eyes and looked around. Yep. I was out in the open with a boner. I also was very alone. *Hmm. Could be fun.* But I didn't want to think about Oliver. That door would be too difficult to close once I'd opened it. I didn't need a memory of a sex daydream to add awkward embarrassment to all the other uncomfortable feelings Oliver seemed adept at pulling from me.

Maybe *long hair* was my type.

Laura and I had met in Seattle at the university's copy center, where I'd worked for five years, since graduating from high school in Eastern Washington. Her hair fell in golden waves over her straight shoulders. She'd been in her third year of undergraduate school, going for a double major in business and psychology. Her blue eyes, healthy skin, slim body, and the way she'd known exactly what she wanted had seemed so *California* to me. She told me she couldn't wait to graduate and return home to get an M.B.A. "Back to the sunshine," she'd said.

To get in the mood without reverting to Oliver, I conducted a mental survey of Laura's hairstyles over the years. When we met, she wore her hair loose, with long bangs swept to the side. After we married and moved to Los Angeles,

Laura's hairstyles became more professional. I'd liked the sleek chignon best, for wicked reasons of my own.

In the early years, when Laura still assumed I'd manifest the potential she claimed she saw in me, she allowed me to unravel her careful chignon and unravel her. After her long days of work in the spare bedroom she'd turned into an office, I would take my time undoing her, mesmerized by the flow of her hair around us as we made love.

A glop of spit slicked my cock, made it easy to remember Laura's capable fingers, insistently pulling me toward her.

I had always, in the privacy of my mind, thought of myself as Laura's consort—a monarch's indulgence on the side. She had wanted me to step up beside her as co-ruler. I couldn't. Her strong opinions about what I should do with my life filled me with static. I worked the whole time Laura and I were together, but never at jobs she considered good enough. It took me a long time to figure out she meant good enough for her, not good enough for me.

Maybe *consort* was too generous. *Male escort* felt more accurate, with all it implied about the transactional nature of the arrangement. My income from copy center jobs paid for our groceries and my clothing. Laura's corporate coaching business paid for everything else, including upgrades of homes and cars and wardrobes when we moved to Santa Barbara.

It struck me that Oliver lording it over me with his stipulations and assignments felt familiar. My chest tightened with the memory of Laura's escalating disapproval. When I signed Oliver's contract, I entered into another arrangement I'd probably botch.

And... I was back to thinking about Oliver.

With determination, I backtracked along my train of thought to Laura's chignon, to the times I'd run the backs of my hands across her tense face, watched her eyes close with relief, reached up to pull out the clips and pins, dropped them to the floor. I lifted her into my arms, held her close, carried her to the bed. The memory pulled me under, gave me something familiar for my body to work with, until my hand flew on my cock and I lost myself to remembered sensations. I kept at it, dragged it out, held off as long as I could, until I shook and moaned and let go.

Afterward, I felt exhausted.

I hadn't counted on the effort required to keep the body I held in my arms from being Oliver.

Chapter 30

GRANT

That first week, Oliver's labor assignment consisted of running errands for him in town and doing hedge maintenance. Easy stuff. Easier than the journaling and self-portraits.

I felt like I was in school again, rolling my eyes at classwork I didn't see the point of, but doing it anyway so I'd get to go outside for recess. I went outside, but I didn't play. I spent most recesses doing homework, to finish before school ended and I had to start my afternoon shift at the print shop—that was my *real* work.

If I could do that, I could do Oliver's assignments.

The morning after my happy-ending bathe in the woods, I walked to Oliver's and found the keys in the van's glove compartment where he'd said they would be, along with a shopping list and five folded twenties—bounty I reminded myself wasn't mine.

Oliver himself was nowhere to be seen.

At the bottom of a shopping list, written in a cursive fluid enough to leave no doubt Oliver was an artist, he'd left me a note. *If you have errands of your own to run, feel free, but have the van back by 11:30. I have a meeting in Tacoma this afternoon.*

I took the smaller roads to town, north along Wax Orchard Road and Westside Highway, past apple orchards and sheep scattered over fields. Large mailboxes poked up beside long driveways that spun away to houses lost in the woods.

Clouds scuttled in from the west above the Kitsap Peninsula. A few times, I caught glimpses of the sea down to my left.

A right turn onto Cemetery Road took me to the east side of the island, to Vashon Highway and town, where my first stop was the public library. I scored a comfy chair in a back corner by an electrical outlet and plugged in my phone to charge it.

I had one phone message, from Mitch's phone.

Kai's voice sounded small, like he wasn't sure he was willing to commit to expressing himself. He didn't say much. "Hi, Uncle Grant. I liked seeing you." There was a pause, long enough I almost checked to see if the recording had ended. I put a finger in my other ear to block out the subtle sounds of the library and heard Kai breathing. "Thank you," he whispered.

And that was it.

He'd made the call around the time he and his dad would have been on the ferry to Seattle the day I'd seen them. Maybe Mitch's presence had kept Kai from saying more.

The weight of Kai's message settled on my shoulders. I slouched in the upholstered chair, remembered Kai's pinched face, and didn't know what to do about it.

Mitch and Sonya and the boys had probably settled into the trailer on Vashon. Maybe if I did Oliver's errands quickly, I could drive by to say hello. I bent my head and took a discrete sniff of my armpit. *Ugh.* I couldn't do it. I needed to see Kai, but it would have to wait until I'd showered. And devised a game plan for my future that wouldn't collapse under the inevitable cross-examination by Mitch Martensen, Esquire.

I had a sudden memory of a dinner at Mitch and Sonya's house in Seattle, when Laura and I had flown up for a weekend. Sonya had hosted with terrifying capability. We'd sat around the dining table for hours, for conversation and delicious food. Laura, Mitch, Sonya, and Kai's older brother, Joel, were all loud, social, outspoken, and aggressive. The air had rung with good-natured debate, shouts of laughter, sharp questions, opinionated answers, jokes, and barbs. Five-year-old Kai and I, the only quiet people at the table, had eyed each other until after dessert, when Kai had crawled into my lap without a word. I'd held him loosely, rested my chin on his head. No one seemed to notice us, and I'd felt Kai slowly relax. Eventually, he snuggled back into me and pulled on my forearms until I understood he wanted to be wrapped up and held close, as if he'd found safe harbor in the storm of his rambunctious family and wanted more.

I spent a few minutes mulling over the possibility of Mitch or Sonya—or Joel, for that matter—doing anything inappropriate to Kai. I really didn't think they would. It seemed more likely that Kai's life with the aliens he called family stressed him out, and he didn't know how to ask them for help.

I had so little to go on. It had been years since I'd last spent time around Kai. Since then, his aunt and I had divorced. *Bless the boy for still liking me.*

I checked my phone—forty percent charged—and willed it to hurry up. I wasn't sure how long Oliver's errands would take and I didn't want to bungle my first day on the job by returning the van late.

I grinned to myself. *I had a job.*

Well, sort of.

While I waited, I checked my emails. I had one, from the copy shop, asking where to mail my final paycheck, since I hadn't picked it up. I'd totally forgotten. *Way to be financially responsible.* The check wouldn't be much, but it would be enough to add a few more calories to my meals.

I yanked the charger out of the wall and drove the few blocks to the post office.

"Sure." The man behind the counter nodded. "We can hold mail for you, as long as it's addressed with your name and the words *General Delivery.*"

In the post office parking lot, I sent an email to the copy shop. I'd stop by the post office to get my check the next time I ran errands for Oliver.

I honked the horn to celebrate the bounty of grocery money for a summer on Vashon. A dog in the next car over barked at me for disturbing his nap. I barked back.

Across Vashon Highway, the big grocery store took up most of the town's mini-mall. I parked and checked Oliver's list. Hardware store first, groceries last.

An hour later, I shuffled forward in the grocery store checkout line with a full cart and idly scanned the array of items designed to tempt shoppers as we waited in line.

A small box of scrolls snagged my attention.

Start Your Day the Zodiac Way.

They hadn't yet put out the July box. I poked a finger through the few remaining June scrolls. I may have had a creative idea or two in June—like proposing a trade to Oliver—but I remained convinced *trying* to be creative would result in more harm than good. Not everyone had the capacity for it. Writing in a journal and doing self-portraits for Oliver weren't creative acts but menial tasks required to earn the basic necessities and survive. *Story of my life.*

The line at the checkout moved forward.

"You're up," the woman behind me said. She almost nudged my ass with her cart.

"Hang on," I told her.

One. There was *one* Cancer scroll left for June.

I bought it. Without removing the paper clasp, I tucked the scroll in my front pocket to serve as a homeopathic treatment, a minute dose of the unwanted to make me stronger.

I almost drove off without remembering to get a journal.

I chucked the groceries in the van, checked the time, and jogged across the parking lot to Easel & Desk, the art and office supplies shop tucked between the hardware and grocery stores.

It didn't take long to find the section of blank books. A hardbound book cost more but would be more durable than a spiral notebook. I found one that fit in my back pocket. If I had to write a page a day, I wanted it to be a damn small page. I studied the pens on offer and a rack of Sharpies caught my eye. *Heh.* That sucker would fill a page fast.

The older man at the counter narrowed his eyes at me. He probably didn't get many customers who chuckled over their office supplies.

By the time I got back to the van, I couldn't wait to do my daily journal page. I had about five minutes before I needed to leave. *No problem.*

I dug around in my groceries to find the box of cheap saltines I'd bought to crunch on when I felt hungry after I'd used up my food ration for the day, ripped off a flap of cardboard, and slid it behind the first page in the journal. For a few seconds I tapped the steering wheel and thought. With another chuckle, I turned the book sideways, uncapped the Sharpie, and wrote *HA HA* in capital letters to fill the page, pleased with myself for gaming the system.

And that was my journaling done for day one.

When I dug in my front pocket for the van key, I felt the zodiac scroll and tried to convince myself *gaming the system* wasn't the same as *being creative.*

Perspective shift.

I couldn't tell if the shift was a break or a mend.

The zodiac scroll had gotten me fired. On the other hand, getting fired had led me to Vashon and spending five weeks outside in the woods.

My unfocused gaze sharpened on the grocery store entrance. I grabbed the key from the ignition and ran back to the store to buy a box of expensive, double-sealing Zip-loc plastic bags.

Working quickly in the van, I dropped the scroll into one of the bags, sealed it, and shoved it into my pocket. The plastic made my thigh sweat, but it was worth it. I needed my frenemy the scroll to survive my terrible camping skills until I figured out what it all meant.

On the way back to Oliver's house, I watched the scenery pass and didn't think about rules I lived by. Or the fact that I hadn't asked for job-hunting help at the library.

Chapter 31

OLIVER

The day after Grant took the van to town, I finished the drawing for the mural and hit a snag. Paper was easy to roll and hide if Grant came around, but I couldn't hide a mural.

When I imagined painting my vision onto the great room wall, my face heated and my heart sped up, like the start of a panic attack. I couldn't do it. Grant would read too much into the subject matter. Even if I painted on canvas in the great room, moving a wet painting at a moment's notice would be too risky. Oil paint had a lot going for it when it came to color depth and luminosity, but it took weeks to dry.

The house originally had two bedrooms—Dad's and the one I shared with Granddad, but after Dad died, I'd converted his bedroom into a library, a room too nice to paint in. Which meant I'd have to work in my bedroom if I wanted privacy.

I rummaged through a storage cabinet in the art corner of the great room. Dad had stocked up on panels for a show he'd done in Toronto, and I thought I remembered a surplus. I found three, backed by wood frames to prevent warping. They could be hung flush against one another to create a nine-foot-wide painting.

I lugged the panels to the side porch and spent most of the morning sanding and applying nontoxic sealant. While the final coat dried, I moved two heavy lights on stands and a large floor fan into my bedroom. My painting methods didn't produce toxic fumes, but the fans and lights would speed the drying time.

The thought of trying to sleep in a room with a painting of Grant... No. Better to save that thought for... *never*.

Great. I'd booted myself out of my own bedroom.

I sighed and took stock of my new private studio. If I hung the panels on the wall beside the bedroom door, they wouldn't be visible from the great room as I went in and out the door.

I relocated a dresser and a club chair, and clipped a canvas tarp to the gallery rail just below the ceiling. The tarp covered the wall and a couple feet of floor. I spread another tarp on the floor between the wall and the bed, and wrapped a tarp around the bed—the bed Freddie and I hadn't used since he'd been back, and wouldn't before he left again. That would be problematic, but I didn't want to explain the mural to Freddie. I couldn't even explain it to myself. I'd have to paint it to understand it.

I kept saying *mural* in my mind, but it wouldn't be a mural if I didn't paint directly onto a wall. I decided I didn't care. My problem with the project wasn't semantics but secrets. I'd never hidden my art or my creative process. When I needed to focus without interruption or lose myself in the thrill of creation, I put up the red flag.

What I was doing with the mural was different. I didn't want to share even the *existence* of the painting. I already regretted letting Freddie see my drawings.

I was going to hide it.

It took the better part of an hour to move the panels from the side porch to the bedroom and affix them to the wall over the canvas so they wouldn't shift as I painted.

Using Dad's formula, I mixed and applied four layers of white ground to the panels, to achieve a smooth surface for the detailed realism I wanted to paint. The fan dried the ground in record time. Before I applied each new coat, I smoothed the dried surface with a sanding block in each hand—an old habit begun as an impatient child who couldn't wait to start painting.

While the ground layers dried, I moved paint supplies from the art corner to the bedroom.

Hours later, after I'd sanded the last layer of ground and wiped it clean, I sat on the end of the bed to think. The next step—transferring the drawing to the panels—would be a commitment of sorts, and it made me pause.

I turned to stare at the panels.

They stared back, their stark whiteness a question.

Hunger scrambled my thoughts, allowed the bigger questions to slip through.

With the exception of Dad dying too early, my life at thirty-five was the ideal life I'd fantasized about as a kid, the only life I'd ever wanted.

Consider what's missing, the panels seemed to say.

I *knew* what was missing: Granddad, Dad, Aza. My mother was missing too, but she'd left so long ago I almost didn't remember her.

In my imagination, one of the panels winked at me, as if we shared a joke.

"Are you saying a man is what's missing?" I spoke out loud, like a lonely recluse who discussed his life with animated art supplies, which maybe I was.

You're going to paint a man, the panel pointed out.

"I've painted men before, even men I've been sexually attracted to."

You never tried to hide those paintings.

The panels and I stared at one another. After a while, they seemed to smirk.

"I *get* it," I snapped. "Yes, Grant and Kai are placeholders for a family of my own. But I don't want them specifically. Kai belongs to someone else, and Grant is... too invasive and broken and pissed off." I pointed at my rolled-up drawing in the corner. "But *that's* the image that seared into my brain, while Grant was asleep, before I even met him. He's only the Ophelia stand-in for my riff on Millais's painting."

Make up your mind. Is Grant a stand-in for Ophelia or for a family of your—

"Shut up. No. You're missing the point. Ophelia is about... Millais's scenery, that almost supernatural intensity of vegetation. The *man* in my painting is... a placeholder for a man who... could hold a child that tenderly."

You're so confused.

I sighed and flopped back on the bed to stare at the ceiling.

For years I'd been on standby with Freddie, letting him call the shots in our arrangement of spontaneous convenience. Maybe it was time to push.

I reach over to pick my phone off the bedside table, curious to see if I could tempt Freddie to come back from Whidbey sooner than later.

"I think the man in the mural should be Freddie," I told the panels.

GRANT

On Friday afternoon, at the end of my first week of working for Oliver, I returned to my campsite after a hike, dumped a big can of beef stew into the cook pot, and set my one-burner camp stove on low. While I waited for the stew to heat, I munched on a carrot.

With better food at the campsite since my trip to town in Oliver's van, and with my final paycheck from the copy center on the way, I'd stopped being a tent potato to conserve energy. As amazing as my hikes were, they hadn't improved my mood. I couldn't stop mulling over Mitch, Kai, my failed marriage, my parents and their rules, and Oliver's assignments long enough to strategize about work.

I could eliminate one of those distractions by completing my assignments for the week. The trip to town had taken care of most of the required hours of labor. Work on the hedge would be easy and take care of the rest. That left a self-portrait and the daily journal entries.

I set the timer on my phone for five minutes, to give myself a hard limit on the self-portrait. My art supplies consisted of a pencil, a Sharpie, and my journal. Everything else in my world was dirt, leaves, and the damned sharp rocks under the tent I could never seem to...

Three minutes later, I took a photo of a mixed media creation I'd decided to call *Self-Portrait with Sticks and Stones*. From a standing position, I aimed the camera down at my arrangement of rocks, twigs, moss, and leaves. On a whim, I included the tip of my boot in the frame. I'd show it to Oliver when I went to do the hedge.

The day's journal entry required most of a carrot. I chewed and contemplated, then took my time filling a page with the word *TREES*.

I finished before the stew was ready. Crappy canned stew, warmed in my crappy pot on my crappy camp stove. I made a racket with the spoon against the pot as I stirred, resentful of the eight minutes I'd spent on Oliver's assignment while he lounged in his big house with the kitchen and the running water, playing lord of the manor.

To calm down, I took a pre-lunch jog around campsite. Stomped the ground. Punched my fists in the air. I felt ridiculous, but I needed to expend my pent-up frustration before I tried to eat.

Someone laughed.

I froze and held my breath.

Silence.

"Penelope?" I lowered my fist and caught sight of her crouched in the undergrowth.

She stood and bestowed her full metal grin on me.

"What the heck, honey?" I said. "Please don't sneak up on me like that. I know I'm staked out here on your path, but you need to yell or something to give me a warning. I worry about you seeing something you shouldn't if I don't know you're there. Okay?"

"Oh." Her smile wavered briefly. "Sorry. I didn't think about that." She pointed to the rhododendron she'd been crouched behind. "I brought someone."

I cocked my head at her. "Are you introducing me to your secret friend, the shrub? I'm pretty sure we've already met."

The rhododendron snickered.

I took a step toward the bush. Kai stood from behind it. He didn't look any less wan than when I'd seen him last, but he was *there*. In two steps, I reached him and lifted him off the ground in a bear hug—a very noxious bear hug. *Ugh*. Reluctantly, I set him down.

"I stink, guys," I said. I took a few steps away and waved a hand at the campsite. "My apartment didn't come equipped with a shower."

It was a relief to hear Kai let loose a small laugh. I thought my heart would burst from seeing him again so soon—and without having to persuade Mitch that I was worthy.

"Please come in," I said with a bow. "My home may be humble, but I'm glad to share what I have. Can I interest you in a vintage beef stew with a side of hand-washed carrots?" The green tops of the carrots flapped as I waggled them.

Penelope and Kai grinned and nodded.

"Sit wherever you'd like." I pointed to the logs I'd dragged in for seats and a table. While they settled, I poured stew into my two metal cups. I could eat out of the pot.

"Use the handles," I said as I passed the cups over. "It's hot." I handed Penelope my only spoon and gave Kai the fork. "We'll take turns."

"I didn't think you knew anyone on Vashon," I said to Kai.

He gave his cup of stew a sniff.

"Art camp started this week," Penelope said. "It's all day on Tuesdays, Wednesdays, and Thursdays. We do arts and crafts stuff—drawing and plays and sewing and dancing. I've been going since I was little."

Kai spoke for the first time. "Penelope was talking about you."

"About me? At art camp?"

Kai nodded. "I heard her tell some girls she found a man camping in the woods. The girls thought it was creepy and asked Penelope if she was afraid. Penelope told the story about the rain and the tarp. It made me wonder."

"Sure," I said. "Some guy's inept in the woods, and it has to be me, huh?"

Penelope scraped the last bit of stew from her cup and handed me the spoon. "Kai came over to me later and asked what you looked like. That's how I found out you're his uncle."

"And now here you are," I said with wonder.

Kai chewed a morsel of stew tentatively, like he'd wait and see if he wanted to swallow. "Mom dropped me off at Penelope's today for a playdate."

"I'm surprised your parents went for the art camp idea," I said. Mitch and Sonya hadn't struck me as the arts and crafts type. More the computer camp type. Or golf camp. Or young attorneys camp.

I remembered an evening at Mitch's when Kai was around six. Kai and I had stretched out on our stomachs on Mitch's living room floor to work on adjacent pages of a coloring book. We hadn't talked, but I'd loved it. The grownups—the *other* grown-ups—talked around us as if we couldn't hear them. Sonya remarked on how different Kai was from Joel at that age. Meanwhile, Joel ran around the house with a plastic hockey stick, jumping over me and Kai, making a menace of himself. No one had remarked on *that*.

"All Kai does is check out library books and abuse coloring books," Mitch had said.

I'd gently pulled the coloring book out from under Kai's marker and flipped through it, charmed by his experimentation with color and the boundaries of how things "should" be. At Kai's questioning look, I'd shaken my head, patted his back, and slid the coloring book back into place. Kai refocused his attention on filling in a mermaid's hair with blue and green, adding curlicues past the black lines printed on the page.

I returned from my memory when Kai said, "Art camp wasn't Mom and Dad's first choice. I told Mom how much I liked Mr. Oliver's house. I said I'd only go to camp if it was art camp." Kai forked up another small bite of stew. "Joel's going to hockey camp and football camp."

"Well, good for you." I washed the spoon with a dribble from my water bottle and said to Penelope, "Does Oliver teach at the art camp?"

"No. I wish he did. They ask him every year. He always says no."

"Hmm." Something niggled at the back of my brain, like an almost invisible dot on a distant horizon.

"Oliver *says* it's because he doesn't need the money." Penelope's expression seemed to say, *If he doesn't need money, he could teach us for free.*

"Hmm," I said again.

Penelope tipped her cup to drink the broth. "Thanks. That was delicious."

"I agree." A final scrape of the pot and I'd finished my stew too.

"You look skinny." Kai's gaze dropped from my face to my chest. He handed me his half-full cup. "I can't finish. Do you want the rest?"

God, what a sweet boy.

I took Kai's cup and finished the stew quickly, before I got weepy. The dishes received a rinse into the pot. I'd toss the rinse water out in the woods to keep food scraps away from the campsite.

"Okay, troops," I said. "What do you two have planned for the day?"

"What are *your* plans?" Kai asked.

"I'm going to Oliver's to give an unruly hedge a haircut."

Kai's eyes lit up. "Can we go with you?"

"Do you think Oliver would mind?" I asked Penelope. "I mean, I'm not asking you to do any work, or to take responsibility for whether—"

Penelope interrupted me. "He won't mind, not if the green flag is up."

"Right. Then we'll take the driveway route, like proper visitors."

Penelope led the way along the narrow paths. When we reached Violetta Road, Kai took my hand.

"Doing okay there, buddy?" I gave his hand a squeeze.

Kai looked up at me and nodded.

The green flag was up, so we forged ahead down the driveway. I left the kids in the front yard to play on an ugly metal sculpture I decided to call *Where the Dump Truck from the Steel Plant Puked on the Lawn*, and went up the porch steps to ask Oliver where I could find hedge clippers.

Through the open front door, I heard Oliver's laughter. I couldn't help but move toward it. I poked my head inside, nudged the door open farther, followed the sound. He was in the bedroom, which I'd never seen. A white tarp covered part of the floor, like maybe he was getting ready to repaint the walls.

I approached with stealth, tried to stay hidden, to watch Oliver before he saw me.

He lay on the bed. If he didn't turn his head and I didn't make a sudden movement, he probably wouldn't notice me. It felt wrong to watch him as he lay there and talked on the phone, but I did it anyway. There was too much of him I needed to take in. I considered snapping a photo, but my internal Creep Monitor vetoed it.

Oliver's voice took on a more serious tone. "When will you be back? There's something I want to talk with you about." After a short pause, he said, "Yeah? Really? That would be great." After another pause, he said, "I wasn't ignoring you. I was in Tacoma that day and forgot my phone."

As Oliver talked, he played with a hair band. The blue of the tarp on the bed made Oliver's skin and the spread of his golden red hair *pop*.

I took a slow step backward, then another, and left the house.

About an hour later, after I'd found hedge clippers in the outbuilding, which turned out to be a workshop, Oliver shouted a greeting from the porch, his hair back up in a topknot.

I called out a hello, then turned my back on him to study the next section of hedge.

Tough to do with my eyes closed, but I gave it a shot.

Chapter 33

OLIVER

After my call with Freddie, during which he'd told me he'd wrap things up early on Whidbey, I felt lighter. My smile stayed put as I copied the drawing from the butcher paper to the panels using quick strokes.

I moved the pencil over the man's elbow, crooked to hold the boy close, and thought I heard a child's laugh. I stopped my hand and held my breath to listen. The laughter seemed to come from the front yard. I closed the bedroom door behind me and went out to investigate.

"Hi, guys." I raised my voice to be heard from the porch, not sure I wanted to do more than say hi before I returned to the mural.

"Hey," Grant said. "Hope we're not bothering you."

Oh. Grant wielded my heaviest trimmer, the one that hung on the far wall of the toolshed, which meant he'd gone in without my permission. I didn't want to jump on his case in front of Penelope and Kai, so I only said, "Carry on."

"Yes, *bwana*." Grant lifted a hand above his head in a mock salute.

"What's a *bwana*?" Penelope asked Grant.

Grant stopped clipping to look at her. "Guess."

"Boss man." Kai's soft voice carried just far enough for me to hear.

Grant's delighted chuckle was affirmation enough for the kids. They all turned to grin at me, and I felt uncomfortable in my elevated position on the porch. Grant said something to Kai I couldn't hear then shifted a couple of steps down the hedge. The three of them moved as a cohesive unit. Neat and tidy with their jokes and smiles.

I went back inside and closed the door.

At the kitchen sink, I washed a pear and wandered to the front of the house to eat it as I peered out the open window.

Penelope circled Grant like an eager puppy, chattered in her bright voice about art camp. Kai kept in touch with Grant at all times. He put a finger through Grant's back belt loop, or leaned on Grant's hip, or sat on the grass with his back against Grant's legs. Grant didn't seem to mind any of it. Before he moved along to trim another section of the hedge, he'd swipe clippings off Kai's shoulders and set his gloved hand on Kai's head, or squat to talk with him for a minute. Kai would answer, nod, offer a fleeting smile.

I couldn't quite understand Grant's words, because his voice was so deep. He must have asked the kids excellent questions to prompt Penelope's long, engaged answers. Kai's answers ran to short paragraphs rather than only a few words.

My hands itched to pick up a pencil and sketch an idea for a garden sculpture. *Happy Kids Orbit the Gardener.*

No. I already had enough to do. The pear core hit the bottom of the compost bucket with a *thunk.* I fled the chatter in the front yard, fled the house, in favor of a long carving session at the throne.

Les Charbonniers pissed me off sooner than usual.

I kept going. The chisel rubbed a hot spot on my palm through the gloves, but I kept at it until I could barely lift my arms and the early twilight meant Grant and the kids would be gone.

When I dropped my tools onto the floor of the shed, I squinted at the back wall, but I couldn't see far enough in the gloom to make sure Grant had returned the hedge clipper, and I didn't want to turn on the light.

Silence from the front yard.

I walked around the house to the driveway roundabout.

The hedge looked like it had been trimmed by a precision instrument. Maybe it had been.

I couldn't stop thinking the phrase *trim my hedge.*

The summer after our senior year of high school, Freddie and I landed part-time jobs with a landscape company in Tacoma. Freddie would pick me up in his old Crown Victoria and drive us to the south dock for the 7 a.m. ferry. We'd lay the car seats back and nap while the coffee we'd brought from home grew cold. In Tacoma, we met the crew at the job site and spent the morning doing the menial tasks, to free the full-timers for the more professional work.

We'd trimmed a lot of hedges that summer. On the job and off.

Something about the stink of our sweat made our mid-day ferry rides back to Vashon torture. Maybe the physical exertion mimicked the exertion of sex to our teen psyches, because we inevitably shot off the ferry on the Vashon side lusty and primed. Freddie would floor the Crown Vic down a narrow road, onto a gravel track, and park at a dead end where we knew we wouldn't be found.

Snickering, aware of our comical desperation, we'd meet in the back seat. The Crown Vic saw a *lot* of action that summer.

Years later, on my knees in my bedroom in front of the white panels of my mural, I bowed my head. The buzz of summer filled my ears. I smelled cut grass and Freddie's skin on the sun-heated vinyl car seat and gave myself over to the memory.

I lean against the door in the back seat, laugh as I untangle my arms from my T-shirt.

Freddie wraps a hot hand around the back of my neck. His lips land beside my nose and rest there, on the tender skin beneath my eye. I burrow into the sun-dirt-sweat smell of his neck. We're close enough to the dock to hear the clatter as vehicles load for the next sailing. Freddie keeps his lips on my cheek, stills me until I've stopped laughing and the sound of the ferry engine has faded away, until the whoosh of the sea against the shore slows and the subtle sounds of high summer under the trees reign again.

When the moment begins to feel too still, I open my eyes, lashes brushing the stubble on Freddie's upper lip. He lifts his head to look down at me. I know he's thinking of the end of summer and our routine drawing to a close when he flies off to college on the East Coast.

Not yet. I close my eyes again and wait to find out what Freddie will do.

Strong hands yank my legs to lay me flat.

I moaned on my bedroom floor, not because the memory turned me on. It *did* turn me on, but in the fantasy, the yank on my legs shifted me into a different car.

The worn vinyl of the Crown Vic gives way to smooth leather.

Not Freddie's hands. These hands are bigger, like Grant's hands. The body above me is bigger. I don't want his fierce movements, so unlike Freddie's gentle care. I don't want the rougher stubble or the knit cap that covers his head.

I push off the cap to feel his hair, coarser than Freddie's, rub my hands over him. I do want him.

He folds my legs into my chest, noses into the hair around the base of my cock, licks and bites me there, pulls my ass up into his face. Hungry for me.

I'll give him whatever he wants.

Wherever we're going, it's nowhere I've been before. No one does me like this, with rising urgency, like my skin, my scent, my hair, my cock are the antidote to his pain. With a press of my feet, I lift into him. He seems to want to be smothered by me, and the thought that I could be someone's air brings a whine up through my parted lips.

He uses his thumbs to separate my cheeks and slobbers over my hole until I cry out and reach for my dick. He beats me to it, lunges up to cover my cock with his mouth. I want it. I want him, more, all of it. I show him by pushing down on the back of his head.

Here, take more of me.

We find each other in the rhythm and whine. In the press and fall and thrill of being in sync. When I feel the jerk of his orgasm in the stutter of his mouth around my cock, I grip his hair—hair I know without opening my eyes is black, not Freddie's brown.

I lift into his wet mouth, giving up, giving it all up for him.

Some time later, I returned to my bedroom floor.

It took a while.

I stood carefully from where I'd knelt in front of the mural, disturbed by the feeling that I'd been paying homage to it, and set the pencil on the dresser. In the bathroom, I left the light off while I wiped myself down and changed into clean underwear and shorts.

Before I left the house, I closed the bedroom curtains and locked the bedroom door.

Outside in the almost darkness, I unhitched the bike trailer then pedaled out across the lawn, pedaled harder, flew into the woods, driven and reckless.

I had a fantasy to outrun.

And it was gaining on me.

Chapter 34

GRANT

The fourth of July Saturday passed without fanfare. I was asleep in my tent before dark.

The next day, I took a hike to celebrate the final day of the week and to distract myself from my irritated skin. I wished I'd asked Oliver for early collection of shower privileges if I finished all my assignments early. I didn't want to show up at Oliver's to collect early and be turned away, so I walked and waited out the week.

On Monday morning, I trekked to Oliver's on an alternate path Penelope had recommended. It wound uphill to a view through a gap in the forest where a giant tree had fallen. I dropped the empty water buckets and sat on a moss-covered log to check out snow-capped Mount Rainer in the distance to the southeast.

As they often did, my thoughts returned to Kai. The day he and Penelope showed up at my campsite, Kai hadn't said much. With Kai latched onto me, the hedge job had taken longer, but I hadn't minded. Penelope entertained us with stories from art camp in years past. When I asked her about school, she said, "That's not as fun as art camp." She'd gone as quiet as Kai for a while.

After I'd cleaned and replaced the clippers in Oliver's workshop, the three of us tromped back to my campsite. Penelope motored on through with a wave over her shoulder—her normal farewell. "I'll wait for you up ahead, Kai," she said, like they'd prearranged a private moment for Kai and me.

Kai lifted his worried face to me. "Will you be here a while? You're not leaving yet, are you?"

I sat on the kitchen log to look him in the eye. "Yes, I'll be here a little while longer."

"How long?"

With my palm, I swept Kai's long bangs up off his face to get a better look at him. "Kai, hey, what's going on, buddy?"

"I don't want you to go yet. Can't you stay?"

"I expect I'll be here a few more weeks." I didn't want to get Kai's hopes up, in case things bombed with Oliver. "At some point, I'll have go back to Seattle to... um..." Kai had problems of his own. I didn't want to saddle him with my problems, but I couldn't lie to him. I sighed and made the decision to expose my ineptitude rather than make excuses.

"I'm out here to try to get my act together about work so I can get a job. Then I can visit you on Vashon or in Seattle without your parents freaking out."

"I don't care if you have a job," Kai said.

"Thank you for that, and I really do want to be in your life more than I have been."

I saw more sadness in Kai's gaze than seemed warranted by the possibility that I'd leave Vashon before he was ready for me to. His expression was so open and vulnerable it was almost painful to witness.

"I thought about you a lot," Kai said. "I was worried about you after Aunt Laura divorced you. I wanted to call, but we didn't have your number, and Dad said it was too soon to ask Aunt Laura for it."

"Wow." Kai kept surprising me. "Okay. Well, I'll tell you how I was doing: I stuck my head under a rock and I only recently thought about standing up for a change."

The tiny upward flick of Kai's mouth hinted at a smile.

"I'm sorry I didn't call you," I said. "Thank you for thinking about me." My surge of joy at the discovery that *someone* had thought kindly of me during the past difficult year seemed pitiful and tragic. "I want to give you a bear hug right now, but I still really stink."

"I don't care." Kai lunged at me and wound his arms tight around my neck.

"Please talk to me soon," I whispered in his ear. "I know something's bothering you. I want to help. Okay?"

He drew back and nodded, but didn't look at me again, only slid across the campsite to follow Penelope down the path.

It had felt awful to impose on Kai the eye-watering funk of my unwashed body that no amount of cold-water bucket-baths seemed capable of fumigating.

As I sat on the moss-covered log with the view of Mount Rainer, I remembered that feeling. I *really* needed a shower, but I dreaded the crapshoot of another interaction with Oliver.

Keep it simple: report in, shower, leave.

I roused myself, hiked on to Oliver's house, and knocked on the front door.

"Come on in," I heard Oliver call out.

He wasn't in the big room, so I took a seat. The overstuffed chair I chose turned out to be so soft I might as well have flopped into a goddamned beanbag chair. I focused on that irritation to scrub my mind of the remembered vision of Oliver on the bed setting off sparks against the blue tarp.

Oliver emerged from his bedroom and shut the door with a click.

I focused on my knees, which was easy, since they were at eye level.

Oliver approached until he stood in front of me in his bare feet. He wore the pants he'd worn the day he found us in the ditch, the ones with drawings on them. The beautiful vines and ferns on his arms had faded, scrubbed away perhaps, but he'd filled in the intricate drawings on his pants with painted color in some places, transforming his pants into camouflage gear for hiding in a masterpiece.

I squeezed the arms of the chair with my spread hands. I needed to *focus*.

The man might be a talented artist, but he was also an entitled prick who considered it fun to play puppet master. The sooner I added *shower access* to my side of our twisted ledger, the sooner I'd be able to strategize about putting a roof over my head before the cold rain of autumn settled in.

Oliver frowned down at me.

I ignored my own orders to keep it simple and asked, "What's up with you and that workshop?"

"Hello?" Oliver's frown deepened. He took a step back.

I waved my hand to indicate the odd crap Oliver had to live with every day. "You're artsy and strange, but not a total slob indoors. Except for the workshop. Why is that?"

"It's a toolshed. And it's none of your damn business."

"Fine," I said. "You have unresolved issues around the *toolshed*. Who cares? Not me. I'm only here to tell you I did all the stuff you demanded, so get on with bestowing my shower."

The freak crossed his arms and nodded. I took that as a request for information.

"Trip to town, *check*," I recited. "Daily journal entries, *check*. I'll show you a photo of my self-portrait, *check*. And I cut the bushes out front. Final *check*."

With a sharp adjustment to the knot of hair at the back of his head, Oliver turned and strode away.

"Congratulatory head pat optional," I raised my voice to say.

I'd never met anyone who exasperated me as much as Oliver. His combination of withdrawn and confident made me suspicious of his motives. On top of that, his coppery beauty emptied my brain.

Oliver goddamn Rossi. A guy like an onion unwilling to give up its outer layer, the reluctant skin coming away in thin strips. A poke into the juicier layers would only provoke a sharp sting.

Reluctant skin. I lifted my head from the back of the chair. Oliver stood at the dining table, bent over a sketchbook, hand flying with a pencil. All I could see of his freckled skin was the back of his bare neck under the sloppy topknot. To shift my train of thought, I looked past him, caught sight of the dartboard on the back door, and blinked.

"Jesus. What did you do?" I fought my way out of the obnoxious chair. "That's my self-portrait." He'd pinned my stick figure painting to the dartboard and *thrown darts at it*. One stuck out of my forehead. Another pierced my crotch.

"It looks like a spider," Oliver said with a shrug.

I torched the back of Oliver's head with my death rays and waited for an apology—or at least a better explanation—for why he'd defaced my self-portrait, but I got nothing.

Oliver glanced up at me. "Why did your marriage end?" His pencil scratched noise from the paper as he drew.

"What?" I felt like I'd landed in one of those sadistic plays Laura used to take me to, where everyone thought they were so clever but nothing made sense.

"Was it her fault or yours?" Oliver asked. "I mean, in your opinion."

"This is the most useless non-conversation I've ever had. You know what? Never mind. Since you're busy with your leisure activities, I'll try again later to address my basic necessities."

"Keep your hair on." Oliver lifted his head. "Hey, would you mind sitting at the dining table and glaring at me for a few minutes? I just want to—"

A rage rose up inside me. "I'm an *inch* from falling off the edge of the earth, and all you do is *push*." I couldn't stay in the room with him one more second.

My footsteps across the lawn took up the cadence of Oliver's final words, lobbed at me from the porch. "Grant, you need to let go."

Let go. Let go. Let go.

Chapter 35

OLIVER

One by one, I removed the darts from Grant's self-portrait.

I'd relished the release of those throws, the *thwack* as the darts punched into the board through the image Grant had painted, like I could kill his harsh opinion of himself if I landed enough direct hits. The vigor of those throws had bled off some of my discomfort around my sex fantasy about Freddie in the Crown Vic that had gone off the rails.

I opened a few more windows, to rid the house of Grant's surly vibe.

He'd walked in with a defensive squint, stinking up my house with body odor and bad attitude, then run out again before I could switch gears from focusing on the mural.

I studied Grant's punctured self-portrait for clues. He showed unwavering patience with the kids, then badgered me to the point of war. Compared to Grant's demands on my time and attention, Freddie's easygoing nature felt like a vacation.

Grant's final words, his parting shot about me pushing him off the edge, told me how cruel I must seem to him.

At the dining table, I flipped his self-portrait to write him a note on the back. I began with *I'm sorry*, fished an eraser out of a drawer, and scrubbed the words away. I *wasn't* sorry. Grant needed a push. Maybe no one had cared enough to give him one, or to push in the right direction—out over the edge of the known into flight. I wasn't going to apologize for being the one to do it.

It took me a while, and more scrubs with the eraser, but I got it in the end.

Grant— Thank you for your help this week. I'll consider the first week of assignments to be in order if you show me your self-portrait. You're welcome to use the courtyard shower for the remainder of your time here. You don't need to check with me before you use it. I put towels and shower basics out there for you. Please keep in mind that the freshwater supply on the island is iffy, especially in summer. When you're ready, we'll talk about week two. —Oliver

I rooted through the linen closet, emerged with an armful of dark green towels and washcloths, a new bar of soap, and bottles of shampoo and conditioner. Peace offerings, to show Grant I considered his first week a success. The fact that he'd done the assignments at all meant he was willing to change—that was all I'd wanted from his first week.

I turned on the water supply to the courtyard, then went out to set my offerings on the bench that ran along one side of the shower stall. Note in pocket, I set off to look for Grant's campsite and check on him. He didn't seem desperate enough to resort to self-harm, but I didn't know him well.

I followed the path Penelope took from the side yard and found Grant's campsite right where I expected it to be, on the spur of land Dad had bought when I was twelve. I remembered the discussion Dad and Granddad had for thirty seconds when it came up for sale. "View of Mount Rainer," Granddad said. "Longish walk from the house," Dad countered. They'd grinned at each other, shrugged, and we'd all taken a ride to the real estate office.

Grant was not in residence at his campsite, which looked pitiful. Beyond pitiful.

A camp stove balanced on a log. Metal cups. Fork. Spoon. Battered pot. A bungee cord secured the lid of the ice chest. I peeked inside. No ice. Five family-size cans of beef stew, cheap peanut butter, a bag of apples, half a loaf of reduced-price bread.

Fuck. I stared into the cooler. Grant had been skinny when I'd found him in the ditch—skinnier than I'd thought he should be. If *that* was all he was living on, he wouldn't put on weight anytime soon. No wonder he'd scarfed half a dozen muffins in five seconds that first day.

Grant was obviously trying to make camping work, but there was no getting around the fact that if the campsite was his current home, he *was* an inch away from the edge.

I felt ashamed of myself suddenly. I *had* been toying with Grant's life, and I had no business doing so, not really, not if he was as destitute as he seemed to be.

I remembered the day he'd shown up on my porch to propose a trade of labor for basic amenities. That must have required a fuck-ton of courage. I looked around the campsite again, to divert myself from the shame of sending Grant away that day without even an offer of a drink of water.

The open window flap of the small tent caught my attention. I put my face against the mesh, hoping I wouldn't discover Grant sleeping inside, because wouldn't *that* be awkward. But the only things in the tent were his backpack and a grubby sleeping bag on a thin pad. The bit of space the pack didn't take up seemed too cramped for Grant to be able to lie flat.

An outer mesh pocket of the backpack held a cell phone and charging cord. I took the note out of my pocket to add a P.S. to tell Grant he could use the electrical outlet in the courtyard, and to give him my phone number, but I didn't have anything to write with.

On second thought, I realized I didn't want to leave the note at the campsite. I felt sure if Grant knew I'd been there without an invitation, he'd consider it a breach of trust. I hoped he'd risk a trip back to the house sooner than later, so he'd know about the shower and the electrical outlet. And to get his poor, abused self-portrait.

The neatness of Grant's campsite didn't cancel the tragedy.

I felt horrible as I trudged back to my beautiful home, where I'd been blessed to live all my life. I'd known Grant's life wasn't good, but seeing his campsite gave me a visceral ache, made his desperation palpable to the point I sort of hated myself for worrying about Grant's emotional well-being when I should have addressed his physical status first.

I wondered what had befallen Grant to bring him to a state of desperation in my woods. If Kai was Grant's nephew, Mitch was family of some kind. Why wasn't Mitch helping Grant? And what was Grant running from?

At home, I added the P.S. to the note and taped it to the front door.

I tried to work on the mural after that, but the walls closed in on me. The careful motion of my hand as I pulled the brush along the faint lines of the transferred drawing jarred with my mood. My shame about Grant required *bigger, louder, messier*.

I excavated my overalls from the clothes hamper in my bathroom and pulled them on, laced my heavy boots on the back porch, and headed out to the toolshed.

I would face a tragedy of my own when I finished the throne. I'd miss the therapy of it, the physical effort and the simplicity. Tap chisel with mallet. Move chisel. Tilt chisel. Check placement. *Thwack. Move. Tilt. Check. Thwack.*

I would make it up to Grant.

I promise.

A revised plan for week two formed as I littered the ground with rejected wood and pretended I could make a difference in Grant's life. The penalty for my hubris would be to give Grant food without the fanfare of manipulating his psyche—though I reserved the right to do that later. For a week, I'd take a break from being a petty tyrant.

I'd try, anyway.

It was possible I'd forget in Grant's actual presence. His presence that filled the air around him, filled up my house. I was glad the location of the outdoor shower made it unlikely I would hear the water fall over Grant's naked body.

A long pause followed that thought, during which I tried to erase it.

With my mind's eye, I studied the image of naked Grant in the courtyard shower.

He smells of days of rough living in the woods, of fear and anger and raw energy. I can smell him from my side of the campground shower partition, where I stand frozen, all attention on his moans and the steam rising above him into the sunlight. When I can't wait any longer, when I need details, I step around the divider.

Hands up, he rinses his black hair, flattens it, sleek and shiny, against his head.

I clear my throat.

He opens his eyes, his hard scowl a strike, and I tense, poised to run, but he lowers his hands slowly from his hair, like he doesn't want to move too fast and scare me off. He watches me watch him. Runs his hands down his neck inch by steady inch, over his chest, across his stomach, down.

What? No.

I could *not* go there again. Not when Freddie was due back from Whidbey. I had a *plan*, a solid, good plan for a life and maybe a family with Freddie. We'd been headed in that direction for years. Freddie hadn't, in fact, brought home a Japanese man. He still came home to me.

"*Ouvre la porte,*" sang Les Charbonniers. *Open the door.*

Chapter 36

GRANT

In the morning on Tuesday, the day after I fled Oliver's in a huff about the shower, I decided to try again to collect my reward. I found his note on the door and jogged around to the courtyard, grateful he'd softened toward me, hoping it would last.

The first blast of hot water hit my back, and I closed my eyes to savor it, the sound of water hitting the flagstones around my feet the sweetest music I'd ever heard. Respectful of the water supply, I luxuriated efficiently. A few minutes had to be enough, and so it was.

By the time I'd toweled off in the fresh summer air, I felt like my body could breathe again. My brain turned over and restarted.

In my clean clothes, I gave myself a tour. The courtyard was about fifteen feet wide by twelve feet deep, enclosed on three sides by the house. The fourth side consisted of a stone wall with an arched entrance. Vines, overarching trees, and a profusion of plants around the archway and inside courtyard created a lush private garden.

Across the courtyard from the shower stall, a row of louvered windows lurked behind a wild rose on a trellis, the only windows looking onto the courtyard. The span of tall panels on the back wall seemed to be folding doors, but they were locked.

A honeysuckle bush cascaded over a picnic table, or maybe had grown around it.

From the state of Oliver's property—overgrown hedges, neglected workshop, mothballed courtyard—he'd stopped caring at some point.

I sat on the end of the picnic table bench to tie up my boots, ready for a walk around the house to see what else I might have overlooked, to explore for clues about Oliver's life.

I almost missed the painting behind a row of ornamental fruit trees outside the kitchen windows. A sheet of plywood bolted onto the blue siding of the house had been treated with some type of white background and then painted on. Dotted lines marked the adventures of a red-haired boy and his pals on an illustrated map. The accompanying images, detailed in some places, rough in others, included spots of sheer brilliance. I smiled as I followed the gang's route around Vashon Island—through town, along the cliffs, out to sea and back to shore. At the end of their journey, a treasure chest with an open lid revealed Oliver's signature and a date. If my guess about his age was correct, he'd been about ten.

Ten years old. *Jesus.* The man's artistry blew my mind.

I continued around to the front door to ask Oliver about the painting I'd found and to thank him for the shower, but he didn't seem to be home. The van and bicycle were parked under the carport. I knocked on the back door. When I stood still and listened, I heard nothing but the rustle of leaves.

I set off across the yard to the path to the stump chair, but he wasn't there either.

My tour around the stump to admire Oliver's recent work was cut short when I stepped on a chisel. Which lay beside a mallet. When I found the tool belt on the seat with a set of earbuds, I collected everything and took the liberty of ferrying it all to the workshop.

When I'd gone inside to find hedge clippers, I'd see the jumble of tools clustered on the concrete floor inside the door, like a deposit made by a receding flash flood. I added Oliver's things I'd brought from the stump to the pile, then felt around on the wall for the light switch and flicked it on.

Oliver's workshop was bigger than the house I'd grown up in with six people. Built-in worktables ringed most of the perimeter and two long tables dominated the central area. Closed cabinets, open shelving, and pegboard covered much of the wall space above and below the outer worktables. A clear plastic sheet covered a *very* nice table saw in the near left corner.

At some point in its past, I felt certain, the workshop had been a hive of activity.

I noted the dust and cobwebs, and reluctantly turned off the light, leaned into the heavy door to slide it closed, making sure the latch engaged securely.

I was dozing on the back porch, basking in the freshly showered feeling, when I heard footsteps. Oliver, at last.

I stood and lifted a hand to wave.

Oliver scanned me from head to toe. "You look clean and rosy. You got my note?"

I nodded, distracted by the tight furrow of worry between Oliver's eyes. "You okay? I found your tools out by the stump."

"I'm fine. Give me a minute to clean up, then we can talk about week two and you can show me your self-portrait from last week."

I followed him inside and wandered to the living area.

Oliver paused at the bedroom door. "Thanks for putting away the tools."

"Yeah. Sure."

Soon after Oliver disappeared behind the bedroom door, I heard a shower go on, which meant he had a private bathroom.

I wedged myself into a corner of the orange couch to wait for him and lined up my questions. If I used my full set of conversational skills, maybe I could peel away more of Oliver's outer protective layer without inciting an argument. *Nice and easy.*

By the time Oliver emerged in shorts and a T-shirt, hair up in a loose bun, damp tendrils framing the strain on the sharp features of his face, I'd worked myself into an almost meditative state of readiness.

Oliver nodded at me and made a sharp right turn into the kitchen area, where he bustled about for a few minutes. "I'm sorry to keep you waiting," he said. "I'll be right there."

"It's okay." I'd miraculously found a comfortable position in Oliver's living room. Calm, clean, and cushioned, I could barely keep my eyes open.

"Here we go." Oliver set a large tray on top of the magazines, sketchbooks, and colored pencils that covered the coffee table. "I haven't had lunch. You're welcome to join me."

I swallowed hard at the sight of the laden tray—sliced ham, black grapes, carrots, cucumber slices, a bowl of what looked like hummus, thick slices of brown bread, tall glasses of iced tea. "Wait. Seriously?"

Oliver passed me a plate and shrugged. "Dig in."

"I want to clean up your workshop," I blurted, grateful enough for the food to want to return the favor. It wasn't what I'd planned to say. A big bite of ham and bread shut me up. I stuffed in a few grapes to make sure I wouldn't talk for a while.

Slowly, as if under the influence of a stronger gravity, Oliver loaded his plate. "You could do that, if you really wanted to, but it would be in addition to your main assignment this week, which is to stock the kitchen. I'd like you to do the grocery shopping, food preparation, and cooking. I started a painting project. If I don't lay in some easy meal options, I'll gnaw on ice cubes and call it a meal. You can have half of whatever you make. There's a chest freezer on the side porch, so there's plenty of space. At the end of the week, I'll give you access to the outdoor kitchen in the courtyard. Not a complete kitchen, but better than cooking at a campsite."

My mouth was full, but I couldn't swallow. The folding panels in the courtyard hid a kitchen. I chewed and swallowed until my throat opened up again. "Okay." My plate was already clean. I set it back on the tray.

Oliver gestured with a cherry tomato, which I took to mean, *You can't possibly be finished. Eat more or I'll be offended.*

So I did.

The awkward stretch of silence while we ate ended when I remembered the painting on the side of the house. "How old were you when you did that painting on the side of the house? *The Adventures of Young Oliver and His Pals*, or whatever you call it."

"Eight."

"*Eight.* No way. Holy hell. You must have taken a lot of art classes as a kid."

"Yes. No. Not... formally. Just here... at home. Granddad, my dad's dad, was an artist. He lived with us. Or, I mean, my dad and I lived with him, until he... died and it became Dad's house. Dad was an artist too. Between the two of them, they had about every medium covered."

"That's why you have so many art supplies and tools. You inherited all of it? No siblings?"

Oliver shook his head.

"How long since your dad died?"

Oliver put down his half-eaten sandwich. "The electrical outlets in the courtyard are hard to find. You can charge your phone in the one under the rose trellis." With a little jerk, Oliver sat forward to dig around under the tray. He came up with a blue pencil and a corner torn from a sketchpad, on which he drew a rose trellis and the location of an electrical outlet.

I took the scrap of paper. "Uh. Thanks." I was stuck on my question about his dad.

When Oliver's warm fingers touched mine, he looked up at me. "Why do you need to camp out? Why don't you have a job, or a home, or anyone to help you?"

"Well, Jesus Christ, Oliver. Don't brace me for the tough questions or anything," I huffed. "Or bother answering *my* tough question."

Oliver only stared at me, intent and waiting.

Onion-poking standoff.

I could be the better man and give a little. "I mooched off my wife, Laura, for a decade, until she got fed up. Haven't had much luck since. My family in Eastern Washington wouldn't be interested in helping me, not in a way I could live with."

"You didn't work while you were married?"

"Sure I did. I worked full-time, but not in, like, a career type of job."

"Copy shop?"

I nodded. "Copy shops. We moved a few times. So, where's your mom?"

Oliver's golden brown eyes narrowed. "I'll put recipe cards, grocery list, and cash in the glove compartment of the van by ten tomorrow morning. Add whatever you've been craving to the grocery list. My treat. Get enough of everything for big batches, so there's a lot to freeze. Also, Freddie's back on Vashon tomorrow afternoon. I'll need the van by two."

I couldn't believe it. "You order me around, expect me to answer *your* invasive questions, but you won't answer mine? That's not fair."

With a shrug, like what I thought of him didn't matter and I was dismissed, Oliver picked up his sandwich.

I took the hint.

I left food on my plate, even though I wasn't full.

Chapter 37

OLIVER

On Thursday and Friday, the days Grant cooked in my kitchen, I thought about helping him, to try again to find out what had led him to my woods. I also thought about asking to see the self-portrait he still hadn't showed me. Instead, I painted. I painted to redirect my guilt about Grant and my fears about Freddie.

When I had to leave my bedroom while Grant was in the house, I'd power walk to minimize contact. "Smells great," I'd tell Grant as I breezed past. "Yum. Looks delicious."

Friday afternoon, Grant finally finished up and left. I shouted a goodbye through the bedroom door.

On Saturday, Freddie showed up with a boner.

"Hey, you. How was Whidbey?" I asked.

Freddie pushed me against my closed bedroom door. "Who cares? Let's go to bed. I want you now, and that guy could come around any minute."

"His name is Grant."

"*Grant* doesn't respect your mailbox flags."

"True."

"And you let him get away with that shit?"

"Apparently. He's been doing some work for me."

My phone pinged with a text message.

"How nice. Turn off your phone and let's get private in the bedroom."

The bedroom was off limits, due to the mural, but I had to give Freddie something. He'd cut his Whidbey trip short for me. Plus, I wanted him receptive when I asked him to be more committed.

"Library." I pushed him off me and took his hand.

"Have you put up curtains in there?"

"Dad hated curtains."

"Yeah, but it's not his room anymore and curtains mean privacy, like from oddball men who nose around uninvited."

Freddie's complaints about Grant sounded like jealousy. Maybe I could use that. I pulled him past the art corner, through the archway into the other half of the house, and took a right into the library, where he plopped onto the blue velvet couch.

"Come here." Freddie patted his lap, his expressive eyes broadcasting need.

I straddled his legs to perch on his knees, but when he leaned forward to kiss me, I leaned back. "Wait." I flattened my palm on his chest. "I need to ask you something first."

"What?" He stared at my lips.

"What would you think of us being exclusive?"

Freddie answered immediately. "Why would I want to do that?"

"Well, where do you see us going?"

With a leer and an arm around my shoulders, he tried to lay me onto the couch.

I shifted my knee to stay upright. "No. *Wait*. Do you see us going anywhere... *more* with our relationship anytime soon?"

"Not really," Freddie said with a frustrated sigh. "But it sounds like you do. What brought this on? It's that *guy*, isn't it?"

"His name is Grant, and why are you being hostile?"

"I don't trust him."

"You've spent zero time in his presence when *you* weren't being hostile."

Freddie laughed and tucked a strand of hair behind my ear. "Touché. But I have to wonder if it's a coincidence that you're asking about being exclusive a week after he arrived?"

I thought about that, tried to put the situation into words I'd be willing to share with Freddie. "It's not a coincidence. The state of Grant's life is making me look at what I want in my own life. What I want is to get serious—with you." I smiled and kissed Freddie's forehead.

He made a circular motion with his hand. "Okay, then. Go on."

"Grant is... lost and alone. Struggling. You and I are not any of those things, but I've been... *floating* long enough. I want more."

"Like what?"

"A family. Kids."

"You do?"

I nodded and put my hands on Freddie's sturdy shoulders.

"With me?" He seemed pleased about that.

"Why not?" I asked.

"I'm sure you've noticed I'm not around much. Why would you want a family with me when I'm usually thousands of miles away?"

"It would basically be what we're already doing, just... more, maybe plus a kid or two."

Sadness wasn't what I wanted to see on Freddie's face. He pulled me close and patted my back. It felt like an attempt at comfort before a letdown. "In case you haven't noticed, I'm kind of a slut," he said.

"You have been. But you've also said you want kids." Freddie's heart pulsed steady and regular. My own heart raced.

"I like being with you when I'm here, Oliver. I'm exclusive with you when I'm on Vashon. But, hey, one of the joys of world travel is traveling the world's bodies. You know how I feel about that."

"I know you sleep with other people when you're on your big trips."

"Honey, I hooked up on Whidbey."

I pushed back against Freddie's arms until he dropped them. That didn't feel far away enough, so I stood.

"Wait. Hey." Freddie reached for me, but I slid away.

I'd been with other men, but not for a long time. For more than a decade, I hadn't been with anyone except Freddie, even though I knew he slept around.

It had never bothered me before.

I lifted the pillow from an armchair and sat with it on my lap. Freddie watched me with an affectionate smile, arms spread over the back of the sofa, waiting for me to get up to speed with reality.

I tried. Freddie staring at me didn't make it any easier.

I remembered the text message and checked my phone, in case it was Talia reporting on her meeting with the neighbors to discuss Edward's suspicious presence in the vicinity of a dead chicken.

It wasn't Talia. Grant had sent a photo with a message: *Week one self-portrait in sticks and stones.* Somehow, he'd arranged natural objects into a recognizable image of himself. He even looked stubborn and angry. With a grin I couldn't suppress, I tapped the photo to enlarge it.

Freddie's patience with my silence ended at that point. He cleared his throat and lifted an eyebrow in a silent request for me to rejoin our conversation.

I blew out a breath, put away my phone, and tried to focus on the issue. Or *issues*, the most immediate of which was whether I wanted to have sex with Freddie if he didn't want to be exclusive.

Freddie snorted and nodded at the window. "Check that out."

Grant strode into view from the right, hands waving as he talked. Kai and two girls I didn't know walked behind him in a line. A papa duck and his ducklings.

"What a weirdo," Freddie said. "Should he be hanging out with kids? I wish you'd be more careful about giving him so much access."

"He's harmless. And maybe I like having someone around more often." What I wanted, I realized, was for Freddie to want me the most, enough to forswear all others.

With a sigh, Freddie said, "Even if I were willing to be exclusive, I wouldn't be here very often. I'm a single-minded, egotistical bastard fixated on a Pulitzer. *That's* my destination. Hookups are side trips."

"I've been a side trip?"

"The very best kind." The twinkle in Freddie's eyes reminded me of all the good times we'd had with our bodies.

"I think... I don't want to be a side trip anymore," I confessed.

"I get that. But you've got a lot going for you, babe. Don't settle." His gaze flicked to the window.

"Yeah. You're right. I should look around for someone I can be exclusive with."

That made Freddie sit up. I'd found a fracture in his bring-on-the-men attitude.

"Wait. You mean..." I could see him connecting the dots. "You'd be exclusive with someone else, so we wouldn't get together? Like, ever?"

"That's right," I said.

"And if you and I were exclusive, you wouldn't want me to be with anyone else, even when I was away from Vashon?"

"Well, yeah, Freddie. That's the whole idea about being exclusive."

"This *is* about Grant, isn't it?" His expression turned hard. "Don't lie to me."

"This is about me wanting to be more than your *kept man*—here for you when you need to get off, but otherwise forgotten. We've been friends a long time.

I've been *available* to you physically since we were seventeen. Casual, familiar, and occasional has worked for both of us for years. Now *I'm* ready for more, even if you aren't."

"But... Grant?"

I threw up my hands in exasperation. "For the love of all that's holy, this is *not* about me trying to get with Grant. He's not in the same league as you. I want to move *up*. If I can't move up with you, I want to find someone who's better for me than you are. Obviously, that's not Grant. But if you don't want to be exclusive, then I'm going to... you know... look around."

Freddie scoffed. "How? Like on a dating app?"

That made me laugh. "No. I know a lot of people on Vashon. I'll ask around. I can ask my friends who they think I should meet."

"And then go on dates?"

"Sure. Why not?"

"You'd be under a microscope if you dated on Vashon," Freddie said.

"So we'll go on dates in Seattle or Tacoma, or go for a hike on the peninsula. Why do you even care?"

Freddie frowned. "We haven't gone hiking in way too long."

I didn't say anything. I was reeling him in. I needed him to keep drawing conclusions.

Freddie drew out his next words. "Hypothetically, if we *were* exclusive, I wouldn't get with anyone when I traveled *and* you wouldn't get with anyone here while I was away?"

I nodded. I had to work hard to keep my smile to myself.

"Well, then I'll think about it."

"Thank you."

"But, Oliver, hey, you could come with me on my trips." Freddie's face lit up. He took his arms off the back of the couch and leaned toward me. "If you were with me, being exclusive would be a lot easier. Man, we could have so much fun. I could show you places that would blow your mind. Think of the art you could create from those new experiences."

As if the distance between us remained fixed and unchangeable, Freddie's forward lean made me sit back in my chair. The best response I could come up with was to parrot Freddie.

"I'll think about it." I said.

His suggestion perturbed me. He'd never asked me to join him on a trip. *Ever.* It rankled that he'd turned my bid for exclusivity into a negotiation.

Freddie slouched back into the couch. "Remember when we made out in the DeVille?"

"What on earth made you think of that?"

My dad's pride and joy had been a 1968 Cadillac Sedan DeVille he'd restored to mint condition. Shined to a high gloss, she'd lived in the garage down an off-shoot of the driveway. Except on rare occasions, Dad had only driven the DeVille on Saturdays for our weekly trip to town for groceries and errands.

"I miss the DeVille," Freddie said. He'd ridden with us sometimes, as had Aza. "Did your dad ever find out?"

"No." I shivered at the thought. "*Hell* no."

"God. You were so worried and hot and cute and distracted. I could have done anything to you if you hadn't shut us down. It would have been fantastic."

"For you maybe. The possibility of cum on the leather was a boner-killer. I would have been grounded until I was thirty."

"At least."

I laughed my agreement. "What made you think of the DeVille?"

"Let's take her for a spin."

"We, um... can't." My throat constricted. "I... Well... I sold it."

The shock on Freddie's face seemed genuine. "You did not."

"I had to. My heart was... broken. The DeVille... It was too much... Dad."

"Well, shit." Freddie stared at me for a while. "Who bought it?"

"Some guy in Oregon."

"When?"

"Long time ago." I waved a hand, ready for Freddie to accept it and move on. "You haven't answered my question about what made you think of the DeVille."

Freddie looked into my eyes. "Remember what you said after we stopped making out?"

"Stopped *trying* to make out."

"*Failed* to make out."

"No, I don't remember."

"You said, 'You'll go away and be famous and I'll stay here and be famous.'"

"Oh. Yeah. I do remember."

I expected Freddie to ask me why I wasn't famous yet. Or to get up from the couch and try to kiss me again. But he didn't. He only slouched and stared out the window.

He'd said he would think about being exclusive. I'd said I would think about traveling with him. Maybe that was progress. I had too many new questions to be sure.

I stood and went to the kitchen to make us something to eat.

Freddie's hand on the small of my back as we talked, as I stood at the cutting board to chop celery for a chicken salad, felt too familiar to be uncomfortable and too tentative to comfort.

Chapter 38

OLIVER

The mural obsessed me.

After Freddie left on Saturday, I sat on a stool in front of the mural and began to paint the plants around the man's bare feet. His and the boy's discarded shoes lay half-buried in the tall grass, roughed in with a ghost of beige paint.

Most of the mural consisted of wild nature, details gleaned from the stacks of botanical reference books beside me on the floor, fetched from the library I'd inherited. I'd also printed images from my digital reference library of nature photos taken on our property over the years.

Honeysuckle blossoms tickled the man's toes.

The blare of an incoming text made me jump and wish I'd thought to turn off my phone.

The text was from Grant. *I'm in the workshop. Want to stop by? Some kids from art camp are eager to meet you. Apparently, the Vashon tween set considers you a celebrity.*

Within a few minutes of receiving the text, I'd cleaned my brushes and changed into dark green pants and a brown T-shirt. On my way out the front door, I grabbed a large pair of binoculars from a coat peg.

The driveway spur behind the hedge Grant had recently trimmed continued past Dad's garage as an overgrown track. I veered right onto the spur, then right again onto the path that circled the yard from the cover of the woods, didn't slow until I neared the small offshoot trail I wanted. When it petered out in thick underbrush, I stopped to peek through the leaves at the back of the toolshed, which butted up against the woods. The shed's tin roof drew the day's heat inside. As I'd expected, Grant had opened the windows.

I could hear voices.

A few minutes of careful progress took me to a perch on my favorite tree limb for spying into the toolshed. I'd discovered the spot the spring I turned eight, when Dad and Granddad banned me from the toolshed for a few days to build a collapsible easel for me. Weeks later, they'd presented it to me on my birthday and I'd acted surprised.

During the twenty-seven years since then, the tree limb had grown, but so had I. I settled in and lifted the binoculars. Through the foliage and the open window, I had a decent view of most of the interior.

A surge of distress over the state of the toolshed made me take a deep breath. Maybe Grant had the right idea about cracking the seal on that time capsule.

"What's this thing?" The pale girl held up something I couldn't get a good look at. She wore a sleeveless orange-and-white striped shirt, and her shoulders looked like they'd never met a sunray. I could tell from her voice and manner she wasn't as young as she looked.

"It's a spud wrench," the taller girl said.

Grant laughed. "Huh. I had no idea. What's it for? If your potato gets stuck?"

"Ha ha. No, it's for plumbing stuff," the tall girl said.

"How the heck do you know that?" Grant asked.

The girl shrugged. "My dad and brother like to fix things. I like to help." She turned away, but Grant kept his eyes on her, followed her to the other side of the table. They stood with their sides toward me.

"Jill?" Grant didn't lean down to make eye contact, like Dad would have, and he folded his arms. Grant was a *big* guy. He loomed with a scowl. "Is something wrong?"

I would have thought his stance would be intimidating, but Jill didn't seem to take it that way. She slumped toward him. I looked closer, trying to see what she saw, and it hit me all of a sudden that Grant's stance wasn't threatening but protective.

"I like helping Tony in the garage," Jill finally said.

"Tony is your brother?"

Jill nodded. "But only when no one else is around."

"What do you mean? Who else?" Grant asked.

She looked nervous, and what she said next came out so soft I couldn't hear it. Luckily, Grant hadn't heard either.

"Sorry. Say that again," Grant said.

"Like his friends."

"What about his friends?"

The other two kids, Kai and the pale girl, had migrated to Grant and Jill. Kai leaned against Grant's hip. I expected Grant to reassure Kai, but he didn't take his focus off Jill.

"Listen, kid," Grant said, "I don't know much, but I know you're not happy about something. Spill it and I'll share my hummus and cucumber sticks."

"Can I have the hummus first?" Jill asked.

"Nope. It's at my campsite, and I'm not going back until I've made a dent in the mess here."

Jill narrowed her eyes at Grant. "Are you calling me a mess?"

With what seemed like a parody of Jill's earlier shrug, Grant said, "You tell me."

Shoulders hunched, Jill turned away to face the workbench. "Tony's friends call me *pretty*, but only when Tony's not there, like if he has to go to the bathroom. I don't like it. It feels bad."

"Do they *do* anything to you?"

"They stare at me, I guess. I don't know. It's silly."

"What does Tony say about this?" Grant asked. "Or your dad?"

Jill fiddled with something on the table.

"Don't you think it's time to tell someone at home about this? How are things with your parents?"

"Her mom and dad are really nice," the pale girl said. "They pick her up at camp, both of them. And they don't start the car until after they look at all the things Jill made." The wistful way she spoke made me think she didn't have the same type of parents.

"Thanks, Clover," Jill said. "But..."

"But what?" Grant asked.

"But Tony's friends haven't *done* anything," Jill said. "And they're Tony's *best* friends."

"Ah." Grant lowered himself to sit cross-legged on the floor with his back against a table leg, which put him below all three kids. He looked up at Jill. "Then you have a tough choice to make."

Jill stared at Grant for a while, then heaved a huge sigh and nodded.

The tension of staying still tightened my grip on the binoculars. I would have gone ballistic at that point, like Dad would have, and launched a crusade against Tony's friends.

That wasn't the tack Grant took.

"So, what are your choices?" he asked her.

When Jill made a quarter turn away from Grant, I saw that she was crying. Not making a production of it, but crying enough that tears fell off her chin.

I moved the binoculars to study Grant, who didn't respond to the tears, or not that I could tell.

Clover nudged Grant on the shoulder to get his attention, then nodded toward Jill and put her fingers up to her own face to mimic tears falling.

All Grant did was smile up at Clover. He didn't reach for Jill to try to comfort her. Nor did he respond to Kai, who leaned sideways against Grant's shoulder.

Grant didn't do much of anything. Sat there. Smiled. Waited. *Fuck, the man was brilliant.* Dad would have wanted the glory of being the one who solved the problem. The scene in the toolshed was more about Jill than Grant, and yet Grant held all three tweens in thrall. He gave the kids the space to be themselves, and he accomplished it by doing nothing more than being his own flawed, unfinished, surprisingly perceptive self.

Clover broke first. She gave Jill's shoulder an awkward pat, which seemed to make Jill take another huge breath. I sharpened the focus on the binoculars.

Jill wiped her eyes and said in a strong voice, "I think it's not right to choose my brother's friends over myself."

All three kids looked down at Grant, as if for his reaction.

Here it comes. Grant's going to applaud, lay down the law about self-care, get all Papa Bear with the hugs.

Instead, Grant stood—careful not to bump his head on the tabletop overhang—removed a tissue from his pocket, handed it to Jill, and turned to resume sorting tools the kids had brought to the central tables from my pile by the door. Tools I'd sprinted into the toolshed to fetch, then tossed onto the floor when I was done with them.

I squirmed on the branch, disappointed in myself.

Grant grouped similar types of tools into piles.

None of the kids moved.

All three kids stared at Grant's back as he worked, until Jill wiped her eyes, blew her nose, and smiled at Clover. Clover smiled back and the two of them wandered away to pick up more tools from the floor to take to Grant.

Kai took a while longer to move on. He didn't unlatch from Grant until Grant put his big hand on Kai's blond head and... left it there. Grant continued to sort tools with his other hand. After about thirty seconds, Kai scooted out from under Grant's hand and went to help the girls.

When they'd cleared everything off the floor around the door, Jill drifted to the workbench at the back of the building, away from the others but closer to me. I couldn't see the surface of that workbench from my angle, but I knew it had been strewn with drill bits for a decade, ever since I'd dumped them from their drawers in a flying fury, on a mission to get what I needed to repair a shelving problem in the laundry closet.

Head down, Jill moved her arms back and forth, maybe running her hands over the loose drill bits to roll them.

I kept still and watched.

Over the next five minutes or so, Jill's expression shifted from serious to thoughtful to peaceful. She began to lift drill bits to read their sizes, and made movements like she was putting them back into the labeled drawers in the storage units under the window.

I remained perched in the tree for another hour as my ass fell asleep. All the while, as the kids helped Grant clean up my mess, they revolved like satellites around his steady gravity.

Chapter 39

GRANT

I finished cooking in Oliver's kitchen on Friday and left with containers of warm lasagna and green bean salad. For a blissful hour, I sat on a log at my campsite and fed myself creamy, meaty lasagna with the wrong end of my spoon, to make it last as long as possible. Stuffed to the point of stupor, I fell into the tent and a hard night's sleep, unbroken until the next morning when Kai and two new friends showed up on their bikes.

"Sorry we woke you," Kai said as he hugged me.

"No problem. You're my all-time favorite alarm clock."

I ran my hands through my sleep-mussed hair and smiled at the two girls. "Good morning. I'm Grant."

The taller girl held out her hand and said, "I know."

"Uncle Grant, this is Jill," Kai said with shy formality. He pointed to the other girl. "And that's Clover."

Though Clover hid behind Jill and didn't speak, I detected a mischievous glint in her eye.

"Penelope's not with you?" I asked.

"Not today," Kai said. "She has a family event. What are you doing today?"

"I thought I'd give Oliver's workshop a makeover. You guys want to join me?" I grabbed a carrot and a cheese stick from the cooler to take along for breakfast. When I'd shopped for Oliver's week of stocking up, I'd picked up my final paycheck at the post office and splurged on more journals and more food for my ice chest.

The kids left their bikes at the campsite so we could walk together. As soon as we came out of the woods, I saw Freddie's crapmobile in the driveway and the house took on a sinister air. I steered clear, tried not to imagine what Freddie and Oliver might be doing inside.

Clover gravitated to the workshop's small bathroom and began to clean it—a job I would have left until last, or never. Kai brought stuff from the floor to me at one of the central tables. Jill cruised the workbenches and cabinets, then went to help Clover.

Outdoor living had heightened my awareness of the natural world. Out of the corner of my eye, through the greenery pressed against the back window, I picked out the unnatural colors of Oliver's clothing, his skin, and the copper of his hair and beard. Flashes of reflected light probably meant he had binoculars.

Hours later, when the kids and I left to go back to my campsite for hummus and veggies, Oliver was still there.

There had to be a way to find out what Oliver problem was—why he'd let parts of his property go untended, and why he'd retreated so much. A devious idea came to me. Perhaps I'd get a closer look at his wound if I invaded his precious space with my unruly presence even more, bothered him enough to let his guard down, drew him into the open to tell me off.

The prospect thrilled and scared me.

I was beginning to suspect the tool of creativity was sharp at both ends, as troublesome for those of us who rejected it as for those who embraced it. Oliver's project in his bedroom seemed to capture him for long stretches, like a descent into a vortex, only to eject him back into the real world haunted, paint-stained, and pensive.

After the kids sped off from my campsite on their bikes, I took my journal out and wrote *HIDING* as my entry for the day, then idly flipped through the pages from the beginning. In a week and a half, I'd filled most of the book's pages. The journal read like private investigator's surveillance notes on Oliver.

I stared down at a blank page and wondered where I fit in.

That was the first day I wrote more than one word on a page. *WHAT AM I HIDING FROM?*

The next day, a text message from Oliver woke me from an afternoon nap. *Come over for an intro to the courtyard kitchen?*

I roused myself, stuffed my toiletries and a can of stew into my daypack, and took the path at a jog, livened by the prospect of another shower and warm food for dinner.

Oliver smiled when we met in the courtyard, but he didn't meet my eyes. He looked weary and moved like an old man.

"Paint fumes getting to you?" I asked.

Oliver ignored my attempt at humor. "You'll need to keep the panels closed and locked whenever you're not here, even for a few minutes, or you'll get wild visitors."

The panels folded and rolled to the sides to reveal a long counter, a single-basin sink, a two-burner stove, and cabinets above and below. Oliver ducked down and stuck his head into the cabinet beside the small fridge, to plug it in.

I pointed to the narrow slot above the panels. "Awning?"

Oliver's answer was to show me the crank. When I turned it, a sturdy green awning slid out from the slot.

"This is a great set-up," I said. "Thanks so much for letting me use it."

"No oven, but you can thaw meals overnight in the fridge, then warm them on the stove."

The guy really didn't want me in his house anymore. *Message received.* "Tough week?" I asked. "Vortex problems?"

A blink and a frown were all I got in response. It was like we were on different planets.

Oliver offered me the key to the panel doors. "I'll tell you the assignment for week three tomorrow."

"Why not now?"

"I'm not... ready." He pivoted and sped away through the archway.

After that brief interaction with the elusive creature, I only wanted more.

In the shower, I handled my cock with some urgency, replayed Oliver's crouch at the cabinet as I squeezed and pulled on my dick with soapy hands.

Escaped tendrils of auburn hair trailed down Oliver's back.

Paint-splattered pants plastered his round ass.

I came too fast to worry about wasting water.

Chapter 40

OLIVER

I should have asked Grant to show me his self-portrait for week two before I gave him access to the outdoor kitchen, but I was distracted by the painting, my conversation with Freddie, and the sleep creases on Grant's cheek. I almost went back to the courtyard to ask him to show me his self-portrait, but Freddie called me from the grocery store.

"Hey, if you're in town, you're already halfway here," I said. "Do you have your writing stuff with you? The dining table is available."

"Hmm. No. I can come over if you want to hook up, but I'm going to write at Mom's."

"That seems like a step in the wrong direction after our talk yesterday."

"It's that guy," Freddie said. "He's intrusive. I don't want any interruptions while I'm writing."

"Don't I interrupt you when you work here?" I asked.

"Not really. You focus on your own stuff. I can ignore you. I can't ignore him."

"Okay." I had to stop and think about what I wanted. "I'm too involved in painting today to hook up."

"I understand. I'm pretty focused on my article."

We hung up, but I couldn't get Freddie's comment out of my mind. *I can ignore you.* It reverberated like a summary of why we were stuck.

I put on headphones, pulled up a playlist from high school, picked up a paintbrush, and lost myself. The playlist repeated until way past bedtime. I finally stopped and cleaned up.

Two hours later, I woke curled on the tarp-covered bed.

The world had gone quiet. Moonlight seeped in around the curtains.

Right there, a few feet away, a man slept in my bedroom.

Time ticked by. My eyes turned gritty from staring at the mural.

Even if Freddie didn't change, I wasn't stuck, I reminded myself. I had other options. After a life spent on Vashon, and with Talia's propensity for gossip, I knew the island's dating pool pretty well. Stewart Abernathy, for example. Ten years older than me. Owned a software development firm. Made me laugh. Very kind eyes.

In my imagination, I took Stewart for a test drive. Over a lovely meal in a Seattle restaurant, he talked about his work and appreciated my creativity. We spent the ferry ride home in fits of giggles. When Stewart walked me up my porch steps at the end of the evening, he paused to see if I wanted to be kissed. My weary mind made his hair thicker and darker. His body bulked and morphed into a version of Grant with more meat on his bones, more peace on his face, more success in his life.

That man, that hybrid concoction, stalked me up the front porch steps, reached around me to open the door, and walked me inside, certain he knew what I wanted. He pulled the band from my hair and laid me on the floor under the coat rack, too eager to appreciate me to wait another moment.

I added my reflection in his dark eyes, to make the dream seem more real.

At dawn, I woke stretched out on the cold tarp, falling for a metaphor.

Chapter 41

GRANT

Voices and bike clatter woke me from a hard sleep.

"Don't any of you scamps go to church?" I yelled from my sleeping bag.

"Yes," Penelope said.

"Only on Christmas and Easter," Jill said.

"It's Monday," Kai said.

"No," Clover said from very close.

I opened my eyes to see her face pressed against the mesh window of the tent.

"Penelope?" I called out.

"Yes?"

"Remember what I told you when we first met?"

"Hey, Clover," Penelope said. "Give the guy some privacy, yeah?"

"Oh." I heard the revelation in Clover's voice. "Sorry, Grant."

"No prob." I zipped up the window flaps and spent a tricky few minutes getting dressed in the too-small space. When I emerged, Jill stared at my T-shirt and scrunched her nose. "Um?"

"Yeah?" I checked my clothes, but everything seemed in order. I even turned my back to check my pants zipper. "I didn't do anything wrong."

Kai snickered from his perch on the kitchen log.

"You wore that shirt on Saturday," Jill said.

"Well, duh. And the day before that. It's still the cleanest shirt I have." To mask my shame, I stood tall and faked a proud lift of my chin. "You guys rate my best."

Jill and Penelope exchanged a look, but Clover was the one who spoke. "It's dirty and you smell."

"Well, then." I pressed my arms tighter against my sides and tried to develop a sudden talent for telekinesis to keep my stink molecules to myself. "I showered last night, so it must be my clothes that stink. I'm sorry. I'll go to a laundromat when I do Oliver's errands this week." I glanced at Kai, hoping he didn't count my stench against me.

Kai gave me a rare smile.

"Oh, I get it," I told him, relieved. "It amuses you to see me on the hot seat?"

Kai's smile widened and he nodded.

"We can show you how to do laundry in the sink in your new kitchen," Penelope offered. I'd texted her about the courtyard.

"I tried handwashing in a bucket already. It doesn't work. And stuff takes a zillion years to dry. And *then* it rains," I groused.

"Penelope told us you have an awning at the kitchen," Clover said.

"You're ganging up on me." They were, and it felt spectacular. I told myself it was because they cared about *me*, not only the purity of their air space.

"Well?" I asked Kai. "What do you think?"

He studied me with his serious eyes. The girls and I all watched him and waited.

"You're camping," Kai finally said. "You're supposed to smell."

I grabbed Kai and raised my arm to give him a playful dose of my shirt's stink. I expected him to recoil and push me away, but he plowed into me like he'd been dying for me to reach for him. I decided I was done waiting for him to tell me in his own time what troubled him. *Somehow* I needed to get it out of him before I left Vashon.

With a pat on Kai's back, I let him go and began to gather my dirty laundry and stuff it into my daypack. "Come on, then. Let's go get me some basic life skills."

The kids biked on ahead. Kai had insisted on taking my daypack. It made him wobble down the trail, off-balance and slow. I draped Mitch's cloth shopping bags, which I'd filled with cooking gear and cans of food, over my shoulders, hoisted the ice chest, and followed.

The picnic table—another handmade Rossi creation, I assumed—was heavy enough it required most of us to haul it across the courtyard. Kai and Clover declined to help until the table had cleared the honeysuckle bush and the risk of bees.

We sat at the relocated picnic table and grinned at one another.

I faked an impatient scan of the courtyard. "Has anyone seen our waiter? I can't believe our food is taking this long."

Clover, bless her, laughed so hard at my joke her sweet, round face lost its tension.

It should have worried me that awkward, artsy tweens were becoming the best friends I'd ever had, but it didn't. I wasn't artsy, but I was enough of a sad loser to consider myself lucky to have some pals.

"Sorry I don't have much to offer you as my first guests," I told the kids.

"What *do* you have?" Clover asked.

"Let's have a look in the cabinets for plates or bowls." I stepped backward off the bench and lifted Kai up and out by his armpits. "Kai and I can fix us a snack."

The girls found art supplies, tablecloths, kitchen gadgets, and baskets with handles. In a plastic bin pulled from a lower cabinet, Clover found dishes in the colors of Oliver's hair and skin. I turned over the plate she handed me. *L Rossi 1978* had been scratched into the clay—a year or so before Oliver was born, I thought.

I wondered what it was like for Oliver to live in a home stuffed with beautiful items made by people he adored. *People gone forever.* It struck me that Oliver's life might be harder than I'd realized.

I clicked the lid into place on the bin of dishes and shoved it back into the cabinet. "Let's not use these."

Clover nodded. "Good idea."

"Here's the plan." Penelope put her hands on her hips. "Work first, snack after. It's time for your hand-laundering lesson, Grant."

"Yes, ma'am," I said.

"We'll use the dish soap I found in the cabinet," Jill said. She instructed me at the sink, then Penelope showed me how to spread my washed T-shirt on a towel, fold in the towel edges, and roll it. Clover watched the entire process with intense focus, as if her life depended on learning it.

"Totally. Freaking. Brilliant," I said.

Kai looked up at me. "Mom lets me sit on the towel sometimes to mash out the water."

We hung damp towels, pants, and shirts from the clothesline Penelope had strung across a corner of the courtyard.

I was hanging up the last towel and listening to Clover and Penelope discuss a teacher at art camp when I caught movement beyond the courtyard entrance. I kept my eyes fixed on that spot until I caught another movement. It wasn't Oliver. It was a kid.

I hustled into the yard, but he'd gone. A glimpse of black hair at the edge of the lawn, just for a second. A moment later, a boy stepped out from behind an oak tree, like he wanted to make sure I saw him before he disappeared.

I turned back to the picnic table. "Is there a tall boy with long, black hair at art camp? I saw someone watching us, but he ran away."

"No," said Penelope.

Clover looked thoughtful. "Not at art camp, but if he was skinny, it could be Abelino. He lives down the road from me. He wanted to go to art camp, but his mom didn't have the money." She dipped a carrot stick in the puddle of peanut butter in her bowl and shrugged. "I only get to go because I save up all year."

"Really?" Penelope asked.

I could tell Clover felt embarrassed.

"Well," I said, to distract Penelope from taking charge of Clover's finances. "If you see Abelino around, tell him to join us."

"What's he like?" Jill asked Clover.

"Nice, I guess. I don't really know. He's from Mexico. He and his mom only moved in a couple of months ago. I know he doesn't have a bike."

"We might have an extra bike at home Abelino could use," Penelope said. "Except it's got a problem with the brakes."

"My bike has a problem with brakes too." Clover set down her carrot and shivered. "Scares me every time I have to go down a hill."

I felt a tingle of inspiration. "Hey, guess what I saw in a cubby in the workshop?"

"A sailor's hat?" Kai muttered.

The girls and I stared at him, but Kai didn't lift his head from his drawing of a man in a boat.

"Um. No," I said with a laugh, "but that's a very interesting guess. I saw bike tools and repair manuals. Who wants to be our bike expert?"

Jill's hand shot into the air so far she stood up. "Me. Me, please. Can we go and look at them now?"

I pointed at her. "You're it."

We cleaned up and I locked the panels. When I glanced around the court-yard to make sure we hadn't left out any food, I noticed one of the louvered windows behind the rose trellis had been opened an inch. I took a step toward the yard to hide behind a rhododendron.

The kids chatted about their bicycles as they walked to the workshop.

I adjusted my vision to try to see into the house, saw only indistinct darkness. And then a flash of copper hair.

Chapter 42

OLIVER

My friend Maddie showed up Tuesday afternoon with a staffing issue at the auto supply store she'd taken over from her dad. I wasn't a business expert, but she came around now and then for my sideways solutions, as she called them.

When she arrived, I was trying on a pair of homemade socks Clementine had brought me on her way home from work.

"Hi, Maddie," I said. "Mind if Clem joins us?"

"Oh, I don't want to be in the way," Clem said.

Maddie gave us a big smile. "Not at all. Hey, Clementine."

I settled us in the library with a tray of tea paraphernalia. Maddie and Clementine updated each other on their lives, which provided a welcome distraction from my new obsession—an uncomfortable awareness that I was jealous of Grant's posse of tweens.

I was having issues with reality.

The cozy domesticity I'd witnessed as I spied on Grant and the tweens setting up the kitchen—their humor and gentleness with one another—had cast a spell over me, turned me into a wraith who lurked and longed but lacked the substance to join them.

On the surface, the conversations I overhead between Grant and the kids were nothing remarkable. Grant chatted, light and breezy, but he was almost painfully *real*, and the kids seemed compelled to share their pain and suffering with him. Grant never pushed, but his interested, relaxed silence spoke of acceptance. The kids opened, invited him into their aches.

I'd formed a theory that significant pieces of Grant remained locked in his childhood, keeping him stuck and unable to engage more effectively in the world of adults. The notion of Grant in the midst of a childhood do-over on my property intrigued me.

No wonder the tweens doted on Grant, included him, and confided in him. He was one of them.

While I mulled, Clementine solved Maddie's staff problem without me, even down to the details. When they were finished, they turned to stare at me.

"What?" I poured myself another cup of tea and settled back in the armchair. "It's a great solution. You didn't even need me."

"You seem..." Maddie started.

"Distracted," Clementine finished.

"I didn't want to butt in," I lied. I couldn't wait for them to leave. I wanted to find Grant and tell him his assignment for week three and see how he reacted.

"Clem says you're taking July off this summer, in addition to your usual August break," Maddie said.

"That's right." It wouldn't be a hardship for Maddie, but I didn't want her to be counting on me when I didn't have the mental space for her conundrums. All I wanted to do was figure Grant out and paint. After he left, I'd dive into the mural even more during August, come out on the other side in September, ready again for visitors.

Maddie's goodbye hug lingered, like she thought I needed comfort. I slid away from Clementine's pat on the back.

"Call me later?" Clementine asked.

I waved from the porch in lieu of a nod, then turned on my phone, eager to locate Grant. A series of pings alerted me to a cascade of messages, all from Grant and all photos, except for one text message: *Wk 2 self portr.*

The first photo, a bird's-eye view, showed an arrangement of tools and hardware on the surface of a worktable in the toolshed. I recognized Grant's face, detailed in drill bits, with shiny washers for eyes and a spray of black netting for hair. The tips of his boots showed at the edge of the photo. He'd stood on the table to get the shot.

It took me a few minutes to recognize the tweens in the other photos, which I assumed were also self-portraits. Penelope's braces rendered in a row of shiny nails. A metal hoop for Clover's round face.

I laughed with delight. I *loved* them.

I shot Grant a text—*These are fucking brilliant*—and clambered down the front porch steps to jog around to the toolshed to talk with Grant and the kids about what they'd created.

As I neared the toolshed, the silence struck me. I heard only the *shush* of a breeze, and felt an unfamiliar frisson of loneliness.

I'd come out of hiding, but there was no one to show myself to.

I bent over my phone to typed another text. *Want to come over and find out your assignment for week three?*

A few minutes later, Grant texted back, *Sorry, sleeping.*

I checked the time stamp on the self-portrait messages. Grant had sent them the day before. *Shit.* I'd worked on the mural for two days with my phone off, stopping only to topple onto the couch for a few hours at a time.

It's almost six p.m., I typed to Grant. *Why are you sleeping now?*

Water shower food... relaxed enuf to sleep for real.

The dire reality of Grant's situation snapped into view again, dispelling my irritation that he wasn't around when I wanted him to be. For the first time in weeks, Grant had enough resources and comfort to... *rest.*

Fuck, I was such a dick.

A few minutes later, Grant sent another message. *Tell me by text?*

I decided I was too excited about the assignment to wait until I saw him. *Wk 3: Plan a tween adventure and do it. Plus errands in town. No manual labor this week.*

Grant texted back right away: *Reward?*

Washing machine access.

The sweet way Jill and Penelope had shown Grant how to do laundry by hand in the courtyard had been heartwarming, but it had taken hours of dedicated work. After the kids left, Grant had spent another hour washing out his underwear and socks.

I'd decided that since they were all children, including Grant, I'd give him an assignment of a kid adventure, topped with a labor-saving reward, so they'd have more time to play together.

Grant texted back one word: *Understood.*

For ten minutes, I stood on my lawn and scrolled back through the portrait photos.

They weren't enough.

My first few steps inside the toolshed made my heart race.

I swallowed the anxiety and pushed the door all the way open to let in as much light and air as possible, then dared a few more steps. The self-portraits spread over the central worktables drew me farther inside.

They absolutely amazed me.

I took a lot of photos, tried to capture their three-dimensionality, eventually ran out of new angles.

The toolshed door seemed less heavy when I slid it closed. *I* felt less heavy as I walked back to the house.

In the kitchen, I assembled a delicious lunch of food Grant had made, which I ate alone. Afterward, I went to my bedroom, closed the door, and knelt to resume the delicate work of painting grass stems.

The throb of silence made my hand shake.

I traded the small brush for a larger one, and stood to work on the deep shadows in the background, which felt more familiar.

Chapter 43

GRANT

I wasn't at my campsite napping when Oliver texted me the week three assignment, but I was headed in that direction. I'd started on a hike, but then turned around, too weary to manage it.

I paused at the edge of Violetta Road to gaze at a blackberry bush and daydream about blackberry cobbler.

But I don't have an oven.

"Damn it," I said aloud.

I walked on and wondered if Oliver might trade half a pan of cobbler for the use of one of his *three* ovens. As much as I appreciated Oliver's assistance, he remained an irritation. So many ovens and art supplies and wild shit filling up space in the house. So many tools in the workshop. So much free time and creativity. And yet, beneath it all, under Oliver's exterior persona of *eccentric artist*, I detected a sad waif, lost even though he had a home.

The image of a trapped animal came to mind. A burnished red fox, wily but caught, a trickster bested by the unexpected. I closed my eyes, tried to catch the fox's eyes, to see if he'd let me free his paw. He growled, avoided my gaze, bled to death from pride and fear.

I shook my head to clear the disturbing image, to wake myself up, and tripped over a blackberry vine, shoelaces tangling in the thorns.

I squatted to free myself and got an idea.

Maybe what Oliver needed was as simple as an invitation to play. A sweep of my hand cleared gravel to the side. With my finger in the dust, I drew a map, searching my memory for a blackberry thicket big enough for what I had in mind.

A car scrunched behind me. I considered standing, but wasn't ready to abandon my map. I spared a look over my shoulder. A car I didn't recognize emerged from Oliver's driveway and made a right turn away from me. A second car followed—Clementine's maroon Volvo. Since the day I'd heard—okay, eavesdropped on—her session with Oliver, I'd met her briefly, on the front porch. She seemed like a woman of gentle extremes. Extremely polite. Extremely kind. Extremely sad. She drove toward me at two miles an hour—another extreme— perhaps to minimize the dust cloud. When she reached me, she stopped the car.

"Grant," she said through the open driver's side window.

"Everything okay?" I asked.

"Yes. Very well. Thank you for asking." She nodded down at me. "You're looking better these days. Are *you* okay?"

"Yep. Slowly coming back to life. Hey, I have a question for you. Do you know of any blackberry thickets within walking distance of Oliver's that are huge, like *really* huge?"

"That's... um..." Clementine blinked. I considered apologizing for my abrupt question, but didn't. I stayed silent as she thought.

"Honestly," she said, "if there's a bramble anywhere within walking distance of Oliver's, he's the person who would know."

"I get that, but humor me."

"Well, the largest bramble I know of is on Bast Road, but that's not close to Oliver's, even if you hike through the woods instead of go by the roads. I could drive you there now, if you want, then you could walk back to..." She hesitated. "Oliver's house?"

Clementine and I had never talked about where I was staying. I suspected Oliver had told her I was camping in the woods. I gave Clementine a playful, stern look meant to chide her for engaging in gossip about me.

She cleared her throat and said with fake sincerity, "Or wherever you live these days."

I laughed, and we smiled at each other while I considered her offer. As much as I wanted to see that bramble, my body craved a lie-down in my tent with a big bowl of food.

"Oh, what the heck." I shrugged and stood to get into the car. It was too good an opportunity to pass up.

Clementine drove as if she intended to kick up as little dust as possible in her passage through life. We inched along and talked. I tried to make her laugh. I wanted to ask her about Aza, but I only knew about him through my invasion of her privacy. Maybe I could work my way around to it.

"How do you know Oliver?" I asked.

"Oliver saved my son's life."

I kept my mouth shut on my thought that her session with Oliver seemed to have been about a son who'd died. Maybe she had more than one son.

"Oh, yeah? How?" I asked.

"Ages ago, there was a sort of artistic social circle on Vashon that revolved around Matteo and Lucca—Oliver's grandfather and father. My son, Aza, started painting lessons with Oliver when he was five and Oliver was nine."

"Oliver gave art lessons at age *nine*?"

"Aza was his first pupil, but yes. Oliver was a better art teacher at nine than any of the adults we tried out for Aza. Well, except for Lucca and Matteo, who taught Oliver."

In Oliver's mural on the side of the house, the pack of boys who roamed the island included a small, black-haired boy always running to catch up, little legs spinning in a blur. I wondered if that was Aza.

"Aza was sixteen when his dad left me and moved to New York." Clementine's impassive delivery, the way she stuck to facts, gave the impression of a cop briefing a colleague. Clementine slowed the car to a stop when Violetta ended at Bast Road.

"Are you sure you want to tell me this?" I asked. "It seems like hard work. I don't want to—"

"Yes. I do," Clementine said, but then she didn't say anything more.

"Aza stayed here, on Vashon?" I prompted.

"He withdrew. He got in trouble at school." With a sigh, Clementine put the car into park. "My parenting skills were not great. I was out of my depth, but didn't tell anyone. When Robert left, our plan was for Aza to spend the school year with me and summers with him in New York. I figured Robert would straighten Aza out over the summer, so I let his behavior slide."

I reached over to give Clementine's shoulder a pat.

"I'm all right," she said. "It helps to tell it. I know it's heavy, and we don't really know each other. I'm sorry."

"Not a problem."

After a nod, Clementine said, "I caught Aza skipping school too many times and finally told Robert, who threatened to send Aza to boarding school. Aza told Oliver. I didn't know what to do. I had such a bad feeling about Aza going to boarding school."

"What did Oliver say?"

"We got on a call—me, Aza, Robert, and Oliver—to try to figure out a solution. Aza wanted to stay on Vashon. He promised to straighten up if we let him do an intensive painting mentorship with Oliver. Oliver was willing. All Oliver wanted in exchange was for Aza to design and create a piece of art for the property. It was an inspired arrangement. My son always had so much energy. Oliver's plan was designed to help Aza manage his energy, in multiple ways."

"Robert agreed?"

"Yes. Reluctantly, but yes. He knew and respected Oliver and Lucca, so he was willing to try the arrangement."

A dog trotted out of nowhere and barked at the Volvo. I startled and put a hand to my chest. "*Jesus.*" For all its dryness, Clementine's delivery had reeled me in.

"I forgot we were sitting here in your car," I said. "You're a great storyteller, but I'm kind of scared for you to continue. I'm not sensing a happy ending."

"I've only told the story a few times. Each time, I gain a little distance, see the story instead of only the..."

"Pain," I said.

"Yes." She glanced at me. "I do sessions with Oliver to loosen things—sometimes big chunks of grief and guilt come loose. It's hard, but it's always worth it."

Clementine didn't seem inclined to drive on yet.

"What were Aza's paintings like?" I asked.

"Before Oliver and Lucca took him in, the only classes at school Aza did well in were art classes. At sixteen, he was already an accomplished artist, but during his intensive with Oliver, his painting became extraordinary, levels above anything he'd approached before. Dark, to be sure, but when you looked at them, you had to feel."

"What do you mean, 'Before Oliver and Lucca took him in'?"

Clementine let out a slow breath.

"You don't have to tell me," I offered, though I really wanted to know.

"It's easier to talk about since I don't know you. If you don't mind?"

"I'm riveted," I said.

"Aza didn't want to live with me anymore. Oliver and Lucca let him stay with them. Aza finished his junior year with much better grades. It seemed like a miracle. He negotiated with his dad to be allowed to stay at Oliver's for the summer. That saved Aza. I'm certain."

I'd seen Clementine's grief when I'd spied on her session at Oliver's. I almost couldn't bear the suspense of finding out what had happened to Aza.

"It didn't last," Clementine said in a soft voice. "Through Oliver's connections in Seattle, Aza got a show at a gallery near Pioneer Square. It was a very big deal, and the show was a great success. There were only two paintings that didn't sell."

"Wow. That's amazing."

"And that was when we stumbled, all of us except Oliver."

"How so?"

"Aza decided, against Oliver's advice, that he was ready for New York. He packed up and moved to live with Robert and attend public school in New York City for his senior year."

"Damn. That must have been hard for you."

Clementine pressed her lips together, hunched forward to put the car into drive, but didn't take her foot off the brake. "Robert and I thought it was a good idea. Aza was adamant about it. Oliver tried hard to talk us all out of it. All the work he and Aza had done together had given Aza more confidence, and he'd grown up a lot, but Oliver insisted, to any of us who would listen, which was none of us, that Aza wasn't prepared for New York City."

By then my curiosity was eating me alive. Because I couldn't handle the anticipation, I asked a loaded question—a *rude* question, since I suspected Aza was dead. "Is Aza still there, in New York?"

Clementine took her foot off the brake and made a left turn onto Bast.

I kept quiet, hoped her discomfort was greater than mine and would make her talk. I felt ashamed and determined in equal measure.

After a silence that charged the air, Clementine pointed. "There." She slowed to a stop.

Drawn by the largest blackberry thicket I'd ever seen, I got out of the car for a better view. While I gaped, Clementine offered a tip about a trail back to Oliver's. She handed me her business card through the window and drove away.

The Volvo disappeared in the distance, leaving me with a blackberry thicket as tangled and thorny as my unanswered questions.

Chapter 44

GRANT

"**Will we** go even if it rains?" Clover asked me.

"Nope," I said.

The kids and I sat around the picnic table on Thursday afternoon of week three, sheltered by the awning from the drizzle, or "needle rain," as Clover called it, "because of the billion tiny, stabbing raindrops." In spite of the rain, the kids had shown up to coax details from me about our upcoming adventure.

Clover's yellow rain gear squeaked whenever she shifted on the bench.

"You look ready for a deluge," I said to her. "Very cheery. Like a buttercup."

"If you tell us what we're doing, we can prepare better," Jill tried.

I smiled and shook my head.

Penelope, our voice of practicality, stuck to the certainties. "Raise your hand if you can go."

"Saturday, right?" Clover looked at Penelope for an answer, which made me chuckle. Someday I'd stand in a voting booth and look down to see Penelope's name on the ballot. *President Penelope.* It had a nice ring to it.

Jill, Clover, Kai, and I all raised our hands—our informal vote to put Penelope in office. I couldn't help the snicker that slipped out. Everyone looked at me, which only made it harder to contain my mirth.

"What's so funny?" President Penelope paused the proceedings.

I laughed harder.

"Just... oh, *man*." I leaned forward on my elbows and put my head in my hands to pull myself together. "President Penelope," I managed to say through my laughter.

When Jill and Clover started laughing and Kai smiled up at me, I felt a rush of affection.

Clover spoke over our chuckles. "We might have one more person. If that's okay." When she looked at Penelope again, I wasn't the only one who snickered.

"You talked to Abelino?" I asked Clover.

"I walked by his house and he came out. He didn't say much, but he let me tell him things. I could invite him."

"He might like to have an adventure," Jill said.

"Maybe." Clover seemed skeptical.

"Nice of you to want to include him, buttercup."

Kai spoke for the first time. "What should we bring?"

Jill jumped like Kai had poked her.

"What?" Kai's eyebrows pulled together with concern.

"You *spoke*." She patted Kai's forearm. "It just surprised me."

"Let's see," I said, to draw attention away from Kai. "Bring a lunch. And a bicycle—got to have that. Boots or some kind of sturdy shoes. Socks, long pants, long-sleeved shirt. A denim or canvas jacket, if you have one. Um... knee pads would be handy. A hat that's not knit."

I stood to fetch our one notepad and tossed it onto the picnic table with a pen. Penelope pounced, as I'd known she would. She organized everyone, made a list of who had what and who needed to borrow what, coordinated Jill's repair of the extra bike for Abelino.

As I prepared us a snack of saltine crackers, sunflower seeds in the shell, and celery sticks, I mulled over the feeling I'd forgotten something. I had yet to invite Oliver, but that wasn't it. It had something to do with Penelope writing on the notepad. When nothing came to mind, I shrugged and carried the snacks over to the table.

Oliver continued to spy on us from the window in the courtyard or his perch in the tree behind the workshop. Now and then, he would grace us with his presence for a few minutes, say hello, but then wander away before I could get a good read on him.

He worried me. The cavalier, easygoing artist who'd exasperated me in the early weeks seemed more like his normal self than the spying waif he'd become.

On Friday, I emerged from the woods and spotted Oliver through a kitchen window. I snuck around to the back door and pounded on it with both fists.

Oliver's yelp from inside carried through the door. He opened the door with a fierce glare. For some sick reason, it reassured me to provoke him into losing his cool.

"What the *fuck*?" Oliver snapped the sharp words at me.

I took two steps forward, into the house, and Oliver backed away.

"I didn't invite you inside," Oliver said.

"Cranky today, are we?" I made my voice cheerful and bright, part of my devious plan to irritate Oliver into exposing more of his layers. "Don't worry. This won't take long."

Oliver's loose shirt—a *smock*, I remembered him calling it—sported fingerprint paint smudges at the hem. Strands of glossy hair had fallen from the topknot. One strand had dipped into a puddle of blue. Without thinking, I lifted my hand to touch it.

Oliver's flinch reminded me of my mission, and I let my hand drop.

"I'm taking the kids on a blackberry adventure for my week three assignment," I said. "We want you to join us. Tomorrow at ten in the courtyard. Don't tell the kids about the blackberries. I want to surprise them."

The annoyed furrow between Oliver's brows relaxed for a second. His eyes softened. "That's... nice."

"Interested?" I prompted.

"Which bramble? There's one out past the throne. It's only a twenty-minute walk, but it's hard to find. Did you find it? Is that where you're going?"

Oliver's motormouth reaction was cute. I ignored his questions. "Throne?"

With a roll of his eyes, Oliver said, "I know you know about the throne I'm carving. Out past the toolshed?"

"Oh. You mean your *stump chair* past the *workshop*." I folded my arms over my chest and put some challenge in my stare, just to mess with him.

"What's your point, Grant? That we don't live in the same world? That's old news."

I ignored his jab. "So. Are you in?"

"Which bramble?"

"Why do you care?"

"I just... do." The shrug Oliver tried to pull off as casual was anything but, due to his tense shoulders.

I bowed my head toward him and whispered, "It's a surprise."

The rise and fall of Oliver's chest sped up. A slight flush overtook his tanned cheeks. I pulled back, curious about what had upset him. Whatever I'd said or done, Oliver considered it offensive enough to shut down the conversation.

"Get out." He tapped my chest with a fist, a reluctant touch to push me away.

I shrugged and stepped back onto the porch. "The invitation stands, if you change your mind."

"I never said I wouldn't go," Oliver bit out before he slammed the door on my smug smile.

Chapter 45

GRANT

Saturday morning arrived with a glorious, sunny flourish. By ten o'clock the courtyard echoed with excited laughter and young voices.

I shoved a bag of carrot sticks into my daypack on top of the splurge of snacks I'd bought in town to share and the collection of tools snagged from the workshop, wrapped in shop cloths to minimize the rattle. It all made the pack heavy and lumpy. I was too eager to care.

I asked the kids to line up in a row in front of me. Clover had persuaded Abelino to join us and I got my first good look at him. His name, height, and long hair—jet-black and down to the middle of his back—likely didn't do him any favors at school. Or maybe I was a cynic. Maybe Vashon schools were more enlightened about bullying than the rural schools I'd attended near the Idaho border. I hoped so.

I sat on the picnic bench with my back against the table and gestured Abelino forward. He came with reluctance and a quick glance at Clover.

"Hey, Abelino," I said.

He stopped a few feet in front of me.

"I'm really glad you could join us."

Abelino nodded, very serious. I thought I saw actual fear in his eyes, so I leaned back to rest my forearms on the table and make it easy for him to keep track of my hands. "Your hair might be a bit tricky. When we get to where we're going, could put your hair up in a hat? I don't want it to get hurt."

Abelino said, "I brought a hat. And a…" He held up his arm to show me the hair band around his wrist. His voice was deeper than I'd expected, but gentle.

"Perfect," I said.

Abelino returned to stand between Clover and shy Kai, who stole a look up at Abelino out of the corner of his eye.

I inspected each kid in turn. There wasn't much else to tweak. The extravagant way they'd overdressed—bulky layers, full pockets, odd hats, work gloves—evoked sci-fi movie rebels up to no good on purpose. "We've got a bunch of overachievers here," I said. "You look like a gang of tough guys I wouldn't want to meet in a dark alley."

"We might have to rough you up if you don't tell us what we're doing soon," Penelope fake-threatened.

"Dream on." I stood to shrug on my daypack.

Since I didn't have a bicycle, I'd decided I would hike while the kids biked. I didn't want to wear them out before we got to the brambles. I could have asked to borrow Oliver's bike, but if he joined us, one of us would have to walk anyway.

I resigned myself to going without Oliver, but at the last minute he joined us.

A hush fell over the courtyard.

Lord, the man was cute.

"Smart get-up." I gestured at the padded, plaid shirt tied around Oliver's waist and his zip-front coveralls. *Oliver,* rendered in machine-sewn cursive, personalized his coveralls on a patch above the breast pocket.

My plan was to talk to Oliver as we walked, dig a little, then surround him with misfit kids.

I sent the kids ahead on their bikes, with instructions to wait at the green bench where two trails crossed.

"I know where that is," Penelope yelled back to me, and they raced off.

Oliver hadn't said anything beyond greeting the kids.

"Nice day, yeah?" I tried as a first foray.

All I got was a nod.

At the edge of the yard, Oliver insisted I go first down the narrow trail, thus foiling my plan to bring up the rear so I could perv on his hair and body without him seeing me do it.

"What are you working on in your bedroom?" I asked. "A painting?"

"I don't want to talk about it." The flatness of Oliver's voice sent off alarms. I wondered again where all his sass had gone.

"Okay," I said, and we walked on in silence.

It was hella tough to keep quiet. The mystery of the guy tugged at me. I pretended I needed to retie my shoelace and Oliver finally passed me.

The long walk won't be long enough. Shafts of light sprayed sparks off the fire in Oliver's hair, and I sighed through a close study of his easy gait.

By the time we got to the green bench, the kids were manic with excitement. They seemed to have multiplied into a horde.

"Dismount," I bellowed, and took the lead on the trail. I wanted the kids walking their bikes so we arrived at the brambles together. I didn't want to miss the looks on their faces when they saw it.

Oliver remained at the back of the line.

The rough trail of switchbacks ended at Bast Road, across from the monster bramble Clementine had shown me. I crossed the road, turned to face everyone, and spread my arms. "Ta-da!"

"What?" Clover looked around, not yet seeing what was right in front of her.

"We're here," I said. "Stash your bikes back in the woods before you cross the road. Put up your hair or tuck it away." I made eye contact with Penelope and Abelino, the only kids with long hair. "Because we're going in."

It took another moment for the kids to get it. Kai got it first. "In *there*?" he asked, awe in his voice.

"Yes, sir," I said.

They whooped and ran to sling their bikes into the underbrush, then huddled around me by the brambles to scramble into kneepads and heavy shirts. Kai put on a ratty canvas jacket he said his dad had given him. It hung down past his knees.

While they got ready, I handed out the smaller cutting tools, making sure each kid understood how to work the safety latches and had a designated secure place to tuck the tool when they weren't using it.

I pulled a giant pair of loppers from my pack for myself. The kids stepped back and stilled. I approached the bramble at the spot I'd sussed out on a previous visit as a decent point of entry.

Before I made the first cut, I turned to check on Oliver, to see if he'd lightened up yet.

He stood on the far side of the road, arms slack, face blank.

"Hey, Jill," I said. "Would you mind seeing what's up with Oliver? Maybe he forgot his kneepads or something. See if we can do anything to help, yeah?"

"Sure." Jill tucked her clippers into a back pocket, checked the road in both directions, and jogged over to Oliver.

The other kids and I watched Jill talk with Oliver. I couldn't hear what she said, but the whole time she talked, Oliver shook his head. He looked terrible—pale, angry, and sad.

Jill put her hands on her hips, like she was about to get stern. For a drawn-out moment, Oliver met my eyes. Then he took out his phone, put it to his ear, and walked back into the woods.

When Jill got back to us, she shrugged.

"What was that all about?" I asked.

"He *said* he forgot he had an appointment. But... I don't know."

"Oh. Well, okay." I was disappointed, *really* disappointed, and more curious than ever, but Oliver would have to wait. A gaggle of kids crowded me from behind. If I didn't get busy with the loppers, I'd face death by thorn bush.

A few dozen calculated snips later and we were in.

Chapter 46

OLIVER

When Grant directed the pack of tweens north, trepidation silenced me.

I knew where they were headed.

For decades, Mrs. Montgomery's blackberry patch had threatened to take over her house. She refused to use pesticides and couldn't beat it back fast enough by herself. Every summer, half the island's high school students wrestled, chopped, and hacked at Mrs. Montgomery's bramble for summer cash and cookies.

I *tried*.

I really tried to go with them.

Grant's excitement, on a feedback loop with the kids', pulled me harder than I'd been pulled in a long time, but I couldn't even step onto the road.

I hated myself for that.

Jill listened with skepticism to my excuse about a forgotten engagement. I faked the need for a call to cover my panic, and withdrew.

As I walked away, I held onto the burble of tween chatter and Grant's rumble of words for as long as I could. The voices faded with each step I took toward home.

I didn't want to go home.

The prospect of removing my bramble adventure outfit, putting on painting clothes or throne-carving clothes instead, made my arms feel heavy and inert.

I turned right onto the forest loop around the house, followed it to the track the driveway spur became past Dad's garage. Low tree limbs met overhead. I stooped to push through. After a while, the track veered to the right along a high bluff. Far away and below, beyond a carpet of treetops, lay the island's southern shore, a stretch of sea, and the mainland.

The trail took me to a wall of holly ten feet high and impenetrable, impossible to see through. Granddad had planted the holly trees in his mid-twenties, to create a secret holly hideout for future generations.

I swept my left palm over the prickly leaves as I followed the curve of the wall, missing the old man whose smiling presence had suffused my childhood. After the social events Dad hosted around a fire pit in the middle of the holly hideout, Granddad and I had always been the last to leave. The embers trapped us, we liked to say.

A gate bit into the holly wall. I let myself inside and locked the door behind me, studied the grain of the wooden gate until sunshine warmed my back and comforted me. When my heart had slowed, I turned and walked to Dad's Cadillac Sedan DeVille to begin my routine.

I opened the trunk and gathered supplies—spray bottle, squeegee, new blue cloth—then got to work. When the windows sparkled and I'd rubbed away pollen, dust, and months of grime, I dropped the cloth to the ground to take with me when I left. With a fresh chamois from a bulk pack in the trunk, I wiped the black finish with slow circles from the back to the front, around the hood, and down the other side, to refresh the gleam. Finally, I burnished all the chrome, including the thin stripes of molding along the sides.

I hadn't visited the DeVille in almost a year. I teased dried leaves from the gap between the upper edge of the hood and the windshield, to procrastinate. I dreaded the next part of the ritual as much as I needed it.

The chamois joined the blue cloth on the ground. I closed the trunk, unlocked the driver's door, and slid the key into the ignition to unlock the doors and crack the electric windows.

The holly wall stopped at the edge of the bluff, to preserve the view. From my slouch into the black leather of the back seat, I saw mostly sky out the front window. The DeVille interior embraced me like the best kind of cave, safe and secure as a hug.

The things I missed most about Dad were his bear hugs and the way he could persuade me to tell him the truth. He was never squeamish, and he always wanted to know everything.

I wasn't great at getting to the truth on my own.

When inside Dad's DeVille, I had an unbreakable rule: I wasn't allowed to avoid the truth. I *hated* my own rule. Dreaded it. Needed it.

To get myself started, I let my mind go blank. Inside the DeVille, that was the equivalent of a white lie. After an hour or so of blue sky and sighs, truths began to nudge through.

Watching Grant with the tweens makes me... ache.

I want to be one of those kids.

I didn't want to think about Grant, but the truths I'd avoided pulled him forward anyway.

I don't like being left out.

That was my own fault.

It's easier to watch.

With that thought, the luxurious DeVille, memento of a bygone era, felt less like a hug and more like a moveable throne, a coach in which the liege rode in state, sealed off from the day-to-day activity of his realm. Protected to the point of isolation.

The weight of time and sadness decayed my slouch until I lay on the back seat. Between the truths I didn't want to face and the blank space I courted to avoid them, I drifted to sleep in the warmth and dreamed of being a king.

The ping of a text woke me and I fumbled to unlock my phone, then wished I hadn't.

Grant had sent me a group selfie from inside the bramble.

The tweens leaned toward Grant against a background of thorns. Dots of sunlight on skin smeared with dirt and berry juice. The faces of the children so open it hurt to see. Red scrape of dried blood across Grant's neck. He looked euphoric.

I could have been in that photo.

I turned off my phone and set it on the floor, rolled to press my face into the seat back, closed my eyes, searched for some way to feel better.

A discarded king held hostage in a black cave, hidden away while a usurper rules his lands. No one from his kingdom knows where he is. No one looks for him. No one cares enough to release him from the spell that binds him. All he has are memories of his father and their once-great realm... and jousts with the emperor's son.

Oh, stop it.

If I started a fantasy in the DeVille, the emperor's son wouldn't be Freddie.

I had no idea what I wanted.

The *truth* was that I was afraid to find out.

In the safe, sacred space of the DeVille, I admitted that Grant attracted and frightened me in equal measure. When I thought of building a life with Freddie, I felt... *good*, the same, normal. When I thought of Grant—on my property, in the toolshed, cooking in my kitchen, lighting up outcast tweens, challenging me, arguing, resisting, questioning, pushing—I broke into a sweat and rolled into a ball.

I covered my face with my hands and gave in to the fantasy, let it carry me away.

The plush furnishings of the suite don't hide the fact that it's a prison, or that I'm here against my will. I pace the row of tall windows in the main chamber and scan the treetops far below. Trees as far as I can see. In clear weather, when I've slept enough to make my vision sharp, I can locate the thread of track that cuts through the forest up the mountain slope on the distant horizon.

That's where someone who's come for me would appear.

Pacing, glances out the windows, and waiting have stacked into a crush of years. I've paced holes in my shoes again and again. A cobbler from the village on the other side of the fortress comes in to fit me for a new pair when my shoes fall apart. The eyes of the soldiers pin me as the cobbler works, hawks prepared to lunge if I do anything but sit quietly.

I'm forbidden to speak to the soldiers, or to anyone. I no longer try. Long ago, when hope remained, I tried to reason with them. They didn't bring me food for a week. It's been years since anyone besides me heard the sound of my voice.

It's been months since I had anything to say to myself.

It's possible I no longer exist.

In the deep of a night following a day exactly like any other, I startle from a blank sleep, woken by a faint sound. Blink into the blackness, strain to hear.

Just when I decide it must have been a sound I dreamed, I hear it again. A flick of something soft against stone. Up and out to the main room in no time, I lean over the windowsill to scan the stone wall below.

Nothing.

There's no one there. The sound was a dream after all.

I turn and step into a hard body. A hand presses over my mouth. The rumble of a man's deep voice against my ear. "Look up now and then."

I breathe him in, try to back away from his touch, but he's stronger. He's always been stronger. My childhood enemy who bested me when we were boys ordered to fight. He was better. But I was going to be a king, so I'd fought hard, every time.

He always won.

I've never forgiven him for that.

The emperor's son has come to kill me, win my kingdom, best me one last time. A part of me is relived, ready to be dispatched, freed from prison, even by death.

"Hold up now," he says in my ear. One hand still over my mouth, he leads me to the nearest divan and pushes me down. Dim light from the night sky shows me how he's aged.

"Missed you," he says, and replaces his hand with his lips.

Sweet breath.

My lips brush his when I say, "I hate you," my disused voice a croak. I close my eyes to feel him more. "Are you here to grant me a final wish before you kill me? Or until your soldiers kill me, so you won't have my blood on your own hands?"

He pulls back. "I would be your last wish?"

I watch his lips. "Your smile..."

The first time I saw that smile I was eight. He was ten. We'd fought. He'd won. I hated and loved that smile. Hated it because he only brought it out when I lost. Loved it because I knew it was only for me.

He smiles that smile and kisses me like the smile was always supposed to be a kiss. I lift my chin. If it's my last kiss, I want as much as he'll give me.

"Oh, the drama." He pulls away and laughs at me. "I can feel you mooning over your tragic demise."

When I huff to contradict him, he whispers, "You always did give up too soon."

"I only give up when I know I've lost. Like now. What's your plan? Strap me to your back and climb up the wall? Toss me out the window and call it quits?" He must know I can't do what he did, climb stone to escape. If I could, I'd already be gone.

"No, Sir Wails-a-Lot. In three hours, we'll walk out." He nods at the door to the hallway and the rest of the fortress. "Relax. Give the wheels time to turn." One of his wide hands drops to my knee, sweeps up the inside of my thigh.

I yelp and squirm against him.

Hand over my mouth again, he stares down at me. "Gods help me. I knew you'd be this way. Hoped. I would imagine this after we fought. How I'd hold you down, run my hands all over you. How you'd writhe and whine."

I still myself at his words. "I do not whine," I mutter against his palm.

The fondness in his eyes confuses me.

"You do." With a movement so precise it takes my breath away, he strips my loose trousers to my knees.

I whine.

We stare at each other. I count twenty of his slow breaths. My bare legs cool in the fresh air from the window.

He's the one I wait for, the one I watch the horizon for. I didn't see the speck of him on the thread of trail on the horizon, but he came for me anyway.

My breath speeds up. "I only get three hours with the emperor's son?" I whisper.

"Emperor. And there you are." He lifts his hand away and sticks his tongue into my mouth. With the same skill he'd used to best me over and over when we fought, he touches me where I'm hottest, tests the weight of my cock as it hardens, holds me in the palm of his hand. Holds all of me in the palm of his wide hand.

The gate in the holly bushes didn't open, but I heard it rattle.

And then footsteps through the tall grass.

Chapter 47

GRANT

After Oliver ran off, I wrestled with my focus in the blackberry thicket. Clover took advantage of my distraction and muscled past me to take the lead. She turned back and held out her hands for the heavy loppers.

"Are you sure?" I asked. But all it took was one look at her radiant face and I became a convert.

Our advancement slowed, and Clover made different decisions than I would have, like to go around a clump of thick trunks instead of cutting through, but I didn't mind. Behind Clover, the rest of us kept busy carving a bigger, smoother tunnel. The first time I looked back, I had to laugh. The kids had transformed the cramped passage Clover and I clipped away at into a causeway. The crawl back to the road would be a breeze.

No one else asked for time up front. After about thirty minutes, Clover could barely lift the loppers.

"Hey, Brutus the Buttercup," I said. Kai and Jill giggled behind me. "Come on." I tapped Clover on the back. "You're pooped. Trade me."

"*No.*" She stopped but didn't turn around. "I'm not *done* yet."

"I'm not asking to get in front. Just trade me those heavy cutters for this lighter pair." We swapped, and Clover surged forward again.

The kids slayed me. They really did. Over the previous week, all the kids—with the notable exception of Kai—had talked to me at least a little about their troubles.

Baby Clover's teenaged parents had been caught dealing drugs. She'd been passed around in their extended family until her parents pulled themselves together. Sort of. When Clover was five, her parents retreated to Vashon to get their families off their backs. They'd settled into a crappy cabin and minimum-wage career paths. Clover had told me her parents mostly worked and watched TV, and she didn't expect her life to get better until she was old enough to leave home. Random home visits from social workers kept the worst of her parents' behaviors to a minimum, but Clover's self-confidence and sense of security had taken a lot of hits over her short life.

Penelope's large family foisted on her the unwelcome expectation that, as the oldest girl, she would care for her three younger siblings. She pushed against that expectation when she ran away to Oliver's for drawing lessons and to play with us.

Jill had her brother's friends and their inappropriate comments to deal with. I made a mental note to ask her if she'd brought up the issue with her parents yet.

I didn't know much about Abelino—only that he'd been born in Mexico, where he'd lived until he was seven, and he and his mom didn't have much money, due to her illness. In the courtyard, when I'd inspected the kids, I'd glimpsed Abelino's lunch in a battered plastic baggie—a banana way past its expiration date, one white bread sandwich with a thin slice of baloney, and a bag of airplane peanuts worn enough to have been foraged for in an infrequently used suitcase. I'd brought plenty of food to share for lunch. I'd make sure Abelino knew he could have as much as he wanted.

And then there was Kai.

I made a few desultory snips at ground-level vines as I waited for Clover to scoot forward. Kai spoke and smiled more each week, but he hadn't given me any clues about what worried him. I was back to waffling on my decision to push, not wanting to make him retreat again.

"Brutus, you about done?" I asked Clover. "I'm pooped." I wasn't, but I sensed Clover was on a mission to prove something and might need help realizing she already had. "Feels to me like you've led us into the heart of the beast."

"Here?"

"Here looks great to me."

Clover dropped her shears, declared us home, and pointed out where we could widen the tunnel to make a cavern.

Kai and Abelino worked as a team with the loppers to sever stalks at ground level. The rest of us clipped away at the edges, pushed the cut stems into the curved walls with our gloved hands until we'd claimed enough space for all of us to sit. The top of Clover's head brushed the ceiling when she stood.

Abelino put a gentle hand on Clover's shoulder to get her to move aside, then held the loppers over his head to clip a circular hole as wide as his shoulders into the ceiling. When he'd clipped as high as he could, he ducked down to hand the loppers to me to finish our skylight.

I stood on my tiptoes, shored up by the kids leaning against my legs to steady me, and cut through to bright blue sky crisscrossed by the few branches beyond my reach.

The resulting patch of sunlight lit the floor of the cave like a spotlight.

I assumed the kids would horse around, take turns posing in the spotlight, gorge on all the ripe blackberries within reach, or rip into their packed lunches, but they stayed quiet.

We sat in a scatter on bare ground decorated with sun confetti, amid a refined aroma of dust, smashed blackberries, and sweaty kids.

Wonder filled their faces as they looked around.

Our labor had come to an end in reverence, as if we'd created a church. I almost asked the kids what they were thinking about, but stopped myself. The unusual space, the timeless moment, the rough circle of stark brightness in our midst, the birds, the rustle of leaves, the heat, the dirt, and our breaths became my favorite prayer, my best moment. I closed my eyes against an intensity of gratitude.

"I think…" When Kai began to speak, the other kids looked away from him, gave him a respite from observation. Their consideration made my heart contract with joy. His soft voice merged with the dappled, contented silence. "I think I'm gay." Kai kept his eyes locked on mine as his face turned red, and he started to tremble.

I smiled and waited, but he held his breath and didn't seem inclined to say more.

"You're perfect," I said.

His face squinched up and he nodded. The tears that fell from his eyes rinsed layers of dust from his cheeks.

"And you look like a warrior," I told him with a gesture at my own cheeks.

The other kids looked at Kai then.

"Oh." Penelope's eyes widened. "You really do."

I dug into my pack to find the stainless steel camping plate I'd brought to serve the snacks on, gave it a polish with a handful dirt and the elbow of my shirt, then passed it to Kai.

That *grin*. Lord, I'd missed it.

Kai handed Abelino the plate and crawled through the spotlight to me. I wrapped as much of him as I could into a hug. "My brave warrior nephew," I whispered in his ear, "holding such a big secret inside until you felt safe enough to let it out. I am so proud of you."

Kai sniffled and snuggled against me for a while. When he pulled back to look at me, his face looked truly relaxed.

Lunch, after Kai's declaration, became a raucous affair after all, involving extensive food trades, surprise treats from my pack, and fingers dipped in smashed berries to draw purple warrior marks on dusty faces.

Penelope and Jill asked Clover, whose face was the dirtiest, if they could design her marks. What they did with blackberry juice and judicious fingerdots of water made Clover look *fierce*. I managed a couple of good photos before Clover saw her reflection in the plate and transformed their careful work by crying all over it.

Through it all, I took photographs to sustain me when I got back to Seattle and missed the sappy, wholesome camaraderie. I laughed and teased, and *felt* enough to burst.

When we'd eaten all the food, Kai suggested Clover take the lead on the way out. I emerged last from the tunnel into full light, birthed anew with my brothers and sisters.

I **hugged** the kids goodbye at the brambles and set out to find Oliver. I wanted to ask him why he hadn't joined us, and tell him about the adventure while it remained fresh.

He wasn't at the stump chair, where he seemed to gravitate to in times of stress. His car and bike were parked under the carport. He didn't answer the door at the house.

I cleaned and put away the cutting tools in the workshop, dumped my daypack on the picnic table in the courtyard, and considered Oliver's options. He might have gone for a walk, in which case I was unlikely to find him.

One final possibility, before I gave up, was the small building I'd noticed out beyond the hedges the day I'd trimmed them. I approached from the driveway, walked around to the back, and cupped my hands at a window. It was an empty garage. Empty as in *sterile*. Bare concrete floor, bare workbench along one wall, shelves bare except for a few old gas cans.

At the front of the garage, I convinced myself the grass between the ruts of the drive looked freshly trampled and followed it on down the hill, away from the house. A few minutes later, the drive ended in brush, but a footpath veered off to the right, toward a blot of dense green, which turned out to be an *immense* stand of holly trees. To get a sense of its size, I began to walk around it.

The gate came as a surprise. I tried the latch. It was locked, or maybe stuck. The solid construction of the gate seemed excessive. It was too tall to see over, even when I curled my hands over the top—which I could barely reach—and jumped to try to get a view of what lay beyond.

Too curious to give up, I held tight and threw a foot up next to my hands, managed to haul myself all the way up and over. I landed on the ground on the other side in a crouch, hands in the grass for balance.

Why in the everloving hell did Oliver stash a Cadillac behind a wall of holly?

I lifted my eyes. *Holy panorama, Batman.* Sky, distant sea, the southern Kitsap Peninsula —all *right there.*

Subtle movement in the car caught my eye. A bare foot propped against a side window.

Oliver.

I smiled and walked toward the car.

Chapter 48

OLIVER

When I heard the footsteps, I took my hand out of my pants. A shadow darkened the divan where I sprawled, lost in the fantasy I'd spun.

A door opened. A hand caught my propped feet. A man smelling of sweat and sun-heated earth slid onto the divan under my legs. The door closed.

I opened my eyes and saw my old enemy, the emperor's son.

"Did I give you that dueling scar?" I asked. I shook my head. That couldn't be right. I lifted my hand toward his neck. "But... it's new. We haven't seen each other in..." It felt like forever since I'd last seen him.

"Since you walked away?" The voice of the emperor's son, low and familiar, made me blink. The emperor's son who'd become the emperor.

He shook my leg. "Hey, you look like you've been napping. Are you okay?"

"I don't know," I answered, because I didn't. I felt unfinished and wanting.

"You would have loved it, Oliver. The kids were incredible. And Kai finally opened up."

The stone fortress began to fade.

When I didn't answer, lost in the in-between, he went on. "I was worried about you." He brushed the backs of his fingers across my forehead and cheek. "You're flushed."

A slight turn of my head into his cool hand took me closer to his scent. I licked his palm to taste, saw the scrapes and grime on his fingers. "You rescued those kids too, didn't you? Wrecked your hands on the stone."

"What?" His full palm covered my forehead. "I think you're delirious. Let's get you to the house and find a thermometer."

"I don't want to leave."

"The car?"

No, the fortress, I almost said aloud. But why wouldn't I want to leave my prison?

It's not a prison if he's here with me.

He set his heavy arm across my thighs. *No, I really don't want to leave.*

"You're out of it, man," he said. "Take a moment to get a grip and then we'll go."

I nodded, but the nod was a lie.

"This is a stunning car," he said. "I want to hear all about it, but later. You need to be home and in bed."

"Three hours won't be enough."

"Enough for what?"

"For all I want you to do to me before they come for us." I put every moment of my long years of imprisonment into my gaze. I wanted the emperor to feel how much I'd ached for him, and for how long. My hand twitched toward him.

It worked.

The concern in his dark eyes flashed into heat. He stared, then rushed me, shoved my legs apart to lunge between them, to reach my mouth. The thumb of his hand on my face entered my open mouth as his tongue filled me. I scrambled to swallow him, to pull all of him into me, tasting earth and need.

His big hands pinned my head to the wall behind me.

From my neck down, my body twisted and squirmed. It was *beautiful*. A flawless pause in the endless stream of time. If the price of that kiss had been an eon of imprisonment, it was worth every...

I fell off the seat.

"Oh crap," he said. "Damn it. Oliver, I'm sorry."

I looked up. Not the emperor.

Only Grant, a jobless, aimless squatter. Intruder. Threat to my secrets.

I *wished* he were Freddie. That would have been simple. But Freddie thought I'd sold the DeVille. Even if he knew I still had it, he'd never breach the gate. Freddie would respect the obvious.

I rubbed at my head to clear it, pushed away the hand Grant offered to pull me off the floor, and pointed at the door. "Out. Get *out*."

The shock and hurt on Grant's face didn't matter. It was his own doing, his own fault.

"I can't believe you did this," I said.

"But... *you* kissed *me*. You—"

"It is inexcusable of you to invade this space, *my* private space."

Lips pressed tight, Grant studied me for a long moment then untangled his hands from my legs, slid off the seat and out the door. I didn't hear him walk away, because my ears weren't working right, but I heard the locked gate rattle as he went over.

I stayed on the floor. The deeper shadows suited my state of ruin.

I'd thought I was alone and private and *safe*.

As I fumed, summer's long spin toward evening placed a careful hand on the dimmer switch. In spite of my cramped discomfort on the floor, I dozed through the shifting light into a dream more disturbing than my fantasy.

We drive at night. The vibration of tires on narrow roads jars my skull against the door. He drives while I hide under a blanket on the floor in the back. The hard work of hiding requires my full attention.

His official mission is to deliver me to safety, but we've been on the road for as long as I can remember. I suspect his personal mission is to keep me captive.

I wake to the hush of early daylight, to his steady breath as he sleeps in the front seat.

I watch his face and wait.

I'm not restrained. Long ago I had the idea to surge up and overpower him as he slept. Climb into the front, open the driver's door, push him out, drive away without him.

I didn't move a muscle to do anything. I swear. I only had the thought, a flash of inspiration, and opened my eyes. He was awake, watching me, running hands through his dark hair. He always knows what I'm thinking.

Every day, after he sleeps, he takes his payment for keeping me lost.

When he awakens, I begin to shake. Don't want it. Want it. Hurry. Wait.

We rarely speak. He reaches back with his long arm to find my face with his hand, maybe to reassure himself I'm still breathing. Fingers slide into my hair. I sigh before I catch myself and tense. My body wants. I only want out.

He tells me he does what I want him to do. He says he's my servant and I'm his sovereign, but how can I believe him? Why would I choose a life on the run, a kingdom as small as the back floor of a car?

I ask him what I'm hiding from.

"You're the only one who knows," he says.

I ask him where we go every day in the car.

"Only where you need to go," he says.

I ask him when we'll get there.

"As soon as you're ready," he says.

I accidently stretch up into his touch.

He climbs over the seat and pulls me off the floor, his first kiss a confident crush. The thumb of his hand on my face enters my open mouth as his tongue fills me and I scramble to swallow him, to pull all of him into me, to taste his certainty. He drives me as capably as he drives the car.

My ears fill with the hiss of the clock's lit fuse. All the other hours of the day are novocaine, timed to wear off when he touches me, when I remember to feel.

I half-stand to shove off my pants, but he pulls me onto his lap before I'm done, arranges his hand beneath me, fingers closed in a fist for me to sit on and rub. Big knuckles against the skin between my balls and hole. He presses up hard enough to turn the motion of my rubs into the engine that rocks the car.

I beg him to hurry.

He never hurries.

I hurry enough for us both, lift off his lap, struggle out of my clothes, kick away the tangle, peel off his shirt, press the side of my face to his warm chest as I unfasten his pants and pull them down. All the while, he runs his slow hands down my back and lower, down and between. His fingers set me on fire, tickle or push, slide into me, wrap my cock, until I look up at him and he smiles.

None of his weapons slay me like his smile. With his fingers in my ass and his smile an inch from mine, I'm lost to his movements and the gentle regard in his dark eyes.

With a sideways shift, he engineers the scene to lay me out beneath him. I watch him slick himself to get ready, can't look away as he prepares to invades me. His sure hands hold me in place until I remember to open, to let him in. I yield.

I always yield. "Don't wait," I beg. "Please don't make me wait."

He stops mid-thrust to smile-kiss-swallow my mouth, teases the top of my cock and waits for me to moan. Not until I freeze does he give me his cock again, in one controlled pump that restarts me with a gasp.

I'm his ruler.

He only does what I ask.

I can't figure out how to breathe for myself, so he breathes for me, day after day.

All I want is the detonation at the end, shooting me into black space. I squirm and twist when he slides his cock out, hold still when he pushes in, flush hot under his steady gaze. He watches my face, stops when I get close to coming. I can't hide it when I get close. I never can. Only when I give up and sag does he start again. A slow push of his cock all the way into me, a slower pull out.

"I hate you." I try to fold my arms over my chest to put distance between us. It's awkward.

"I know," he says with another smile.

"I command you to give me what I want."

"I am." He smiles. "Your highness."

"Fuck. You."

"Mmm."

When frustration threatens to make me kick him off, I remember I know his body too. I hold the side of his head against my mouth, thrust my tongue into his ear, scrape my teeth along the furled curve. With my other hand, I jerk myself fast.

"Guh," he says, and lifts his body to quicken his thrusts, to finally give me room to hump up against him and pull harder on my cock. When I get the angle just right for him, he starts to sweat. I pull myself closer to whisper into his wet ear, "I'll never let you go."

He comes first. I feel the hot rush deep inside me.

With both hands down my open pants, I floundered on the floor of the DeVille, locked behind a tall gate in a barbed wall in a car aimed over a cliff. My climax crushed my lungs, until I remembered I knew how to breathe on my own.

Chapter 49

OLIVER

I'd never come in the DeVille. The risk of jizz on the leather seats was too high.

Except that time I did.

I unfolded myself from the floor, cleaned up, locked up, and jogged to the house. En route, I called Freddie to tell him I *needed* him.

He was willing to drop everything.

"Thank God," I said. "Drive safely, but hurry."

We finished the call to the sound of the minivan starting.

While I waited, I showered off the heaviness of an afternoon spent wrestling with truth and fantasy in the confinement of the DeVille, and came to the conclusion that it didn't matter if Grant had caught me off guard with a kiss I'd then co-opted to use in a fantasy—his disregard for my privacy was a deal-breaker and I wanted him *gone*.

Twenty minutes after I'd called, Freddie slipped into my house with a leer and a purr. "Howdy, babe."

"Not in the bedroom," I said when he tried to steer me in that direction.

"No privacy in the living room," he countered.

I used his attempt to kiss me as a lure to draw him toward the arched doorway on the far side of the great room.

"Library?" Freddie asked.

"No. No spunk allowed anywhere near the velvet couch."

"Well, then." Freddie reached for the door handle of the room across the wide hallway from the library. "The old hideout it is."

My childhood hideout began as the closet where Granddad stored his collection of textiles—raw material for the strange, magnificent quilts he sold for thousands of dollars. I'd kept the last quilt he made me on my bed ever since Dad died. A dozen more he'd made for me over the years lay neatly stacked in my bedroom closet.

Renovation of the closet occurred soon after I started first grade, which I'd hated. Life at home was theater productions, courtyard parties, art experiments, and everyone treating me like I was special. School was horrible and pointless and far away. I'd rebelled, cried, thrown tantrums, argued. Dad urged me to paint it out of my system, but grew weary of tripping over stacks of dour paintings no one wanted to look at.

As a desperate measure, Dad and Granddad removed the textiles and shelving from Granddad's closet, cut in a row of windows to the courtyard at my eye level, and installed a wall-to-wall mattress. I took to the tiny room like a pasha. Fabric draped the ceiling, layers of pillows covered the mattress, and I hogged the Christmas lights from January to November.

Not much about the hideaway had changed. The mattress made it easy to kneel and spy on Grant and the kids in the courtyard.

Freddie left his shoes in the hallway and flopped onto his back, sending up a spray of pillows. "Batten down the doors and windows." He rubbed a hand up my shin. "I'm going to play you like the fine instrument you are. You'll be loud. I don't want that guy to butt in."

"His name is Grant."

"I don't care. Come here."

Daylight filtered through the wild roses on the trellis to flutter shadows around the room. I smiled at Freddie. He smiled back.

The pause lengthened.

"Well?" I said, still wound up from my fantasy in the DeVille, more than ready to be played.

Freddie didn't move, other than to wink and crook his finger.

I caught myself before I rolled my eyes. I'd forgotten his tendency to make me do all the work. "You *talk* a big game," I teased.

Freddie used his foot around my thigh to try to nudge me closer.

Not what I was hoping for. *Man up*, I chided myself. *Ask for what you want.* "Go on, then, Freddie. *Play me.*"

"Well, I would if you'd get over here. What's the holdup?"

If Freddie stood, he could put his junk in my face and I'd give him everything I had, all the *lick*, *suck*, *slide* he'd complained about missing. I willed a fantasy forward to get me into that desperate space again where I *needed*.

I got... *nothing*. Nothing from my imagination. Nothing from Freddie.

Exasperated, I dropped onto my back beside him. *Then* he roused himself, but only enough to roll toward me and put his hand on my face.

I stuck out my tongue to try to reach his thumb, to pull it into my mouth.

Freddie laughed and swiped the wetness from my cheek.

Only because I was staring at Freddie's neck at that moment, I noticed his nervous swallow. "What?" I asked.

"That guy, Grant, has been making me think."

"He's leaving. He's—"

"Invasive."

I thought of Grant's thumb in my mouth. "He sure is."

The nod Freddie began as we stared at each other extended past its expiration date. Freddie didn't often turn serious. I sat up and leaned against the wall so I could see him better.

"I've been thinking about us," Freddie said. "I got some news yesterday I want to share with you. Good news."

"Yeah?"

"That exposé series I proposed to the news journal was accepted. It means I'll be leaving Vashon a bit early."

"How early?"

"Mid-August instead of mid-September."

"Oh." The heaviness I'd washed away in the shower was back. Freddie and I hadn't had sex since his return, and he'd already be leaving. "In four weeks?"

"It's a big opportunity for me, Oliver. Really big."

"Well, then... um. Congratulations. What's the series about?"

"Japanese-American trade issues. I want to spend a month in D.C. doing research and interviews before I fly to Tokyo."

"I see. So how long will you be away this time?"

Freddie held my gaze. "Six months."

Half a year before I'd see him again.

Freddie patted my leg. "I know. It's a long time."

All I could do was blink.

"I've been thinking about our talk in the library," Freddie said. "If you came with me, I'd be willing to try being exclusive."

"Huh," I said.

"Think about it. If you went somewhere new, your art would flourish."

A flare of irritation made me look away. Freddie and I rarely discussed my art. What did he know about what would make it flourish? Maybe my art was already flourishing.

"Clementine and Talia can take care of your place while you're away. I mean, it's not like you have any pets or..." Freddie's expression turned thoughtful.

"Or what?"

"I was going to say 'or livestock,' but I can't decide if your hobo is more farm animal or wild animal."

My burst of laughter ended with a snort. "Stop it. We're talking about us."

"*I* was talking about us. You weren't saying much."

With an actual offer of exclusivity on the table, my doubts rose to the surface. I thought of the photo on my fridge. "What about your Japanese-guy preference?"

"Excuse me?"

"Come on. We've never talked about it, but I know you. Even in high school, you mostly dated Japanese guys."

"You're not Japanese. Tommy wasn't Japanese. Neither were Alfie or James or—"

"Okay." That time I did roll my eyes. "The fact that you could make a list that long off the top of your head makes my point just as well. I'm wary of your ability to be exclusive, with or without me."

"You know what, Oliver? I'm trying here."

"Okay. I know. But... what if I go along with you on your trip and you don't like it? Or what if I don't like it and want to come home? Would you still want to get together then, when you're on Vashon?"

Freddie's silence confirmed my suspicion.

"There's an *or else*, isn't there?" I asked.

"I don't want to use the *or else*. Come with me and I won't have to."

"So... what? If I don't go with you you'll... Wait. I know. You'll stay in Tokyo and find a guy. If you're based in Tokyo instead of on Vashon, you can be at home with your guy all year."

"My guy could be you. I want it to be you," Freddie said.

Well, that was something, at least. "Yeah?"

"Yeah. Our history comforts me." Freddie must have seen my skepticism. "Oliver, all I'm asking you to do is take a chance. I'm not asking you to sell your place. I'm not even asking you to move to Tokyo—or not yet anyway. Just get off the island, leave the state, have an adventure. Come with me to D.C. as a start. We can see what happens from there."

Leave the state. Have an adventure. I pictured my suitcase on the front porch. Freddie's face softened. It struck me that he really did love me.

"Thank you for the offer," I told him. "Let me think about it, okay?" I mentally added a second suitcase for art supplies.

"Okay." Freddie sighed and laid his head on my chest. He smelled clean and felt solid and familiar in my arms. Not a fantasy, but a real man I could really have. I imagined us holding our child's hands as we ambled around a Japanese Shinto shrine and Freddie regaled us with legends.

A series of loud thumps coming from the great room made Freddie startle and bump his head on my chin.

"Ow," I said. "I'll get it. It's probably Grant."

"You're leaving? Now? Can't you ignore him?"

"The kitchen lights are on. He knows I'm here. He'll knock until I answer."

"I can't believe you put up with that."

"Not for much longer." I'd decided to cut a week off my arrangement with Grant, which meant he'd be gone in a week, at the end of week four. Then my life could return to normal for four whole weeks before I—*maybe*—joined Freddie on an adventure.

I dawdled down the hallway, in spite of Grant's clamor of knocks on the back door, to enjoy the press of Freddie's hips against mine as he walked close behind me, his arms around my shoulders.

In the great room, Grant's thumps sounded much louder.

"What?" I yelled as I flung open the door.

Grant's gaze shifted up from my feet to my mouth and went cold, probably when he saw Freddie behind me. I stomped a mental boot on the memory of Grant's kiss. *It was a violation.*

"Don't you have a home to get back to?" Freddie asked Grant.

I was sure Grant would take offense, but all he did was laugh and take a step into the house with his duffel bag.

"Sure, come on in." Thick sarcasm dripped from Freddie's words.

"Don't mind if I do," Grant said.

Freddie turned to look at me. "I *really* can't believe you let him get away with this shit."

"I did your bidding for another week," Grant said to me. "I know it's a day early, but I'd like to collect my reward now. Good sir," he added with a leer. "Also, side note, Freddie can go fuck himself."

"Hey," I said. "Freddie is a guest in my home."

"Sure. I get it. Freddie is a guest, so I should talk nice to him, but I'm the hired help, so he can insult me as much as he wants. Understood. Now show me belowstairs to the laundry so I can leave your lordships to your very important and majestic business."

I held my ground to keep Grant from coming farther into the house. "No. Not unless you come in with your grown-up manners."

"Manners? That's all it takes to be invited in as a guest? Duly noted, and yet totally unnecessary. I have no interest in spending any more time than absolutely necessary in this..." Grant looked around the great room with disdain. "Yard sale waiting to happen."

Freddie stepped between me and Grant. "You are not welcome here."

Grant didn't budge.

"Oliver," Freddie said, "I'm not leaving you here with this asshole. You'd damn well better come with me to D.C. in August."

Grant's face remained set on *hard-ass*, but his eyes turned vulnerable.

"I've got this." I laid a hand on Freddie's shoulder. "Back off, please."

"You heard him, big guy." Grant sneered down on Freddie from his great height. "Back off and give your creepy curator boyfriend a chance to defend his own honor."

I kicked at Grant's duffel bag. "At least I have more to my name to curate than your... filth." If I didn't rein myself in, I was going to get too mean and regret it.

Grant gave me a sly look. "Was I too filthy for you in the—"

"*Stop*. Stop right there. That is not at all relevant." Since my open relationship with Freddie remained in force, my kiss with Grant didn't matter, but I really didn't want Freddie to find out about the DeVille. I hadn't wanted *anyone* to find out about the DeVille, but Grant was a nosy son of a bitch. "It doesn't matter."

The hardness on Grant's face shifted to sadness. He closed his mouth, picked up the duffel bag, and backed out the door.

"Good riddance," Freddie muttered.

Grant looked past Freddie and caught my eye. "You should make up your mind who you want to help."

When Freddie tried to close the door in Grant's face, I stopped him. "What do you mean?"

Grant waved a hand at me. "You stick your sharp, coppery face into my business, trying to help me, but you can't even help yourself. You're like a lost penny, driven over so many times you forgot what you were made for."

I slammed the door.

"What in the—" Freddie started.

"It's over. Come on." I took Freddie's hand and led him out the front door toward the garage, in search of distance and privacy, and to ask about the timelines for D.C.

If I asked, if Freddie told me, it didn't register. Nothing much registered after Grant's parting shot, except Freddie's description of an apartment he'd found in D.C.

I sent Freddie away with an apology for my lack of focus, and then went for a walk.

When I arrived home, I entered through the back door and tripped over Grant's flattened duffel on the floor in front of the laundry closet. I'd been gone long enough for a washer load of flannel shirts to finish.

I transferred the shirts to the dryer. Turned it on.

Waited, but Grant didn't come back.

Ate dinner on the couch with a tray on my lap. Watched nothing happen on the empty stage. Felt the hours of evening slide into night.

In my bedroom, I pulled Granddad's quilt out from under the tarp on the bed, carried it through the great room to my old bed in my old hideaway.

Chapter 50

GRANT

When I arrived at the back door with my laundry, Freddie and Oliver looked like they'd been having sex. Oliver's hair band had slid way off to one side, and Freddie hovered around Oliver, handsy and close, like maybe they hadn't finished.

I enjoyed the idea that I'd interrupted them more than I had a right to.

After my spat with Oliver and Freddie, I lugged my duffel to the courtyard and sulked at the picnic table until I heard faint voices. I snuck around the house to pinpoint them, then peered through a line of trees and rhododendrons to watch Freddie and Oliver bump shoulders as they ambled toward the empty garage. Maybe they'd continue past the garage to the car behind the gate, where *I'd kissed Oliver.*

The memory made me surprised to be me all over again.

I couldn't believe I'd kissed Oliver, or that he'd responded the way he had, with loose, dreamy eagerness—until I accidently pushed him to the floor. I wished I'd touched his hair. Mostly I wished we hadn't stopped.

Near the garage, Oliver looked up at Freddie and they... Yep. Damn it. They kissed. I held my breath, undecided about whether I wanted to watch, but the kiss only lasted two seconds before Oliver pulled away, tugging Freddie onward.

Forget it.

I retrieved my duffel from the courtyard, let myself in the back door, and set out to explore the house, on the pretense of looking for the laundry room. What I really wanted to find was the room with windows facing the courtyard.

I found it, but I wished I hadn't.

The pillows in Oliver's nooky palace were still warm. I knew because, like a pitiful loser, I bent down to feel them.

Back in the main room, I found the laundry area behind a set of folding doors to the left of the back door. I shoved shirts into the washing machine and started it.

My first priority was to solve my destitution problem, but, *Jesus*. The moment I landed a job and a room, I was going to get busy on a hookup app. In the meantime, I reassured myself with replays of Freddie and Oliver's tepid kiss.

Back in the courtyard, away from the temptation of opening Oliver's bedroom door to see what he was painting, I sat at the picnic table, journal open in front of me, and wrote *BOUNDARIES*.

Oliver was all about boundaries, which I tended to ignore. Because I was an *ass*. I sighed. A mental audit of my marriage gave me a measure of relief. Laura had expressed concern about a lot of things, but never about me being inappropriate with her boundaries.

PERMISSION, I wrote on the next page.

For the first time, my capital letters looked like yelling, and I suddenly knew what had bugged me before the bramble adventure. I turned another page and wrote *PERMISSION SLIPS*.

I hadn't considered my activities with the kids from the perspective of a parent. I remembered Penelope walking into my campsite the day we met and felt a jolt of panic. If I wasn't careful, I was going to provoke a parental shitstorm.

The Sharpie and I spent an unpleasant half-hour of debate about what to write next, if anything. Finally, I turned the page and wrote, *NEW RULE #1: ASK FOR HELP*, which struck me as long overdue.

Oliver can do better than tepid.

That thought woke me from a doze at the picnic table, the side of my face pressed against the edge of my journal.

I couldn't understand what Oliver saw in Freddie, a poser who missed half of what Oliver said and who wanted Oliver to go to D.C in August. Oliver, the zany, gorgeous ignoramus, would probably do it. Bad news for me. I'd hoped to finagle an extension of our deal and hang around through August, instead of leaving at the end of July. It wouldn't surprise me if Oliver, under Freddie's hostile influence, banned me when our contract ended. I wouldn't blame him. I tended to be a freeloader when I could get away with it. Laura had pointed that out to me more than once.

I brushed at the indentation in my cheek from where I'd slept on the journal.

The word *OLIVER* sailed into view as worthy of capture, but I didn't rush to pick up the Sharpie. Despite most of my journal being *about* Oliver, I had yet to write his name, and I didn't want to. To get him out of my system so I could move on, I picked up the ballpoint pen I'd found in a courtyard drawer, wrote an *O*, and circled it few times to turn it into something less personal, a doodle of overlapping circles.

I slowed the circular motion of my hand. My eyes lost focus. In my meditative state, the sloppy circles made me think of an onion. *All those layers.* I squirmed in my seat as I remembered perving on Oliver's *reluctant skin*. I didn't hide the same way Oliver hid, but I was also reluctant, like when Oliver asked questions and I got angry. He got under my reluctant skin too. He had from the very beginning.

I drew a round *G* for *Grant* next to Oliver's onion and brooded over it, circled the roundness of my onion again and again, until the lines of our two onions began to touch.

We intersected, Oliver and I. Poked each other with our sharpness. Pierced and stung each other. *Invade and evade. Lie and spy.*

A flick of the pen and our two onions became a loop of infinity, a mess of swirls with mass and spin and hidden depths, an endless intrigue.

Chapter 51

OLIVER

Grant had opened the toolshed's sliding door all the way. Bright sunlight illuminated the interior into the far corners. He sat on a stool at one of the central tables with his head bent over a little book.

I tripped when I stepped inside, caught myself on the bicycle I'd brought over.

"Oops," Grant said. "Watch out for those sudden patches of thick air."

When I didn't respond to his comment, Grant leaned sideways to slide the book into his back pocket. "See you next fall?"

I smiled before I remembered I was there to get rid of him.

Grant nodded at the bicycle. "Where did that come from?"

"It was Dad's. I thought... you could borrow it, as a consolation prize, because I need to cut our deal short. This week will be our last." In truth, I wanted Grant gone immediately, but I couldn't quite make myself do that to him. My compromise was to give him week four plus the loan of Dad's bike, to prompt Grant to leave the house more often before he left for good.

His brow furrowed and he stood. "You're kicking me out? Already?"

The shock on Grant's face made me look away. I wouldn't back down on my decision. "You have until Sunday. I'm sorry." I wasn't sorry. I was desperate for Grant to be gone, but softening the blow seemed prudent.

"But what am I going to do?" Grant sat back down with a thump.

I shrugged, unwilling to do all the work. I'd given him space and time to find a job and a longer-term place to live. From what I could tell, he hadn't done anything about either.

"How's the job hunt coming?" I asked, to be a heartless prick.

The way Grant lowered his head and fidgeted said it all.

I'd given considerable thought to Grant's final assignment. One of his fundamental challenges seemed to be envisioning a better future for himself. I'd come up with a way to give him a taste of something better. He would have to stretch for it.

"I have one last assignment for you," I told him.

"Well, that's a sucker's deal." He shot me a frown and a glare. "Why would I do an assignment if I won't be around to use the amenity reward? What's my motivation?"

Grant's oblivion depressed me. If that was his attitude, it would take longer than a week, or even a whole summer, for me to persuade him to step up for himself. "I assume from your comment that the purpose of my assignments has gone undetected."

"And there's the Professor Snooty Pants I haven't missed," he said.

Our stare-off ended when I remembered Kai's quiet voice the day I'd found them in the ditch: *Uncle Grant is going through a rough patch because Aunt Laura refused to budge an inch.* Sorrow for Grant and his tough life made me blink and look away. *Get it over with.*

"No shopping or manual labor this week," I said. "Just an assignment, which is to write a proposal for a one-day workshop for tweens, including a financial plan, such that you net at least one hundred dollars. If I like the proposal, I'll give you a hundred dollars to send you on your way."

"You'll... *Jesus.* Okay. Hell yes. I'm in."

"You can use my computer at the desk, if you want. And you probably have more laundry to do." Grant in the house meant I'd be stuck in the bedroom, but that was a small price to pay for full reclamation of my home in a week.

"I'll try to remember to text you before I come over," Grant said, "so you don't freak out when I show up."

I opened my mouth to reply, but the sound of girls' voices stopped me. Jill, Penelope, and Clover biked into the yard and mobbed us with bright chatter. I said hello, smiled, tried to join in. They all seemed so far away, even though I was right there.

Jill saw Dad's bike leaning against the wall and lunged for it.

"Oliver loaned it to me," Grant told her.

"Can I?" she asked him.

"Have at it," he said with a laugh.

She took the bike and rolled it to the bike repair cabinet.

Penelope pointed at Grant and said to me, "Grant's doing a lot better since you let him use the outdoor kitchen. His camping skills still suck."

It took a moment to process Penelope's words. "Uh... good." It was time for me to go, before I spaced out altogether and embarrassed myself. "Saturday works best this week for your trip to town in the van," I told Grant before I turned to leave.

Penelope surprised me by walking away with me. "I wish you could have come with us into the blackberries."

I had nothing to say to that.

She didn't say anything else until we were halfway across the yard. "Oliver, do you think Grant's going to be okay?"

"Oh. Sure. He'll be fine." I didn't believe it.

Penelope gave me a funny look. The concern in her expression sharpened my attention. I didn't want her to worry about me too. "It's all fine," I offered with a smile I had to act the heck out of to keep from coming across as fake.

"Well. Okay. You take care." She patted my shoulder and jogged back to the others.

For a few heartbeats, I watched them in my toolshed, then backed away, faded into the house, disappeared in my bedroom to resume work on the mural and think about Freddie.

His gentle kiss after the squabble with Grant had been... *nice*. I'd dreaded going into the garage to get Dad's bike, so asked Freddie to go with me. With a rag grabbed from a drawer under the workbench, I'd brushed cobwebs off the bike where it leaned against the far wall under the window. Dad's absence hit me hard. I lost track of Freddie's cheerful words as I brushed away the years.

When I tuned in again, I heard Freddie say, "This place I found in D.C. is perfect for us, right in the city. You can walk to all the big museums. Best of all, it has two bedrooms plus a living room. I was going to use the second bedroom for an office, but you can have it. I know how much you like your privacy."

What Freddie described sounded good. It also sounded like a theory, something that *could* be real, not a place where I might spend days of my actual life.

I lifted my head. A sloppy smiley face decorated the grime on the window glass. Grant, the intrusive jerk, must have drawn it during a snoop around the garage.

It wasn't fair of me to push Grant to get real if I wasn't willing to try it myself.

"That's very thoughtful of you." I turned to give Freddie my smiley face.

Chapter 52

GRANT

When Oliver delivered the loaner bike to me at the workshop late Monday morning, I scanned him for signs he and Freddie had gone beyond the kiss I'd seen at the garage.

Inconclusive.

Then Oliver hit me with an eviction notice and walked away.

To tamp down my panic and avoid the issue of my future, I hopped up to sit on the edge of the worktable near the girls and the bike and asked, "How's everyone doing today?"

"Kai and his family have visitors in from out of town," Penelope said.

Clover nodded and added, "And Abelino's not here because his mom is sick today."

"Is the bike your reward for last week?" Penelope asked. Both of her parents were lawyers. She'd asked about the contract I'd signed with Oliver, and then pored over it when I'd shown her.

"I think the bike is more like a bonus," I told her. I didn't say I thought it was Oliver's way of getting me off his property. "The main reward was washer and dryer access."

All three girls exchanged eye contact then executed a synchronized cheerleader move that managed to be both ironic and cute.

"I can take a hint." I laughed and hopped off the table. "I'm going to check my laundry. If the bike gets Jill's seal of approval, what do you say we go for a ride when I get back? You can tell me about your weekends, and I'll tell you about my assignment from Oliver for next week. Maybe you can help me with it."

Jill nodded, which I took to mean the bike would pass muster, and I jogged off to the house. Oliver had taped a note on the back door saying to come on in, which I did. I heard faint sounds from the bedroom.

Plenty of times since he'd woken me in the ditch, Oliver had tried to get me to respect his privacy. I'd bitched, barged into his space, criticized his lifestyle. No wonder he'd resorted to avoiding me. My invasive presence had turned a recluse into a prisoner in his own home.

I berated myself the entire time it took to transfer a load to the dryer and start another washer load. After a grope in my pocket for the zodiac scroll, to confirm I hadn't washed it, I ignored my internal smackdown and bellowed at Oliver over the laundry noise, "Thanks for the bike. We're going for a ride. Want to live a little and come with us?"

As expected, no answer.

From what I'd seen, the people in Oliver's life gave him plenty of alone time. I wasn't convinced it was healthy. Oliver seemed to sleepwalk more and more as the days went by—maybe in response to my invasion. Or maybe not.

I stomped across the back porch to make more noise.

Before I left for good, maybe I could wake Oliver up.

"**How did** you learn to work with bikes?" I asked Jill as we rode north along a trail toward Bast Road. The competent way she had adjusted the bike to fit me made me feel like I floated on a cloud as I rode, even on the bumpy trail.

"It's just basic stuff," Jill said. "I read a manual."

"Like, *read* it?"

"Yeah. I got it from the library," Jill said.

"You are so cool." I turned around for a second to blast Jill with a grin.

When we got to Bast Road and the girls turned left to head up the slight slope, I lagged behind to crunch a few gears.

Penelope slowed to ride beside me. "What's your next assignment?"

I waited until we'd caught up with Jill and Clover to say, "Oliver wants me to plan a one-day workshop for kids that earns a hundred dollars after expenses.

That means good enough for kids to want to do and for parents to be willing to pay for."

"I think you already did a one-day workshop." Penelope lifted her chin toward the blackberry bramble within view up ahead. "My parents definitely would have paid you for that."

We rode on amid a constant stream of ideas the girls had for workshops. Penelope and Jill, whose families seemed to have plenty of money, had attended many camps and taken lessons in a range of subjects. The issues they brought up in the form of stories about things gone wrong made me cringe. That would likely be my fate, since I didn't know what the hell I was doing. The more they talked and the more excited they got, the less capable I felt. Even Clover, with her sketchy parents, seemed to have a better sense of how to plan and budget than I did.

Deep into a discussion with Jill about pricing, which I could barely follow, Penelope said to me, "Your workshop wouldn't have to be only for us. If Clover, Jill, Kai, Abelino, and I were the only ones to do the workshop, you would have to charge us each more than twenty dollars."

"Inviting more kids makes the fee less per kid," Jill said with an approving nod and a glance at Clover.

Asking kids for money when all we wanted to do was play outside felt terrible. I hung back a little, then a little more, and lost track of the conversation. The girls were being so nice, but I didn't feel worthy of their excitement.

"Hold up a sec, guys." I didn't want to fake an excuse, like Oliver had done at the brambles, but that didn't stop me from doing it.

The girls braked and turned to face me.

"I... um... suddenly don't feel very good. I think I need to head back." I held up a hand to keep them from coming at me with their sympathy. "Thanks for all your great ideas. You keep riding. Next time you see me, tell me what else you came up with."

From the skeptical looks on their faces, I could tell they didn't believe my flimsy story.

"I'm sorry," I said, and I meant it.

It took a little more persuasion, but they eventually rode on without me and out of sight. I breathed a huge sigh of relief and bent to puke my breakfast onto a cluster of pretty yellow flowers by the side of the road. "Sorry," I said again, bummed my inability to solve basic life problems like earning a living had caused me to murder some innocent flowers.

There was just enough water in the bottle I'd tucked in the bike's wire holder to give my mouth a rinse and to pour over the flowers to give them a chance at recovery.

I sat at the edge of the road and closed my eyes. For the first time, I saw a connection between my problems and the rules I lived by.

Huddled there beside my own puke, I gained a new level of respect for the devious jerk who'd crafted my assignments, because the tasks Oliver had given me—tasks I'd considered worthless and unnecessary—had shifted something, in spite of my resistance.

My gaze lost focus on the asphalt between my knees as I considered the rules I'd identified. Rules repeated through my childhood in the monotony of my parents' voices.

Beggars can't be choosers.

No playing until your work is done.

There's always more work to be done.

School is play.

I added the rules I'd unconsciously made for myself.

Creativity is play.

If I don't like it, I leave.

Which I'd just done when I excused myself from riding with the kids.

Annoyed, I stood and picked up the bike from where I'd dropped it. I needed to go lie in my tent and think for a while, even if it hurt. Then I needed to follow New Rule #1 and ask for help.

I rode toward the sharp left turn onto Bast Road, stared at the pavement in front of the spinning bike tire, and mulled over the possibility of another new rule. I could feel something trying to muscle its way into my awareness, something to do with Jill and the bicycle, and with Penelope poring over my contract with Oliver.

A spurt of tires on gravel interrupted my thoughts. I looked up, expecting to see a car.

It wasn't a car. It was Oliver on his bicycle.

I caught a glimpse of hair as Oliver flew in from the left on Bast, blasting toward the sharp turn that would put us face to face. Before I could brace myself for an interaction, Oliver veered left instead of right and shot off into the woods. He disappeared in an instant, absorbed by the thick forest.

I didn't think he'd seen me.

My new rule snapped into focus.

New Rule #2: Follow the fascination.

Chapter 53

OLIVER

Grant's invitation to join them for a bike ride, shouted from the great room in the rumble of his deep voice, gave me an idea. Instead of brooding indoors, I would practice taking a trip away from home.

I cracked the back door to watch Grant and the girls bike away, then ran to get my bike from the carport and follow them. At Bast Road, I hid behind a tree to let them ride on down the road. They stopped at Mrs. Montgomery's bramble and huddled close, bikes clacking against one another with metallic pings. Grant listened with a huge smile as the girls relived the experience. I could hear them when I stood very still.

Bast Road ran due west, toward the cliffs on the western side of the island. Grant and the girls carried on to the end of Bast Road, until I could barely see them, then took the right onto Willow Way and rode out of sight.

I eased my bike onto the pavement and found my balance, averted my eyes as I passed Mrs. Montgomery's bramble. I needed courage, not a reminder of failure.

At first, I thought the itch at my neck was a bug. I lifted a hand to brush it away. After the tenth time, with no change in the tickle when I brushed at it, my vision pulled in from the sides. The road ran on in front of me, on and on.

My mouth went dry. My heart sped up.

I pedaled faster, to force myself not to turn around in defeat, but the erratic beat of my heart drained my legs of coordination. I thought if I could get to Willow, catch sight of Grant, I might be okay.

The tremors in my legs and arms became a full body shake. I couldn't keep my balance when I hit a patch of pebbles and veered onto the left shoulder with a jerk. I made it through a jarring descent into the ditch and a hard pedal up the other side, dodged a tree trunk, then another, bumped hard through the sparse underbrush, and scraped my knuckles on a branch when I didn't course-correct fast enough.

Fucking fuck it. I've practiced enough.

I shook with overwhelm, hot and disheartened and eager to be home.

The red flag was up at the mailbox. Freddie was busy writing at his mother's house. Grant and the kids would be out for a while yet.

If I rushed home, I'd have the place to myself.

I'd be safe.

Chapter 54

GRANT

The gravel track ran straight ahead of me, like an extension of Willow Way to the south. I stood on the pedals, leaned over the handlebars, and sprinted down the hill after Oliver.

The secretive weirdo must have followed us at a distance.

My brief sighting of Oliver included an impression of brown shorts and a forest green T-shirt. All that separated Oliver from the forest was his hair. I kept the reddish glint in sight until he made an abrupt right turn off the track onto a small trail, heading away from his house.

I hesitated.

The track continued south. By my reckoning, the abrupt edge of the island wasn't far off to the right. For Oliver to get home, he'd have to recross the track at some point. Or... *hell*... maybe the track dead-ended.

I dithered too long.

I followed Oliver onto the trail, but didn't see him again.

The cloud cover and the curving trail messed up my sense of direction until I became well and truly lost. I thought I'd turned to ride east, only realized I was still riding west when I had to brake hard on a patch of bare ground at the edge of the cliff. Thirsty and disoriented, I began to worry I wouldn't find a road before twilight, or I'd make another wrong turn and pitch off into the cold saltwater of Colvos Passage.

I'd ventured way past the familiar.

Hours later, the sun's slant toward the strip of bare sky at the horizon made it easier to get my bearings. I decided to dogleg north and east to intersect Bast

Road. The paths in front of me blurred in the fading light, and I had to back-track a few times after riding into the undergrowth.

The sun dipped below the horizon before I'd found the road.

Alone in the long northern twilight without a phone or flashlight, I dismounted and did my best to aim north and east. Chill flooded the air with silence.

By the time I bumped onto the asphalt of Bast Road, twilight had given way to spare moonlight. I rode as fast as I dared, guided by the contrast of beige gravel at the dark edge of the road. The slice of moon winked out behind a cloud and I got off the bike again to walk, turned right onto the gravel of Violetta Road, picked my way down the hill to Oliver's driveway.

When I neared Oliver's house, I moved onto the narrow strip of grass beside the driveway until I reached to the yard, wary of making noise. I left the bicycle under the carport and felt my way down the familiar path to my campsite.

In the tent, I succumbed to a post-adrenaline tremor, guzzled a bottle of water, and collapsed onto the sleeping bag with a long moan of relief.

I didn't wash off the hours of sweat and tension. I didn't eat, though my belly was empty. I didn't remove my shoes or even zip the tent door. I didn't do anything before I plunged into sleep except declare myself the detective in charge of solving the mystery of Oliver.

The next morning I woke in a vile state. Clothes stiff with dried sweat. Body a mass of aches. Stomach at DEFCON 1. I splurged on a double helping of on-sale strawberries and on-sale pepper jack cheese as I gathered stuff to take to the courtyard for a shower.

All the while, my mental map of Vashon Island pestered me.

It took me a while to locate the brochure I'd picked up on the water taxi. I found it in an inner pocket of my backpack and unfolded it to locate the area between Oliver's house and the western edge of the island.

No roads. No *anything*. Solid, white-paper blankness.

Partway through my stiff shuffle to reach the shower, I thought of Google Maps. To get a signal on my phone, I had to be within sight of the house, which was on a slight rise. I paused under the trees near Oliver's yard, pulled up Google Maps, and zoomed in. Same result. In map view, the area west of Oliver's consisted of blank, gray nothingness. Satellite view showed a solid mass of green treetops.

I glanced up when I got to the yard. Two bicycles under the carport, but no van.

I shot off a text to Oliver. *Did you decide to do your own errands this week?* *In Seattle for the day,* he texted back. *Not that it's any of your business.*

The jerk knew I was looking for work in Seattle. He could have let me ride along.

Something bothered me about Oliver leaving with the van, teased at the back of my mind.

Like a dork, I decided to take a bike ride to mull things over, even though I'd just showered and I really *hurt* from the day before. I moseyed back along Bast, made the right turn onto Willow, and rode on past the spot where the girls and I had gone our separate ways. Within a few more turns, I'd reached Westside Highway. I took a left to head north.

A couple of miles on, I commandeered a homemade bus shelter and flopped onto the bench to munch my peanut butter sandwich and check the view of the Kitsap Peninsula and the clouds beyond. The view from our school bus stop in Eastern Washington had been the family's print shop and Dad's office. I'd watch Dad wave his arms at Mom, check the clock on the wall, and readjust his cap, which he did when he worried we'd miss a deadline.

I knew what my dad would say about my summer on Vashon: *Stop wasting time, boy.*

I fished out my journal and the ballpoint pen and scribbled a drawing of the scene in front of me, to distract myself from Dad's voice in my head and so I could take the view with me when I left Vashon.

In the margin, in small letters, I tried out an idea: *WORK + NATURE + KIDS.*

My phone rang.

"Grant," Mitch said in his brisk attorney voice. "Kai and I will stop by soon."

"Today?" I sat up straighter, buoyed by the prospect of seeing Kai.

"No, but soon. Kai has been talking with us and I want to talk to you. Also, the father of one of the children you've been..." Mitch hesitated.

"Hanging out with?" I proposed.

"That's not a phrase I would use, all things considered. Jill's father approached me on the ferry with some concerns about you."

"Really? What did you tell him?"

"Not much. I wanted to talk with you first."

"Can't we talk now?" I asked. Mitch getting on my case at Oliver's place, where Oliver might witness my humiliation, seemed like a terrible idea. Oliver already thought I was a big loser. I rubbed my abdomen where the sandwich sat in a hard lump.

"I don't have time now," Mitch said, "and Kai wants to show me around Oliver's. I'll try to get to you before Jill's father finds you, but I…"

"Wait. What? He's coming to Oliver's?"

"It sounded like he might. I know you wouldn't do anything untoward with the kids, but he seemed suspicious enough that you should probably watch yourself. I wanted to give you a heads-up."

"Well… hell."

"I have to go." Mitch hung up, leaving me with my journal open on my lap to an idea that seemed impossible.

On my way back south, I passed the yellow flowers I'd puked on the day before, wished them well with a repentant nod, and coasted down toward Bast Road. On a whim, instead of making the left to return to Oliver's, I kept on straight, onto the track, like I had the day before, enticed by the prospect of taking another shot at figuring out the trails in the area where I'd failed to chase down Oliver. So what if I got lost again and ended up a quivering puddle of overused muscles. I wouldn't be on Vashon much longer. I wanted to make the most of it.

Out beyond the spot where I'd lost Oliver, I veered east onto a trail up a hill so steep I had to walk the bike. Rhododendrons swiped at my bare legs as I huffed up the last few yards. I'd hoped for a view, but the trees at the top blocked the sky. I paused to assess the state of the trail down the far side of the hill, at the bottom of which, on a dirt turnaround by a creek, sat Oliver's orange van.

Seattle, my ass.

With an almost audible click, the pieces fell into place.

The morning of my second day on Vashon I'd hiked through the woods from my new campsite and crouched under the carport to spy on Oliver. A little later, when I'd eavesdropped on him and Clementine, I'd heard Oliver tell her he'd driven to the hardware store that morning.

It didn't add up.

I laid the bike on the ground with care and sat on the trail. With my phone silenced, I checked for cell reception, which I had, barely, probably only because I was on a high point, and settled in to confirm my suspicions.

I'd woken early that first morning, excited by forest sounds and slanted sunbeams. My fingers flew over my phone. Sunrise on June 22 had been at 5:12. I thought back, trying to estimate the timelines with accuracy. I'd stuck my head out of the tent at 5:30. I'd explored, found the spigot at the vacation house, moved my campsite, and fetched water until a little after 8:00. I closed my eyes to remember. It couldn't have been any later than 8:15 when I crouched at Oliver's van to watch the birds. I bent my head over the phone again to find websites for the island's hardware stores. The one in the mall opened earliest on Saturdays, at 8 a.m.

The van had been cold. Chilly Pacific Northwest overnight *cold*. I'd put my hands and then my back against the rear of the van, where the motor was, to brace myself and remain hidden, to free my hands for my binoculars so I could watch the birds and then Oliver.

I checked one more thing—the driving time between the hardware store and Oliver's house.

Thirteen minutes.

Even if Oliver had been at the store when they opened, shopped and paid in less than five minutes, then driven straight home, the van would have been warm when I leaned against it.

I put my phone away and stood. From my angle, I could see the driver's side of the van. I didn't see Oliver. Maybe he'd gone for a hike.

I thought of calling out to him. I put my hands to my mouth to direct the sound, took a big breath, but didn't follow through. He would evade, fabricate a story, hold tight to his outer skin. I wanted to pierce through his lies.

I left the bike, retraced my steps down the hill a ways, then circled around. From the new position, I could see the back of the van and... Oliver.

He lay on his back on a log, head on a sweater, open book held above his head. He lifted a hand from his chest to turn a page.

I pulled out my journal, set it on the ground, took a photo of it, then texted the photo to Oliver with a message. *Hey, mind getting me one of these journal books in Vashon on yr way home?* If he'd actually been in Seattle, he could have stopped in town on his way south from the ferry dock.

I didn't expect him to have cell coverage down in the hollow, but of course his service was better than mine. I heard his phone ping.

Oliver ignored the notification. Read a while. Turned another page. Recrossed his legs.

I typed another message: *On second thought, get two?*

Ping.

Oliver took his phone out of his front pocket, probably to turn it off. Just in case, I confirmed that my phone was on silent and watched my screen.

Swipe & Swivel? Oliver texted.

At first I didn't understand his message. The tiny store where I bought the journals was called Easel & Desk. I managed to slap my hand over my mouth and laugh without making a sound when I realized "Swipe & Swivel" must be local vernacular for Easel & Desk.

Yep, I texted back.

No prob. Ferry's pulling in now. Back soon.

For a full, unblinking minute, I stared down at Oliver's message.

The little shit.

My thoughts spun as I watched Oliver lie there and read. When my ass fell asleep, I lay back and watched the treetops.

Whatever Oliver's reasons were for his secret life, they were strong enough to cause him real pain—I'd seen it on his face at the bramble thicket before he'd walked away. I wanted to confront him, but I didn't want to risk provoking a psychological event of some kind.

The sound of the van door closing interrupted my internal debate. I sat up to see Oliver already in the driver's seat.

I'd followed trails far to the south on the bike without seeing any eastward tracks wide enough for a van. Unless Oliver knew of a secret tunnel, he'd have to wind around to exit the woods at Willow Road, where I'd come in. By bike, I could make a beeline for Oliver's house. I was fifty percent sure I could do it without getting lost.

The idea of catching Oliver arriving home without my books took possession of me. I wanted to study the look on his face when he told me he "forgot." It might give me a clue about his mental state.

I scurried to the bike, flew down the hill the way I'd come, and hooked a right toward Oliver's house. I pedaled like mad, almost killed myself on the rough trails as I opted for speed over safety. When I blasted through a bright spot, I glanced up to check the position of the sun.

I dug deep and drove my body hard, but when I burst into the backyard from behind the workshop the van was already there. *Unbelievable.* I carried on to the carport and heard the tick of the cooling motor.

When I pounded on the front door, Oliver opened it, calm and cool, and handed me two little books. Exactly the type I'd asked for.

I couldn't speak.

Oliver took in my breathless, wrecked state and raised his eyebrows in a question.

After a while, when I hadn't said anything, he shrugged, bent to set the books at my feet, and closed the door.

Chapter 55

OLIVER

Grant looked like he'd run to hell and back.

I expected at least a *thank you* when I gave him the books. I'd unearthed them from the back of a drawer full of notebooks and sketchbooks Dad, Granddad, and I had stockpiled over the years.

All I got was a wounded glare.

After I closed the door, Grant didn't knock again, which was fine. I'd taken the morning off and was eager to return to the mural.

My painting technique required many thin layers to achieve the luminous, rich colors I craved. In the damp air of the Northwest Coast, each layer took a couple days to dry. The mural was big enough that I could paint a layer in one area and leave it to dry while I worked in another area. It would take months to finish the whole painting.

In the corners, I'd managed to make bits of nature pop with lush super-reality. I felt very proud of myself for that. It had required false starts and more than a few intense hours of research online and in my home library.

As I extended the super-reality toward the sleeping figures, tiny vignettes began to form in the shadows, under the dense mass of leaves, flowers, and vines. The first vignette emerged when I set out to paint the dim space under a large vine maple leaf. With my smallest brush dipped in gray, I painted a scene from my mind's eye. A tiny man stood at a worktable in a barely suggested toolshed, his hand atop a boy's head. The boy sat at his feet, leaned against his leg. I dipped the brush in gold for the boy's hair.

I wondered what Freddie would think if he saw the vignette and the recognizable lines of Grant's body. I set the brush down and stepped back to look at the entire mural. I'd roughed in the two large figures of the man and the boy, but left their faces blank.

I didn't want to see Grant as the man in the mural, but I couldn't seem to see anyone else. I wanted him to be Freddie. Either choice would require more explanation than I felt ready for.

The solution to my dilemma came as I stared at the oval placeholder for the man's face: *No one I know ever needs to see this painting.* If I never showed it to anyone at home, I could paint to discover, explore to resolve, and when I'd finished, I could sell it online, ship the panels to someone far away.

I would never have to see it again.

I expected Grant to return to use my computer for his proposal on Tuesday, the day I gave him the books, but he didn't. Nor did he return the next day. Maybe I'd find a draft of his proposal scrawled on the back of a soup can label stuck to my front door with pine sap.

On Wednesday afternoon, clouds moved in and settled, thick enough to muffle sound. No breeze. No sunlight. No people. *Eerie.* I closed the curtains in the bedroom and sat on the floor with my back to the bed to consider what area I wanted to paint next.

The protective way "the man" wrapped his arms around "the boy," captured my attention. If the man was Freddie, the child could be ours. I leaned my head back on the edge of the bed and tried, for a long while, to imagine Freddie sleeping in a ditch. I couldn't.

What if the man in the mural is me?

I slid down to lie on the floor and mirror the man's position, lifted my arms to hug an imaginary child.

Aza flashed through my mind, shrouded in Clementine's pain, too ethereal to grasp.

I hugged myself instead, felt more like the child in the painting than the man.

Dad's hand on my head.

He thinks I'm asleep.

I'm not.

I leapt up and left the bedroom before I'd made a conscious decision to move. *What the fuck was that?* I snatched my phone off the kitchen counter and sprinted to the toolshed.

In the dirt in front of the toolshed door, someone had drawn an infinity symbol, which I obliterated in my rush to grab my carving tools. Someone had moved them from the floor to a wooden bin on a table set just inside the doorway.

Late that night, I huddled in my sleeping bag on the couch, muscles cramped from how long I'd carved on the throne. In my dreams, my arms ached from how tight I held myself as I floated face-up in a stream.

Rain began during the night, a patter of white noise pressed against the house.

I woke to grim daylight, waded through the murk to root through my bedroom dresser for a sweater. After I'd turned on the heat and eaten a muffin and an apple, I felt better by a few degrees, prepared enough to venture down the rabbit hole of the mural again.

For a fresh perspective, I left the bright lights off, turned on a bedside lamp, and walked around to stand on the far side of the bed to resume contemplation of my next move.

I was a very good painter—that had been inevitable, considering how I'd been raised and by whom—but the mural stirred something new within me, brought forward a phantom I hadn't meant to paint, sinister and unnerving.

A few swipes of my palms down my thighs didn't brush away the fear, and my body went cold, even in my sweater. I sat cross-legged on the floor to watch the mural with the bed between us.

Nothing moved.

I turned my head away and caught sight of Grant's contract on my dresser, closed my eyes.

Darkness.

Keep my eyes closed.

The dark space in the back of my mother's car. City sounds far removed. Smooth seats. A man drives in front, behind a wall of glass. My heavy head against Dad's strong shoulder.

"I cannot believe you're serious about this," Dad says.

I make my arms and hands wet noodles so Dad and my mother won't know I'm awake. Dad pets my hair just the way I like it, rests his big, warm hand on my head.

The chill deepened and I began to shake, in spite of the heating vent's blast of warm air against my back.

Those few seconds of *somewhere else* carried the stink of a memory trying to rise from the dead. *I don't want it.* I moved to lie on my stomach on top of the heating vent, pressed my cheek against the floor under the edge of the tarp covering the bed. Out past the shadows, the boy's pale hand drooped onto the bottom edge of the mural.

I closed my eyes tight, fell asleep half under the bed.

When I woke, I found my phone and sent texts to Freddie and Talia to set them in motion toward me. I didn't tell them why I wanted company.

Thank god, Talia texted back. *I've missed you.*

I scrolled up and saw texts she'd sent over the past week. I hadn't seen them. Or maybe I'd ignored them.

Friends on their way meant a shuffle to the kitchen to cook for them. *What meal would be appropriate?* I didn't know. The scrap of memory I'd had and the dark day had stopped time. I stood in limbo at the kitchen sink, watched the leaves on Granddad's cherry tree bounce in the rain.

Car tires on gravel.

A knock on the front door.

Voices.

GRANT

All day Wednesday, I explored the area where I'd seen Oliver with his van. I dedicated myself to the task as if I'd never get to roam free in the woods again, finally retreated to my tent at the end of the day with a miserable, achy groan.

After a rainy night, a fitful sleep, and a slop around my campsite Thursday morning, I knew I had to get somewhere dry for a while or I'd risk getting sick, so I slogged through the woods to Oliver's workshop to do my self-portrait assignment.

With a hammer, a roofing nail, and a scrap of wood from a bin of cast-offs, I got busy on a self-portrait of nail holes—time-consuming, but I didn't have anything better to do. Well, I *did* have better things to do, like worrying about Jill's dad showing up and writing the workshop proposal, but I convinced myself I could ponder my life situation while I hit the same nail with a hammer over and over—my one-man interpretive dance entitled *If It Doesn't Work, Do It Again*.

There wasn't a good place to hammer in the bathroom. I studied my face in the mirror over the sink, trudged back to the worktable and hammered in a few more holes.

It would have been a great project to do with the kids. Penelope had sent a text to say it was too rainy and they wouldn't come by after art camp. I missed them. Their presence made things seem more real.

Weary of the trip to the bathroom and back when all I wanted to do was sit, I went free-form and gave myself wilder hair. I enjoyed the sound and tempo of the hammer on the nail, a counterpoint to the steady rain on the roof and the *jerk-squeak* when I pulled out the nail.

I thought I might understand Oliver's attraction to his chisel and mallet.

When I ran out of wood for more hair, I tapped in a final nail hole and checked my phone. I'd texted Oliver to ask about using his computer, but he hadn't responded. I tucked the scrap of wood under my shirt, pulled on my rain poncho, and dashed across the yard to the back porch. It took a few knocks before Oliver opened the door.

"Here." I shoved my self-portrait at him so I could take off my clammy poncho and hang it on a hook to drip on the porch.

Oliver stared down at the silly thing I'd made. And stared some more.

Something seemed to have flipped Oliver's sign to *Out to Lunch*. He blinked but otherwise didn't move.

"Back up." I gave Oliver's chest a light shove so I could get inside and close the door. He wore the pants with the fern drawings on them, from the day at the ditch, and new drawings covered his arms. Blackberry vines spread up past Oliver's forearms to disappear into the blue sweater he wore. Wreaths of thorns, barbed leaves, juicy berries. They made me want to lick him.

"You okay there, bud?" I asked Oliver.

He nodded, but I wasn't at all convinced.

Low voices floated over from the living room area. I looked up to see Talia and Freddie on the couch. *Ugh*. Not my ideal circumstances for writing a proposal.

"Hey, Grant." Talia walked over to stand beside Oliver. "Whoa." She pointed at my self-portrait. "Check that out," she said. "It's you."

"Yeah," Oliver said in his faraway voice. "It is."

Freddie barged in to look over Oliver's shoulder. "Let me see."

"Won't win any prizes," I said.

Their little huddle of focus on what I'd done made me roll my eyes. "That's enough." I snatched the wood out of Oliver's hands, walked it to the art supply shelves, and shoved it on top of a bin of crayons. "Can I use your laptop?" I asked Oliver.

None of them had moved.

"Oliver?" I waved my hands. "Hey. I need to type stuff or my noggin' will self-destruct." I took my journal, full of notes and ideas about the assignment, out of my back pocket and waved it at him. He didn't take the bait of my wink, which tried to convey my awareness of his fancy shenanigans with my journals when he hadn't actually been to town.

Oliver's dazed look told me he was in no shape to catch subtleties.

I sighed and turned my back on them all. To make space for my journal on the desk, I had to relocate a bottle opener in the shape of a hand, a wire head massager, and two books—*The Encyclopedia of Color for Oil Painters* and *Frogs of the Pacific Northwest*. Oliver's sleek desktop booted up without a password.

"Is he always like this?" Talia asked. "Like he thinks he lives here, when he actually doesn't?"

"Pretty much," Freddie grumbled.

That made me smile.

Oliver's visitors seemed unaware of his altered state. They asked Oliver more questions when he hadn't answered the previous ones. Oliver didn't need Freddie to badger him about going to Whidbey Island "for a practice run." Even with my back to them, I could tell Oliver needed to be around people without having to interact with them. If I'd been an actual friend of any of those jackasses, I might have said something. Instead, I withdrew my attention.

After I typed up my journal notes and organized things a bit, my proposal for a fort-building workshop began to feel real. I cruised the internet for tips and stories about outdoor forts, hooked on the photos I found of kids' faces and the same expressions of transformation I'd seen during our bramble adventure.

My fingers froze on the keyboard.

Transformative play.

I opened my journal and wrote in small, careful letters, *WORK + NATURE + KIDS + TRANSFORMATIVE PLAY.*

No way could I—with barely a high school education and approximately one and a half clues to my name—rise from rock bottom to make *that* career happen before I reached retirement age. Contemplating it made me feel like loser crap, so I returned my focus to the proposal.

The biggest glitch would be convincing the parents to pay. I was *terrible* with parents. I was too big and too gruff. I tended to loom and glower and say rude things to adults when I wasn't in The Zone. Plus—minor details—I was unemployed, had no credentials for working with children, and, I suspected, was unemployable. Also, I lived on someone else's property without permission, in a one-person tent I shared with a giant backpack. *Massive parental nightmare.*

Before I had a panic attack, I grabbed my phone to call Mitch, the only parent I knew personally. Overachiever that he was, Mitch answered on the first ring.

"Hi. Got a minute?" I asked

"No," he said.

"Well, why did you answer?"

"What do you want?"

"When are you coming over? I want to talk to you too."

"We could do Sunday. Two o'clock."

"Great," I said. "Jill's dad hasn't shown up. I'm relieved. I'm not ready."

"They had guests. Probably distracted him."

I didn't say anything for two seconds, which, in Mitch's world, meant we were done. "I've got to go," he said, and hung up.

I could have called Mitch back, but I wasn't sure what I wanted to ask him.

I swiveled in the desk chair as I thought. I couldn't justify asking Oliver for help. I'd loaded enough of my problems on him. Freddie and Talia wouldn't help. I based that assessment on their frowns telling me to leave them alone.

Oliver sat on the edge of the stage. His stiff posture and spaced-out expression made me think he was in the midst of an out-of-body experience. Back bent in a slouch, he nodded at what Freddie and Talia said... and *said*. Jesus. Couldn't they tell Oliver wasn't listening?

The stage made me think of Clementine. I stood to take my phone out of my front pocket.

"Do you have something to add?" Freddie asked in his sarcastic voice from his spot at the end of the orange couch closest to me.

I took a couple of steps so I could loom over him. "You bet." I made my voice boom to fill the large room, to annoy Freddie even more, and to give Oliver a little comic relief. "The rubber needs to meet the road before the shit hits the fan." It was the first thing that came to mind—something I'd written in my journal.

Oliver's lips lifted in a quick smile, there and gone.

"That's all for now," I said. "Thanks so much for asking, Freddie." I walked away and tuned them all out again to call Clementine, using the phone number on the card she'd handed me the day she drove me to the blackberry bramble.

I told her about my workshop idea and invited her to help, curious to see if the prospect of spending time with tweens would be a hard limit after whatever had happened to her son. "I'm most concerned about the parents," I admitted. "I thought maybe you could help me with that part? If you want to."

"I would love to." Clementine sounded quiet but strong. "I could stop by after work today."

We made a plan to meet in Oliver's workshop. Back at Oliver's computer, I emailed my draft of the proposal to Clementine and to myself, so I could access it on my phone, then closed down the computer.

"Bye, everyone," I called out as I headed for the back door.

They all ignored me.

On the dartboard hung a piece of paper on which a thick infinity symbol had been painted. I leaned close. A faint, penciled crown hovered above the loops of black paint.

"**I'm not** a very good example of a parent," Clementine said from the stool beside me in Oliver's workshop. "But I'd like to help. If I can. I can try."

By the end of the conversation that followed, I'd decided to wait to do the workshop until after I had a job, a place to live, and some official volunteer experience working with kids.

"Bummer," I said. "Waiting seems right, but that means next summer."

"Have you thought about looking for work on Vashon?" Clementine asked. "If you were here, maybe the workshop could happen sooner."

"Yeah, but... Kai."

Clementine nodded. "You want to be in Seattle."

"I want to be around for him in case school sucks. I think I understand him in a way his family doesn't, or doesn't yet."

Clementine nudged my cell phone on the worktable. "I think you'll be great at doing this workshop, even if it takes a while."

Chapter 57

GRANT

I woke on Friday energized enough to continue my exploration of the western woods. The clouds had lost their heft overnight and the rain had tapered to a drizzle. I ducked into my poncho and set out on the borrowed bike. Wet ferns and salal crowded the edges of the paths and soaked my legs and boots.

The area had become familiar enough that I was surprised to come across a patch of uncharted territory. I pedaled slowly up a gentle rise, followed the trail around a curve, and then had to walk the bike over a rocky stretch.

I would have missed it if I'd glanced left instead of right.

I rolled the bike back for a closer look.

Someone had dumped a wooden step stool into a thick patch of undergrowth a few yards off the trail. A very *nice* step stool. I leaned the bike against a maple tree and waded through the ferns to investigate.

It wasn't a step stool.

A circular staircase wound up around a massive oak. I craned my neck but couldn't see what it led to. The branches of the maple blocked my view.

The staircase suspended from ropes that seemed sturdy when I yanked on them. I straddled a maple branch and risked a first step. The entire staircase wobbled—and held. A banister began ten steps up, right when I needed it. I wrestled through vines and underbrush to climb above most of the maple tree, then paused to hug the oak's trunk and look up. And *up*. Through leaves and branches, I glimpsed the underside of a platform. After that, the wobble intensified as I climbed higher, and I didn't try to look up.

Every ten steps or so, a heavy rope circled the tree to anchor the staircase, which nevertheless flopped and swung as I moved. I tested each step before I put my weight on it.

The staircase ended high above the ground under a trap door. I gave one of the platform supports a shove to test for sturdiness and hauled myself up through the trapdoor to collapse on the... porch. A porch attached to a treehouse.

The tiny house had been engineered to suspend from the higher branches. Clever metal gadgets and more ropes secured the house to the trunk. The gadgets looked adjustable, maybe to loosen the ropes as the tree grew. *Fucking brilliant.*

I wondered if the treehouse was Oliver's. If so, he'd ignored it for a long time. Dead leaves and bird shit covered the porch. I brushed spiderwebs from the wooden door and turned the handle.

Locked. Dang it.

A small window in the door at eye level succumbed to my ministrations with spit and the hem of my T-shirt until I could take a look inside.

The interior space was about eight feet by four feet, furnished with a narrow bed along the wall shared with the porch. Built-in shelves at the head of the bed surrounded a window. One other window, in the short wall to my left, completed the room's spare perfection.

I wanted *in*. And I wanted it bad.

I spun to the left and braced my hands on the porch railing to support my weight while I leaned out to take a look around the corner of the house. The near edge of the window was maybe three feet away.

Close enough.

I pressed my chest into the corner of the treehouse so I could stretch out my left arm and grip the window to give it a push upward. It *seemed* locked, but my awkward position didn't provide much leverage. After a moment of thought, I sat backward on the railing and leaned out sideways toward the window, which gave me better leverage. With a tight grip on the railing with my right hand, I pushed up hard on the window with my left arm.

Yes.

Another few upward shoves and I managed to raise the window all the way.

With my feet back on the porch floor, I leaned forward again over the railing to judge the size of the window opening in relation to the size of my body.

I really shouldn't have looked down.

My brain locked. I froze for a breathless few seconds before I jerked back and plastered my spine against the door.

I could ask Oliver for the key. But if the treehouse *was* Oliver's, its neglected state likely meant he considered it booby-trapped, like his workshop, and he wouldn't want me nosing around.

That only made me more determined to get in.

I did it by not thinking. I put my brain, including the self-preservation lobe, on pause and lifted one leg then the other over the porch railing until I stood on the wrong side, facing the porch. Chest plastered to the treehouse, right hand tight on the railing, I grabbed the window edge with my left hand, swung my left foot inside, did the splits, and *freaked out.*

I hung there for too long in a burning groin stretch, ass splayed over a dead drop.

It was hella motivating.

Deep breath. Don't think. Lunge.

My crotch took a beating and I bashed the top of my head on the window frame. I landed on the floor inside the treehouse in a heap, one hand pressed to my mouth. My other hand hovered over my crushed balls. My eyes watered from the pain.

I stared out the window at the leaves until I'd recovered enough to get up and check the door. It unlocked from the inside without a key, thank *fuck.* I left the door open to air the place out and gave myself a tour.

Under a tarp, I found a beauty of a mattress, unstained and firm, resting on a wooden frame. When I sat on the edge of the mattress, my knees almost touched the wall across from the bed. The whole set-up was tiny, but I loved it.

Hi, honey. I'm home.

I wished I could stay forever instead of having to go back to Seattle and get a job.

My gaze zeroed in on a nail in the wall across from the bed, which gave me an idea. I tore a blank page from my journal, drew an infinity symbol on it with the Sharpie, and impaled the page on the nail.

Once upon a time, a life in which I stared at an infinity symbol on the wall of a treehouse as the seasons changed around me would have seemed ideal. A part of me wished Oliver hadn't woken me to my deeper flaws, like my reluctance to take responsibility for my own trajectory. I did love the treehouse, but I also wanted more.

I would go to Seattle and get a job, use it to aim myself at a better job. Until then, I had a few more days on Vashon. The treehouse lay buried in acres of deep woods. No one would know.

Two hours later, I'd eaten an early dinner at my campsite, ferried my sleeping bag, water bottles, headlamp, and breakfast to the treehouse, and biked off to explore some more.

After a night on a real mattress, I felt like a new man.

When I visited to the courtyard to shower, I didn't see Oliver, but I found cash, keys, and a shopping list in the van's glove compartment. I bypassed the scenic route and headed for town on Vashon Highway, eager to get to the library. Restful sleep had coalesced vague thoughts into questions.

The librarian on duty at the reference desk—a Black woman with beautiful posture—listened intently as I told her what I wanted to do as a career. "I *want* to do it, but I'm not sure I'll be *allowed* to," I confessed.

"Basically, you need to woo parents in spite of being a mess."

I laughed, delighted my librarian had a sense of humor. "Ha ha, but, well... yes."

"Would you want to work outside without kids, to avoid having to impress parents?"

"No. *God*, no. Who would I play with?"

"Gotcha." She smiled and winked, and I wanted to be her friend.

"I'm Grant," I said. "It's nice to meet you. Thank you for helping me."

"Isis," she said, a challenge in the lift of her eyebrow.

"No shit."

"Truth. Let's start with state and local child care regulations." With focused fury, Isis typed on her computer for half a minute.

I'd feared info overload, but Isis stuck with me. She made sure I understood each factor I needed to be aware of before she moved to the next one. The result was a list of websites for me to study, which she emailed to me, and a handwritten action plan we colluded on, which included enrolling at a community college and applying to volunteer with a Seattle parks program, to gain experience working outside with kids.

The first item on my action plan was to get a job at a copy center as close as possible to Mitch's fancy Madison Park home.

"Isis, may I be frank?" I asked.

"Of course."

"This first task feels like the toughie. All the stuff after it doesn't even feel like work."

"Hmm." Isis bullied her computer keyboard again. The printer spit out a list of copy shops around Madison Park, with contact info and manager names. "I also emailed it to you," she said.

"Um... *Wow.*"

"What else you got for me?" The tough-guy voice Isis tried and failed to use cracked me up. We chuckled quietly to each other.

"Seriously, though," she said, "can I help you with anything else?"

With the worst shit dealt with, I felt like I'd earned a snoop into Oliver's life. "What Vashon Island maps do you have? I'd love to get a detailed look at a particular area."

"Topographical map?"

"Okay. Maybe. I'm not even sure what I'm looking for."

Isis got up to fetch a large volume that turned out to be bound topo maps. She opened it on the desk and helped me find the map I wanted. We leaned forward and I used my index finger to touch the tiny black square of Oliver's house. That gave me a sudden idea.

"Is the general public allowed to see property records? I mean, would I need the owner's permission? Or... would I have to go to King County headquarters in Seattle? Is there a fee? God, I hope there's not a fee." I held my breath.

"All you have to do is sit there," Isis said.

"You're shitting me."

"Nope. King County property records are online for all and sundry. Here, I'll show you." She typed and then turned the screen toward me. "I zoomed in on the area where you put your finger on the topo map. Is this what you're looking for?"

It took me a moment to understand what I was seeing, and then I couldn't answer Isis because I was speechless. With Oliver's house positioned in the center of the screen, we could also see a few surrounding parcels, overlaid with owner names.

I swallowed hard. "Could you... um... zoom out farther?"

On parcels all over the screen, Oliver's name repeated in tiny type. *Oliver Rossi, Oliver Rossi, Oliver Rossi*. On parcel after parcel. All around his house. In the vast area I'd explored by bike. Farther south. Much farther than I'd ventured.

"Holy everloving *fuck*," I whispered to the computer screen.

Isis, bless her, sat back and let me look without interruption.

The bramble thicket where the kids and I had our adventure was *not* on Oliver's property, but was across the road from a parcel Oliver owned. I remembered his distress when I wouldn't tell him which blackberry bramble I'd chosen for the adventure.

I felt tears come to my eyes.

Oliver can't leave his property.

That was why Oliver lied, why he'd been lying for God knew how long. He lied to hide, and none of his friends knew. No wonder I freaked Oliver out. From the beginning I'd challenged his boundaries, pushed him out of his safety zone.

"Isis," I finally said.

"Yes, Grant."

"You have blown my mind. Can we print some of this?"

"Sure, and I'll show you how to find it online. Then you can access it by phone when you're out and about."

"With respect," I said, "in some other version of reality, we are totally married."

"All in a day's work, my friend."

After we'd taped together the three pages Isis printed, I used her orange highlighter to outline Oliver's holdings. Isis checked to see if Oliver owned any other property in the county. He didn't, and all of his Vashon properties connected.

"Do you know him?" Isis asked. "Oliver?"

"Yeah. He's been helping me get my shit together."

"He's on Vashon? I'm surprised. I haven't seen him in a long time—not since before his father died, I think."

I let out a long breath and set down the highlighter.

Isis must have seen something in my eyes, because her smile faded. "Is he okay?"

I couldn't think of an answer that wouldn't invade Oliver's privacy more than I felt comfortable with. *He's in pain. He's hiding from something big. He's amazing. He's an imperious jerk. He's in love with the wrong person. He'll be better when I'm gone.* In the end, I summed it all up with a shake of my head.

I could tell that made Isis sad.

It made me sad too.

A text to Clementine from the grocery store led to her invitation to stop by for tea and cookies on my way back to Oliver's. The rain picked up again as I drove. At Clementine's, I tucked my taped-together map inside my jacket and dashed to the front door.

At the kitchen table in her small, elegant cottage, we sipped herbal tea from small, elegant cups while I told her what I'd discovered and showed her the map.

Clementine didn't seem surprised. "Oliver's grandfather bought the property the house is on in the early 1930s. I knew Matteo and Lucca bought more property over the years, but I didn't know their holdings were this extensive."

"And it all went to Oliver when they died." I felt like I could stare at the property lines for a week and my discovery wouldn't have sunk in. "What does he *do* with it all?"

Clementine laughed her small, elegant laugh.

I looked up from the map.

Green eyes twinkled at me. "He loves it," she said.

Of course he did.

Chapter 58

OLIVER

Do you *have a minute?*

I glanced at Grant's text and ignored it, too engrossed in painting to stop.

I'd begun the morning on the honeysuckle blossoms above the heads of the sleeping figures, then gotten lost in a series of vignettes under a tangle of blackberry vines and salal. A group of children cut a tunnel into a dark bramble, crawled into a cave of speckled light. Painting the scene made me feel like I'd been included in their safe bubble of community.

As I painted, I mulled over the facts around the scrap of memory I'd had. My mother had worked downtown in Seattle. She'd traveled between Vashon and Seattle in a limousine with a driver. I could picture the exterior of the car. Until that snippet of memory, I hadn't remembered being inside her car.

Are you home? Grant texted.

I sighed and set down the paintbrush. *Yes.*

Can we talk for a minute at the workshop?

Toolshed, I corrected.

I cleaned the brushes and grabbed our contract off the dresser.

Mist rose from the lawn, evaporated in sunlight and treetops. From across the yard, I watched Grant pace inside the toolshed. He'd opened the door all the way again.

When I drew near, he looked up with a frown. "We need to talk."

"I agree." I waved the contract at him. "Today is the last day of week four. Your interruptions have gone on long enough. As of today, our arrangement is over. I appreciate your work in the toolshed and with shopping and cooking and all that, but this is where it ends. If you show me your proposal today and I think it's good enough, I'll give you the hundred dollars."

The contract fluttered as my hand shook. I hadn't seen Grant in a while. I'd forgotten the *scope* of him. He'd been emaciated when I found him, and brutal in his regard for the world, with an underlayer of childlike fear. That combination had called to me to help. But he'd become something else in the weeks since, and not who I'd intended him to be. His healthier, bigger body emanated intensity that made me want to curl away into myself.

"This is where it ends," I said again.

Grant dismissed my presentation with a shake of his head. "That's a piece of paper. Our arrangement worked because we wanted something from each other. What you're saying is it stopped working for you, but you're wrong about why." He took three long strides toward me.

His force field pulled me in.

I tried to stand my ground. Loose strands of hair around my face lifted toward him.

"Maybe," Grant said in a softer voice, "you want me to leave because it's hard to keep lying to yourself about what you want from me."

I held up the contract between us, to watch Grant's face as I tore it in half with a sharp rip.

Grant's expression didn't change. "Did that give you a thrill?"

"It did. It means you'll be gone soon."

"I bet I can give you a bigger thrill."

I crunched the pieces of paper into tight balls in my fists. "Get off my fucking property today or I *will* call the cops." I tried to sound resolute.

Grant's amused look said he didn't believe me. "Tell me something, Oliver. Why can't you leave your property?"

My lungs tightened and froze. *He knows?*

"Hey." Grant reached for me. "Oh, damn it. *Hey.*" His fingers touched my face. "It's okay, Oliver. I didn't mean to—"

I want to sit next to my mother in the back seat of her big car.

I jerked away, dropped the balls of paper, and yelled with all my might, "Leave me *alone.*"

Flee. Now.

I became a fox to escape into the forest, turned and ran.

I want to sit next to my mother in the back seat of her big car because I don't see her very often and because she looks like me. No one else has skin like mine, muddy and white at the same time. Dad calls it russet, but that makes me feel like a potato. My mother has the same hair as me, shiny and really like a fox. I want to touch her pretty hair, to touch someone who feels like me, but when I try to climb onto the seat, she puts a hand flat on the stack of folders by her leg. A briefcase the same color as our hair takes up the seat on her other side. Before I can crawl into her lap, Dad scoops me up and buckles me into my car seat on the seat facing backward. I think it's mean not to let me sit with my mother, because we don't get to be together very often.

When the car starts to move, I'm not allowed to get out of my car seat, so I watch her with my painter's eyes. I look like her, but she's more still than I am, more like a statue. Dad has to take photos to paint me because I get up and run around, but I could paint my mother as a still life. She keeps her gentle hands in her lap when she talks. I have to use my hands to say things, like my granddad and my dad. Dad is Dolphin Father, because he's so playful. Also because he needs his pod. Dolphin Father is tall and big all over, like my granddad, The Eagle. That's how it is with animal people—an eagle can have a son who's a dolphin, and a dolphin can have a son who's a fox. Dolphin Father and The Eagle call me Coyote, but I call myself Fox, like my mother.

The dark car windows make the neon lights wrong, like we're not really in Seattle but in an old movie when someone remembers Seattle. I keep my eyes on my mother in the gray light. Sometimes neon gets all the way inside to make her foxy hair flash and sparkle.

Their voices together in our car bubble sound like a song just for me. Their song goes on and on in circles around my head. The musical notes float in the air, pull us tight together, make me sleepy in our cozy darkness.

I let myself fall sideways against my dad.

Their song stops when Dolphin Father puts his warm hand on my head and leaves it there. We ride together as a pod through the silence, close and safe, up and down the hilly waves in the sea of Seattle. I want to stay awake and not miss anything, but I have to close my eyes.

When my mother starts the song again, she uses a little voice, a voice like trying to hide in a too-small cave. "I must decide by the end of this week."

Dolphin Father sings back to her in his voice that gets everyone's attention when we have our entire, biggest, everyone pod over for dinner and shenanigans. The

Eagle calls it Dolphin Father's open-sea voice and says it can get the party started or shut it down. It's not nice for Dolphin Father to use his open-sea voice in our car bubble, especially when my mother wants to sing quietly.

"I cannot believe you're serious about this," Dolphin Father says from the middle of his giant chest.

I keep my eyes closed and try not to move.

Chapter 59

GRANT

Oliver blasted across the lawn like I'd shot him from a cannon.

Okay, maybe a direct confrontation wasn't my best idea.

He was on foot and fast, but I had a bike. I kept him in sight, but didn't try to catch him. A hard run would bleed off his panic. When he crashed, I'd be there.

The route Oliver took didn't follow any paths I could discern. He ran through a stand of alders so dense I had to walk the bike, and then leave it behind to keep him in sight. The undergrowth thickened. Wild rose vines grabbed at my clothes. Sunshine after all the rain had made the vegetation burst. The air swam with pure oxygen.

I popped free of the vines to see Oliver about fifteen feet away to my right. Half his hair had come loose to hang around his face in sweaty strands. I started toward him, concerned by his harsh breaths and shaking hands.

A blackberry thicket rose at his back, vast enough to rival the one Clementine had shown me. He had nowhere to go.

The pair of work gloves Oliver plucked from the grass protected his hands as he lifted a section of brambles and swung it to the side, like a hinged door. In the time it took me to run to the doorway, Oliver had crawled inside with the gloves and pulled the door closed, leaving me staring at a wall of thorns.

I took off my flannel shirt to use as a makeshift glove, yanked away the chunk of bramble, and ducked inside. A mental replay of the naked longing on Oliver's face the day of the bramble adventure drove me forward. Whatever pinned him to his property was no joke. I felt compelled to find the painful barb and remove it.

My suspicion that Oliver's lair included a second doorway, an escape hatch, cost me scrapes as I hurried. My shoulders were wider than the Oliver-sized tunnel. I felt my T-shirt rip and kept going.

When the tunnel ended, it wasn't at another door.

I wouldn't desecrate the space Oliver had created by calling it a cave.

Atrium.

Conservatory.

Palace boudoir.

Fortress of thorns at the heart of a kingdom of thorns.

Rugs stained by fallen berries overlapped to cover dirt and the vine stumps Oliver must have cut at ground level. The walls curved upward in a dome. Specks of light floated and swayed in the fragrant gloom, reflections from shards of broken glass hung by strings from the ceiling.

When I saw Oliver's fury and tears, I almost felt bad about my invasion. But *someone* needed to confront the slippery critter about his lying, and I seemed to be the only person in his world with the backbone to do it.

Oliver charged me on his knees to try to shove past me and out.

"Nope." I squared my shoulders to block the doorway. "Not happening."

"Then get *out* of my space."

I was sure Oliver wanted me gone, but he hadn't put an exclamation point at the end of his order. A flush bloomed over his face and body, tinted the bramble drawings on his arms. I had to close my eyes to collect myself. *On his knees in the boudoir. Pinked copper skin.*

Focus.

"I'll leave," I said, "if you tell me why you ran. What did I say? What are you so afraid of? And don't lie."

"You!" *That* was an exclamation point. A big one. Oliver flung his hand up to point at me with an unsteady finger. I admired the way he could yell and cry at the same time. "You're not welcome here! Why won't you just... *leave*? You make me..."

Like a toddler bent on prolonging a tantrum, Oliver flipped between hurt and outrage as he yelled on. I watched and waited and listened with all the compassion I could muster. He swung his arms, tried to catch his breath between angry sobs and repetitions of the same basic message to *Go away!* He dripped snot, swiped at his tears, scratched his hands and arms on the thorns, tried so hard to stop showing me his pain.

I didn't interfere.

Oliver finally deflated with an exhausted sigh and used the bottom of his T-shirt to wipe his face. "I really hate you," he gulped. "So, *so* much." He stabbed me with his best effort at dagger eyes.

Maybe Oliver did hate me. If so, his hatred had helped him expend a heck of a lot of energy—old, nasty energy that had been bottled up way too long.

"It's pretty safe to hate me," I said. "I'll be gone soon."

Oliver tried to stand. His shoulders curved against the sharp ceiling. A blue shard of glass bounced off his neck. "What do you want from me, Grant? Whatever it is, say it, so you can take it and go."

I decided to give Oliver a breather before I took another shot at exposing his wound. There was plenty else I was curious about.

"Well, since you asked, I want to know why you're with Freddie. He's all wrong for you."

"Does this look like a slumber party to you?"

"Sit down. You look ridiculous trying to intimidate me in a crouch. And you're bleeding." I nodded at his hand. Blood dripped from his finger.

In a graceful collapse, Oliver folded to sit with his legs crossed. He dabbed at his hand with the hem of his shirt and flicked a wary look at me. "I won't discuss Freddie with you."

"I see. When I kissed you in your secret car, you kissed me back, but Freddie's your boyfriend and you don't owe me any explanations. Makes perfect sense."

"You stole that kiss under false pretenses."

I shook my head. "Any false pretenses were yours, buddy. You were begging for it."

"Was not."

Oliver's petulant resistance made me snort. "What would Freddie say about the kiss you were so adamant he not know about?"

"Freddie and I have an open relationship. It was the DeVille I didn't want him to know about."

"Whose side are you on in this argument? Why kick me out of the car when you so obviously wanted to kiss me *and* you and Freddie have an open relationship? Did you wish I were Freddie?"

Judging from the flash of surprised distaste on Oliver's tear-streaked face, his answer was no.

"Then I don't get it," I said.

Oliver squirmed and dabbed at his hand again, though the bleeding had stopped. "A guy's allowed to get off on his fantasies in private. You... interrupted me."

"Mmm. Juicy. What was your fantasy about?"

Oliver's answer was to turn bright red, unfold a long leg, and kick me half-heartedly. I grabbed his ankle and took the conversation in a different direction to try to shock some truth out of him. "At your house when I was working on the proposal, I overheard Freddie talk about his trip to Whidbey next week and how he wants you to go with him."

Oliver's inability to leave his property hung in the small space between us, a live, almost visible thing.

"So?" Oliver jerked his foot out of my grip and folded his arms.

"Wow. Whatever has you by the throat must have happened when you were a child. Look at your pout. Just... Come *on*. You need to share this stuff with someone. Talk to me."

"There is *nothing* I want to talk with *you* about."

I rolled my eyes. "So. Freddie doesn't know about the car?"

"Don't call it *the car*. It's a *DeVille*. It's a 1968 Cadillac Sedan *DeVille*."

"For God's sake, Oliver. What I call the damn thing isn't going to change the fact that you're lying to Freddie, and not only about *the car*. *Super* basis for taking your relationship to the next level. Kudos to you."

My pissy tone seemed to please Oliver. He looked at me directly for the first time, calculation in his gaze. With a sinuous move, he uncrossed his legs and arms and crawled toward me across the rugs. "You know... it *was* a pretty good kiss."

I'd seen that look before, during our brief tryst in the car. Over the past week, I'd remembered it while I stared at the top of my tent and imagined more, imagined being stuck in that car with Oliver for hours.

"Stop it, you devil." I put my fingers up in the sign of a cross. "I know that trick. You're trying to use your... your creative, messed-up, intuitive..."

Oliver didn't stop slinking toward me, and it rattled me.

"Your intuitive... um. Thingies. Your stuff," I stammered. My skin tingled under all the dust.

"My *stuff*, huh?" Oliver inched toward me.

"You're trying to distract me, using... um, a diversion. To keep me from poking at your wound." I scooted sideways to unblock the doorway.

"*Now* you let me go?" Oliver lifted his eyebrows. "After you went to all the trouble to corner me and make me bleed?"

"Yup." I waved at the tunnel. "Have at it."

"Remember what happened in the DeVille?"

Even though I knew what Oliver was doing, I could barely keep my thoughts together. "Whatever you're so determined to avoid must be big if you're willing to seduce me just to prevent me from helping you confront it."

"In the DeVille that day, I was fantasizing about you," Oliver said.

He was probably lying. I pressed my eyelids together.

"I imagined you pinning me down so I couldn't escape. I hadn't invited you into my fantasy, and yet there you were. And then there you were in person. Right there with your hands on me."

In the patience of the clear afternoon, Oliver's long sigh filled the air, trailed off in a gasp that sounded like arousal. "Remember how you rested your weight on me when you kissed me?" he asked in a whisper.

"No." I squeezed my eyes tight, backed into the thorns to get away. "I have no idea what you're talking about." I'd lusted after Oliver for weeks, but I didn't want to get sexy under circumstances that might compromise him in the vulnerable state he was in.

"Who's lying now?" Oliver asked.

I reached blindly for the tunnel opening.

Oliver touched me. He ran his hot palm up my arm.

I remember. I remember what your mouth feels like under mine.

"After you kissed me, after you left, I revised my fantasy." Oliver's knees pressed against my thigh. "I imagined you driving me around all night while I hid on the floor in the back under a blanket."

Oliver's words and slow voice pulled me under.

"You stopped the car where no one would find us." I felt Oliver's breath on my cheek. His lips brushed my ear. "Every day, after you slept, we had sex. That was the one thing, the *only* thing that kept me safe."

"That is so messed up," I muttered.

"It's *my* fantasy. I can do what I want in my own mind."

"Is this a fantasy you tell to Freddie?" I tried to push Oliver away. I didn't want to hear a reconstituted fantasy about Freddie. "You know what? Stop."

"Shh." Oliver pressed his fingers hard to my lips. "I've never shared my fantasies with anyone."

"That only tells me how desperate you are right now to stay hidden. You're using your fantasy as a weapon. That's not—"

Oliver took his fingers off my mouth and kissed me.

My hands clenched with the heat and wrongness of it, with the effort required to resist him. I opened my eyes, to make sure I wouldn't push Oliver into the thorns when I shoved him off me and left.

I shouldn't have opened my eyes.

Pink lips, red beard, sharp eyes.

This is such a bad idea.

Oliver scurried to block the tunnel. "You woke up and climbed into the back seat to get to me. Yanked my legs." Eyes locked on mine, Oliver stretched his legs toward me, freckled shins under a light brush of hair. "I resisted."

"To hell with *this*. And to hell with *you*, you jerk." I rose to my knees and shoved a hand down my pants to shift my hard cock up from where it pinched.

Oliver wiggled his feet. "You pulled me onto your lap."

To hell with rug burns too.

I grabbed Oliver's ankles and pulled hard, manhandled him onto my thighs. The stark pleasure of my hands on him burned away all my reluctance. I ripped out the band holding Oliver's hair, shoved my hands deep into the thick mass, and buried my face in it, in *him*. He smelled like oranges and sweat and berries and hot metal. I breathed deeper.

Oliver rippled his body, rubbed at me with his hips. "And then you kissed me."

I did. *God help me.* I kissed Oliver Rossi. Used my thumbs to lift his chin, covered his entire mouth with mine and rushed him, my hunger a hurt I pushed into him.

Oliver flailed. His feet stuttered on the rugs. I thought he was trying to escape so I followed, kissed him across the open space, unwilling to let him go. Only when his back hit the thorns and he pressed into me did I realize he'd been trying to find a foothold to keep his balance. I put an arm around Oliver's back and hugged him close.

He felt dangerous in my arms, like a wild animal I'd trapped, an untamed creature who might chew through me to get free. But he spread his legs and leaned into me, ate me back until I had to pull away to protect our teeth. I closed my eyes against the onslaught of sensory input.

As soon as our mouths separated, Oliver panted more of his words into the humid air. "You... made a fist. Put it between your legs so I could—"

I held Oliver's thrumming body closer, clenched my fingers at my crotch. When he wrapped his legs tight around me and humped onto my fist, his mouth savage on mine again, I opened my eyes.

Spangles of light on scraped caramel skin.

Loops of satin hair snared by thorns.

His *mouth*.

His astonishing mouth.

I hung on with all my might.

Chapter 60

OLIVER

I don't want to remember.

But what I wanted didn't matter.

The memory came for me anyway, tracked me as I became a fox and fled to my safe den, followed me inside. I couldn't block the memory or stop it, even as I raged at Grant. If I'd been alone, I could have turned my back on it.

Grant took that option away.

When he brought *the car* into the crowded space of my den, I became Coyote-Fox.

For the first time since I was a child, I felt the shift, stretched into my Coyote-Fox pelt, my protective fur, grown to fit the man I'd become.

Fox smelled sex in the air.

Useful, Coyote mused.

I knew Grant, knew him well enough. He'd cut off my paw to try to save me, slash a new wound to fix the old one, force me to leave part of myself behind in the trap.

Only if I let him.

I slid my right paw... *hand* up Grant's arm, my same hand that had rested on Dad's thigh in the back of my mother's car.

I shook my head to clear it.

Don't remember. Let the trap keep my paw. I don't want to be free.

Coyote told Grant the fantasy of being together in the car in the safety of hiding. Told him and told him, until Grant took over the telling. I followed along in my mind.

It's one of those days when we crash together. I thrust my hand into the heat-shocked space inside his shorts and find a dick so hot my hand blisters. My squeeze makes him hiss and kiss my ears and yank my hair. I like that so I pull his dick harder, make noises against his ear to fill in the backbeat. That fast, he comes in my hand with a groan that tells me he hadn't meant to, not yet.

His huge fist beneath me blooms into a spread hand with fingers against my hole in a hard dig. Right there. There. He knows when he gets it right. He slows everything then. Slow kisses up my neck to my mouth. Slow tongue inside my open mouth that I can't close to kiss him back. There. He moves his other hand from my back to my dick. Slow hands right... there. I slow all the way to stop. Freeze while he does things to me like he knows a better fantasy.

I came with a full-body spasm that lasted a year.

His fingers kept at me until I reached into my shorts for a swipe of my cum to feed him. When he turned to take my thumb into his mouth, I yearned toward him again.

But the trap yanked at my hair, pulled me sideways.

Vines snapped tight around his leg.

Slash of red blood. Spooked eyes. Hard breaths like pain.

Frightened animals, both of us, wounded by need.

It made it easier, not hurting alone.

Chapter 61

GRANT

I stared into Oliver's open face, into eyes filled with more than I had time to catalogue.

My phone rang.

Oliver closed his eyes, thus ending the best moment of my life.

The call reminded me I had an appointment with Mitch. "Damn it. *Damn it.*" I took my thumb out of Oliver's mouth and wiped it on my shorts.

I expected Oliver to withdraw from me, but he didn't. Without a word, he laid his head on my shoulder and sagged, sighed into my neck. To hold his weight and reach into my pocket for the phone, I had to shift the leg I'd shoved into the brambles when I'd lost my balance.

"Ow. Hello," I said into my phone. My voice sounded as scraped up as my leg.

"Where are you?" Mitch said. "We're here, but there's no one around. Did you forget?"

"Sort of. I'm so sorry. We'll... I'll be right there. Please don't go. I really do want to talk with you."

Mitch wasn't a bad guy, but he also wasn't a go-with-the-flow guy. I pictured him checking his watch. Right on cue, he asked, "How long will you be?"

"Um..." I looked around to assess, considered how far Oliver had run from the house. "Twenty minutes maybe?"

Mitch sighed and hung up.

"Hey." I patted Oliver's back. When he didn't budge, I rested my chin on his shoulder. *Just for a minute.*

When I glanced down, the tattered rips of Oliver's shirt caught my attention. I lifted my hand from his back to find it smeared with blood. "Aw, hell."

Oliver answered with a soft sigh.

We might have roused ourselves then—disengaged and wiped down—except Oliver's hair had tangled with the barbed vines. We would have needed scissors for a quick exit. Grateful for the excuse to savor Oliver's relaxed weight, I carefully reclaimed his hair from the grip of the brambles. It took a while. I wasn't willing to sacrifice a single hair, not if I could help it. The thick strands draped like cold silk over my hands.

I didn't assume our sexual interlude would change anything between us. It seemed obvious I was a trigger for whatever internal struggle Oliver was in the throes of dealing with. I wished I knew how to help him. My qualifications for determining what was best for Oliver were nonexistent. *Which Oliver pushes me away? The Oliver who needs me to goad him to heal, or the Oliver who needs me gone in order to heal?*

After I'd freed the last bit of Oliver's hair, I wrapped my arms around his neck and his lower back, to avoid the torn skin, and rocked him for a while, rocked us both.

I didn't close my eyes. I wanted to memorize the scene. In the upper layers of the bramble, in the brighter sunlight, fat blackberries bunched amid the green leaves. In the murky interior of the thicket, shadows shifted as the leaves above fluttered in the light breeze. Out beyond the edges of the rugs, rotted blackberries stained the bare earth.

My gaze settled on the middle distance and lost focus, Oliver's trusting weight and the fall of his hair over my arms all I wanted.

My phone rang again. I poked at it on the rug by my knee to turn it off. I did want to talk to Mitch, but nothing seemed as important as being Oliver's place to relax.

Even if it only lasted until Oliver remembered he didn't like me.

Chapter 62

GRANT

Forty-five minutes after my scheduled time for meeting Mitch, Oliver and I reached his yard. We made a pit stop at the workshop to clean up in the bathroom as best we could, and to put on coveralls to hide our ripped, cum-stained clothes, Oliver's wrecked back, and my bloody leg.

Oliver handed me coveralls with *Matteo* embroidered on the chest patch and mumbled, "Granddad's," like he wanted me to know, but didn't want to have to say it. They were short in the legs and a bit tight in the armpits.

Kai found us as we were zipping up the coveralls.

I hugged Kai quickly, self-conscious about my odor after my romp with Oliver. "How's your dad? If he's still here, he must not be too peeved."

Kai shrugged. "He's okay. I gave him a tour of the workshop and the court-yard and around the house. He's talking to Jill's dad now."

I stopped trying to flatten my hair with my wet hands at the bathroom mirror and stared into my own surprised eyes. "Like... talking on the phone?"

"No. He's here. He called Dad this morning and Dad told him he could meet us here."

"Well, *shit*," I said to myself.

I turned to Oliver, gestured at his coveralls and the wild tangle of hair around his head that he hadn't tried to tame.

"You don't have to do this," I told him. I didn't want Oliver to witness what-ever Jill's dad might say to me about tardiness and kids and credentials. "Hit the shower. We can talk later." I looked down at myself and sniffed my armpit with a sour face to make Kai giggle. "After I've had a shower."

"Are you kidding?" Oliver bugged out his eyes like a cartoon character. "Another Mitch and Grant drama? I wouldn't miss it." He turned to smile at Kai. "Let's go get the show started with snacks for everyone."

They left while I dawdled at the bathroom mirror, remembering how Oliver had stood beside me on the porch the day we met, when Mitch showed up to get Kai. When I decided not to leave with them. Since then, Kai had come out to his family and Mitch's attitude toward me had lost some of its edge. I wasn't eager to disappoint him all over again.

My hair was a lost cause, and the red scratch across the side of my face wasn't doing my image any favors. In the medicine cabinet over the sink I found a squeeze bottle of Bactine that looked older than Oliver. A shake told me it wasn't empty. I squirted some on a folded piece of toilet paper and sniffed it before I applied it to the cut on my face. "Ow! Goddamn it." I hopped around until the punishment abated, then trudged to the front of the house to scare Jill's dad with my bad first impression.

Mitch and a bear of a man leaned against the back of Mitch's BMW. A quick scan assured me Jill's dad wasn't within reach of a shotgun.

Based on Mitch's snort and his down-up once-over, I guessed I looked worse than the last time he'd seen me, the day he'd kicked me off his property. Without a word, I waved them up the front porch and ushered them inside. Jill's dad, who Mitch introduced as Vince Donahue, seemed tense enough to need a drink.

Mitch and Vince recoiled from the onslaught of Oliver's decor. With a nostalgic smile, I looked around at the stage, the art supplies and animal skulls, the potted trees, wall-to-wall framed art, and monstrous orange couch. I picked up my favorite pillow, an elaborately embroidered orange and red creation with *Hell No!* on one side and *Why Not?* on the other, and flipped it to *Why Not?*

When it seemed Mitch couldn't take the overstimulation anymore, he frowned and shifted his focus to me and my state of disarray. "What happened to you?"

"We, uh... were clearing out a blackberry thicket." I rubbed the spot where Oliver's sharp nose had pressed into my neck as I'd untangled his hair. "Sorry. I lost track of time."

That particular lift of one eyebrow conveyed Mitch's skepticism. I hoped he didn't suspect what had actually happened—that Oliver and I had distracted ourselves from our troubles by getting sexy in a thorn bush. *Like dorks.*

"You're not making this easy," Mitch said, a quiet reprimand.

"Yeah. I know. I know I'm not."

Vince emerged from his visual shock at that point, tore his gaze from a swarm of larger-than-life papier mâché insects suspended from the rafters, and tromped to stand beside Mitch in the middle of the living room.

Two against one.

I refused to be the first person to sit down.

While I waited for Mitch or Vince to say something, I watched Oliver in the kitchen, which did nothing to help me shift my post-orgasmic looseness to confrontational readiness.

Oliver stirred something in a small pot on one burner while popcorn pinged the lid of an large pot on another burner. Kai tugged on Oliver's shirt to pull him down to eye level and whisper into his ear. From Oliver's reaction of a smile and a hug, I assumed Kai had taken the opportunity to come out to Oliver, as he'd told me he wanted to. *The boy is unstoppable.* Kai looked up to catch my eye and gave me a thumbs-up.

Oliver dumped melted butter and salt onto two bowls of popcorn and handed one to Kai. They set the bowls and a stack of cloth napkins on the coffee table behind Mitch's legs and settled onto the couch with expectant expressions.

Perfect. Public humiliation, take one.

I started to ask Vince how Jill was doing, but he spoke first, to Mitch. "So far, I'm not impressed."

"Tell Grant what happened," Mitch replied. "He should know."

Vince turned to me. "Where do I start? I'm not in the mood to pull punches, Eastbrook. I gather from what Jill told me that you've been spending time with a bunch of kids like you think you're one of them." His disapproval came across loud and clear. "Even so, I think you're old enough to recognize a problem that requires parental intervention."

I sank onto the couch beside Kai. I'd been slacking about getting a job, but I hadn't thought what I'd been doing with the kids was *bad*.

"I'll be frank," Vince said. "You're too unsettled in your life to babysit without it looking like something else."

A grunt of disbelief escaped me at that point. "For the most part, the kids have been babysitting me." I winced and tried to stifle any more counterproductive comments.

Mitch pointed at me. "Stop talking for a minute." He turned to Vince. "I get that you're angry, but I didn't bring you here to castigate him. What he's done with Kai has been nothing short of phenomenal. Give the guy a chance. Tell him about Jill."

Vince's jaw clenched.

"Jill told me she felt uncomfortable with her brother's friends," I said. "I suggested she talk with—"

"Give you a *chance*?" Vince raised his voice at me. "You had your chance and you blew it. Living in a tent in the woods. No job. Lost your last job over a confrontation with a customer. *Nothing* about any of that is near acceptable if you want to be a role model for my daughter."

Christ. Vince was right. I couldn't breathe. I remembered my anxiety attack in the motel in Seattle and my throat tightened. My next inhale wheezed and failed.

Kai wiped his fingers on a napkin and climbed onto my lap to sit with his back to my chest, a move that put him between the angry dad and me.

Jill's dad stared at Kai in surprise.

"Mr. Donahue, that's not very nice." Kai folded his arms and puffed up his skinny chest, a mirror of Vince's power stance. "Just because Uncle Grant's going through a rough patch doesn't mean he's not a good person. He's a *very* good person. He's *my* role model."

Then we *all* stared at Kai. I had never known him to take a stand before—on anything. Certainly not against an angry adult man. I felt like I'd won the lottery. I put my arms around Kai and squeezed tight. He kept his chin up and his arms folded, basically using me as his throne.

Oliver chuckled.

Mitch blinked and closed his mouth.

Vince let out slow breath and unfolded his arms to run his fingers through his hair.

"You do need to work on cleaning up your act," Mitch said to me.

"I *am* working on it," I said.

"I don't believe you." Vince waved a hand at me. "What do you think will happen in a few weeks? Your parents will show up with hugs to take you out to the mall to buy school supplies for your first day of junior high? *Wake up*, man. Maybe you have a special way with kids, but that's not enough if you can't also be responsible in the real world."

Mitch moved to stand between Vince and me. "Hey. Stand down or I'm going to think it was a mistake to bring you here. Yes, Grant could have handled the situation with Jill better, but he encouraged her to talk to you, and she did."

Vince's angry expression shifted to what might have been guilt, before sorrow settled over his features. "Did Jill tell you one of those boys in the garage touched her inappropriately?" he asked me.

My body went ice cold. *Flash freeze.*

Vince nodded. "You listened to Jill, and I'm grateful for that, but I'm also angry you didn't follow through when she told you she had concerns. Between the day she talked to you and when she finally got up her nerve to talk with her mother and me..."

A wash of shame rolled over me and I squeezed Kai tighter. "Please, please don't tell me they—"

"One boy cornered her in the garage one time. He leaned against her and touched the small of her back. That was the extent of it. His *intent* upset Jill a lot more than what he did physically. We've addressed the issue with the boy and his parents, and with Jill and her brother. Jill assures us she's okay. But I wish like hell you'd called us, or come to see us, or come with Jill to talk to us. I wish you'd done anything except nothing. Do you understand?"

Before my shame could render me useless, I lifted Kai off my lap and stood to go to Vince. "Yes, I understand, and I am genuinely, deeply sorry. You're right that I didn't think it through, and that I don't have my life together. I can't tell you how sorry I am." I held out my hand.

Vince's face finally relaxed. He nodded and shook my hand.

Before things could get awkward again, Mitch said to Vince, "Grant's looking into training programs in Seattle." Kai must have told Mitch about that, because I hadn't. I'd chatted with the kids about my plans over snacks at the picnic table.

"Good," Vince said. "I'm glad to hear it, and I accept your apology. However, that doesn't mean things will go back to how they were. You're not to have any contact with Jill unless you've taken serious steps to put your life in order. Do that, let me know, and then we'll see."

I could barely function, but I managed to nod and say, "I'm going to apply to a volunteer program. I want to work in nature with kids." My voice seemed distant, the sound out of sync with the movement of my mouth. I felt the way I had in high school after a fight, after the adrenaline drained away and left me exhausted, spacey, and ashamed.

Mitch and Vince spoke around me.

I felt for the coffee table and sat. *Jill in a garage with an older boy who wanted something from her he had no business trying to get. And I could have protected her.*

Kai—a boy half the size I'd been when I was his age; a shy, gay boy brave enough to start middle school in a few weeks—stood behind me and placed his hand flat on my head, as I'd done for him many times.

That was the moment I took full responsibility for my own life.

Chapter 63

OLIVER

After I walked Mitch, Kai, and Mr. Donahue out to the driveway, I went back inside to check on Grant. He assured me he was fine. I didn't believe him. His vacant look and stiff legs when he tried to walk made me wish I'd waited to invite Freddie over.

I'd texted Freddie while the oil heated for the popcorn, to ask him to come over. I needed an easy distraction from the crush of memory, though I couldn't decide which memory I most needed a distraction from—being in my mother's car or wrestling with Grant in the blackberries.

Grant stumped on uncoordinated legs across the porch and down the stairs. I followed, worried he might fall, hoping he'd be gone by the time Freddie arrived.

I couldn't suppress a sigh when I heard a car coming down the driveway.

Freddie parked the minivan and approached us with suspicion. "What happened to you two?" he asked. "Catfight?"

Grant came to life enough to say, "You wish." I couldn't see Grant's face, but I heard the braggy sneer in his voice.

"I don't *want* to have a problem with you," Freddie told Grant. "Don't you have anywhere else to be other than mooching off my boyfriend?"

Maybe because of the recent beating he'd taken from Jill's father, Grant took the bait. "Don't fret, studly. Except for the times he can't control himself, Oliver and I maintain a strictly business arrangement."

Freddie's eyes flew to mine. "Oliver?"

"Yes, Freddie? Problem?"

Freddie didn't raise his voice, but I could tell he was mad. "You guys are in this state of disarray because you had *sex*? Where? On a roll of barbed wire?"

"What's with the attitude?" I jumped down the last two steps. "We have an open relationship. Remember?"

"Bye," Grant said. "Good luck with your domestic dispute." He staggered off toward the courtyard shower.

I put my hands on Freddie's shoulders and gave him a shake. "Stop fuming. You're being unattractively hypocritical."

"So this is why I've only gotten chaste kisses from you so far."

I shrugged.

"Well, hell." Freddie closed his eyes and took a few deep breaths. "Okay. I get it. I *have* been a hypocrite. My bad." The hug he drew me into was less graspy and more caring than I'd expected. We stayed pressed together until he pulled back to look at me. "I want to be exclusive, as of now." His hands tightened on my waist.

"Noted," I said. "I'll consider it."

"But... you're the one who wanted to be exclusive in the first place."

"How about this? I'll be exclusive as of when we leave for Whidbey Island."

Freddie's face lit up. "Really? You'll come with me? I can count on it?"

"I wouldn't," Grant said. He stepped into view from around the corner of the house. "Oliver, don't you think you should talk to Freddie? I mean, if he's going to be your *exclusive* boyfriend who assumes you can go with him past the boundary of your prop—"

"That is *not* yours to tell," I snapped at Grant. The air between us wavered and grayed.

Shadows in the back of the car.

"I cannot believe you're serious about this."

They think I'm asleep.

I keep my eyes closed and try not to move. Dad pets my hair just the way I like it. It almost makes me really go to sleep.

"I fell in love with my career," my mother says. "As you did. That's not an atrocity."

"I wish you'd done it sooner, before we got married."

"But then we wouldn't have our Coyote."

I suddenly knew what the memory must be about. It was from when I was five.

"Babe, hey. *Oliver.*" Freddie must have felt me sway. He directed me with his hands to sit on the porch steps.

I dimly recalled the day Dad sat me down and told me my mother was gone. That conversation had been enough trauma. I didn't want to also download the specific memory of my parents talking about it. *Why would my psyche be so cruel?*

To keep the memory at bay, I stared into Freddie's concerned gray eyes, let them pull me all the way back into the present.

"Grant's lying, isn't he?" Freddie asked me. "Or kidding or something? You go to Tacoma to the building supply store, and to Seattle to get art stuff. I mean, you've texted me from the grocery store in town to ask what I want for dinner."

"He lies," Grant said. "Tell him, Oliver. Don't set yourself up for a fall. You should tell someone besides me."

"You're mistaken." I stood to face Grant. "I never told you. You're making things up. I tore up our contract. Your time here is over now, and I'm glad. I didn't want you here in the first place. You don't follow the rules and you don't take no for an answer. I don't care what you do or where you go, but pack up and get off my property within the hour, or I'll have Freddie call the cops. He'll do it."

"What do you mean he didn't take no for an answer?" Freddie's voice rose as he tried to keep up.

"Not what you're thinking," Grant said to Freddie. "Oliver seduced *me* with his..."

"*Stop.*" I used my voice to put up a wall.

Freddie looked like he didn't know who to believe. "Oliver," he said in a tight voice, "The liar here better be Grant. If you've been lying to me about something as big as not being able to leave your property—"

"I'm *not* lying. I promise."

Grant huffed but didn't say anything.

"High school in Seattle, Freddie," I reminded him. "Hikes on the peninsula. Summer jobs together in Tacoma. Of *course* I can leave my property."

"Then I expect you to back up that claim by coming with me to Whidbey. Saturday, August eighth, two weeks from yesterday. Write it down when you get inside. If you're not with me when I get on that ferry, we're over. I'll go fuck Hiroki's brains out for three days, return to Vashon, pack up *all* my stuff from Mom's, and ship it to Tokyo. Then who knows when I'll be back."

Freddie's ultimatum should have given me the shakes, but I only felt calm. With Grant gone, I'd have two weeks of peace before Whidbey. They stretched in front of me, plenty of time to set myself to rights and pack a bag for a weekend away.

I looked Freddie right in the eye. "No problem. I'll be there." I meant it.

"I choose to believe you," he said, "but you'd better come through. After all these years, we're close to going somewhere—not just on a trip but in our relationship. Don't you dare get me this far and then leave me hanging."

I nodded and gave Freddie a big smile I only had to force a little bit. "Deal."

"Fine. Mom's doing a lunch she wants me to attend that Saturday, which means we'll leave Vashon on the four p.m. sailing. I'll pick you up a little after three."

Grant studied us with his steady glare.

"Fine." I leaned in and gave Freddie a peck on the lips.

"Ugh. You need a shower, babe. I'm not feeling it with someone else's sex on you. I'm going to go home and take a run. Call me later?"

Grant kept his eyes on me until the crunch of tires down the driveway faded to silence. Under the livid red of the thorn scratch, his face settled into sadness. *Bye*, he mouthed, then slid out of sight around the corner.

I went inside and closed the door.

On automatic pilot, I gathered a few art supplies—charcoal sticks, acrylic paint, butcher paper, sketch pads—and arranged them on the high work table in the art supplies corner. Sat on a stool with my hands in my lap and stared at them. The silence grew and grew.

It wasn't a decision or a thought that moved my hand to pick up a charcoal stick. Something else, something more, moved through me and I responded. That was how it always was. Under an umbrella of hushed solitude, I drew and painted and drew some more. The shadow of the memories I didn't want morphed into a shade of gray one dollop of cerulean blue away from the color of a cloudless evening sky.

When I felt done, I lay on the couch in my sleeping bag in the moonlight and deconstructed the grays around the room until all the shadows became friends and I couldn't stay awake.

Chapter 64

GRANT

After a final shower, a sullen affair that sluiced away all traces of Oliver's cum and the lingering smell of his sweat, I packed my stuff from the courtyard, abandoned the frozen meals in the chest freezer with my name on them, and plodded through the forest to the treehouse.

My compulsion to replay my molten tryst with Oliver—his toned body's sinuous wriggle, the heft of his hair, the things he'd said, the... *everything*—distracted me so much I stood inside the treehouse in a daze until my arm muscles yelled at me and I snapped out of it.

I dropped the stuff I'd lugged over onto the bed and went out again to clean up the campsite. I jammed the damp tent into its stuff sack and crammed it and everything else into my backpack. I'd spread it all out to dry at the treehouse.

On my way past Oliver's through the cover of the woods, I snuck out to the carport and nabbed the loaner bike to borrow for a little while longer. As perfect as the treehouse was, I knew it wasn't my ultimate solution. The bike would get me to town for food and to Clementine's. Her cottage wasn't big enough for me to stay over, but I thought she might let me use her shower before I headed back to Seattle.

I didn't own much, yet my belongings filled the treehouse. I dropped the pack in the last empty corner and typed out a text to Oliver, grateful I was high enough to get a signal on my shit phone. *I left the key for the panels on the picnic table.*

I could have said more. I could have typed out, *Any chance you still want to review my workshop proposal?* Or *I loved kissing you.* Instead, I tossed the phone onto a shelf and collapsed on the bed to eat my way through the perishables from the courtyard fridge.

Over a bowl of cereal, I mused on our thorny sex wreck. I was dying to know how Oliver was doing in the aftermath. Did he feel bereft without his hands on me? Did he treasure his scrapes? Did he get hard again when he remembered?

I'd *never* had sex like that—primal and thoughtless and reckless. Not even close. It hurt to think I'd never have it again, or if I did, it wouldn't be with Oliver.

What a pair Oliver and Freddie were—the creative liar and the clueless tramp. My huff into the bowl I held under my chin splashed milk onto my hands.

I mooned over Oliver through a pint of generic yogurt, then shook myself back to reality and typed out a message to Clementine. *Oliver needs his space. Can I impose on you for shower and laundry sometime next week before I return to Seattle?*

Of course, Clementine texted back.

Thanks!

Where are you staying? she asked.

The red power bar on my phone gave me an easy out. *Gotta go. Low phone charge.*

I spent the next twenty minutes lost in a meditation on digestion, then got up and rigged makeshift curtains so I could read in bed at night and not worry about someone seeing the light.

I fell asleep before I found my headlamp.

The next day began with a double helping of celery and carrots for breakfast and a bold entry in my journal: *NEW RULE #3: DON'T LIE TO MYSELF.* I scratched it out and wrote a revision on the next page. *NEW RULE #3: TELL MYSELF THE TRUTH.*

I chewed on a mouthful as I pried a nail out of the wall with my multitool and hammered it back in over my infinite onion drawing so I could hang up my new rule. The truth was that I knew my action plan wouldn't work without an upgrade to my self-image.

A rummage through my backpack unearthed my first self-portrait from Oliver's interview. I offered the angry stick figure of my former self a smile and ran my fingers over the punch marks from Oliver's darts.

I wished I had bigger sheets of paper. Also, I needed more nails, and food that didn't have to be refrigerated. And markers in colors besides black.

It took me an hour and a half to bike to town. I could have done it faster if the whole damn island wasn't so pretty. I'd hurry up, then have to slow again to take in the view.

By the time I stashed the bike behind the grocery store, the sunny sky had devolved into clouds. Since I didn't have a lock, I wedged the bike between a wall and a dumpster.

At Swipe & Swivel, I bought a couple more journal books, a pad of eight-by-ten-inch art paper with a bit of heft, and a six-pack of colored markers. I fondled a small paint set, but it was too expensive and I didn't have a sink at the treehouse. At the hardware store, I spent a dollar on a pack of brown paneling nails. After ten minutes in the grocery store to stock up on eighty-nine-cent cans of pinto beans, I was done.

Oliver's bicycle hadn't been stolen, *thank Christ*. I took a look at the sky and decided to forego a visit to the library. I couldn't risk getting caught in the rain with my art supplies.

Yeah. The ironies kept coming.

I promised myself I'd make another trip to town soon to use a computer at the library to focus on my job search.

I spent most of the ride from town making a mental list of things to do on the library computer. Download resume template. Fill in online application for volunteer program. Browse Craigslist for roommate situations as close to Mitch's neighborhood as I could afford.

The sky waited to let loose until ten minutes after I'd returned to the treehouse. To celebrate, I used a forest green marker to draw a picture in the sketchpad of me waving and smiling from the treehouse porch.

I hammered one of my new nails into the wall and hung my drawing, then stood there and grinned at it for a soppy few minutes.

Rain pummeled the roof.

I languished indoors, cozy and impressed with myself, aching to share my success with Oliver.

Chapter 65

OLIVER

After Grant left for good on Sunday, I spent that afternoon and the next two days sketching versions of Freddie as the man lying in the ditch in my painting. On Wednesday, I called Freddie and asked him to come over. I wanted to show him what I'd done, so he would believe I was serious about being with him.

Freddie stood at my dining table and blinked. "You drew *me*?"

"I did. More than once."

He picked up the first drawing on the stack, set it aside, and pulled out a chair to sit. I'd stacked them in the order I'd created them.

I stood behind Freddie with my hands on his shoulders, felt his breath slow as he looked.

"My God," he blurted. "Babe, these are spectacular. You could make a mint with these. I'm talking full-on bidding wars."

"They're only sketches."

When he neared the final drawing, I sat beside him, to watch him see it.

Freddie left the paper on the table and leaned over it, brow furrowed. His fingers moved in the air over the face of the Japanese boy I'd drawn sleeping on Freddie's chest.

I leaned against Freddie's shoulder. "I was thinking he could be... someone we adopt?"

While Freddie bear-hugged me, I checked the clock on the kitchen wall. If he left soon, I could work on the mural a while before night settled around the house.

I would make the man in the mural be Freddie, I decided, but I wouldn't paint over the vignettes. I would only add vignettes, to turn the mural into a commemoration of the summer Freddie and I progressed from fuck buddies to family for the long-term.

Freddie sensed my fixation with the clock. "Too bad," he said as he pulled back. "I wish you didn't have drawing lessons today." He caressed my cheek, studied me with affection and desire.

If Freddie had forgotten I didn't do lessons in the summer, I wasn't going to remind him.

My nod took so little effort it made the lie feel small.

Check out our cozy cottage on Whidbey, Freddie texted me the next day. He'd taken to sending me messages and photos about our weekend trip, to infect me with his excitement.

Cozy seemed an optimistic description of a shed with gingerbread trim. It looked cramped. Or maybe *cramped* was my new feeling about everything.

My property had never felt so small.

I left Freddie's text unanswered, stowed my phone in my cargo shorts, and continued to circumnavigate my lawn in the rain.

I paused on the strip of dirt behind the toolshed to revisit the mystery of Grant's defacement of my property. He'd used blue chalk—probably from Dad's forestry kit—to draw an infinity symbol on the siding beneath the window. The symbol stretched as wide as my spread arms. Like the other infinity symbols I'd found, it seemed purposefully shambolic, as if Grant's intention was to deconstruct infinity into chaos.

The confident trill of a song sparrow turned me toward the woods. My scan for the sparrow's striped chest came to an abrupt halt when something blue in the foliage caught my eye. I squinted and made out a blue-chalked infinity symbol on a branch. *The* branch. *My* branch. Right at the spot where I'd perched to snoop on Grant and the tweens.

He'd known.

My face heated at the thought of him knowing I'd lurked there like a weirdo.

Grant's infinity symbols pulled on my thoughts like a fixation.

I hurried back to the house, kicked off my wet boots, and padded to the computer. According to Wikipedia, a cryptographer named John Wallis had invented the infinity symbol. I diverted my attention from the words "eternal love." I doubted that was Grant's intended message. He and I had chemistry together, and I'd gotten off when I'd used sex to distract him, but that was only physiology and hormones.

A sentence about the artist M.C. Escher caught my eye. I traipsed off to the library to find the Escher books, then spent a pleasant hour lost in clever drawings of endless turns and tricky perspectives, admiring all over again Escher's mastery of Möbius strip infinity on a two-dimensional surface.

Aza had loved perspective tricks. We'd often slouched together on the couch in the great room to study the Escher books. Aza squirmed and pointed and plied me with questions about how to manipulate perspective, sketchbook at the ready for demonstrations as we talked.

Fifteen years later, alone on a couch in the library, I turned to the inside front cover of the book in my lap to revisit the words rebellious Aza had written—*in pen*, to get a rise out of me. He'd known Dad and I didn't write in our books.

Aza Andrew Abrams, he'd inscribed in ornate, mocking cursive. And then a short note, meant for me.

I want this when you're dead.

Chapter 66

GRANT

Monday's downpour gave me an excuse to hibernate.

Tuesday disappeared altogether. I woke, opened my eyes for two seconds, then zonked out all day and all night. I figured since I'd pigged out on all the food from the courtyard refrigerator instead of rationing it, I needed to digest. Plus, I felt safer in the treehouse than I'd felt anywhere, ever. The safety made me sleepy.

Wednesday morning, armed with my new supplies from Swipe & Swivel, I took a break from sleeping and buckled down to do a life review. It was time to deconstruct myself and find a more promising trajectory.

With the sketchpad on my raised knees, I peered at the old rules I'd nailed up beside my first self-portrait with Oliver's dart holes in it. I didn't feel like that anymore—scary and severe.

I picked up the light blue marker, for *sky* and *no limits*, and made a few tentative marks on the paper. I dawdled, determined not to draw another stick figure.

When I began to draw my arms, I discovered I was a tree. Blue leaves sprouted from my elbows. My branches extended to fill the page. I used the forest green marker to fill in the leaves: green leaves with sky blue outlines. Blue roots grew from my feet into the ground.

I look amazing.

I tore out the page and nailed it above the infinity symbol.

Using the light green marker, I wrote out my new rules.

New Rule #1: Ask for help.
New Rule #2: Follow the fascination.
New Rule #3: Tell myself the truth.

I thought about all the jobs I'd worked since I was a child that required the flat line of The Zone to get me through the day, and how I'd assumed I wasn't capable of more. Thought about forest and earth and my feet as roots.

New Rule #4: Dig deeper.

Noon came and went as I excavated and documented. The wall filled with turning points, mistakes, things I'd wished for as a kid. Pages fluttered in the cross-breeze from the open windows.

All I was doing was *noticing* myself.

It felt so good.

Before evening remodeled the treehouse into a cave, I took a break to brush my teeth, then snuggled into my sleeping bag with the art pad to make one more drawing before I slept.

With the orange marker, I drew an *O* that filled a page from the sketch pad—for *Oliver* and for *onion*—then relaxed my arm and drew more circles over and around the first *O*, until I could squint and see Oliver's infinite layers.

Somehow, I wanted to capture Oliver, to remember him.

With a pencil I'd found behind the novels on the shelf, I wrote *Imperious* in stretched letters to fill the narrow space between two layers.

Slender, I wrote in the layer below.

Breathtaking coppery hair and skin. That one I wrote in a long space near the outer edge of the onion. Words came fast after that. I hurried to keep up.

Prisoner. Liar. Renaissance artist. Creative genius. Teaches perspective.

I couldn't find words for all the layers of Oliver I knew, but I tried. *Mistaken about Freddie. Surrounded by ghosts. Funny. Sweet biceps. That ass in those overalls. Infuriating. Lost his mother.*

I wondered how many of his own layers Oliver knew, and how many layers he knew that I would never know.

Ruled by secrets, I wrote. *Kisses like a dream.*

Because I had the good sense to cap the orange marker, I didn't write on my dick when my attention shifted to the memory of Oliver's frantic kisses in his blackberry boudoir. I tried to drag out the pleasure, but Oliver's agile hand around my dick didn't want me to go slow.

I came fast on an explosion of remembered joy, wiped up with a T-shirt, and sank into sleep to avoid the knowledge that I would leave Vashon without touching him again.

On the fourth day of rain, I ran out of art paper.

"It's time," I said to the bookshelf. I pulled out all the books and laid them on the bed, then added the two novels I'd brought from Seattle. They were all paperbacks. The most obscure one—*Underground Art & Theater of the Weimar Republic*—was also the largest. I shoved the other books back onto the shelves and sat with *Underground Art & Theater* on my lap to deliver the bad news.

"I'm sorry," I told it with a sympathetic pat, "but it's for the greater good." I had the decency to wince as I ripped off the front cover.

I wrote and drew on the blank insides of the covers, nailed them to the wall, then started in on the pages. Printed words became background designs for memos, maps, memories, and yearnings—my long-hidden veins of gold.

Chapter 67

OLIVER

A persistent bout of cabin fever punted me out into the rain again. I ended up at the toolshed with my ass on the edge of the concrete floor and my phone in my hand.

For courage, I fired off texts to Talia and Clementine—*I'm off to Whidbey with Freddie next Saturday for a few days. Wanted you to know*—before I scooted back another six inches into the toolshed, to practice moving out of my comfort zone.

My heartbeats sped up. I stared down at my boots in the mud.

That was where Penelope, Clover, and Abelino found me. They splashed over the lawn on their bikes.

"Hey, guys." I coughed to clear the gravel from my throat. "Sorry. Haven't spoken in a while."

Clover let loose a chuckle that sounded as uneasy as I felt. I tried to remember the last time I'd brushed out my hair.

"You all right?" Penelope, always the caretaker, got right to the point.

"Yep. Come on in out of the rain."

The kids huddled in the shelter of the toolshed and told me things. I tried to listen but got sidetracked by how much tween Aza would have adored them. He'd been more trouble than any of the sweet kids in Grant's tribe. I shuddered at the thought of Aza's pushy personality inside a thorn bush. Grant and his tweens wouldn't have minded. They would have adored Aza back—restless energy, wounded soul, and all.

A pat on my shoulder brought me back to reality.

"We're going," Abelino said in his smooth voice. "You take care." His dark eyes told me he saw what I wasn't saying, that I wasn't okay. But he was a kid, so I faked a better smile and threw in a reassuring eye twinkle. That seemed to do the trick.

The kids sped off on a spray of shouts, Abelino's black ponytail tossing arcs of rain as he flew. Hair as black as Aza's had been.

Aza had never bound his hair. *Tangled but free.* That was Aza.

I drew an infinity symbol in the muck with the heel of my boot and wondered how I could remain tangled with Aza—because I loved him—but also set us both free.

After a lunch of a can of sardines, poppy seed crackers from Clementine, and dill pickles dipped in ketchup, I retreated to Dad's garage to prepare for a confrontation with Aza.

I should have turned off my phone. A cluster of text messages from Freddie ended with, *I want to come over.*

When I called him, Freddie answered with, "Well?"

"Not yet, okay? I'm—"

"What the *heck* is that sound?" Freddie raised his voice. "Where are you?"

"In the garage." Rain pounded the roof, echoed in the empty space.

"Doing what? There's nothing in there—unfortunately. Why couldn't you have just covered the DeVille if you didn't want to see it?"

I *knew* I needed to tell Freddie about the DeVille, and I *did* want to stop lying, but I detected land mines. He would ask difficult questions I wasn't ready to answer. I decided I'd come clean about the DeVille on our trip to Whidbey.

"Call me when you're back in the house," Freddie said. "I couldn't hear what you said."

That was convenient, since I hadn't said anything.

We hung up and I settled into the hammock I'd hung from two hooks in a corner of the garage. Bundled in a heavy sweater, boneless in the hammock's hug, I tried to think about Aza. Every time I pulled in my thoughts to focus on him, my mind went blank.

I watched rain spatter the window and erase the remnants of the smiley face drawn in the grime. I wondered if Grant had left his campsite yet. I hadn't gone to check. If he'd stayed, he'd be huddled in the tent, rotting from damp after days of rain. *Might motivate him to stop goofing off.*

The voice in my head sounded bitchy and bitter.

I checked the weather report. Sunshine and clear skies on the horizon— perfect weather for drying out and packing up camp.

Goodbye and good luck.

I shook Grant off and tried again to think about Aza.

The series of portraits I'd painted of Aza the year he stayed with Dad and me swam up in my memory. I tried to hold on to the images, but dozed off. Aza's voice in my mind woke me.

Hey, Ollie. Come visit me.

I rubbed my eyes and sighed. *At least let me wait until the rain stops.*

If I was serious about putting Aza to rest, I knew where to find him.

Chapter 68

GRANT

The absence of rain on the treehouse roof woke me Sunday morning. From the porch, I watched clouds give way to blue sky. *Time to go*.

Laden with my daypack full of dirty clothes, toiletries, phone, power cord, and bits of garbage, I biked to Clementine's through beams of sunlight. Waves of hyperactive photosynthesis filled the air with fresh, pure oxygen.

"There you are," Clementine said at her front door. "I was getting worried."

"Sorry. My phone died."

"Come on in."

"Stand back," I warned. "Until I've showered, I'm the beast you invited into your sweet little home."

Clementine made a show of putting her hand over her nose and mouth and gestured for me to pass her. "The washer and dryer are in the bathroom. First door on the left."

I hadn't bathed in a week, not since my last shower at Oliver's, and the hot water and soap felt so good. I felt ten pounds lighter afterward. I started a load in the washing machine and went to look for Clementine.

I found her in the kitchen. When I held up my phone charger, she pointed to an outlet by the coffee machine and said, "Talia told me Oliver sent you away. Did you move to a new campsite? How did you manage in the rain?"

"I'm... um. Well, to be honest, I'm squatting somewhere, but only for a few more days."

"Do I even want to know where?"

"Nowhere I had to break into or anything. I mean, I didn't *break* anything to get in." My groin gave a twitch of protest.

Clementine lifted one of her eyebrows. "Do tell."

"It's a treehouse—the most beautiful, *perfect* treehouse. It's snug and dry, and there's even a porch. You'd love it. It's classy and well-crafted. Actually, it reminds me of you in some..." I looked up from plugging in my phone.

Clementine's face had gone white.

"Hey, whoa now." I reached out to steer her to a chair at the kitchen table. "What did I say?"

"Aza." She swallowed. "It's Aza's treehouse."

I remembered what Clementine had said in her car on our way to the bramble. "Oliver required Aza to do a project on the property."

She nodded. "He wanted to boost Aza's confidence around something besides painting." Her croaky voice sounded like she was crying, but there were no tears.

I sat beside her and gathered her cold hands in mine, still warm from my shower. "Did it work?"

"Yes. No. Aza gained confidence, but he got ahead of himself." Clementine took a big breath and raised her head to look into my eyes. "He would be thirty-one this year, if he'd lived. He killed himself when he was seventeen. Fourteen years ago. Not that I'm counting."

"I'm so very sorry, Clem."

She nodded and looked away. "In New York, he applied for shows at some of the bigger galleries, but wasn't accepted. I guess he gave up, couldn't adjust his timeline or his expectations, didn't ask for help... something. I don't know."

"Oh, man."

At the end of a long sigh, Clementine said, "There were only a few people on the beach that day. February, freezing and windy. A couple of people tried to stop him, but they couldn't reach him in time. They said Aza..."

I scrubbed lightly at Clementine's cold hands and waited.

"Walked," she whispered. "He walked into the sea. They found him days later, miles from where he'd gone in." Clementine huddled on the chair like an old lady, shrunken and frail.

The washing machine interrupted with a clunk from the other side of the kitchen wall.

I stood, bent to lift Clementine into my arms, and carried her to the living room couch, where I could more easily wrap her up. I set her sideways on my lap and held her close, to help her reinflate. She sagged against me but didn't cry or fall apart.

I felt like I might.

"Clem?" I gave her a gentle squeeze.

"Hmm."

"In the car that day, why did you tell me Oliver saved Aza's life?"

"If Oliver hadn't taken him in, I think Aza would have killed himself sooner. Robert and I pursued so many options—everything from therapy and alternative treatments to pharmaceuticals and institutionalization. Aza rebelled against most of it. Oliver had the magic touch. He told Aza he'd mentor him on painting, but only if Aza went to regular therapy sessions and took his meds. Aza agreed."

"Oliver gave you more time with Aza," I said.

Clementine pushed my arms away to slide off my lap and sit beside me. "I didn't use the extra time well." She pulled a tissue from the front pocket of her slacks and blew her nose. "I get stuck on what if I'd gone to Aza's gallery opening. I'm pretty sure he went to New York because he didn't feel like I cared enough."

"This is a rude question to ask, but why didn't you go to the opening?"

"Your question isn't as rude as my answer." Clementine closed her eyes. "The annual planning meeting for the nonprofit I worked for took place on Orcas Island that year, at a board member's vacation home. I didn't want to miss it."

"Clem." I remembered how awed I'd been when I'd spied on Clementine's session with Oliver. "I think you're brave for looking at your pain and trying to sort it out."

I also thought Oliver was brave to help her.

"I think Oliver saved my life too," Clementine said. "I'd never commit suicide, but without his friendship and our sessions, I wouldn't have lived as much. More every year."

The tissue in Clementine's hand fell apart. She balled the pieces in her fist and leaned her head on my shoulder.

We fell silent, sat together, and listened to the washing machine click and swish as it pulled dirt out of my clothes and sent it down the drain.

Chapter 69

GRANT

While Clementine freshened up in the bathroom, I stayed on the couch and tried to process what she'd told me about Aza.

"Hey," I said when she returned, "after your session with Oliver this week, would you mind texting me to let me know how he's doing?"

"I would, but he's taking a hiatus to focus on a painting project. We texted yesterday. He seemed excited about a trip with Freddie."

"Well... hell." The discrepancy between the Oliver I saw and the Oliver his friends saw weighted my shoulders with sorrow for him. In the wake of Oliver's denials to Freddie, disclosing his private business to Clementine didn't feel like the right move.

"Will you be okay without your sessions?" I asked her.

"I'll be fine. Oliver said if he goes to D.C. with Freddie we can do Skype sessions starting in September."

The sadness took on more weight in my chest. I rubbed my hands over my face and stood to look at the framed photos on the shelf over the fireplace. They all featured a thin boy with an expressive face. In most of the photos, some part of his body blurred. "Looks like a video camera might have been in order."

Clementine chuckled. "Aza never could keep still."

"He looks like a character."

"He was. He would have fit right in with your troop of children."

Drawn by the blaze of auburn hair, I leaned in to study teenage Oliver with his arm around Aza's shoulders.

"I think you could have helped him," Clementine said, "at least for a while."

"I don't know about that." I pretended to look at more photos, to keep my back to Clementine as I told her about Jill and my confrontation with her dad. "I agree with Vince. I need to learn to work with kids more responsibly."

"Play."

"What?" I turned to look at her.

"*Play* with kids more responsibly. Don't focus so much on being responsible that you don't play. From what I've seen, playing is one of your gifts."

The words swiped a slash of white paint over my old rules. "Clem. That's the nicest thing anyone's ever said to me."

She gave me a quick hug and walked away to pick up her purse from the table by the front door. "I'm going to town to run some errands and clear my head. Do you want to ride along?"

She drove up the west side of the island. I filled my lungs with fresh air from the open window, soothed by the twitter and green mayhem. In a scrawl that wobbled from the motion of the car, I captured Clementine's words about me in my journal, to remember them.

She cadged a grocery list from me in the library parking lot. I forced two fives on her. "Have fun," she said, and drove off to get groceries for both of us.

Isis wasn't there, but another librarian parked me at a computer with a resume template. The result was a minimalist spin on the concept. The librarian corrected a few things, and I attached the resume to my online application for the Seattle parks volunteer program.

"You know, I work downtown," Clementine said on our drive back to her cottage. "I'd be glad to treat you to lunch sometime. We could make it a regular thing. You have Kai's family, but maybe you could use another Seattle friend."

"Yes, please." To keep myself from getting weepy over her kind gesture, I asked about her work as an administrator for a coalition of charitable trusts.

Later that afternoon, I folded the last dryer load of clean clothes and zipped open my pack to refill it for the ride back to the treehouse. The groceries Clementine had picked up for me didn't even cover the bottom of the pack. I closed the bathroom door and spread all my money out to count it.

Twenty-three dollars and twelve cents.

I tapped my phone to find Mitch's contact info.

"Grant," he answered.

"Hey. Er... I have a favor to ask." I talked fast to keep Mitch from hanging up. "I've identified six potential places to work, all within easy bus rides from your house in Seattle. I updated my resume and applied to that volunteer program. I've made actual progress. Can I stay in your guest room for a short time, until I find a room to rent? I don't want to stay in a motel. I could help you guys with cooking or..." Surprised Mitch hadn't interrupted, I let my presentation peter into silence. I held my breath. I'd never asked anyone for that much all at once.

"Okay," Mitch said. "Kai and I will be out and about on Thursday. We'll meet you at the dock in West Seattle."

I was stunned. "You're not... *mad* at me for asking? Really?"

"No, Grant. I'm not mad. I admire you for taking action. It shows commitment."

"Well, I'll be damned."

"You have a lot of goodwill in the bank with me and Sonya. We'd be glad to have you with us for a while. Kai will be over the moon."

Jesus. I had actual tears in my eyes. I unrolled a few squares of toilet paper and swiped at my nose.

"Um. Thanks. I'll come over Thursday and try to nail down a job, but I'll need to return to Vashon Friday for a couple of days, to..." I stared down at the toilet paper in my hand, curious about how I'd finish the sentence. I couldn't say, *to make sure my landlord, who doesn't even know he's my landlord, doesn't freak out about leaving Vashon on Saturday when there's no one there to notice he's freaking out.* "To finish packing up an art project I did."

I looked into the eyes of the mirror version of myself. He furrowed his brow and mouthed, *Seriously? You have an art project?* Out loud I said, "You'd really be willing to take time off on a weekday to help me?"

"Things slow at the firm in August. It's no problem. I'd offer you the trailer on Vashon, but it's been turned into the site office."

"You're all back in Seattle?" I hadn't seen or talked to Kai since the day he, Mitch, and Vince visited me at Oliver's. Calling Kai meant going through Mitch, and I'd wimped out. "Also, you told me you wanted to talk to me, but then Vince showed up that day."

"I wanted to get an update on your status, which I got. And, yes, we're back in Seattle. The construction noise bothered Kai, and the crew needed shelter from the rain, so we came back early. Our guest room is yours until you find your own place."

"Well. Gosh. Okay, then. Sure. Please." *Goddamn it.* I had to get off the phone. I'd turned into a guy with decent prospects but only half a brain. "My phone's not always on, to save the charge, but I check it now and then."

"Are you still camping in that courtyard Kai showed me?"

"Oh." I didn't want to tell Mitch Oliver had kicked me out. He wouldn't consider it progress. "I'll... um... update you when I see you?"

"Everything okay?"

"Yep."

"Thursday," Mitch said and hung up.

I blew my nose and went to give Clementine the good news.

Chapter 70

OLIVER

On Sunday morning, six days before my scheduled trip to Whidbey, I received a photo from Grant, a self-portrait taken in a bathroom mirror. White towel around his waist. Bare chest and shoulders. Steam. Grant offered the camera a small smile. *Practicing my interview face*, he texted.

I wished he hadn't sent it. It distracted me, and Aza deserved my full attention.

Armed with the treehouse key and a bottle of water, I navigated the forest to the almost undetectable trail across a rocky hillside.

The treehouse was hell to get to.

Aza had scoured the forest and finally found a tree way out in the hinterlands he proclaimed to be perfect. I'd given in to his enthusiasm. It had been a pain to haul building materials over the rough terrain. Aza and I joked that the distance between my driveway and his tree was a solid twenty minutes of cursing. He'd hidden his treehouse well. Loose rocks, tree roots, and dense undergrowth made access a challenge.

I wished I'd brought the small machete. In the years since Aza left for New York, the forest would have swallowed the...

A flattened tent hung over a tree branch.

I blinked at it for a minute before I understood what it meant.

"*Hey*," I shouted up at the treehouse. Because I knew where to look, I pinpointed a window high above, through the mass of leaves. It was open.

The fucker had broken in.

I leapt up the stairs, shouted as I pulled myself up three steps at a time. *"Get. The Fuck. Off. My. Property."* I wasn't going to knock when I got to the top.

The door I flung open bounced off Grant's half-empty backpack. He wasn't there.

Yet... he was.

Grant was so *there.*

I closed the door and leaned against it to take in what he'd done with the place.

The scent of Aza's patchouli hair oil had been replaced by Grant's unbathed reek. I didn't want to admit I liked it. I breathed in another deep lungful as I gaped at Grant's creation on the wall. His mixed-media installation grew outward from the central point of a messy infinity symbol drawn on a torn page. Everything spun around that fixed point. Like a river eddy, or the swirl of a galaxy.

I *loved* it.

I pushed off the door to take a closer look at a baggie under the central infinity symbol, swiped it off the nail to open it. Hunched over the bed, I extracted the roll of paper and pressed it open on the mattress with my fingers.

Don't get too attached to your job. The planets picked you to mess with this month. Your best bet for getting through is to get creative.

I flipped the paper. "June—Cancer." Hadn't Grant lost his job in June? I wondered if the scrap of paper was the source of his hostility toward creativity. If he somehow blamed creativity for the loss of his job, then *fuck.* No wonder Grant bristled at everything about me.

Suddenly it felt like *I* was the invader. Everything on the wall—the rules, the self-portraits, the drawings and lists—pulsed with vulnerability.

I should leave.

With inefficient fingers, I hurried to push the horoscope roll back into its paper band and return the baggie to its nail. I spared an anxious minute and a fumble with my phone to grab some photos.

On my way out the door my gaze fell on a stack of Grant's journals on a shelf. There were so *many.* I scurried over to nudge the untidy pile. Every book had a number on the cover. I picked one at random. It was filled with Grant's thoughts, drawings, and... *I want them all.*

I stared out the window to distract my conscience as I shoved the journal with the *1* on the cover into my back pocket.

Chapter 71

OLIVER

The next day, I hid in the DeVille for hours and trespassed on Grant's inner life. I combed through the photos I'd taken and the journal I'd stolen, on a search for clues to explain the havoc Grant had wreaked on my life.

One of my photos included a corner of a page with orange lines and a few penciled words—*Prisoner, Liar, Ruled by secrets*. I sat up to swipe through all the photos again, but I hadn't taken any that included more of that particular page. In the midst of my debate about whether Grant's words referred to me, I received a text from Talia.

Clem and I are here. You home?

Edward met me at the garage with an ear-splitting bark, pushed me in the ass with his head. "Yeah, yeah," I told him. I rounded the hedge to find Talia and Clementine on the porch steps.

"Hey, guys," I injected my voice with a double dose of cheerfulness. "What's up?"

"Sorry to barge past the red flag." Talia stood to give me a hug, keeping it brief so Edward wouldn't butt in. "It's a little early, but we wanted to make sure we got to tell you *bon voyage*."

"I can't remember the last time you took a trip off the island just for fun," Clementine said.

Liar. Prisoner. Ruled by secrets.

"I'd invite you inside," I said, "but the house is a mess." *Liar.* "I'm... organizing stuff, in case I decide to be away for an extended time." *I sound like I'm trying too hard.* I cleared my throat and scratched Edward behind the ear. "How's Edward?"

"So much better," Talia said. "I found this retired canine cop in Tacoma who does training. His specialty is doggie rebels. Edward is a total tool for that man." A small smile escaped.

"What's his name?" Clementine asked.

"Jack."

Edward looked up at Talia and barked. We all laughed.

"See?" Talia said. "Besotted."

"What about Brian?" I asked.

"Ugh. Edward broke him. Brian gave me the speech: 'Edward or Me. Your choice.'"

"Aw," Clementine said. "You chose Edward."

Talia nodded. "Of course."

"What's your retired cop like?" I asked Talia. "Are you besotted too?"

Talia's cheeks darkened with a blush, which was answer enough.

"I'm glad for you," I said. "I'd love to meet him. Bring him by sometime."

We all seemed to share an unspoken *but when?* moment.

"Which ferry are you catching on Saturday?" Clementine asked me.

"The four o'clock. Freddie has a lunch thing with his mom."

"You weren't invited?" The lift of Talia's eyebrow conveyed her disapproval.

"Not this time." Not ever, I realized, and wondered why that didn't bother me.

"I could give you a ride to the ferry," Clementine said.

Talia pointed to Dad's van under the carport. "Or you could drive yourself and leave the van in the upper lot. I'll drive it back here when I get off shift. Jack can fetch me." Edward barked twice, maybe because Talia said *Jack* and *fetch*. He trotted to the edge of the driveway and found a stick.

"Deal," I said. I sent a quick text to Freddie to tell him about the change of plans before I forgot.

For ten minutes or so, Talia threw the stick for Edward while the three of us talked. I managed to laugh in spite of feeling melancholy about the prospect of leaving my two best friends if I took off with Freddie to D.C.

Clementine kissed me on the cheek before she drove away.

Edward barked and ran circles around Talia's bicycle while she yelled at him. They made their noisy way down the driveway and out of sight.

The silence grew. My smile faded.

I moseyed up the porch steps—to memorize the background music of the breeze through the pines and the chitter of sparrows, to give each stair step time to imprint *home* on the soles of my shoes.

Chapter 72

GRANT

After two days of bike rides through Oliver's southernmost properties, I rode to Clementine's to freshen up for my trip to Seattle the next day. She persuaded me to stay for lunch.

"That was delicious." I sat back in my chair on the back patio with an appreciative groan. "What can I do to pay you back for all your help?"

"Consider it a gift."

"That's not—"

"Look who's here," Clementine interrupted with a nod.

I lifted my head from contemplation of my full belly to see Penelope, Clover, and Abelino drop their bikes on the grass.

"Aw. Hey, guys." They came in for hugs, but I hesitated, Vince's reprimands fresh in my mind.

Penelope looked at me funny and plopped into the chair next to mine.

"Clementine told us you were here," Clover said. "We wanted to see you."

"I wanted to see you too," I told them. I could have met them in the woods, but I hadn't texted to propose it. "I've kind of been in... um, a limbo situation, really trying to get my, uh—"

"We missed you," Clover said over my waffle of embarrassment. "That's all."

The kids decimated the remainder of the lunch. Penelope slouched against me and regaled us with family drama around her cousin's elopement. Clover confessed to fears about school starting. She and Abelino were saving for a cell phone they could share. Abelino didn't say much, but he smiled and laughed.

After dessert cookies had come and gone, Abelino spoke into a lull in the conversation. "We saw Oliver."

I'd wanted to ask, but hadn't wanted to worry the kids with my worries. "Yeah?" I tried to sound casual. I had a hundred questions. None of them seemed appropriate. *Did Oliver look exhausted? Is he still with Freddie, the wrongest boyfriend ever?*

"It was weird to be there without you," Clover said.

I turned to Penelope, who'd known Oliver longest. "How did he seem?"

"Okay, I guess," she said. "Distracted."

I didn't believe Oliver was okay. Distracted by the creative process was one thing. What I'd seen went beyond that. I suddenly needed to hurry off to check on him. "Clementine, thank you so much for the shower and the lunch."

"You're welcome." She stood to gather dishes. "Say goodbye to the kids while I clean up, then I'll give you and your bike a ride—to keep your shower fresh for tomorrow."

"See ya, kids." I beamed smiles at them, patted their heads, and reached to pick up an empty platter.

"No. Grant." Clementine's hand on my arm stopped me. "You're leaving Vashon tomorrow." She nodded at the kids and their sad smiles.

"Oh." She meant... *goodbye.*

I didn't tell the kids I'd come back to Vashon to visit them. It would be a while before I could spare money for another ferry ride, and I didn't want to get their hopes up. I would return to Vashon on Friday to check on Oliver one last time, but I didn't tell them that either.

Penelope told me she'd share my phone number with Clover and Abelino when they got their phone. I stood at the end of Clementine's driveway and watched the kids who'd become friends and mentors over the summer ride out of sight. Their departure struck me like a body blow. I kept my eyes on the empty road and thought about the kids and Oliver, wished I knew how to take care of myself better so I stood a chance of being able to take care of someone else.

The ride to the trailhead with Clementine passed in silence. In the treehouse, I set my daypack on the bed and called the library. Isis listened through my bluster as I attempted to arrange half-formed thoughts into a question. "Do you know of a good mental health crisis line?"

Isis probably thought I was asking for myself. Hell, after the divorce, I *should* have asked for myself. It had never occurred to me.

"Yes," Isis said. "Let me check. Here we go. There are options, depending on the issue." Isis hesitated, perhaps out of deference to my mental state.

"It's for a friend," I said. "He's withdrawing. More than usual, I think. I haven't known him long, but something seems *off* about him, and no one else seems concerned. I'm leaving Vashon soon and... Isis, I don't know what I'm trying to do. It's actually none of my business."

"I see." Isis drew out the words. "Does your friend seem troubled about a specific issue? For example, does he seem suicidal?"

"Oh, shit. I hadn't even thought of that."

"I emailed you some phone numbers and a website link. I think these could be helpful resources. One of the phone numbers is a help line for you, for people who think someone they know might be at risk for suicide."

I put us on speaker while I checked my email account. "Okay. I've got it."

"You take care of yourself," Isis said before we hung up.

Chapter 73

GRANT

I clambered down the treehouse stairs and set off toward Oliver's house, unable to shake my worry. Except for the self-portrait I'd sent from Clementine's bathroom, I'd left Oliver alone for nine days. I felt the urge to give his tough skin of mistrust another poke, even if all it got me was a sharp sting that made my eyes leak.

The trail took me past the stump chair and I paused for a look. The only place not packed with intricate leaves and wildlife was one spot inside, above the crown Oliver had carved to hover above whoever sat inside. Faint marks in the patch of uncarved wood drew me in for a closer look. An infinity symbol had been scratched above the crown.

Oliver wasn't in the workshop.

The van and Oliver's bicycle were parked under the carport.

No one answered my knock at the house.

I walked around to peer through the French doors. Sleeping bag unrolled on hideous couch. Suitcase open on evil chair. It hurt to see the suitcase.

At the garage I peered in the window, saw only empty space, and walked on to the holly wall. Oliver had insisted his secret car was private, but *tough*. Some things were *too* secret, and if Oliver wouldn't take care of himself, someone needed to prod him in that direction.

My hypocrisy sent up a warning flare, but I ignored it. I would take myself to task for the same crimes later, after I'd assured myself Oliver was okay.

The gate clattered as I went over. Through the back window of the car, I saw Oliver's head whip around. I ran then, slipped in fast and closed the door behind me. Oliver's look of surprise gave way to outrage and a retreat behind guarded eyes.

His topknot had slipped sideways. A few curved strands of hair fanned over the green of his T-shirt. I forced my eyes away from the shape of his chest under the shirt. Maybe no one had paid him in groceries since I'd stopped shopping for him. I felt like a dick about that, but only for two seconds.

"How's the freezer holding out?" I asked. "Still got a meal or two in there?" *The poke.*

"I banished you," Oliver said. "Remember? I fired you for inappropriate conduct in the workplace." *And the sting.*

"Don't forget challenging the status quo. Oh, and insubordination."

Oliver smirked. "Same old story, huh?"

"Nope. I'm off to Seattle tomorrow morning to arrange my new life. Back on Friday to pack up and take one last hike before I move in with Mitch until I can afford a room in a place with housemates." The subtext I tried to convey was that I'd be in the vicinity on Saturday when Oliver tried to leave his property, in case his shit hit the fan before Freddie's minivan boarded the ferry.

Oliver's disdain, which I'd been certain would progress to full-on anger as I spoke, faded instead to a blank expression.

I forged ahead. "I've been worried about you, so I got some information from the library." I opened my phone and forwarded the email from Isis to Oliver. "Call these folks if you need help with, like, you know... Aza, or not being able to leave your property."

Oliver only stared at me.

"Anyway, I also wanted to tell you goodbye." I rushed into the final bit to get it out before Oliver fainted or puked, or whatever his utter stillness was leading up to. "You're annoying as hell, but you kicked my ass into gear. Your ridiculous assignments even helped me find a career. So, yeah. I'm grateful." I waved my phone at him. "Read that email. You might need it when I'm not around."

All the color drained from Oliver's face.

He hadn't moved a muscle.

But he was gone.

OLIVER

"I fell in love with my career," my mother says. *"As you did. That's not an atrocity."*

"I wish you'd done it sooner, before we got married."

"But then we wouldn't have our Coyote."

When I hear my mother say my animal name, it's hard to pretend to sleep, because I want to smile. I try to record her voice in my mind, so I can remember it during the week when she's not home. Her voice sounds the same color as her hair, which is the same color as my hair—red like the leaves falling from Granddad's trees outside the kitchen window, but only after they rest on the ground for a while. I like to kneel and watch the leaves, to see if I can catch the exact second cadmium red turns to copper. When I put my elbows on the ground, my long hair covers the leaves and makes it easier to find the ones that look like my mother's hair.

Dad says, *"You love your career more than you love us."*

A sharp corner of Grant's journal dug into my tailbone. I'd had a split second to hide the book before Grant blew into the DeVille. I pushed into the pain to stop the memory.

"What is going on with you?" Grant leaned toward me.

My fear of the memory morphed into anger at Grant. "What do you *think* is going on? The asshole who torpedoed my summer *still* hasn't left. You're trespassing, and I'm calling the cops." I pretended to mean it. I powered up my phone, which opened on a photo of Grant's collage wall.

Grant's collage on *my* wall, I reminded myself, in *my* treehouse. "Where have you been sleeping?" I asked him.

That made Grant squirm.

"Well?" I put away the phone and kicked his thigh with my foot. I'd taken off my boots, so the kick wasn't as satisfying as it could have been. "You'd better not be camping on my property."

"At Clementine's?"

"Sure you are. So now who's the liar?"

Grant frowned. "I'm seriously worried about you."

"Nice redirect. The irony here is that if you *left*, I wouldn't be—"

"Why do you lie to your friends?"

"That's none of your business," I said. "Like everything about my life."

"I get why you want to be able to leave your property, but why with Freddie?"

You love your career more than you love us. I ground my tailbone onto the journal until it *hurt.* I let out a small yelp.

Grant narrowed his eyes and studied me. His massive body filled most of the back seat.

Hey, Coyote said, *Grant's massive body fills most of the back seat.*

I pushed my toes under Grant's thigh, gave him a thoughtful look with some heat in it.

"Oh no." Grant pushed my feet away and scurried out of the DeVille. He left the door open and leaned in to say, "That's not what this is about."

"Come on," I cajoled. "I told you, Freddie and I have an open relationship."

"I saw Freddie's face when you talked about your open relationship the day you sent me away. You want to mess with your boyfriend like that, go ahead, but keep me out of it. I also saw *your* face during that conversation. You don't want an open relationship. And that's one more lie."

I reached behind my back to wedge Grant's journal out of sight between the door and the seat, then slid across the seat and out. Grant leaned against the DeVille with his arms folded.

"We won't talk about Freddie," I said.

"You brought him up, but no problem. There's no shortage of sore spots to poke."

"Butt *out.* You agreed to my plan, which *wasn't* an invitation to nose around in my life. I only wanted to help you to shift your perspective about work."

"And you did. Thanks. Now tell me about Aza."

I sighed and glared at the pushy jerk. With reluctance, I admitted to myself that if I told Grant a bit about Aza, relieved a little pressure, I might be able to slam the lid on my box of sad memories and rebury it, keep my mother underground where she belonged. When I left Vashon with Freddie, I would leave the triggers behind. *Problem solved.*

I closed the door of the DeVille and leaned against it. "Aza was in high school when he came to live with me and my dad to study painting." I paused and glanced at Grant. "Clementine told you about him?"

Grant nodded.

"What Clem doesn't know, what... no one knows, is that Aza... called me. That day."

"Oof," Grant said, like my statement had punched him in the stomach. He tilted sideways toward me until our shoulders touched. I didn't move away.

"Aza didn't say anything on the call that alarmed me. He'd sounded... happy. Told me about galleries he'd applied to since we'd spoken a few days before. We laughed about some of the good times we'd had together. At the end of the call he... thanked me."

Grant unfolded his arms. His hand, warm and alive, wrapped around my hand between us.

I didn't want to expose more of myself to Grant, but the weight of Aza's last call made my head feel so heavy. "I'd known Aza all his life. We'd lived together. I *thought* I knew him. I thought..."

Grant remained calm and didn't speak, just like he'd done with the tweens. He let me be. It felt... different. Dad would have nudged, caught my eye, tried to make me laugh, fixed me something extravagant to eat, invited people over, filled the house with cheer.

I liked what Grant did better. Grant let my pain be about *me*. Dad, I realized, had made my pain about him, about his ability to distract me from pain.

"I pieced together the timing," I told Grant. "Aza must have called me from a bus stop on his way to the shore. He called me and then... walked into the ocean. Maybe that's why he was so happy on the call." I let go of Grant's hand and slid to a crouch at the thought. "He'd already decided to do it."

"He called to tell you goodbye," Grant said.

I nodded. "He didn't say that word."

"Maybe he didn't want you to worry."

I wished Grant would put his hand on my head. I remembered how Kai had leaned into Grant's legs at the hedge and in the toolshed. I let gravity take me, pressed the side of my face against Grant's thigh. When he didn't move his hand, I picked it up for him and set it on my head.

He left his hand there, grounded me, stood beside me, a sentry on lookout, while I let out a long breath and removed Aza from the box. With the earth beneath me and Grant's patience above, I took a long look, felt my body absorb Aza's story and make it mine, a story of my own, one I might be able to forgive myself for.

After a while, Grant moved his fingers to caress my hair, a swipe of sandpaper to smooth the jagged edges of my new story.

When I tilted my head up to look at him, Grant squatted and put his palm on my cheek. "Aza must have loved you very much."

If they think I'm awake, my dad and my mother will stop talking the way they are, so I act asleep with my whole body, like Dad taught me. I play the role of a noodle in hot water on the stove and go slowly limp. I don't move any part of me except to breathe, and I breathe like The Eagle when he sleeps on the couch in the great room in the afternoon—long and slow.

Coyote leaned me forward. I touched Grant's lips with mine.

Before I could get a taste of his tongue, Grant pushed me away and stood.

They stop talking, even though I'm a noodle. And then there's so much silence in the car it's hard to keep pushing sleep away.

"Are you certain he's asleep? It won't do for him to hear this," my mother says.

"Please." I stood, the memory hot on my heels. All the spaces of my home, spaces I moved through every day, crowded me with traps. My life tangled and tightened around me. Grant was both trigger and escape, the source and the salve. "Please let me."

He shook his head, backed away another step. "Tell me the truth. How long has it been since you left your property?"

"Only about... I'm not sure exactly. Maybe... a year?" My breath sped up at the lie. It was a big lie, big enough to make the memory fade.

"Who can corroborate your claim? Get someone on the phone right now— someone who met you in town for lunch in the last decade. Then I'll believe—"

"He finds the king in the stone prison." Coyote spoke past Grant's confused blink, to hook him before he moved farther away. "That smile..." I passed a finger through the air an inch from Grant's lips, to mark the place I wanted his smile to appear. "He smiles *that* smile and kisses me for the first time, as if his smile was always supposed to be a kiss."

Grant didn't speak, but he stopped breathing.

Coyote loaded my voice with hypnotic allure. "I lift my chin. If it's my last kiss before he kills me, I want as much as he'll give me. He says, 'I can feel you mooning over your early, tragic demise.'"

With a slow shuffle, I reached Grant, brushed my hand down his arm, dropped my voice to a whisper. "He gives in then. 'You don't need to do anything,' I say. 'I'll do everything for us both.'"

The planes of Grant's broad chest felt real under my palm. The dip between his pecs directed my hand downward.

"Oh, Jesus." Grant gasped and snatched my hand away "Oliver. *Stop.* This is wrong. Even now you're lying. Don't you see that? You're lying about why you want me."

"Let me go." I turned my wrist inside the ring of his fingers.

"No." He tightened his grip. "Listen. You rehabilitated me. You *did* it. I have no doubt I'll work my way up to a career I'll love. My next job will suck, but that's okay, because for the first time in my life, I have a career plan—and that's because of you. Yet somehow, in the process of giving me new life, you've lost yours. I don't want to leave you like this. Help me know how to help you. Should I notify someone, send out an alarm? Do you understand what I'm saying?"

I shook my head. I didn't want to understand.

"When you try to help people who come to you, is this how you feel? Like you see what they can't?" Grant pulled me toward him.

Finally.

He wrapped his thick arms around me, buried me in bulk and skin and muscle and warmth, his embrace more like a parent's than a lover's.

"Dad lied." The words flopped out of my mouth.

"About what?" Grant asked.

"Never mind. I don't know why I said that. Dad never lied. He wasn't a liar. He was the center. Our community revered him. He... took care of me when my mother left, filled my life with magic and friendly people and art until I didn't need her, until I didn't even really remember her."

The muscles in Grant's arms flexed and tightened. "There's something unbearably sad about that, Oliver."

All I managed was a shrug, a twitch to shed his pity.

There's so much silence it's hard to keep pushing sleep away.

"Are you certain he's asleep? It won't do for him to hear this." My mother says her words like Fox Mother Queen. That's the name I give her when she sits on her throne with her back straight and her chin up, like her eyes can see trouble coming from far away. When she speaks from her throne, her voice sounds like she's reading a proclamation from a long paper with a curl at the end. Fox Mother Queen likes words to be neat and final and black, with a lot of signatures at the very end. I know because I sit with her at the dining table on Saturdays and Sundays. I pretend to draw but really I watch her work. I can't sit in her lap because Fox Mother Queen is small, like me, and she doesn't like to be climbed on. Dad and Granddad are bigger than enormous. I can climb on them whenever I want to.

Dad's hair is black—blacker than Fox Mother Queen's words. When I paint my pictures of him, I have to add a dab of indigo to make his hair look exactly right. Dad is Dolphin King. Granddad is The Eagle Emperor. The emperor always gets a capital The before his name, because he's the king of kings. Dolphin King and The Eagle Emperor like to relax. They don't care if I make a mess. "Creativity requires a mess." That's one of The Eagle Emperor's favorite proclamations.

"He's asleep," Dolphin King says to Fox Mother Queen in a very quiet voice. "And you're cruel." His voice is the same quietness of Granddad's and my entire bedroom after Fox Mother Queen reads to me at home, after she kisses my cheek and stops saying anything. It makes me happy that Fox Mother Queen likes the same kind of no noise I like. Behind my closed eyes I hear a tiny ocean wave shhhhh when she slides the book onto my bedside table. She stays with me in the beautiful quiet stillness, tall in her throne pose on the side of my bed, and holds my hand as I fall asleep.

Chapter 75

GRANT

Oliver's head lolled back on the arm I'd wound around his shoulders, eyes open but unfocused. I gave him a shake. "Oliver? *Oliver.* Hey, you're really scaring me here." When I started to move to get him into the car so he could lie down, he jerked against me.

"No." Oliver blurted the word before his eyes refocused, and then bowed his head onto my chest.

I kept my arms around him while he took a few deep breaths, curious to see how he'd explain away his trance, or whatever it had been.

"This is not convincing me you're okay," I said against Oliver's soft hair. I kept one arm around his waist in case he flopped again, and swept my other hand up and down his back to soothe him.

In a low voice I felt on my sternum, Oliver said, "My mother left when I was five. She up and moved to Europe, with almost no notice. Left me and Dad for a job. Something about... the painting I'm working on is making me remember that time. It's..." Oliver huffed a weary laugh. "Not fun. I already lived through her leaving once. I don't need to do it again. I'm going with Freddie to... to take a break from my property. See if that helps."

That seemed like too much information for Oliver to tell me, and I wondered why he had. He'd been eager to get rid of me moments before. "Sounds to me like you're running away."

"Maybe. But if I travel with Freddie we can have... a life together. More of a life."

"Okay," I said with suspicion.

"So I have a favor to ask." Oliver pulled back and looked up at me. "As of when I get on the ferry on Saturday, Freddie and I will be exclusive. That will be our start of something new."

"Sure it will. Keep telling yourself that."

Oliver glared at me.

"Why not let the memory come and be done with it?"

The sudden, stark terror in Oliver's eyes told me why.

"Too much?" I asked.

"It's like... watching a movie, but I *feel* it. A scene in horrible detail in which a mother abandons her young son. I don't *want* the details. I know how that movie ends."

"I get it. But if the memory haunts you, maybe it would help to work with a therap—"

"What would *help*," Oliver interrupted, "would be a *distraction*. With you. Now. That's the favor I'm asking."

"God, your reasoning sucks. Don't think I can't see that."

Oliver steadied his gold-flecked eyes on mine, put his hand on my chest and left it there. "I feel it, Grant. Here. You want me." He splayed his fingers over my heart. "I know you want me."

We stared at each other while my heart ran amok.

I put my hand on top of Oliver's, to keep him close.

Oliver lifted his other hand to free his hair from the binding. That would have been enough to get me hard, but he pulled the mass of hair forward over his shoulders and leaned toward me. Glossy strands draped over my arm, caressed my hand.

The Professor Evil leer and loose hair were almost more than I could resist.

"Traveling with Freddie isn't a solution," I managed to say.

Oliver upped the ante, slid his hand out from under mine, leaned in, used both hands to drape his hair over *my* shoulders. I felt its weight on my shoulder blades. *Christ, why is this such a turn-on?* I had a relentless boner for Oliver's hair. My cock pressed its approval into his abdomen.

"You are so messed up," I said.

Oliver's feral smile promised damage and oblivion. "Now or never."

Touch his beard, my cock suggested, and I did. I stroked his moustache, caressed his beard, the hairs sharp and soft at the same time. I lifted Oliver's hair to drape it down his back, then wound the slippery weight of it around my hand.

With a squirm against me, Oliver said, "No false pretenses this time. Just you and me and a tale I call *The King's Rescue.*"

"Another fantasy, huh?"

Oliver pulled against my hand that held his hair, tried to get closer to me. I didn't let him.

"I want you to fuck me," he panted. He mashed his hard cock against my thigh. "One-time deal. A goodbye fuck."

I swallowed my objections, slid my hands along the curves under his ass cheeks, and lifted him enough to show him I knew what I wanted. When I spread my hands to caress the crease of his ass with my fingertips, his eyes glazed.

"A goodbye, good luck fuck." I slid my fingers farther, stooped to reach between Oliver's legs to where I'd pressed my fist when we'd lost ourselves in the brambles.

He lifted onto his toes. "The... *fuck*—the king doesn't want to be rescued. Not really."

Oliver's words meant nothing to me. I almost couldn't hear them over the sound of his body in my hands. I slid my fingers under his shirt to touch his hip bones, his back muscles, the smooth skin of his shoulders. His skin heated. Skin like warm cream, thick and liquid.

I wanted Oliver relaxed enough to pour onto the ground. I slid his arms inside his T-shirt, pulled it over his head and off. Miles of hair took forever to let go of the shirt, then fell around his shoulders with the swirl and splash of a sequined cape.

The contrast of Oliver's hair against his skin undid me. "Stop talking now."

Oliver shook his head. More hair fell forward over his shoulders.

"I'm going to deconstruct you," I whispered. I spread my fingers up into his hair at the back of his head, put my other arm around the small of his back, and lowered him to ground. "I'm going to leave you in pieces for *him.*"

"For who?"

Oliver's dazed look got to me. I wanted him slack and drooling. "You're right," I said. "He doesn't exist. I'm going to demolish you for *me*, before I let you go."

Oliver gave a slow blink and began to talk again. I caught a few words—*stone wall, far horizon, soldiers.* The story wasn't about us. We lay on the grass in the fresh air of Vashon Island, my favorite place on earth.

"You come in through the window," Oliver panted.

"The *window*? Is that what we're calling it these days?" I reached down to caress Oliver's asshole. "Get your pants off so I can get into your *window*."

Oliver jerked to try to sit up.

"No. Keep your shoulders on the ground." I stretched out beside Oliver, used my fingers to fan his hair into a halo while I enjoyed his squirm and fret as he tried to kick off his shorts and underwear without lifting his shoulders.

"You're *hurting* me," he finally said, his face pained.

"Liar." All I'd done was touch his hair. I bent to put my lips on his, settled there and waited.

Oliver opened his mouth, found my teeth with his tongue. Once he got started, Oliver's kiss grew a mind of its own, demanded and teased at me until I shifted to lie on top of him. I bit and sucked at his mouth as I bullied off my own clothes, all of them, down to the truth.

"No more hiding." My voice had dropped an octave during our diss.

"Let's go to the house," Oliver said. "We need lube."

"No. I like it here." I brushed my hand up Oliver's forehead and over his hair I'd spread out on the thick grass. I wanted to stay outside, to be in control for a change, to make something good happen for someone else instead of taking what I couldn't repay. "I have a condom and lube packet in my wallet."

"Seriously? Hopeful much? Go get them." Oliver tried to push me up.

"Just *wait*."

I needed another few minutes with his skin. God in heaven, *Oliver's skin*. I smoothed the worry line between his eyebrows with my thumb, followed the bridge of his narrow nose, ran my palm over his cheek. Everywhere I touched turned pink. *Cream with a splash of cherry juice.* I laughed and slid half off him to stroke his neat chest, down his abs. His cock, sloppy with pre-cum, had turned so pink it was red.

"I'm ready *now*." Oliver wiggled and pushed against me.

"You don't get a vote." I held him down with my leg.

In a deft move, Oliver slid out from under me before I could grab him, and walked away.

From where I lay, I could follow Oliver's progress under the car. I watched his feet as he approached the shorts I'd flung over the car in my enthusiasm to get naked.

Like a caveman who hadn't eaten in a month, I stood to track him.

As Oliver came back around the car, I got my first frontal view of him naked. He loped toward me, eyes locked on mine, hair a gust of autumn leaves around his upper body.

"Goddamn, you're beautiful," I told him.

Oliver walked into me hard enough to take me down, a clumsy move that hurt the arm I put out to break our fall.

Clumsy and genuine and excellent.

When our bodies met, my brain surrendered to my cock.

Full frontal contact, a flash of joy, then nothing but nerve endings and need.

Chapter 76

OLIVER

My hair fell around Grant's head to make a private space for our faces. "Everything falls apart for the king's rescuer." My fantasy had devolved into rubble, but I kept at it. In an unexpected twist, trying to tell the story kept me from coming too soon.

Sunlight sliced across Grant's strong nose through a gap in my hair. "Nothing happens as planned," I said.

Grant didn't seem to hear me, but I didn't need him to.

He bound me to him tight with his strong arms. The head of his cock caught on and slid past the head of my cock, made me spread my legs and... *Keep talking. Keep talking.*

"The soldiers arrive too... soon." I'd lost the thread of my story. "We lie together on the stone floor. Shouts outside the door. So... close. I'm so close already. Grant. *Grant.* Wait."

The slice of sunlight found the smug upturn of Grant's mouth. "Aw, did I get you too hot too soon?" He rolled us into a patch of shade next to the DeVille and landed on top of me. "Your turn for grass wedgies." His thick thighs between my open legs and his cock on mine made me ignorant.

What's grass? my mind asked.

Grant exhaled on my nipple. "It's been a long time."

"Years and years," I groaned, lost between the two worlds. *When he pushes my arms above my head, I stumble and fall, even though I'm already on my back on the cold stone.*

Rough hands, to make sure I stay the way he wants me, open and honest.

It was like before, in the bramble.

Up close, my body reacted to Grant with confusion, our tryst a fight to the finish with someone I didn't want to hurt. *Too intense. Back off. More. Don't go.* My heart goaded me with beats I couldn't keep up with. I pushed my feet against the ground to pull away from his mouth, from his kisses along my hip bone. *He won't slow down.* He wouldn't let me feel between strokes of his agile hands, another bite of his confident mouth, another pivot in a scene I hadn't engineered.

I scooted back until my head hit the front wheel of the DeVille and my cock hit the underside of Grant's scruffy chin. I froze and stared up at him. My hands rested against the tire above my head, even though he wasn't holding them anymore.

"Better," he said. "Now put your hands on me." With a tilt of his head and a sinister smile, Grant lifted my hips and bent to lick my hole.

I *screamed*—I couldn't help it. Slapped my hands on Grant's head, tried to escape, banged my head on the hubcap.

He licked me again and pressed his palm onto my boner.

I didn't know what the hell I was doing. He'd turned me into an animal, into instinct and thoughtless reaction, and it *scared* me. I grabbed his hair, tried to pull him off, but he was stronger, kept at me, followed as I writhed and grunted, pinned me against the tire with his shameless tongue and insistent palm, pressed spit into me, then his tongue, then lube, too much to keep up with.

Without meaning to, I began to use my hands in his hair to direct him. I stared at my fingers wound tight with black hair grown long over the summer. My grunts and exhales changed tempo as Grant figured me out. His *teeth*, for a split second, against the wet rim of my ass, convulsed me. A knot formed where the back of my head hit the hubcap again and again.

"Get *in me*, you *jerk*." I yanked hard on Grant's hair.

Before my next breath, Grant stroked two lubed fingers up inside me with a twist. I pressed my head into the hubcap for leverage to push onto his fingers.

With his free arm, Grant pulled me sideways away from the tire. "Condom," he ordered in a voice deepened to a hard scratch. A wrapped condom landed on my chest. He rotated his hand to rub his fingers against my prostate.

"Holy... *fuck you*." The condom fell from my fingers. "*Stop it*. I can't concentrate."

"Good." Grant pulled his fingers out of me and knee-walked his cock to within range of the condom.

"Holy fuck indeed," I muttered. I left the condom on my chest while I took the measure of him, worried the condom wouldn't be long enough.

"Waiting," Grant said with a load of sarcasm. He wiped his lubed fingers on my thigh.

"Rude beast." I unwrapped the condom and rolled it over Grant's cock, smoothed it down with the last of the lube squeezed from the packet.

Grant grabbed my wrists.

"Go slow," I said. "You're bigger around than I'm used to, and a lot longer."

"I *knew* it."

I inhaled to reprimand Grant's brag, didn't have time, used that breath to manage the ache from his cock sliding in—not far, not *too* far. *Far enough.* I swallowed a mouthful of saliva then left my mouth open.

We watched each other. I heard a distant horn blast from the Tacoma ferry.

The rock of Grant's hips seemed involuntary. Shoulders so wide I couldn't see past him. Dark hair spread down his pecs to become a swirl around his belly button.

"Breathe *now*." Grant patted my chest. "You froze. Take a breath."

I sucked in air, a lot of air, moaned it out, drew him into me, and widened my eyes as he... "*Fuck*, you're long."

Grant slid and *slid* into me. I lifted my chin to make room, as if he'd need my esophagus too.

"Too long? I can stop." He pulled out a little, with a smirk.

"*Don't.*" His cock in me hurt, but not enough to matter.

With controlled movements in and out, Grant filled me. He leaned over me, brought my raised legs with him, and said in his ragged voice, "You make me want to be so filthy."

"Please." I didn't want to get away anymore. I only cared about one thing by then. It wasn't his molten-hot cock inside me or his bulk that blocked the sun. It wasn't his lubed hand from my ass wrapped in my hair or his dirty tongue on my lips or his teeth across my tongue.

It was the way he *found* me.

I open and he captures me.

No. That wasn't how it went.

Soldiers crash against the locked door. He lays me onto the stone and thrusts into me like he owns me.

He captures me and I open.

I found an emperor lying in a ditch. He told the ghosts where I lived, fucked me with a vengeance, and rode away to claim his own kingdom.

I nail the fortress windows closed so I won't see his departure up the thread of road, then turn away to the open door and sail off with the man of my dreams.

Beautiful story.

I came with Grant's urgent hand around my cock and his tongue so far down my throat he touched himself.

The end.

Chapter 77

OLIVER

When Grant came, he drooled onto my throat, eyes open, gone and shaking. He'd humped up into me until he'd driven us out of the DeVille's shade.

We blinked at each other in the sunlight.

I'd screamed so much my voice cracked when I said, "Goodbye." He'd freed me. I wanted to go. I watched his eyes, watched him comprehend my dismissal.

With slow consideration, Grant pulled out of me and backed off on his knees, swiped at the saliva on his chin. The cramp in my ass made me hiss. We'd breached enough walls to fuck ourselves into a new order. When my ass righted itself, I stood to brush myself off, to rid myself of grass and grit and Grant, and looked around for my clothes.

Grant didn't move except to close his eyes.

The strangest thing was how calm I felt. "Don't come see me when you're back on the island on Friday," I said. "This was our final goodbye, and you have my sincerest thanks for it."

Calm wasn't the right word for how I felt. It was more... *distant* or *vacant* or *empty*. Whatever it was, I liked it.

"Promise," Grant said, all traces of flirty desire gone. "Promise me."

"Um. What?" I overplayed my surprise, to make a sarcastic point. "We have no future, so promises need not apply."

"You're different, Oliver, from when we first met. I hope I haven't done any-thing to make you—"

"You didn't *do* anything." The words fell between us with a messy, impolite plop, and my shirt suddenly required my full attention to turn right side out. I pulled it on before I said, "Freddie is leaving Vashon sooner than expected this summer, which reminds me of my mother leaving. That's all. It's not about you." It's *not*, I assured myself.

"Well, whatever you have to tell yourself to get through the day," Grant said. "But I want your promise that you won't do it."

"Do what?" I opened the driver's door of the DeVille to roll up the windows, hit the automatic lock, and grabbed the keys. I was being a total bastard. It felt bracing. I slammed the door. I needed to get in the shower before my fuck-high wore off.

"Promise me you won't do what Aza did," Grant said.

"That's absurd." I pulled my hair up and back, held it with one hand while I dug around in my shorts pocket for a hair band.

"Oliver?" Grant prompted. He looked pitiful, slouched on the ground, naked and sweaty and smeared with dirt. The used condom, still attached to his dick, draped over his thigh. He looked raw and serious and maddening, and I couldn't wait to turn my back on him.

"*Okay.*" My voice came out loud and impatient. I strode to the gate to escape my own harsh word. "I hate it that you even wondered."

"Say it. Tell me what you promise."

"*I fucking promise I won't kill myself.*" My shout propelled me out past the holly wall. In a voice laced with resentment I couldn't hold back, I said, "I promise that if I haven't dispelled the microscopic rain cloud above my head before I leave on Saturday with Freddie, I will reach out for professional help."

"Thank you. Keep the contacts I texted you, for when you try to leave your property and freak out and things blow up with Freddie."

"Fuck *off*, Grant. God, I know I butted into your life, but then I called it quits. Now you need to stop butting into my life."

That made Grant look guilty, on top of the hurt.

I turned away from him, from all of him. "Close the gate when you leave."

We needed a clean cut. The cleaner the better. *Amputate, cauterize, move on.* My body felt loose and coordinated. I broke into an easy trot, certain of my direction, as if I'd been aimed and released from a bow.

In the house, itchy and eager, I stuffed my dirty clothes into the laundry hamper and grabbed my toothbrush to scrub the taste of Grant out of my mouth.

Not until after my shower, as I passed the towel over my clean body, did I put two and two together.

Grant will stay overnight in Seattle.

I could visit the treehouse before Grant returned on Friday. I could put Aza to rest, forgive myself, and let Aza go before I escaped with Freddie.

Drugged from the sex and the shower, I skipped dinner in favor of an early bedtime, toppling onto the couch as if I'd been bashed on the head with a rock.

I remembered Grant saying he planned to go to Seattle in the morning on Thursday. I waited until noon to venture to the treehouse, sneaking through the foliage to check for Dad's bike. I didn't see it, but I stayed hidden, parked my sore ass on a rock behind a rhododendron to listen for signs of activity from the treehouse, to make sure.

The familiar setting made me remember more about Aza. We'd flung ropes, measured, hauled, and hammered for months. After he'd struck the final nail and I'd slid in the last shelf, Aza had moved into the treehouse, for the most part. He did better in school after that. I'd hoped he'd be happy enough to stay longer than he did. He could have stayed forever.

Why hadn't it worked?

For the first time, I confronted my painful questions head-on. Could I have tried harder to persuade Clementine and Robert to keep Aza on Vashon longer? What if I'd realized, somehow, that Aza's call from the bus stop was more than *thank you*? If I'd known it was *thank you and goodbye forever*, could I have stopped him? Or at least delayed him?

Could I have kept Aza alive?

Aza's phone call stumped me. I snagged on it, unable to free myself. I closed my eyes and let the tree trunk at my back bear the weight of my head. A bird chirped and rustled in a salmonberry thicket in a patch of sunlight to my left.

New York City is trippy, Aza had said on the call. *It's so much, Ollie. It's everything I imagined it would be.*

My tangle of emotions flailed a loose end at me. I grabbed at it and pulled.

It's everything I imagined it would be.

On a Sunday before he came to live with us, Aza and I had hiked into the western woods. The sea appeared through the trees now and then, a deep blue down below. As we walked, Aza told me about his classmate who'd killed herself the previous weekend. *I think about it sometimes, you know,* he'd said with a darted a glance at me. I put my hand on his shoulder to stop him from walking on. He turned to face me. *You do?* I asked. Aza shrugged. *It's only a thought. Like a way to tell myself I have something I can control.* The tight clutch of his hug surprised me. He'd whispered, *I'd never, Ollie—not unless I really couldn't imagine anything else.* I'd felt relieved, comforted by the scope of Aza's prodigious imagination, but I'd also told Clementine, who'd called Aza's psychiatrist.

In the forest under the treehouse, I asked myself what else I could have done.

Before those of us who loved Aza could help him imagine something more, imagine something else, *anything else*, the world ate him and spit his empty shell into the cold sea.

Alone in the woods, I let the pain of Aza rise. My failure crushed me for long minutes of a desperate cry. I let it come, slipped through the phone to hold Aza, to stand with him in that frozen phone booth, to imagine for him.

When I'd bawled and sighed enough, I dried my eyes and wiped the snot off my face with my T-shirt. Sat and breathed.

The tangle of Aza loosened and fell to the ground, sorted itself into one long string stretched from me at the treehouse to Aza in the phone booth—a taut line, unbreakable forever. I tugged on it and heard his voice, sent love and sorrow and requests for forgiveness down the line and felt Aza's answering tug.

Grant's infinity symbol settled around us. Aza and I hung our arms over the sides to use the loops as life preservers, the twist a bond between us. I splashed Aza with seawater—a dark joke I knew he would appreciate. He laughed and splashed me back.

The journey up the treehouse staircase felt bittersweet, but in a new way. Grant's discovery of the treehouse felt *right*. In a couple of days, when Grant left for good, that would feel right too. He'd restored a neglected shrine to the work of art it was meant to be.

My gratitude to Grant didn't keep me from doing what I did next, and his unlawful occupancy didn't make what I did defensible. But I did it anyway.

I took careful photos to use as reference, so I could replace everything before Grant returned. Heart on overdrive, I pulled pages off the wall, stacked them, and slid the stack into the bag with his journals.

Then I ran.

I squeezed my upper arms against my sides to feel my life preserver, my secure connection with Aza. His rebel laughter rang out as I raced away with my plunder.

In the house, I filled bottles with water, gathered food and pillows, stuffed my sleeping bag into its sack, then paused to consider. I'd need a flashlight lantern. And extra batteries. Sketchbook and pencils. I filled more bags. I had the afternoon, a night, and a morning to camp in the DeVille and study Grant's inner world, to immerse myself in evidence that I was capable of saving *someone*, even if the only thing I'd done was save Grant from an uncreative life.

I slumped into the back seat of DeVille, turned to lean against the door, and shuffled through the stack of papers to find the one I wanted to study first—the one with Grant's orange circles and penciled words. Afternoon sunlight fell over my shoulder onto the page.

Liar. Prisoner. Ruled by secrets. Mistaken about Freddie. Lost his mother. Imperious. Sweet biceps. Surrounded by ghosts. Kisses like a dream.

In the middle of the page, Grant had written *Oliver's Onion.* I rummaged until I found his page with the messy infinity symbol, from the center of the galaxy swirl.

Suddenly it all made sense.

Two onions, with a turn in between.

I squeezed my arms to my sides again and blinked, mourned the layers of Aza's onion we hadn't found in time.

On a fresh page in my sketchbook I drew overlapped circles and began to write out Grant's layers. *Magic with kids. Smells like pine and dust. Loves to be outdoors. Huge. Funny when rude. Intrusive. Adored by his nephew.*

Kisses like a dream.

I closed my eyes and let the sketchbook slide to the floor. *No. Don't get sidetracked.*

I sighed and refocused, sorted Grant's pages into categories—rules, nature drawings, drawings of the tweens, views of the treehouse, self-portraits. In most of the self-portraits, Grant had depicted himself as a tree. Every drawing burst with honesty.

He'd journeyed so far beyond my assignments.

Except for the *Oliver's Onion* page, none of the pages from the wall were about me. The journals were another story.

I'd already looked through the first journal, the one I'd taken the day I discovered Grant's presence in the treehouse. Journals 1 and 2 seemed to be full of me, though not in a flattering way. Most of those entries made me uncomfortable—*LIES TO FREDDIE* and *WHO IS HIS ART FOR?* and *DOESN'T*

TRUST HIS PALS. Most of the other entries, the ones not about me, made me laugh, like *LASAGNA HIGH* and *MY BEST FRIEND IS A TREE* and *FARTS KILL*. A few of the entries threatened to make me cry, like *TOO HUNGRY TO HIKE* and *TOTAL ASSETS: $35.26*.

I fell asleep Thursday night in the midst of journal 4, woke the next morning under a snowfall of papers I'd somehow managed not to crumple.

After a quick visit to the house to resupply and charge my phone, I settled back into the DeVille. Sketchbook on my lap to provide a white background, I photographed every page from the wall and every page of journals 1 and 2, plus selected pages from the other journals.

Because of me, somehow, Grant had turned a corner. The photographs were proof, in case I forgot. When I finally turned off my phone, I felt *done*—done with the past and ready to move on.

Chapter 78

GRANT

I'd lost control of myself with Oliver, there in the grass by the car. He'd bludgeoned me with sex to protect his wounds and I'd fallen for it. *Again*.

While I berated myself, I couldn't stop smiling.

The man did things to me, unprecedented things, things I didn't regret, even though I probably should. I'd thrown Oliver around like a rag doll, bitten him from stem to stern, immersed myself in the pink pulse of him. His attempts to boss me around while I did whatever I wanted to him had boosted me to all-new levels of arousal.

The captured king fucked like a barbarian.

After Oliver left me at the DeVille, I put on my clothes and returned to the treehouse in a daze. At least my climax fog hadn't kept me from getting a promise out of him. If only I knew whether I believed him. As I reflected on Oliver's emotional extremes, I felt less confident about his promise.

I decided to reach out to Freddie for input. An online search turned up Freddie's impressive website (*Fredrik Tolliver, Award-Winning Freelance Journalist*), and a cell number.

Freddie responded to my first text with, *No, I won't talk with you about Oliver. He's fine. Leave me alone. I'm writing.* I texted again, got no response, and didn't try a third time. I didn't want Freddie to block my number.

The next morning began with a curse when my phone alarm went off at 5:30. I'd worked out the timing for adding a shower at Clementine's before we caught the 7:20 ferry. Grass-stained elbows and the reek of nasty sex wouldn't impress my potential employers, or Mitch.

I pedaled through swirls of mist in dawn's suffused light and mooned over Oliver. Out past the Willow Way corner where I'd seen Oliver zoom into the forest, I stopped to check the yellow flowers I'd puked on, glad to see they'd recovered.

I winked at the dew-laden blossoms. "How would you like to be my lucky charm?" Maybe an early call would irritate Freddie enough to want to berate me in real time.

"What the hell?" Freddie said when he answered. "It's not even six the fuck o'clock. *God*, you're a persistent dickhead."

"Please don't hang up. Give me one minute. Please."

On a heavy sigh Freddie said, "Okay. Whatever. Go."

"I'm genuinely worried about Oliver. He told me he hasn't left his property in over a year, but I think it's been much longer, and his behavior makes me think he's moving toward a crisis point of some kind. Would you be willing to call Oliver before your trip on Saturday and try to talk with him about it? Maybe he'll open up to you."

"Oh, he'll *open up* to me all right—once he's away from you."

I tried to focus past Freddie's hostility. "Don't you get it? I don't think Oliver *can* leave his property, even if he wants to go with you. I'd be surprised if he could leave without therapy."

"Fascinating." The sarcasm in Freddie's voice made me lay the bike onto the road so I could stomp around.

"Come on," I said. "Can't you see that Oliver is struggling? This isn't the time for posturing." I should have stopped there. "Or for being threatened by Oliver's bit on the side."

Freddie laughed. "That's what you think? That I'm threatened by you?"

"I know you are."

"I tell you what, while Oliver and I are away on our relaxing, *sex-filled* vacation this weekend, I'll mention your concerns. If I think your claims have any validity, I'll decide how to handle it. I'm not going to badger Oliver. That's your thing."

I huffed, exasperated. The guy seemed willfully obtuse. "It's like you don't hear a single thing I'm saying. If you see Oliver at the ferry, he will have gotten past the hard part without you."

"Then more power to him. He told me he would meet me at the ferry. Unlike you, I'm not going to second-guess him."

"When was the last time you saw Oliver in person?" I asked.

"He requires a lot of alone time."

"Jeez," I muttered. "No wonder he's got problems."

"I *heard* that. You've made your case. I said I'd mention it to him. Now I'm going to block your number." The line went dead.

I kicked at the bike tire in frustration. I *did* second-guess Oliver, but *someone* needed to. I stomped a bit more and decided Oliver's promise and Freddie's reluctant agreement would have to suffice. I had my own problems to worry about.

I arrived at Clementine's breathless and made a beeline for the shower, mindful of the timeline. When I got out she said, "You look nice."

"Why thank you, ma'am." I'd "ironed" my only button-up shirt by arranging it on the bed at the treehouse, then sitting on it while I read a book.

Our comfortable silence in the car lasted until Clementine turned onto Vashon Highway at the north end and I asked, "Do you know how Oliver's getting to the ferry on Saturday?"

"Last I heard, he was going to drive the van to the upper lot. Talia said she'd drive it back to his place after her shift."

That meant no one would be with Oliver when he tried to leave his property. I wasn't sure what to do about it, if anything. Probably I should butt out.

The line for the ferry snaked up the hill. Clementine eased up to the end of the line and turned off the engine. Ahead of us, commuters stood beside cars, leaned on open doors, fiddled with phones, sipped from thermos cups, chatted, and waved to one another. To pass the time while we waited, I bombarded Clementine with questions.

"What were Oliver's parents like? He never talks about his mom. Did she die?"

"Not that I know of," Clementine said. "I knew Lucca, Oliver's dad, a long time before he met Madeleine. I got to know her a bit when Oliver was a baby. She's where Oliver gets his striking coloring from. Lord, Madeleine was a beauty. Lucca was devoted to her. At first, anyway."

"What happened?"

"Madeleine was very ambitious. She was in her early twenties when she took an art class Lucca taught on Mercer Island, where she grew up. After they married, she moved to Vashon and commuted to Seattle to continue at the university."

Although we couldn't see the dock from our spot in the line-up, I heard the ferry arrive with a *swoosh* of waves and a clatter of metal. A few minutes later, a clump of traffic surged up the hill from the dock.

"Why did Lucca stop being devoted to her?" I asked.

"She got pregnant about a year after they married—right around the time she started graduate school. I think that was when they faltered."

Way down the hill in front of us, vehicles in line began to move forward.

"By the time Madeleine finished her graduate degrees, she was also holding down a full-time job in the city," Clementine said. "She had an apartment near downtown where she stayed during the work week."

"Did she and Lucca split up?"

"Not at first, but Lucca railed against the arrangement. He and Matteo raised Oliver on Vashon while Madeleine spent most of her time in Seattle."

We followed the car in front of us down the hill, rattled over the ramp to board the ferry. I checked the deckhands directing traffic into lanes on the ferry. None of them were Talia.

After a long silence, Clementine said, "Madeleine had a gift for banking and finance. She worked her way up the ranks at a big bank in Seattle, but refused job offers that would have taken her away from Oliver and Lucca."

"I already know this story doesn't have a happy ending," I said.

"She got an offer she told Lucca she couldn't refuse. In Europe somewhere."

My heart gave a sympathetic lurch for Oliver. I tapped my chest with my fist. "Ow."

"I know. It was especially sad because Oliver was devoted to her."

"Do you know where she is now?" I asked.

"No, and I'd be surprised if Oliver knew. I can say with great confidence that since Madeleine left, I've never once heard Oliver mention her."

"That seems extreme, even for Oliver. There must be more to the story."

"Probably. But by the time Madeleine left, I'd moved to the periphery of Lucca's community. My own marriage wasn't going well. I had a new baby and I felt..."

"That was Aza?"

Clementine nodded.

"You felt what?" I raised my voice to be heard over the rumble as the ferry pushed away from the dock.

"I was going to say I felt *ambivalent*, but that makes me sound like a heartless bitch about my only child. I wish to God I knew how much Aza's problems had to do with my ineptitude as a mother."

I tapped my chest again with my fist, to prevent the hollow sensation from growing.

Through the openings in the side of the ferry, we had a view northwest over Puget Sound. The mass of Bainbridge Island floated past.

"I guess Madeleine didn't visit after she moved to Europe?" I asked.

"Not that I know of. I once heard Lucca refer to their divorce as a 'documented amputation.' Madeleine abdicated all claims to Lucca's properties, income, art assets... everything." Clementine cleared her throat. "Including Oliver."

"Man, that's harsh," I said.

"It wouldn't have been a financial hardship for Madeleine. She had her own wealth, from her family and her career."

"Must have been a hell of a hardship for Oliver, though."

"Yes. A big one."

Clementine's mention of Lucca's art assets made me remember something else I'd been curious about. "Why doesn't Oliver share his art? I don't know much about art, but even the guy's doodles seem brilliant enough to knock the world on its ass."

"I really don't know." Clementine shook her head. "I used to push him to do more shows. He did several in Seattle, others in San Francisco and Chicago, but all before Lucca died."

"Died how?"

"Heart attack. Very sudden."

I wondered if that had been the trigger for Oliver to stick to his property. "How old was Oliver when his dad died?"

"Twenty-two. I was no help to Oliver, I'm sad to say. Aza had died the year before. It took me a long time to notice how much Oliver had withdrawn." Clementine looked out at the view for a few minutes, then said, "If you ever get the chance, you should ask Oliver for a tour of the archives room."

"Every *inch* of that house is an archive," I said.

"Yes, but there's more, and very little of the art on display is Oliver's. The decor in the house is mostly a memorial to his ancestors. He comes from a long line of Italian artists. Matteo, Lucca's dad, emigrated from Florence in his early twenties with his parents and his wife, Violetta. They were all artists descended from artists."

I remembered the sign on Oliver's mailbox: *24281 Violetta Road.* "Doesn't Oliver have cousins or uncles or any other relatives?"

"Not in America. Not that I know of. After Matteo's parents died in Boston, he and Violetta came west, drawn by rumors of the quality of the light. They brought their art collection with them—heirloom pieces from Italy, from Matteo's and Violetta's families, plus the artwork they created, and pieces they acquired on their journey across the country."

"I hope they had a security team." I paused to marvel at the travel logistics and expenses.

"I wouldn't be surprised if they did," Clementine said.

"Was Violetta alive when Oliver was born?"

"No. She passed when Lucca was a young man. Matteo lived on for thirty more years. He and Lucca showed their art in galleries and museums all over North America. So many art shows I lost count. They made and collected more art, adding to their legacy. They designed the house to include a museum-quality archive room."

The day I'd lugged my duffel bag of dirty laundry to Oliver's house and nosed around, I'd seen a closed door next to Oliver's little nooky room. That must have been the archive room. I took a mental walk around the house. "Yeah. Wow. Not a small room."

"Lucca gave me a tour of it once."

"Really?"

"It was..." Clementine shook her head. "I spent the entire time in tears. The sheer beauty packed into that one room. He showed me a pile of letters from museums, from collectors and curators—requests to borrow or buy pieces from "The Rossi Collection," or to at least be allowed a tour."

"Damn. That's cool," I said.

"People sometimes came to the house, by invitation only. Business-suited, very deferential people who'd spend hours in the archive room. That all ended when Lucca died."

"So—what? Oliver makes amazing art and lobs it into the archive room?"

"I think so. He's always creating—he's proficient in a wide variety of media, and I've seen many pieces in process, but the decor in the house rarely changes, so those pieces must go somewhere. When I asked him about it, he shrugged and changed the subject."

"I don't like this," I said. "It doesn't seem healthy."

"At some point, after all the losses, I think Oliver—"

"He stopped trying. Shifted his focus to helping others."

Clementine gave a curt nod. She clammed up after that, like she needed time alone with the thought of not trying. She closed her eyes and reclined her seat back a few inches.

I gave her space, listened to the wet *shushhh shushhh* of the ferry's passage, and digested the new information. Though our circumstances differed, I could relate to Oliver's losses.

My family's printing company would have failed if not for the hours my siblings and I worked. That was what our parents told us. For the first time, I saw how our parents valued their business more than their children. We represented labor-hours. They created us, then sacrificed our childhoods for the company's greater good.

If my parents had liquidated their business and gotten regular, nine-to-five jobs, I could have slept until school started instead of working an early shift. I could have done my homework at home instead of working an afternoon shift. I could have played outside. We could have eaten dinner together. I could have had a birthday party.

I suddenly wished someone had reported my parents to Child Protective Services.

I put my fist to my chest a third time, blinked hard, and tapped my heart with gentle beats, a request to come back to life, an attempt to save my own life. No wonder the overburdened, neglected child in me didn't want to work. No wonder he needed a summer off. He'd never had one.

I lost my childhood.

Clementine slept—mouth slightly open, hands together in her lap—while I leaked tears. To keep from disturbing her with my sniffles, I got out and walked to the opening in the side of the ferry to look out over the water and feel the moist breeze on my face.

I'd lost my childhood.

Oliver had lost all the people he loved most.

Maybe the broken place in Oliver broke more every time Freddie flew away. I could understand how going with Freddie might seem to Oliver like a good solution, a salve for his pain. But Freddie wasn't the layer where Oliver hurt.

And finding a job I didn't hate wasn't the layer where I hurt.

Our answers, the answers with the power to mend our breaks, lay deeper, way down in the hurt at the original wound, where neither of us wanted to go.

Deep inside, the lonely children we still were sewed the scar tissue closed, sewed again, sewed through trial and terror, groped for tools small enough to fit our small hands, tried and tried to rise above the bleeding.

Shouts for help through layers and fears and years.

Don't forget about me.

Chapter 79

OLIVER

Friday noon found me at the kitchen sink washing fruit for the Whidbey trip when a text came in from Grant. I dried the last apple and picked up my phone.

Got an interview at a copy shop by a park. Couldn't have done it without you. Back to Vashon this evening with Clem.

Grant's timeline meant I could finish packing for Whidbey before I returned his stuff to the treehouse. I stashed the apples in a plastic bin in the fridge with the bag of homemade protein bars I'd discovered in the bottom of the chest freezer.

I wondered how much Freddie would need to work while we were on Whidbey, and whether I trusted him to stick to work with the man he'd hooked up with there.

When all I had left to pack were conundrums, I called Freddie.

"Hey, you," Freddie said. "Listen, when you get to the dock tomorrow, don't look for Mom's minivan. Cathy's loaning me her Jetta." Cathy, Freddie's sister, must have driven up from Oregon for a visit.

"I don't know what a Jetta looks like," I said. "What color is it?"

"I don't know. Silver? I'll stand by the car. Look for me."

"Should I bring a pillow? And how much food will we need? Will you bring an ice chest?"

"Sure, bring a pillow." I heard the smile in Freddie's voice. "It's not a wilderness trek, babe. It's two ferry rides with an hour and a half of driving in between. And there's plenty of food on Whidbey to buy when we get there."

"Oh."

"You're being very cute about this."

"I feel ignorant," I confessed.

"Hey, it's understandable. You've been the head honcho at your art ranch for a long time. This trip is taking you out of your comfort zone. Relax. I'll take care of you."

With my packing questions answered, I was too distracted by the need to return Grant's things to the treehouse to dwell on the note of condescension in Freddie's voice.

"Thanks for your help, Freddie. See you tomorrow." I ended the call and headed to the DeVille, which pulsed with magnetic force. I power walked past the garage, sprinted along the trail to the holly gate.

Splayed over the back seat in the afternoon warmth, I allowed myself a last look at the page with the orange circles and tried to justify keeping it. The steady drone of a bee too fat to slip in through the cracked window made my eyelids close for longer than a blink.

"Are you certain he's asleep? It won't do for him to hear this."

I startled and widened my eyes. It had been days since I'd felt the memory stalk me. It crept up most often in the house, when I tried to sleep. I'd lie awake on the couch in the great room as the house filled with ghosts.

I was ten when Granddad found the orange couch in Tacoma. He'd brought it home and filled half the great room with it, then persuaded me to park on it for hours while he worked on a new quilt. I'd lounged and sketched, lounged and read, lounged and eaten, tried to ignore him as he draped fabric over me and the couch, muttered about geometry and math, flashed his compass and scissors, conducted an opus at his sewing machine. Granddad had named that quilt *How the New Couch Complements You, Especially When You Glare at Me and Your Face Turns Red.*

Granddad always named his quilts starting with *How.* On my first day of third grade he gave me a quilt named *How You Spent Your Summer Painting Green Portraits That Made Everyone Look Sick.*

After Granddad died, Dad and I loaned the quilt with the longest title to the Museum of Contemporary Art and Craft in San Francisco under a twenty-year agreement. It was Granddad's most intricate and famous creation, a quilt he made for me when I was twelve. The sign holder on the wall at the museum had to be specially made to fit the title: *How You and I Went Camping and It*

Rained the Whole Time and We Didn't Go Home, Even Though the Playing Cards Got Wet and We Ran out of Blueberry White Chocolate Muffins and You Made up a Story You Told Me for an Entire Day While That One Asshole Bird Chirped in the Background.

I grew up ferrying scraps of fabric and bits of thread on the bottoms of my socks and inside the legs of my pants and pajamas. Knowing they were there, the flotsam of home, helped me fall asleep. I missed them.

My heavy hands pinned Grant's drawing with the orange circles to my chest in the DeVille. Granddad's sewing machine stitched at the edge of sound, piecing together a new quilt. *How the Ghosts Finally Found You.*

I don't want to fall asleep.

The bee buzzed above my head in a constant hiss of tires on rain.

"Are you certain he's asleep? It won't do for him to hear this."

"He's asleep," Dolphin King says in a very quiet voice. *"And you're cruel."*

Fox Mother Queen takes a big breath. *"Me not taking this job would be like you giving up art. I'm not asking you to do that. I would never ask you to do that."*

When she stops talking, Dad doesn't say anything.

"Lucca," she says, *"We can really be together. You would love Geneva. I know you would. Please move with me."* My mother sounds sad when she says that part. Sad gray edged with opalescent gold, like she's sad that being in love with her work means we have to move, but also happy because in Geneva she can be with her Fox Son every single day instead of only on Saturdays and Sundays. I keep my smile to myself and don't snuggle into Dad with happiness.

"You already know my answer," Dad says.

"Won't you please compromise? Please. I don't want to hurt him."

"Then don't go. It's your choice."

"Lucca, I'm begging you." I hear a rustle and open my eyes just for a quick second. My mother's emerald green dress sounds like a gust of dried leaves when she moves off her seat to kneel in front of my dad. *"You career is more mobile than mine. I love you both so much, but if I don't take this job I'll... I'll waste away. It's a great honor to be asked to take this position, a great opportunity. I'll help so many people. Please let's do this together, for all our sakes. We'll bring Matteo. You'll take Europe by storm. We have more than enough resources to do it however we want to. Isn't there any way at all you'd be willing? If not for me or for us, then for... him. Imagine him growing up immersed in the art and history there. He would love that."*

"How the hell would you know?"

"His favorite book is Hart's History of Italian Renaissance Art.*" Fox Mother Queen sounds calm and sure. I know Dad will say yes.*

Moving to Europe is the hardest thing to keep still about. My favorite painting, by Mr. John William Waterhouse, lives in the United Kingdom. It's the one of Ophelia in a bright blue dress. If she wore a crown, she would look exactly like Fox Mother Queen, even including her sad face. Granddad showed me the United Kingdom in our atlas. He tells me stories with his fingers in the atlas, like about when he was a boy in Florence, Italy. When we live in Europe we can all go on a trip to visit the United Kingdom and Florence. On a train!

I have to put a bubble around living together in Europe to freeze my wiggle so I can be still and listen and record all the words they say. I make it a pretty bubble with tiny rainbows, like the ones Granddad knows how to paint. After we get to the ferry dock and I tell my Fox Mother Queen goodbye-for-now until Friday night when she comes home again, and after Granddad tucks me in tonight, I'll pop my pretty bubble and listen.

Dad clears his throat and bounces his leg. "If you do this... Madeleine, if you leave, I'll get a legal document. To keep you from... To keep..." Dad's hand on my hair stops petting. "To keep... him. Do you understand?"

My Fox Mother Queen takes a fast breath, like she stepped her paw on a steel trap under the trickster grass.

I shut off my hearing more, to make more space between their words and my ears so I can be still.

"I will fight for sole custody." That voice isn't Dolphin King. It's only Dad, my Dad who really means it this time.

The next silence inside the car is longest. At first, to stay awake, I add black specks to my bubble that holds Europe and living together all in one place all the time. Granddad showed me how shiny bubbles reflect, but I can't get it right. I don't know how to paint a bubble trapped in black.

My dad doesn't breathe for the whole long silence. I try to breathe for us both while we wait for Fox Mother Queen to say what I know she will say, that if her king and her Fox Son won't go to Europe, she will stay with us. Of course she will. Breathing for two people makes me much sleepier. It makes me sleepy to death, as Granddad says. I want to hear Fox Mother Queen say she'll stay, but I can't wait. Sleep takes me with grabby hands. I soften in the claws and dream. I dream what happens next.

"He'll never understand." Dad starts to cry—that's how I know I'm dreaming. "You don't see him after you leave on Monday mornings, Madeleine. He cries for hours. All day Tuesday he mopes. On Wednesday, he tells me how many hours until you get home Friday evening." Dad cries harder. His leg moves away from my foot.

Since it's only a dream, I don't have to worry about anything. A dream is a story about something that didn't really happen. In real life, I'm only taking a nap on my bed. Across the room, The Eagle talks to his sewing machine. Dad is out in the courtyard telling stories to our friends to make them fold onto the picnic table with laughter.

My life, the one with Dad laughing, is my real life.

I hear the rustle again. I feel my mother's hand on my chest and her breath on my face and hear her quiet voice above my head. "Tell him it's my fault. If you think it will make it easier for him, tell him everything painful is my fault."

Fox Mother Queen bends closer. I smell her Monday morning perfume for going back to work in the city. She whispers to me in my ear. "I will always, always love you, my Coyote-Fox. Always and forever." One kiss on my cheek, soft and exactly right.

One final kiss before she stops being my Fox Mother Queen.

After that day, she is only Fox, a lady Fox in the stories Dad and Granddad tell me, a glittering red fox who sneaks around our property on many secret adventures.

I sometimes catch tiny sudden pieces of her. A flash of copper fluff at the tip of a tail behind a tree. A sigh of paws over dried leaves. One red hair in a spot I've never been. Maybe.

Dad and Granddad's stories of Fox make me laugh. I ask to hear them again. Their stories are perfect.

They keep my mother from being Fox Mother Queen who didn't choose me. Their stories are perfect.

They keep my dad from being the king who stole his son for himself.

Chapter 80

GRANT

"**You did** well, Grant." Mitch slowed the BMW so we could look for Clementine's Volvo among the vehicles lined up along Fauntleroy Way. Friday afternoon commuters and island weekenders crowded the road and the boarding lanes at the West Seattle ferry dock.

"I did do splendidly, didn't I?" I bragged.

Kai snickered from the back seat.

Mitch's praise made me feel less like a sad ex-relative and more like an equal. He'd even trusted me with a spare key to his house.

"There." Kai raised his skinny arm to point over my shoulder. Clementine must have left work early. She'd almost reached the dock.

Mitch stopped beside the Volvo and put on the BMW's flashers. "See you Monday?"

"Yep. I'll ride with Clementine to the ferry dock on Vashon, then catch the water taxi to downtown." Monday was shaping up to be a big downer. "Maybe I'll go to a park on my way to your house." The life seemed to have gone out my voice. I got out and opened the back door to tell Kai goodbye.

"You'd like the botanical park," Kai said. "It has trees and trails and islands. It's *big*."

"That sounds super." I didn't have the heart to tell him it wouldn't be big enough.

Kai almost tore my neck off with a fierce hug. "See you soon," he said.

All the way back to Vashon on the ferry, and then to Clementine's cottage in her car, I chanted to myself. *Kai, income, botanical park, Mitch*—a litany of city gratitude to distract me from *Vashon, deep woods, Oliver, Clover, Abelino, Penelope, Jill, Clementine.*

Clementine and I shared a dinner of sandwiches at her kitchen table until we'd talked long enough to make a bike ride to the treehouse unwise in the twilight.

"I really did not mean to do that," I told her.

"Sleep on the couch," Clementine said. "Consider it a bon voyage gift."

We made up the couch with sheets and a blanket, took turns in the bathroom, and told each other goodnight.

I slept hard and woke uncertain.

Over brunch at Clementine's kitchen table, I felt like I could barely lift the fork. "I guess I should go," I said, but I didn't want to. Saturday, the day Oliver would try to leave his property to meet Freddie at the dock, and I dawdled over the crumbs on my plate, reluctant to reclaim my role as the asshole who invaded Oliver's space to check on him.

I biked to the treehouse in the mist and trudged up the stairs. Maybe Mitch would let me and Kai build a treehouse in their backyard.

My first thought when I opened the door was that I'd slipped through a time warp, back to the first time I'd opened the door, before I'd put anything up on the treehouse wall.

But the nails were still there. My backpack slouched in the corner. My sleeping bag lay on the bed with the sweater I used as a pillow. Clean clothes on a shelf.

Empty shelf where my journals had been.

So this is what invasion feels like.

It felt *terrible*, like an emergency surgical procedure.

I don't have permission to be here, I reminded myself. I was lucky Oliver hadn't taken all my stuff. What shocked me most was the realization that the things Oliver took were my most valued possessions.

I memorized how it felt to discover that a space I'd thought was *safe* and *mine* wasn't. I'd done that to Oliver—bypassed his red flag at the mailbox, stomped into his house with hostility, presumed to overhaul his workshop—*toolshed.* I'd even ignored Oliver's names for his own things.

What a pair of jackasses.

I pulled my journal from my back pocket, snagged the ballpoint from the shelf, and drew an infinite onion across a two-page spread. *Something...* I clicked the pen and stared. Something about our invasions nagged at me.

Layers accumulated over time, stories of buried pain and hoarded joy, a mystery at the center. One glimpse of the mystery in each other and our curiosity bound us with a twist and a compulsion to expose, a need to know, the endless intrigue of a connection with the promise of depth.

Oliver and I had looped around each other for weeks. I'd goaded him with my attitude—a dagger aimed at an internal organ. I'd gouged into his inner layers, wounded him so I could see more, drawn false conclusions, poked again. He'd done the same with me.

But we'd gotten it wrong.

I slid the pen along the loops, slowed and softened as I thought of Oliver's sweetness in the brambles when he sagged in my arms and I held his warm body close, then when he leaned against my leg at the DeVille and told me about Aza.

I'd learned the most about Oliver when I'd been quiet, patient, and present.

Connection isn't a cold poke to the center with a dagger, but a gentle peel with a warm hand over time.

I didn't have time.

I dropped the pen and put my head in my hands to talk myself out of invading Oliver's space again.

One last time. To retrieve my art and journals. To apologize for the ways I'd invaded his life. To assure him I wouldn't do it again. To wish him and Freddie a happy life together. To apologize for anything Oliver wanted me to apologize for. And I would mean it. I would apologize for all of it.

Infinite apology. Sorry for the sting. Safe travels.

Goodbye and good luck.

Chapter 81

GRANT

According to my calculations, Oliver had to leave his house by 3:25 p.m. to catch the 4:00 p.m. ferry. That meant I had an hour to find him and help him leave. Or to sweep up the pieces when he fell apart in the attempt. Neither option felt like a win.

A jog from the treehouse through a drizzle of rain delivered me to Oliver's yard. No suitcase in the van under the carport. Oliver didn't answer when I knocked on the front door. Sheer curtains over the porch windows allowed me to peer inside. I noted pillows arranged in symmetrical rows, a towel over the computer. An excess of unusual tidiness. I didn't see my journals or drawings, but I couldn't see the entire room.

On the side porch, I pressed my face against a pane in one of the French doors and saw papers on the dining table that might be mine, and kitchen counters cleared to barren.

At the windowless back door, I stared for a while at the door handle. When I finally tried it, with a heavy sigh, I found it to be locked. Ditto the other doors when I went back around to try them. The whole place had been battened down tight.

I considered the implications of Oliver's closed bedroom door, and the closed bedroom drapes I'd noted on my way around the house, and the hairs on my arms stood up. But I wasn't willing to break into the house. Not yet.

Like a determined thief, I tried the toolshed door, found it to be locked, and circled to the back windows to case the joint. The table I'd set inside the door for Oliver's carving tools had been tucked under a workbench. I pressed my cheek to the glass to try to see into the near corner. Oliver's carving tools hung on the pegboard in their white-outlined spaces.

It was all too *definite*, as though Oliver planned to be gone longer than a weekend. None of it was my business—I knew that—but I couldn't shake my unease. The longer I didn't find him, the more my conclusions stuttered on a sentence that began, *Oliver put his world in order and then...* My mind refused to complete it.

Oliver wasn't *ready* to leave. I felt sure of it.

Aza hadn't been ready to leave either.

I tried calling Oliver's phone. A robotic voice invited me to leave a message. Maybe he'd finished his carving project, hung up the tools, and gone back to try out the throne, but forgotten to keep track of the time. If Oliver wasn't at the stump, I'd check the DeVille.

I sprinted down the path. When I arrived at the stump, I lifted my hand to trace the images with my fingers—sparrows in flight, rabbits tucked under blossoms, bursting life in a forest of leaves—all brought into being by Oliver's unfathomable talent.

He wasn't curled onto the seat as I'd hoped. I leaned in for a quick look at how Oliver had finished the blank area, and came face to face with a carved person, eyes so full of expression I reeled back and banged my head on the roof of the enclosure.

What. The. Hell.

I leaned in again. The crown and the infinity symbol hovered over a king whose arms extended to encircle whoever sat on the seat.

I recognized the king's face. I'd seen it in the mirror.

My thoughts fractured. I hadn't checked the DeVille, but I also hadn't been able to see into Oliver's bedroom.

My body took over. I ran flat-out back to the house to try the windows. In the courtyard, I found a louvered window that had been closed but not locked. I pulled it open as far as it would go then contorted myself to squeeze behind the rose trellis and into the house. It was awkward as hell, but I managed to land in Oliver's nooky room with my muddy boots in the air and shimmy over the pillows and out the door before I put my feet down.

The archive room was locked, of course. I banged on it anyway, called Oliver's name, in case he'd hidden himself away with all the other artwork. Empty library. I carried on to the great room. Nothing but ice crystals in the freezer.

In the fridge, a bottle of HP Sauce and a tub of miso huddled in the otherwise empty space.

The papers on the dining table weren't mine. I flipped through the first few drawings in the pile and wished I had more time to look, even though they were drawings of Freddie with an Asian boy asleep on his chest. They were *exquisite*. I tore my eyes away and moved on, gave the guest bathroom a cursory check.

Oliver's bedroom door wasn't locked.

I *had* to know if he was okay.

I gave the door a push and strode right in, passed the bed to reach the doors in the far corner. Closet. No Oliver. The other door led to Oliver's bathroom—his large, empty bathroom. No Oliver unconscious in the bathtub. I blew out a breath and turned around. Also no Oliver in a mess on the floor between the bed and the window. I exhaled another sigh of relief.

I'd lock up the house, check the garage and behind the holly wall, and then call it quits. If I had to offer my infinite apology by text instead of in person, so be it. Oliver could share a laugh with Freddie about me as they floated off to Whidbey.

The tarp on the floor of Oliver's bedroom was gone. I caught a glimpse of a large painting on the wall—bare feet and grass—and averted my eyes. If the drawings I'd found on the dining table were preliminary sketches, I didn't want to see more. I didn't need Oliver's larger-than-life painting of Freddie burned into my retinas for all time.

I would have slid out of the room without a closer look, except the utter beauty of the few inches I'd caught sight of made my breath hitch.

I turned my back on the painting, walked to the bed, closed my eyes, and sat. Before I looked up, I gave myself a lecture. *You butted into the guy's life when you weren't wanted. You know you shouldn't be here. Now do what he told you to do and let go. Accept reality. Freddie will be Oliver's other loop, the man who peels Oliver's layers over time. Just... let him go, buddy.*

I lifted my eyes to the left side of the painting, to avoid Freddie's face. Most of the surface remained white under tangles of grey sketches. The few painted areas shimmered and pulsed with life. Small scenes, like painted stories, filled the shadows under Freddie's feet. I stood to take a closer look.

My bramble adventure with the kids played out under an umbrella of salal leaves. Tiny versions of me and the kids in a bramble cave—and Oliver. His smile must have required the world's tiniest paintbrush, yet the speck of red paint depicted Oliver's smile to perfection.

Beyond the vines twirled around Freddie's bare toes, Oliver had conjured the darkened interior of a car. A woman with auburn hair sat opposite a boy with auburn hair who slumped in a car seat beside a large man. The man covered Oliver's head with his hand.

A blond boy climbed the steep slope of Freddie's finger, the colors of the rainbow flag on a staff in his hand vivid against the black of the sleeping boy's hair.

I held my breath and risked a look at Freddie's face.

Closed my eyes again, certain I'd conjured the image.

Not Freddie.

Me.

I held the sleeping boy.

The viewpoint was from slightly above the sleeping figures, as though Oliver had sat at the edge of the road to paint every loose thread of the tattered clothes I'd worn that day, every eyelash and blade of grass. All in living color, exactly how it had been.

Almost exactly.

An infinity symbol, white-gold against the greenery, glowed above Aza's black hair. I recognized him from the photos in Clementine's living room. He lay peaceful in my arms, no sign of pain on his tranquil features.

My painted face turned toward the viewer, toward the artist, toward Oliver. I gazed out at Oliver with enough love to make my knees wobble. In my eyes, as Oliver had painted me, I saw what I'd been missing, what Oliver had noticed that I hadn't.

I love him. I had looked at Oliver like that. I felt the memory of it on my face.

I didn't want to leave the painting. I couldn't bear to leave it, but I needed answers.

Oliver had noticed *that* look, painted it, put his house in order, and... *Jesus, then what?* Sent me packing and gone off to be exclusive with Freddie? Or had Oliver done something much worse? I needed to go, but the painting drew my attention again. The subtle crown of leaves and birds above my head almost disappeared against the flowering bush in the background.

I closed my eyes and shuffled out of bedroom to escape.

Outside, with the front door locked behind me, I checked the time. Oliver needed to go, if he hadn't already gone, or he wouldn't make the ferry.

My head spun with confusion.

The distant sound of an engine filtered through the woodland chitter and bustle. I paused to listen, thought it might be someone come to fetch Oliver, but no one came down the driveway.

I managed to hoist my heavy body over the locked gate in the holly wall on the third try, only to land in an uncoordinated heap on the other side. I brushed myself off and turned to confront my fear that Oliver had—

A patch of blackened earth. Parallel rows of bent grass. I followed them out beyond the curve of the holly wall, where a track ran along the bluff and away to the right.

Jesus Christ. Oliver had done it.

He'd stowed his fucking suitcase in his dad's Cadillac and driven himself to meet Freddie and their future together.

The track would only lead to a road that would lead to the ferry dock. I scrambled back over the gate and bolted for Oliver's van.

I could make it.

I hoped I could make it.

GRANT

After I passed through town on Vashon Highway, I jammed the accelerator to the floor and kept it there.

Top speed in Oliver's van turned out to be two miles over the speed limit.

I had less than ten minutes to find Freddie's car at the ferry, see if Oliver was okay, and apologize.

I slowed when I reached the ferry line-up, but didn't see Freddie's shit minivan. All the while, the ferry floated closer.

On the dock, I drove to the end of the row of parking spaces and pulled in next to the waiting room building. I'd put the van in reverse, to turn around and go back up the hill for another look at the vehicles, when a shout came from behind me. Foot on the brake, I checked the rearview mirror, expecting to see a pedestrian from the waiting room who'd been alarmed by the van's reverse lights.

Fucking Freddie trotted over from the line of vehicles on the dock.

He pushed his smile into the open driver's side window with happy laugh. "Why didn't you park in the upper lot?" When he realized I wasn't Oliver, his face twisted into a grimace.

"Oops," I said, to acknowledge his blunder. "Surprise."

"*You*. What are you doing here?" Freddie's scan of the van's interior put a scowl on his face. "Where's Oliver?"

"Hang on." I put the van into park and got out, tapped Freddie's shoulder to urge him back.

"Keep your hands off me," he said.

"Then move your snarl out of my face." I took a step toward the dock railing.

"Why are you driving Oliver's van without him in it?"

From where I stood, I had a clear view of the road down from the upper lot.

"If Oliver doesn't show, I'll blame you," Freddie said.

"If he doesn't show, you probably should blame me."

Freddie moved in close again. "He was *fine* until you butted in."

"By *fine*, I assume you mean Oliver seemed content to stay home alone while you fucked around elsewhere for months on end."

"He made his own choices."

"Sure. And yet you're in a huff because Oliver called you on your bullshit and *chose* to fuck someone else." The unfairness of Freddie's misdirected anger made me lean into his face. "Namely, *me*."

As if I'd given Freddie permission to have at me, he tensed and took another step toward me.

"You want to hit me?" I said. "Go for it." The top of Freddie's head came up to my chin. I crossed my arms to display my biceps, squared my shoulders, and puffed out my chest. It was fun.

Two spots of pink on Freddie's cheeks spread into a full flush. He stomped off to fume, but didn't go far. I guess he wasn't done with me yet.

Freddie's minivan rust-bucket wasn't in the line-up, but a Ford pickup halfway along the dock caught my attention when two guys in jeans and flannel shirts emerged from it and made a beeline toward Freddie and me.

Green Flannel reached us first. "Problem?" he asked Freddie. It must have been obvious that I could put Freddie down with one hand behind my back.

Green Flannel cocked his head at Freddie and narrowed his eyes. Freddie ignored him.

Red Flannel approached me. "Do you know Rossi?" He nodded at Oliver's van.

"Maybe," I said. "Who are you?"

"Oh my God," Green Flannel said. "You're Fredrik Tolliver."

Freddie nodded but kept his eyes on me.

With a laugh, Green Flannel stuck out his hand. "*Man*," he gushed. "I can't believe this. Those articles of yours in *International Culture and Business* kicked ass—the ones on the Japanese space agency. My wife and I read the whole series aloud to each other in one evening. We couldn't put it down."

"Seriously?" Freddie said. I felt sure he hadn't intended his voice to come out that high.

"Yeah. Sheri and I were both hoarse the next day."

How sweet. Freddie has a fan.

"Is Rossi back on the island?" Red Flannel asked me. "I haven't seen him in way too long."

"Yeah," I told him. I turned my head and raised my voice to say, "Freddie. Can I talk to you?"

He shot me an eye roll and continued to talk with his admirer.

"Real quick," I added. For privacy, I walked the few yards to the dock railing.

"Be right back," Freddie told Green Flannel. "What?" he snapped at me.

I waited until he got closer before I said, "I'm a real dick to do this, but I have to say it, in case it's my last chance. Now that I'm in your presence again, I remember the many ways you're wrong for Oliver. If he shows up and goes with you, it will fall apart before the ferry docks in West Seattle."

"I don't give a fuck what you think. Stop talking to me." Freddie turned to go.

"Wait," I said. "Just wait a sec."

Oliver had driven off in the DeVille before I headed out in his van. *Where did Oliver get stuck?* I wished I'd followed the track instead of driving to the ferry. Then I might have found him, frustrated and falling apart at the edge of his property, and stayed with him so he didn't have to fight that fight alone.

"It's likely Oliver won't show at all," I said.

Freddie's hand came up fast and I grabbed his wrist out of instinct.

"I'm not trying to hit you, *loser*," he said. "I'm showing you my phone." He wiggled it in front of my face.

I turned Freddie's wrist and saw a text message from Oliver: *Running late. On my way.*

"Well, then." I exhaled and let go of Freddie, took a step back. *Good for Oliver.* The moment narrowed to a dramatic roar in my ears, until the seawater beyond the railing swelled and the roar sorted into the sound of the ferry closing in on the dock.

Deckhands tied up the ferry. Freddie returned to Green Flannel. The dock ramp lowered with a reverberating clang. Vehicles began to file off the ferry in two parallel lines.

Now or never, Oliver.

Freddie chatted with Green Flannel but kept his eyes on his phone and on the road from the upper lot, which remained empty.

Walk-on passengers emerged from the waiting room building and milled around, waiting to board the ferry. To avoid them, I slunk back until my shoulder blades hit the building, slid sideways into a wedge of shadow at the railing. I didn't want to be seen trying to keep my shit together if Oliver ran down to the dock at the last minute and got into Freddie's car.

The last few cars rattled off the ferry.

Time's up.

In the relative silence, the blare of a car horn sounded in the distance, high up the hill on the main road. Someone tapped a few staccato horn blasts. A different car honked. Then another. Before the sound died, the DeVille swooped around the curve of Vashon Highway and onto the dock, Oliver's loose hair blowing out the open car window.

Freddie let out a whoop and turned toward me. The combination of victory and shock on his face gave me a small, bitter thrill. *I already knew about the car,* I mouthed to him, to be a jerk, but he'd already turned away. Oliver eased the massive car into a parking spot at the shore end of the dock.

I watched it all from the shadow. Wished I'd stayed in the treehouse. Wished I hadn't found the throne or Oliver's half-finished painting. Wished I knew what any of it meant. Wished to be anywhere else.

Freddie's hug twirled Oliver off his feet, made Oliver's hair float—hair Oliver had let down for Freddie.

Based on Freddie's smiles and the sweep of his arm at the DeVille, he was thrilled. He wrapped a protective arm around Oliver's shoulder, grabbed the suitcase Oliver lifted from the trunk, and walked him down the dock to a car I didn't recognize, near the front of the line-up.

I wished I didn't have to know—would always know—how Oliver looked as he walked away with Freddie. His pinched expression of the past weeks had been replaced with... I didn't know what to call that look. Determination? Confidence? Peace?

To get out of sight even more, I crouched down. Saltwater lapped at the pilings beneath the dock. I couldn't wait to get back to the woods where I belonged. My crouch and the van hid me from Freddie's car, but gave me a view down the dock to the DeVille, polished to a high shine. A few people must have left their cars in the line-up to check it out, their smiles so big I couldn't miss them, even from the other end of the dock.

Drivers of the vehicles at the front of the line started their engines.

I could swallow my pride, run to Freddie's car, and blurt my apology before Oliver left. *Do it*. I swallowed hard.

I got as far as the back of Oliver's van. A deckhand, poised to wave vehicles onto the ferry, noticed me and stopped me with a hand and a stern look. He gestured the first car forward, pointed them toward the loading ramp.

Five cars back, Freddie started the engine.

From where I stood, all I could see of Oliver in the front passenger seat was his knee.

Freddie stuck his arm out the open window and raised his hand above the roof of the car to give me the finger.

The deckhand waved Freddie forward.

I threw the van keys into the glove compartment and started walking.

I let him go.

Chapter 83

OLIVER

At the end of the gravel road from the holly wall, I punched the gas pedal and left my property for the first time in thirteen years.

Freedom.

What a ride.

My nervous laughter and a cautious yell reverberated inside the DeVille. I felt shaky, but *I'd done it.* At Reddings Beach Road, I pulled onto the shoulder and stopped to collect myself. A tap of my fingertips on the electric controls lowered the windows. I took in a deep lungful of fresh air.

Move it. Ferry won't wait.

I drove on, slowed to gawk at the Steiner's new barn, slowed again to enjoy the repaired potholes at Lisabeula Road. Trees along the road had grown or were missing. I recognized Clementine's cottage from photographs she'd shown me.

Wind pushed tears into my ears. The world had moved on and I'd missed it.

That morning, I'd woken after an unprecedented twenty-two-hour snooze in the back seat of the DeVille, covered in Grant's papers and journals and in possession of the full memory of my mother's goodbye. I'd discovered the truth, and it gave me *momentum.*

Traffic picked up at the north end when I reached Vashon Highway. *Pay attention.* I rounded a curve and checked the line of vehicles on the side of the road. Someone honked. It wasn't Freddie in a silver car. More people honked. I wondered if they remembered Dad's Saturday Tour DeVilles.

At the bottom of the hill, I slipped into a parking space and turned off the DeVille, rested my forehead on the steering wheel. *Ferry won't wait. Get out.*

"You made it." Freddie's bright voice sailed in through the open windows. *Windows up. Lock the doors. Move it.*

Freddie gave me an extravagant hug, then hurried me across the dock. At the silver car, he ushered me into the passenger seat, tossed the suitcase in back, and landed in the driver's seat with a bounce.

"*That* was cutting it close." Freddie's laugh seemed manic. "You sure know how to make an entrance. I'll forgive you for lying about the DeVille if you tell me why you—"

"Hand me your phone," I said to interrupt Freddie's ramble. "I want to follow up on a hunch."

He shot me a wary glance. "Um... *no*." His answer came out breathy.

"I'm not joking around." I held out my hand. "Open the text app and hand me your phone."

Freddie stared at me but didn't move.

"We're running out of time," I said.

With more force than necessary, Freddie tapped his phone to unlock it. "Just remember—you lied too," he said when he handed it to me.

I backed out of Freddie's text conversation with me to check his other recent text exchanges.

Freddie made a grab for the phone. I blocked him with my elbow.

"So," I said with a nod, "Hiroki looks forward to your trip to Whidbey today." I read Hiroki's most recent text out loud. "'Can't wait to suck your dick again. Hurry up and get here and ditch the boyfriend.'"

"That is none of your... You shouldn't..." Freddie spluttered.

"Also—*wow*—based on his photo, Hiroki is a lot younger than I'd expect for someone who's retired."

"He came into some money, not that it's any of your—" Freddie lunged over the center console.

"Get *off*." I pushed him back. "Your outrage would be a lot more believable if you hadn't answered that message from Hiroki ten minutes ago with a photo of your dick, which at least you didn't take while sitting here in the ferry line-up. I know because it's the same photo you sent me a few weeks ago."

I tilted the phone to assess Freddie's cock, then scrolled up to see the earlier texts. "I can see why you like him. He's shameless. Aw, but boohoo for Hiroki and the biggest dick he's ever had in him. I had a bigger one in me a few days ago. *Mmm*... gotta get me more of that soon."

"You mean *Grant*?" The rancor in Freddie's comment twisted his face.

"Yeah, Freddie. It turns out I'm more into dicks who don't want other assholes. And I'm not talking about body parts."

The car in front of us rolled forward.

"Keep your foot on the brake," I said. "You'll get on this ferry. But not quite yet."

Cars passed us from behind, driving around to board the ferry.

"You're not coming with me, are you?" Freddie asked.

"Funny man. No, I'm not *coming* with you ever again."

"Let me guess. You want to be exclusive with someone who has a bigger dick."

I raised my eyebrows and held up his phone. "You told me you wanted to be exclusive."

"And you told me you'd sold the DeVille."

"Yeah. I lied. I'm sorry about that. I also lied about leaving my property."

"Are you kidding me?"

"Nope." I handed Freddie his phone.

"That was true?"

"Well, up until about thirty minutes ago."

"Ha. I got you to leave your property, even if it was to break up with me." His arrogant look was pure Freddie. "How long has it been?" Freddie asked. "Since you left?"

"Thirteen years. Since right after Dad died."

"Fucking *hell*, Oliver."

"And *you* didn't get me to leave my property. I don't think you paid enough attention to me to be able to pull that off."

"Ouch, man. But—"

"It took Grant a few weeks to figure it out."

"I hate him. He ruined us."

That made me laugh. "*He* ruined us? There was nothing between us to ruin. You made plans to get with Hiroki behind my back this weekend. I concocted a future with you to escape from my real life. That's not a relationship. That's the ongoing bullshit of two liars using each other."

"That is not true. We've been together for *years*, great years. We—"

"Oh, for the love of God, Freddie. *Stop*. Yes, we've been friends for years, and we still can be, but without sex, and only if we stop lying."

"What about the suitcase? Is that just for show?"

"It's everything of yours from my place. After all our 'great years,' it's not even half full. Consider the suitcase itself a gift. Go be a famous journalist, Freddie. I won't hold a grudge."

Freddie stuck his arm out his window. The scowl on his face didn't seem directed at me.

"What are you doing?" I asked.

"Giving Grant the finger."

"He's *here*?"

"You didn't see your own van parked by the waiting room? He came to—"

I shoved open the door and got out. There was Dad's VW, surrounded by a scrum of people, but I didn't see Grant. Some of the people saw me and waved me over.

I checked for traffic and started across, scanning faces, searching for Grant's frown. All I saw were smiles.

"Bye, Oliver," Freddie said behind me.

I turned back long enough to say, "Send me a postcard. And give me a call when you come back to visit your mom."

When I reached Dad's van, Talia sidled toward me, a sport bag slung over her shoulder. "I got off early," she said with a sly look. "So as not to miss any potential drama."

An old man hobbled over with a kind smile—Mr. Wong, Granddad's accountant. He hugged me close then passed me to Natalie, my babysitter after Granddad died. I wanted to hug them back and answer their questions, but not as much as I wanted to find Grant. I craned my neck to look farther back, out over the tops of people's heads.

The dock ramp motor whined behind me as it lifted off the ferry. I saw Grant then, way out at the other end of the dock, past the DeVille and walking away.

"He thinks you got on the ferry with Freddie," Talia said.

"But I didn't."

Talia rolled her eyes and cupped her hands around her mouth. "Hey, Grant," she shouted.

I pushed through all the people who weren't him.

Chapter 84

GRANT

I tracked the rumble-swish of the ferry's departure behind me as it moved away, taking possibilities with it. *Oliver did it. Good for him.* I repeated the words over and over.

Talia yelled my name. It didn't matter. She'd find the keys if she looked hard enough. I only had one mighty wish: *Get under the trees.* I marched on toward the upper lot.

Running footsteps behind me. "Grant. Wait."

At the sound of Oliver's voice, my heart lurched. I turned around.

He stopped a few feet away. "Hey." Miles of copper hair lifted around his shoulders in the salty breeze. A fiery Medusa against a backdrop of blue sky and bluer sea, Oliver stunned me with his smile. In the distance, the ferry escaped to the mainland.

I balled my hands into fists. To my dismay, I was *angry.* I turned my back on Oliver, not wanting to confuse him with my confusion, and walked faster up the hill.

A minute later, I heard the DeVille's powerful motor start.

Oliver drove up beside me and slowed to match my pace. "I didn't go with Freddie," he told me out the open passenger window. "We broke up."

"Go to hell," I muttered. Anything I felt like saying, Oliver wouldn't want to hear. When I reached the parking lot, I started across it with the hope of finding a street at the far corner that would carry on past the houses and yards to a trail.

"Would you please get in?" Oliver shouted from the road. "We can talk."

With any luck, I'd find a trail with a view of ocean between the tree trunks.

In the time it took Oliver to drive around to the lot entrance and weave through the scattered vehicles, I'd made it halfway across the lot. He maneuvered the DeVille in front of me and stopped to block my way.

"*Move*, goddamn it," I growled.

"What is going on with you?"

More than anything, I wanted to not be angry at Oliver. I felt bottled up and pressurized. Everything had happened too fast. I just needed... something. Something else. *Relief.* I needed relief. I walked around the back of the DeVille and moved on toward the trees.

Oliver drove to stop in front of me again and leaned across the seat to say through the passenger window, "I'm not leaving until you tell me—"

"*You scared me*," I roared. "You *scared* me when I couldn't find you." I blasted my remembered fear into the car.

He's safe, I tried to tell my fear. *He's right there.*

"I'm sorry," Oliver said. When I didn't answer, he said, "Please get in." His bright eyes pleaded.

Anger welled up to push at the fear. "I couldn't find you. The house was so clean and empty."

Oliver gave me a wry smile. "You didn't think I'd be able to leave."

He was right. Even when I knew Oliver had driven away in the DeVille, I hadn't believed.

A station wagon rolled into the lot and disgorged two adults and three children who began to walk in our direction to reach the sidewalk down to the dock.

I didn't want strangers to see me cry. That was the only reason I got in the DeVille. I opened the back door. I wanted to be as far from Oliver as possible while still being inside the car. The door was heavy enough to make the slam satisfying.

"Fasten your seat belt," Oliver said in a calm voice.

"Fuck. Off." I found the seat belt ends and buckled up. It was going to be a bumpy ride.

Oliver rolled up all the windows and we floated across the lot. We sat together in the quiet space. The air vents sighed. I slumped into the plush leather and ignored Oliver.

After he'd made the right turn onto Vashon Highway, Oliver asked, "How did I scare you?"

I sighed my irritation and made him wait. We passed a few cross streets in silence. "Couldn't find you," I muttered, sullen and rude and unable to look at him. "Saw the van. Didn't know if you'd disappeared somewhere to... hurt yourself."

"Oh." The car slowed a little.

"I thought it was too soon." I kept my eyes focused out the side window. "Too soon for you to try to leave your property." .

"You thought I'd try to leave, fail, and then... what? Commit suicide?"

It sounded absurd when Oliver said it, but it hadn't *felt* absurd, not when I'd been careening around his property with fear and love and grief warring inside.

I felt embarrassed, and I regretted getting into the car. If Oliver would slow enough... I put my hand on the door handle.

"I wouldn't kill myself," Oliver said. "I wouldn't do that. Not ever. I promised."

My overtaxed mind delivered a new tangle. "I saw what you painted. In your bedroom. And your drawings on the dining table." I felt like Oliver owed me an apology. Or at least an explanation.

"You broke into my house?" Oliver asked. He didn't sound upset.

"Why did you lock all the doors? You never lock the doors."

"What did you have to break to get in?"

"I didn't *break* anything," I snapped.

At the fork in the road, Oliver veered left to stay on Vashon Highway, instead of turning right onto Cedarhust and the quietude of the west side of the island. That made me angry too.

"Answer my question," Oliver said.

"*You* answer *my* question."

"Oh, for heaven's sake."

I folded my arms and glared out the window, longing for the trees of Westside Highway.

"I deserve an answer," Oliver said as we passed Cove Road.

"Unlocked courtyard window."

"Okay. Good. Well, to answer your question..." Oliver cleared his throat. "I locked the doors to keep the, um... ghosts inside. I was trying to avoid... a memory."

"Did you?" I asked before I could stop myself.

After a long exhale, Oliver said, "No."

"Are you okay?"

When Oliver didn't answer right away, I huffed and gave him the silent treatment again, watched scenery go by, tried to understand myself.

"Your infinity symbols kept showing up," Oliver said. "They made me think things I hadn't thought before. Like how long I'd been running in place and going nowhere."

We'd reached town by then. Oliver slowed to a stop at a crosswalk. People with cloth bags and bunches of carrots, children with dogs and smiles, and a slow man with a cane moved from one side of the road to the other. Summertime on a sunny Saturday on Vashon Island, and I hated everything—the tourists, the islanders, the specials in chalk on the cafe blackboard, the buckets of fresh flowers at the farmer's market. I closed my eyes, aware of how much I'd missed while I'd been running in place too.

I kept my eyes closed until we picked up speed on the far side of town and I heard Oliver open the glove compartment. "Here," he said.

I took the stack of papers he passed to me. My life-review pages from the treehouse. Seeing them in Oliver's hand refreshed the feeling of being invaded.

"I have your journals too." Oliver glanced back at me. "I'm sorry I took them, but... No, that's a lie. I'm not sorry."

He'd stolen my careful work and he couldn't even apologize.

"Your creations, your art... helped me leave the property," Oliver went on. "I sat on your journals, spread your pages over my legs. I tried to be as courageous as you are."

My head cramped, tight enough to turn my ears hot. "I am so mad at you right now."

"About what?"

"So. Many. Things."

"Like...?"

"Like I wanted to be in the car with you when you left." My voice rose and I let it. "Like driving us through town instead of to the west side. Like *you stole my stuff*. Like your beautiful drawings of Freddie. Like your painting of me. What if I left and never knew it existed?" The thought shortened my breath. I set the papers on the floor behind Oliver and turned to press my forehead to my window. To try to calm myself, I named the trees we passed.

Cedar. Holly. Cherry. Cherry. Douglas fir.

I think Oliver took pity on me then. He stopped talking, made a right turn onto Cemetery Road, which took us to Westside Highway. By the time we approached the turn onto 220th, which would take us to Violetta Road, I couldn't wait to escape the car.

But Oliver didn't slow down.

"What are you doing?" I shouted as we passed 220th. "Turn the goddamn hell around."

"No. We need to talk. And I want to drive. I want to see the island. So much has changed."

I hadn't thought of that.

It made it harder to stay angry.

Oliver turned left onto 248th, blew past Old Mill Road, steered with apparent ease through the curves of Shawnee Road.

"Now what?" I said, to break the silence.

Oliver shrugged. He looked like a fucking *badass* driving the enormous Cadillac. I spent a while staring at him as we skimmed along the road, protected by the DeVille's fabulous shocks. Mostly I stared at his topknot. He'd put his hair up after that Medusa moment at the dock, before he'd followed me in the car to harass me.

"I broke into your house today," I said. "After you'd banished me."

"So you said."

"Then why aren't you upset?"

"Because I love you."

My jaw fell open, stayed open until I blinked and swallowed.

"That's not a reason. I love you too, but I'm still angry." I glared at Oliver's bare neck under the topknot so hard my eyes hurt. *He took his hair down for Freddie.* I had too many feelings to care about being rational.

My slouch devolved into a flop. I loosened the seat belt and gave my hips a twist so I could lie back on the seat and fume out the window at the trees instead of at Oliver's neck.

Now and then, as we sailed by, people honked at us. The DeVille's sound-proofing must have been state of the art. Between the honks, I sank into the hush of our plush capsule.

Oliver's stomach growled.

We slowed. Slowed more. I sat up to see why.

The DeVille drifted into a parking spot in a far corner of the grocery store lot. Oliver turned off the engine and got out. "I need groceries."

"Fridge wouldn't be empty if you'd asked your friends for help," I muttered.

He leaned down to ask through the open door, "You coming with?"

"Hell no."

"See you in a few, then." Oliver smiled at me, then loped away across the lot. I lay down again with a huff.

I waited. Stared at the ceiling. Sighed.

He loves me.

The silence ran on and on.

When Oliver closed the trunk with a solid *thunk*, I startled out of my drowse.

He drove us out of the lot onto Vashon Highway, the blinker's *tick-tick-tick* marking time until he completed the turn.

"I fell asleep in the DeVille yesterday," Oliver said, his calm voice calm. "Right before I fell asleep, the... memory I've been avoiding... found me."

His hesitations sharpened my attention. I held still to listen.

"My mother left when I was five. In the... memory, Dad and I were with her in her car, at night, in Seattle. They thought I was asleep and... talked. She'd gotten a job offer from Geneva and wanted us to move with her. She... *begged.*" The DeVille didn't waver, but Oliver's voice broke.

"My mother never begged. I once overheard Dad tell Granddad she was... cold. To me, she seemed calm and strong and... aloof. I thought she didn't care about me, not as much as I wanted her to. But maybe she just didn't care the way I was used to with Dad and Granddad. She begged Dad to go with her so we could be together as a family, and Dad... refused. We hadn't all lived together since I was a baby. My mother only came to Vashon on weekends. Some weekends. Dad never took me to the city to see her. That memory of us in her car— that was last time I saw her."

I sat up and watched Oliver's shoulders rise and fall, his breaths slow as he lapsed into silence. His courage, the fears he'd confronted, stunned me. I didn't know what to say.

He'd steered around a few more curves before he spoke again. "Dad gave my mother an ultimatum. If she took the job in Geneva, he would fight for full... custody. Of... me. He said so, right there in the car..." The breath Oliver took sounded painful, and he exhaled it for a long time. "He told her if she took the job, he would make sure she never saw me again."

"*Jesus.*" What a thing for a five-year-old to hear. "How did she respond? Did you remember that?"

Oliver nodded and swallowed. "She said it was the job of a lifetime and giving it up would be like asking Dad to give up making art. She said Dad could make art in Geneva but she couldn't do her work in Seattle anymore. She..." Oliver's hesitation became a full stop.

I stared at the faint freckles on Oliver's neck. At the age of five, his neck would have been so precious as to be unleavable, wouldn't it? I couldn't bear the suspense. "She what?"

"She told Dad to tell me it was all her fault, to make it easier for me. Then she whispered in my ear that she would always love me."

I pictured the little boy who'd heard that conversation and buried it deep. *That boy.*

Goose bumps rose on my arms.

That boy was who I wanted to help in my career. I felt his deep pain as he grappled with the invisible thing too scary to know, tucked it way down, below the layers he pulled over himself to keep it hidden. Helping that boy would require a hell of a lot more than a few volunteer hours. I'd need a psychology degree or something, enough training to trust myself to peel children from their buried depths into sunshine filtered through a forest canopy.

Oliver glanced back at me then away. I heard the whisper of a tissue pulled from a box. Without looking at me again, he stuck his left arm between his seat and the door. A white tissue fluttered down onto my papers from the treehouse.

After I blew my nose, I said, "How did you bear it when she left?"

"I didn't have to bear it, not consciously. Dad and Granddad worked hard to make me... forget. Forget... her."

"How?"

"They turned her into fiction—an elusive red fox they told me stories about, until that was all I really remembered."

"Your dad lied." I suddenly remembered Oliver's blurted words as we stood by the DeVille.

"He lied to me most of my life, about her, anyway. I continued that legacy of lying—lied to my friends, lied to myself, persuaded myself I'd be okay if I let Freddie take me away—"

I snorted my disapproval.

"I also distracted myself by clearing the air with Aza, which I'd needed to do for a long time. Aza led me to the treehouse... and your art. The memory stalked me through it all."

"I think I'm glad it finally caught you," I said.

"Me too. But... I thought I was resisting a memory of my *mother* rejecting me. My world feels... topsy-turvy now. My mother wanted us to be together. My *dad* kept us apart." Oliver cocked his head to the side, maybe to try out his new perspective.

He kept his foot on the gas and we passed the turn-off to his house again.

"What happened after your dad died?" I asked. "Did you try to tell her?"

"No, but she found out. Maybe she saw it in the newspaper. She contacted me, after the... funeral. It was our first direct contact since... before. She sent voice mails, letters, emails."

"What did she say?"

The strained pause between my question and Oliver's answer bowed his shoulders. I waited. Oliver drove. The majestic starship DeVille bent time in grand sweeps as Oliver wrestled with his answer and the last remnants of my anger fell away.

When the road straightened out, Oliver said, "I don't know what she said. I deleted her messages without opening them. I never responded." He let out a heavy sigh. "I'd been devoted to her before she left. I do remember that. After she left, Dad and Granddad helped me blame her. It was like I chose one parent to be loyal to, and that was Dad."

Oliver took a hand off the wheel and rubbed a knuckle over the corner of his eye. "I grieved so hard after Dad died—months of fear and loss. That was when I stopped leaving the property. Whenever I tried to leave, I felt like I was leaving him."

"Might have been a good time to let in someone else," I said.

"Probably. But not *her*. Dad had... painted over her. She didn't exist."

"I'm sorry." Out beyond the massive hood, the straight shot of Vashon Highway ran on to the horizon. Oliver's capable hands high on the steering wheel, his glorious hair and tanned skin, the calm presence of him, lifted another layer of tension from my body. "I'm sorry for what you went through. Thank you for telling me."

He shifted in his seat and pulled the seatbelt strap away from his chest. "I remembered something else."

"Uh-oh," I said.

"Yeah."

"More about your dad?"

Oliver nodded. "Dad used to host fire circles, out at the holly wall, at the full moon. We'd drum and dance and eat. On one of those nights, after all the guests had left—"

"How old were you?"

"Seven or eight. I was supposed to be brushing my teeth and going to bed, but Dad hadn't come inside yet. It was late. Granddad fell asleep on the couch. I put on my sneakers and padded outside in my pajamas. The holly gate stood ajar. I saw Dad standing over the glow of the fading fire with papers in his hands. His face and his body seemed... small. He fed the papers into the fire, one by one."

"Did you go in?"

"No. I hid. Watched. After he'd released the last... paper, he doused the fire with the buckets of water we kept handy on those nights. I moved back around the wall and waited until he'd gone, until I couldn't hear his footsteps on the gravel anymore. Then I found a stick and poked through the mess of wet ashes."

"Did you have a flashlight?"

"Full moon," Oliver said.

"I saw the place where those fires must have been. A patch of scorched earth. You'd parked the DeVille right on top of it."

"Huh." Oliver let out a small laugh. "So I did. Not consciously."

I marveled at Oliver's clever psyche. "Was there anything left?"

"Enough. Tiny scraps of paper. A corner of a smoked envelope. The tiniest edge of a postage stamp. Bits of postmarks. One swirl of... handwriting. Handwriting I recognized."

"No way."

Oliver nodded. "It's hard to accept, but I think Dad was the parent who left me."

"Your new topsy-turvy world." We cruised along Cemetery Road again, which seemed appropriate. "How do you feel about them now? Or is it too soon to say?"

We'd pulled up to the stop sign at the intersection of Westside Highway. There was no one else anywhere near us.

"They were human," Oliver said. "My parents were only human."

"You too."

"Yes. Me too." He resettled his hands on the steering wheel.

"Wait," I said. "Stay here a minute." I unfastened my seat belt and slid across the back seat to wind my arms around Oliver's shoulders and whisper in his ear, "Why did you let your hair down for Freddie?"

"I didn't. I mean, it wasn't for him." Oliver took his hands off the steering wheel and rubbed them over my forearms. "I've always worn it up, but since I had the memory, I feel like..."

"Like what?"

"It's *her* hair, my mother's hair. Or it was. I don't even know if she's... alive."

It took me a few seconds to connect the dots. "Your hair reminds you of your mother."

Oliver nodded. "I could have cut it off, but..."

I lifted a loose tendril of hair and kissed Oliver's cheek. "But it reminds you of your mother."

Oliver turned his head to kiss me. Without the undercurrent of his desperation, the kiss felt like his first kiss, Oliver's *true* kiss, a kiss with enough heat to lure me into the front seat to sit beside him.

With his thigh pressed against mine, Oliver roused me with another kiss, an unrepentant slide of tongue and arms and hot breath, brash and honest and—

Someone behind us honked.

Oliver reached out and put the blinker on for a left turn before he removed his mouth from mine and his hand from the back of my head.

It took me until then, until the blinker prompted me to pay attention, to realize what Oliver had done.

We'd traveled the same route over and over, toured the island from north to south and back again, the twist of Cemetery Road at the middle of the infinite loop. Oliver's serene focus told me he would have driven me forever, as long as it took to retrieve my truth from beneath the anger and fear.

When I told Oliver I'd figured out his devious route, he lifted my hand from his thigh, pressed it to his hard cock, and said, "The 1968 Cadillac Sedan DeVille showcases a powerful 375-horsepower engine, six-way power seat adjustment, and a fuel tank capacity of 26 gallons. Would you like to take me for a drive?"

"God, yes."

"Did I mention the cruise control?"

Chapter 85

OLIVER

I'd been half-hard since Grant stormed into the DeVille and slammed the door. After he thawed and touched me, my focus was shot. I put the DeVille into park and waved the car behind us to go around.

"Your turn," I told Grant.

We resettled, refastened our seat belts with Grant driving and me in the center front seat. I kept my hands to myself for a minute, to let Grant get a feel for the DeVille. For one whole minute. Then I gave in to temptation, wrapped my left arm around his massive shoulders, and kissed his neck.

"You are a bad person," he muttered.

With my right hand, I roved Grant's bristly jaw and neck, devoted myself to his skin. "You're too gaunt. I need to feed you more." The wiry muscles of his chest and torso twitched under my touch. By then I was cursing the seat belt, the only thing keeping me from humping his thigh.

He elbowed me a third time as he slowed for the turn onto 220th.

I bit his shoulder.

"Get *off*, Oliver." With a harder shove, Grant put a few inches of space between us. "At least wait until I'm off the highway, you prick."

I laughed and put my hands in my lap. *Mistake.* A flick of my thumbs rubbed my dick through my shorts.

Grant kept his eyes on the road and his hands on the wheel—all very nice and proper, but his jaw muscle twitched and tightened, and when we reached Violetta Road, he clamped his hand over both of mine to stop them.

No problem.

I braced my feet on the floor and lifted into the firm pressure of Grant's hand. "Yeah." I did it again, intoxicated by his touch, by all our breakthroughs. *High on life and horny.*

"You are a foul, vicious bastard," Grant snarled. He slapped my busy hands off my lap. "No. Not fair. Wait."

Before we reached my driveway, Grant slowed to a stop and turned off the engine.

"Don't stop." I moaned. "I can almost see my mailbox from here."

"Get out." Grant found the button to undo my seat belt and shoved me toward the passenger door.

"No." I fell onto my side on the seat. "We're almost home."

"I'm not asking." The freed end of Grant's seat belt thudded against his door and he got out. He slammed the door hard, like he was mad at me again. Two seconds later, he opened the front passenger side door.

I looked up at him, raised my eyebrows, and palmed my cock.

Grant's answer was to grab me under my arms and haul me out of the DeVille. I was too turned on to coordinate anything not directly related to my cock, including my feet. It didn't matter. He managed my limbs for me, laid me out on the edge of the road.

"What in the fuck are you doing?" I asked.

Grant's answer was to stretch out on top of me.

I pushed at his shoulders and tried to get up. "Move. We're on the side of the road. Rocks? Shoulder blades? Ow?"

"I can fix that." Grant held me tight and executed a half-roll away from the DeVille, which put me on top. It seemed like a crappy solution when my house was *right there.*

"Stop rolling," I said, "or we'll end up in the..."

Grant watched me with a self-satisfied smile.

"Ditch," I finished. *Oh. The ditch.*

"Reenactment, anyone?" Grant lifted his eyebrows. "I've fantasized for weeks about a do-over."

I laughed, and the motion caused my cock to rub against Grant's. *Firestorm with a side order of whimpers, please.* "*Ungh.* Yeah. Say something else funny."

Grant clutched my ass with enough fervor to convince me he was serious.

"Okay, then." I'd give Grant his do-over—with a few crucial edits. I clamped my knees around his hips and rolled us through the tall grass, all the way down. Grant landed on his back with a splash.

"Oops," I snickered.

"*Agh.*" Grant scrambled to get up. "It's *cold*. Get up!"

I couldn't. I could only draped my boneless body over Grant's and shake with laughter at my reenactment skills.

"Goddamn it, Oliver." Grant's attempts to get up amped the friction at my crotch. I pressed my ditchwater-soaked knees into the wet earth and drove my cock over Grant's in a burst of movement I couldn't restrain. I'd been hard for too long. For a decade, it felt like.

I came fast, without trying to stop myself, with an unselfconscious groan and a laugh to chase the satisfaction, relieved and ridiculous in equal measure.

A splash of water doused my back. "Seriously?" Grant sounded peeved.

"Hang on." I slithered down Grant's body and rifled through his shorts to find his dick and get my mouth around it before he could scramble away.

Grant's upward thrust with his hips almost threw me off him. When he'd splashed back into the ditch, I swallowed him again, shoved one hand down into his underwear to work at his balls. In seconds, with a litany of nasty curses, Grant spewed down my throat and all over my hand. Rivulets of cum ran out of my full mouth and over my hands. Ditchwater flowed past, carried our cum away downstream.

In spite of the chill, I felt better than I'd ever felt in my entire life.

Grant heaved up, lifted me out of the water with him, and stood. Clouds rolled by above us in the twilight. We squished our way up to the road.

"Still think I'm a bad person?" I asked.

"Yes."

"*Wait.* Stop. Don't touch the DeVille. I mean it. We're too wet and dirty."

"See?" Grant said. "Still a bad person."

We stripped naked, slopping our clothes and shoes into a pile in the grass.

"I suppose we'll have to air dry," Grant said with resignation. We stared at each other and shivered.

"Kiss me again," I said. "You taste like pine sap."

"I should say no, you freak." He smiled and pulled me close. "But you don't taste like lies anymore, so I'll make an exception."

We kissed until shivers made my teeth clack against Grant's.

For our final wipe-downs, I snagged chamois cloths from the trunk, scrubbed myself, then ran my cloth down the middle of Grant's back where he couldn't reach. "Ready?"

"More than."

"Guess what you have to do now?" I raised my eyebrows at the pile of wet clothes and shoes.

"The hell I will."

"It's either that or you walk."

Grant knelt on the passenger seat with his upper body out the window to hold our dripping clothes away from the side of the DeVille. I sat on a fresh chamois and drove.

"This is *not fun*," Grant groused.

My careful study of the spot where Grant's white thighs met the lower curve of his round butt caused me to miss my own driveway.

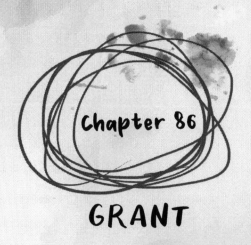

Chapter 86

GRANT

When we got to the house, I dumped the pile of wet clothing on the porch. Oliver backed away from me toward his bedroom and said, "I'm going to wash the ditchwater out of my hair. *Alone*, or it'll take forever. Use the guest bathroom."

"Fine." I showered fast, wrapped a towel around my waist, and sat on Oliver's bed to stare at his painting while I waited.

"Not here," he said when he emerged from his bathroom.

"But I want to look at your painting."

"Tomorrow. Tonight I need your help to reclaim the great room from the ghosts."

Oliver loaded me up with pillows and comforters, turned off the bedroom light, and we decamped to the orange couch. Moonlight seeped in through the windows.

I swung a comforter around my shoulders like a cape and watched Oliver get the couch ready. He stretched out when he was done, looking scrumptious in navy-blue pajama bottoms on the light blue comforter.

"You're going to sleep with wet hair?" I asked.

"It'll dry overnight. Come here and be my blanket."

I shook my head. I wasn't ready to touch him yet. It would turn off my brain, and I had a few things on my mind—things that wouldn't wait until morning.

"I flipped through those drawings." I nodded at the dining table.

The *come-hither* expression on Oliver's face turned into a frown. "When you *broke in*. Give me that comforter. I'm cold."

I draped it over him then stood back and folded my arms.

"Mmm. Yeah." Oliver wriggled and his eyes went dark. "I require you to stand over me naked and glare at me at least once a day."

"You drew a lot of pictures of Freddie. How far did you guys go?" I hadn't been able to ignore my memory of the two of them touching, or my imagined scenes of what they'd done when I wasn't around. It *bothered* me. "Did you guys have sex?"

Oliver smiled a private smile I *hated*, because it probably meant he was remembering.

"You did, didn't you? That day I came to do laundry when Freddie got mad. He was angry because I interrupted, wasn't he?"

"I'll tell you." Oliver threw back the comforter. "I promise. But only if you lie on me."

"Why the hell are you wearing... anything?" I held up the comforter while Oliver shoved off his pajama bottoms. To make room for myself on the couch, I pushed him toward the back and lay on my side. I needed to minimize contact until I was done talking. "Well?"

"A few pecks with closed lips. That was all I could manage. And one slightly tonguey kiss."

"That's all? Really?"

"Yeah. He was Ready Freddie, like always. Usually I was pretty into it too, but this visit was different."

"Why?"

"You know why," Oliver said. "You affected me, even without my permission. It made me hesitant about Freddie."

"Good."

"Freddie thought he was ready for more of a relationship," Oliver mused.

"Bullshit. Freddie wanted things to stay the same. *That's* why he didn't like me."

"Freddie didn't like you because he could tell I was falling for you."

I puffed out my chest.

"Asshat." Oliver rolled toward me. I couldn't resist petting his damp hair, smoothing it down his back to make him squirm and rub against me.

"You painted *me*." I heard the wonder in my voice.

"I did."

"You made a ginormous painting of a *ditch*."

"Only because the ditch had you in it."

I felt my face shift and recognized my expression as the one from Oliver's painting. He beamed at me, and I bent to touch my lips to his, to taste the red-gold beauty of him. When he opened his mouth to draw in a breath, I closed my eyes and became the man who kissed Oliver Rossi until he clutched at me and bound me tight in his limbs.

To torture him, and to look at him some more, I pulled back. "Now that you're free, I bet you're going to be more social, like your dad. You're going to be community glue."

"Stop talking."

"Not yet."

"I can't believe it," Oliver muttered. "You're a *savorer*. Fuck my entire life. Why did I let Freddie get away? *He* understood the value of a quick fuck. *You*—you're going to drag this out, aren't you?"

"Still waiting for you to join the conversation and tell me why you painted me." I smiled, pushed Oliver against the back of the couch, and petted his hair until he gave in and talked.

"Whatever wizardry you did with those kids," he said, "you did with me too. That's your gift. You get kids to play, but you let us bring our sorrow. You put your big hand on the tops of our heads and we know we're okay."

I blinked hard. "Bastard."

Moonlight shone across Oliver's grin. "Here's what I believe. I believe you were coming to see me that day I found you in the ditch."

"Oh, I see you all right." I shaped Oliver's damp beard with my palm and fingertips. For the first time in my life, I wished I knew how to paint. "You brave and majestic Celtic king."

I'd never seen a brighter smile than the one my words brought to Oliver's face. He put his warm lips to mine and kissed me slowly but *more*, more than I'd ever been kissed. More filthy lust. More sweet tenderness. More willingness. More strength.

I needed to *absorb* him.

I shifted Oliver to lay him flat and straddled him, felt his cock pulse hot against my balls. With my hands, I rubbed up Oliver's sides to his armpits and over his biceps to push his hands above his head. "Your arms drove me to distraction from day one. Those overalls..."

Oliver smirked and flexed his biceps.

Pre-cum slid down my cock onto Oliver's belly. Drawn by the complex scent rising from Oliver's armpit, I buried my face there to lick at the sparse patch of hair.

"Oh. Agh." Oliver shot me a hateful glare.

I chuckled and took an extra minute to enjoy the heave of his defined chest. It inspired me to pet his pecs and nipples. "I have another question."

Oliver trembled. Squeezed his eyes closed. Cursed and rocked his pelvis up against me. Pressed the length of his cock against the base of mine.

"Ask your damn question," Oliver snarled. "Then get the fucking lube and fucking *fuck* me."

Yeah. I stayed quiet, watched Oliver writhe, loved that I could so easily rile him. We were going to have so much fun in the sack. Or, well, I was. Oliver looked rather conflicted.

"Question?" Oliver said in a peeved voice. "Lube? Fuck? Hello?"

"Can I renew my contract?"

He froze. "You...what? Really?"

I nodded. "I know what I want to do for a career, but it feels too big. I want you to do what you did this summer—pressure me, annoy me, show me what I can't see on my own."

Oliver's face took on the calculating look of Professor Evil Pants. It gave me hope.

"That's it," I said. "Think of all the dastardly things you can require of me now that we're..." I gave his dick a hard grind with my taint. The sharp pleasure made my eyes roll up.

"Deal," Oliver said. "I just now drafted a new contract in my head. It's *good*— nice and nasty. Here's how it starts: *Fuck me now or no deal.* Get the lube under the pillow." He wiggled his wrists within my grip.

I slid down to put my mouth on his, to kiss my love into him. I couldn't kiss him enough. The love kept flowing, and I needed Oliver to know *how much*. I loved him with my mouth and long grinds of my cock into his pubic hair, against his slick cock, along the hard bones of his hips.

Oliver quivered and hummed. With a gasp, he turned his face away and drew in a big breath. "Stay, Grant. Stay with me. Live here. Please don't say no."

"But I want to get a degree so I can be a child therapist."

"You are really frustrating me right now with all the talking. Also, you do?"

I nodded. "A child therapist who specializes in nature cures."

"That's... Fuck, that's perfect. I'll pay for it."

I laughed at the absurdity. "Um. No way. It'll take me approximately a hundred years to get that degree, but I'm sure I can figure—"

"You're not hearing me. Go ahead and volunteer at a park in Seattle, take classes, do overnights at Mitch's to spend time with Kai, bring Kai here—but *take the van* and come back home to me. Get it, Grant? *Live* here. *Visit* Seattle. New career. No copy shops. We'll find a university with minimal onsite requirements. I'm serious. I have a *lot* of money—more than you can imagine—and I'm going to spend some of it on you. There. It's settled."

Oliver's proposition caused a cranial power-wash event in my skull, a life trajectory reset. It went straight to my cock. "No more copies?"

"That's your takeaway?" Oliver asked.

"I can't—"

"Say yes or I won't let you fuck me."

I slid my hand between our bodies and gave Oliver's dick a hard jerk to get him squirming again, then pressed my fingers between his ass cheeks, right up onto his hole.

He tried to close his legs, to shut me out, because I hadn't said yes to his offer, but he couldn't manage it.

"You shouldn't make threats if you can't follow through." I pressed the tip of my finger, slick with his pre-cum, up inside him, just for a second. I found the lube under the pillow with my other hand, flipped the top, and took my finger away from Oliver long enough to slick it up. When I pushed into his ready heat again, I hooked my finger onto his prostate, making him moan and shimmy.

"Looky here." I teased. "Caught me a live one."

Oliver swallowed hard and tightened his asshole around my finger. "Tell me," he whispered. "Say yes to my offer or I'll... I'll stop right now."

That made me smile. He'd wrapped his legs around my waist. We both knew he didn't want to stop me. "Love this wiggle you've got going, Professor Squirmy Butt. Condom?"

"Must we?"

"Dream on. I know you haven't been tested. Your open relationship with Freddie the globe-trotting tool means we'll use a condom. Also, quick memo, your scowly face doesn't work on me. Well, it does, but it only makes me really hot."

The ruddy flush of Oliver's skin, the glaze in his eyes, his roving hands trying and failing to reach my dick *all* did it for me. My focus narrowed. For a long while, I got off on Oliver's pleas and small surrenders. I slowed my fingers inside him, avoided his prostate.

"Never mind," Oliver panted. "No deal. You're a loser with no future. I don't want you anywhere near—"

"Yes, you do."

"Anywhere near me," Oliver finished on a slow moan.

"Mm-hm. Right." I reached under the pillow and found a condom, which gave me an excuse to stop my too-slow finger-pump into Oliver's asshole altogether. "I'd better check the expiration date. Not much light in the room. Could take a while."

He lunged up to grab my cock and I threw the condom into the air.

"Give me *that*, you freak." Oliver tore open the condom wrapper. In record time, my dick was covered and he'd scooted up to put his hole within range.

"Here's the deal, you *fucker*," Oliver snarled. "You stick your cock in me within the next ten seconds, as your binding agreement that you'll move in with me, let me pay for your degree *and* your food, and *any other fucking thing* I want to pay for, or else—"

I didn't let him get to past the *or else*. I suddenly remembered Oliver's desperate animal sounds when I'd fucked him in the grass by the DeVille.

"Yes." I pinned Oliver with my eyes as I pushed my cock into him. "Yes."

Oliver smirked and keened and went limp, all at once.

I took advantage, bent to kiss his desire. His mouth tasted pure and real and true, like island air spiked with seawater. Even freshly washed, Oliver's hair smelled like the art supplies corner, as if his lifetime of creating had transformed him cell by cell into a masterpiece.

I pushed my cock into Oliver all the way, pushed farther, until I'd pushed him half off the end of the couch. I wanted *in there*.

With one of his long arms, Oliver reached between us to circle his fingers around the base of my cock, his fingers right against his own hole. The hard squeeze he gave my cock made me remember I didn't only have to push. I could pull out too.

Oliver's tight grip, *right there*, answered all my questions. I became one of Oliver's creations. I snapped my cock into the heat of him, pulled out when he gave me a vicious twist. I held him close in my arms, shoved my face deep into his hair, slobbered on the secret heat of his jawline as he put the finishing touches on his reconstruction of me.

Like he'd done in the bramble boudoir, Oliver stuck his pointed tongue into my ear. I acted the part he'd written for me, came with a flourish, slid against his hot cum on my belly to flail above the surface of the sea and sparkle down at him.

"I see you too, dickhead," Oliver panted at me.

Hook, line, and sinker.

Chapter 87

OLIVER

I woke hungry and too warm, in spite of the swirl of cool air from the open windows. At first I thought I'd been rolled up in a rug.

Grant, it seemed, was a possessive sleeper.

I lay on top of him, my face mashed sideways against the groove between his hairy pecs. His arms pinned my arms to my sides. He snuffled into my hair as he snored. One of his heavy legs twisted around both of mine.

I felt safer than I'd felt in a long time.

Safe, but also *starving*. I put off trying to extricate myself long enough to replay my mental movie of the night before. Tried and failed to figure out how I could have hated every one of Grant's torturous, teasing delays, and yet loved the experience as a whole.

My attempt to take a deeper breath woke Grant. I expected him to release me when he realized how tightly he held me, but he only gripped me tighter.

"Can't breathe," I squawked.

"Mmm. Morning, wiggly puppy," Grant whispered. He licked my face in a big swipe, up my cheek and temple.

"Ugh, you weirdo. Let me go." I flapped my useless hands against his thighs.

"Nuh-uh. Not unless you have to pee. Do you?"

I considered lying, thought better of it, and sagged onto him.

"Good," he muttered. "Be still. I'm not done."

I decided I had nowhere better to be, and we languished until I felt Grant's blink against my hair when he finally opened his eyes.

"Won't you hate living with someone else, having me here all the time?" he asked.

I let the question settle, gave it a chance to trigger a backpedal on my offer. All I felt was a deep relief that I wouldn't be alone. "I lived in close quarters with people for the first twenty-two years of my life. Dad and Granddad were as in-my-face and in-my-business as you are."

"Is that good or bad?"

"I'll love having you here, Grant. It feels like I'm coming home, even though I didn't go anywhere."

Grant squeezed me harder.

I kicked him on the shin.

That brought out the devil in his eyes and led to me making an extensive mess on the comforter and Grant getting himself off in my mouth. He wiped cum from his hand onto my pubic hair.

"Gross," I whined. "You disgust me."

"You sure have a funny way of showing it."

I pushed him away. "I have to—oh, *fuck*. I left the groceries in the trunk of the DeVille."

Grant's hand on my chest kept me on the couch. "Calm down. I got them when I heard Talia deliver the van and went out to say hi. After I debauched your lovely ass and you conked out."

"Oh. Thanks. Now get up and fix me some breakfast."

"Okay," Grant said. "In a minute." He stroked my chest with one hand, traced the edges of my pecs, swiped a nipple, caressed my hair and beard.

I tried to bat his hands away. "You're drugging me again."

"My coppery sex flame."

"Agh. *Stop*. I had a thought a minute ago I wanted to share," I said. "Before you—"

"It'll keep."

"No. I remember now—we should have a party."

"We just did. Pretty noisy one too. I almost called the cops to come over and shut you up."

I ignored Grant's attempt to wind me up. "A party to celebrate you finding a home and me leaving home."

"Yeah." Grant's hand settled on my sternum. "A party with a gallery showing."

"What you did on the treehouse wall *should* be in a gallery," I said.

"Your painting should be in a museum. Except I never want to not be able to see it."

"It's not even finished." My stomach growled so loudly Grant released me.

"I'd better feed the beast," he said.

As we ate, I told Grant about the archive room, and about Pascal, the Tacoma auto mechanic I'd sworn to secrecy.

"Doesn't a Cadillac as old as the DeVille run on leaded gas?" Grant asked.

"Pascal changed out the valve seats to run on unleaded."

"He made a house call? That seems—"

"No. Well, yes. Twice a year he comes to Vashon at night, stows his car in my garage, and takes the DeVille to Tacoma on the last ferry of the night."

"Sneaky."

"She gets a thorough checkup and detailing the next day, and the next night he brings her back, along with a resupply of full gas cans for the van."

"*Brought* her back," Grant said. "You don't need that arrangement anymore."

My breath stopped. I stared at Grant and felt my eyes go wide, so wide it felt like my eyebrows slid off the top of my head.

I forgot I could leave.

"Well, you don't," Grant said. "You should call and invite Pascal to our party."

I stood so fast my chair clattered against the stove. "Let's go invite Pascal in person."

Grant's surprised laughter made him look like a child. A child who got to ride in a big Cadillac and daydream about the fun things he'd do when he grew up. A happy child who lived in a pretty house in the middle of a big forest and got to play under the trees with his friends.

Chapter 88

GRANT

A month or so later, on a warm Saturday in September, the day of our party found me perched atop the fridge.

From across the great room, Oliver directed the placement of his painting-in-progress. He'd stopped working on it for a week to let it dry enough to temporarily relocate it for the party. "Lift the left corner of the right panel a *touch* higher."

"Screw that," I snapped. "I'm looking at the bubble in the level. It's dead even."

Oliver smiled his smile that meant he'd wound me up on purpose.

He'd pay for it later.

"Nervous about your first art show?" Oliver pinched my big toe and grabbed the grocery list on his way past the fridge.

I peeked across the room at my treehouse collage, which Oliver had installed with great accuracy on the wall by the stage. "A little." It was going to be strange to share that private stuff with our friends.

"Good," Oliver said.

"Hey, Penelope took a break from play practice. She wants to go with you." Our party didn't start until dinnertime, but we'd invited a few people over early to help out, including the kids, who'd taken over the stage. "She's already in the van."

"Of course she is."

Oliver and I had reinstated the Saturday Tour DeVille, with a route change to honor the day Oliver unraveled me as he looped around the island, and so we could pick up and drop off kids and parents along the way. After the first

Tour, over lunch with the kids, Mitch, and Jill's dad, and with the aid of a map unrolled on the dining table, Oliver had confessed. "Basically," he'd said. "I hadn't left my property since before any of you kids were born."

Penelope had taken it the hardest, the shock evident on her face. She'd peppered Oliver with questions and appointed herself Oliver's guide to the world "out there," as she called it.

I slid off the fridge with a thump and headed for the French doors. "Big night tonight, kids." Jill, Clover, Kai, and Abelino didn't acknowledge me, too intent on final preparations for opening night of their play about a boy who came out in a bramble patch.

In the courtyard, I squished myself into a lawn chair near Vince and Mitch and let the rumble-chuckle of their deep voices sedate me, dozed with my head buried in the rose trellis until Kai ran into the courtyard and barreled into Mitch, nearly knocking over his chair.

"Watch it," Mitch said.

"Dad. Hey, *Dad*." Kai patted Mitch's knees and hopped from foot to foot. "I decided."

"Okay. I'll bite," Mitch said. "What did you decide?"

Kai squeezed between his dad's knees to hug him. "I'm going to be an *actor*."

Mitch held my gaze over Kai's head. I nodded to acknowledge his unspoken thanks.

After Kai ran off, in the lull before Clementine and Talia arrived to help with dinner prep and Oliver returned with the groceries, I heeded a finch's complicated warble from the yard and stood, drawn to take a minute alone in advance of the chaos. "Back in a few, guys. Need anything?"

Vince shook his head. Mitch held up his half-full beer bottle. "All good."

When I'd walked far enough into the yard that I could no longer hear voices, I stopped to study the expanse of lush grass bordered by dense forest.

"I sort of have a yard," I said out loud with a smug smile.

YARD was a decent idea for my journal entry for the day, but I thought I could do better. I held my open journal on my palm, twirled the ballpoint pen in my other hand, and waited for inspiration. The moment unspooled until I lost track of time.

Tires on gravel. The slam of the van doors. Penelope's high, bossy voice. Oliver's indistinct answer. Edward's bark. A sharp hoot of laughter from Isis, who'd traded shifts at the library so she could attend our party.

In letters big enough to fill the page, I wrote *CLAN* and put the journal and pen away to scan the forest. At some point, I'd begun to memorize individual trees, to include them in my clan. *Can't have too many pals.*

I recognized Oliver's footsteps through the grass. I'd memorized that too.

"Notice anyone new?" Oliver asked when he stopped beside me.

"'Tween western hemlock. Ten o'clock. Just beyond the cedar."

"Hey, buddy."

I loved it when Oliver talked to the trees I introduced him to.

"Want help unloading the van?" I asked.

"Kids are on it."

After a few silent seconds Oliver took a deeper breath and turned to face me. Serious eyes above his broad smile. "Do you have a minute?"

I snorted. He knew I had all the minutes in the world for him. "Sure. What's up?"

"I've been thinking about... a lot of things. About the forest, about... Aza."

Uh-oh. Whatever Oliver had to say, if it put him in hesitation mode, it was big.

"About kids." Oliver went on, "Your current kids and... other kids you'll work and play with." With a sly glance at me from under his eyelashes, Oliver brought a folder out from behind his back and handed it to me.

"Hey, did you update our contract?" I'd started classes at a community college in West Seattle, in preparation for applying to university, and had asked Oliver to reward me for homework.

Oliver didn't answer, except to gesture at me to open the folder.

The papers inside looked more official than Oliver's contracts. I scanned the top page, saw the word "Deed," flipped to the next page and the next. My hands began to shake. "Oh my God."

A small laugh escaped Oliver. "I thought it would be nice if you had a... forest. Of your own."

I didn't mean to, didn't plan to, but sunk to my knees on the grass. To my dismay, I began to cry. I tried to stop, to close the breach, but I couldn't. All the fears and disappointments I'd weathered over my thirty-nine years seemed to gush out all at once. I held the deeds off to the side so I wouldn't get snot on them.

Oliver came down with me. He didn't make fun of me for crying, only knelt in front of me until I could find my voice. "Oliver. You can't." I pushed the folder at him. "Why is my name the only name on—"

"Hush." Oliver didn't take the folder. "Hush now. I have something to say."

I nodded, eyes locked on the folder. The deeds quivered in the double-handed clutch of my outstretched hands.

"To me," Oliver said, "these deeds are a scholarship you've more than earned—compensation for the hard work you did as a child when you should have been playing. Now you have somewhere to play forever, and no one can take it away from you."

I commanded my arms to refuse the gift, to set the folder on the grass if Oliver wouldn't take it, but rebel fingers clamped tight, the disregarded boy in me demanding reparation.

"It's done, Grant. Suck it up." Oliver tapped the folder. "In total, it's a little over thirty-six acres—contiguous parcels from the western edge of my holdings. I suspect we'll eventually add you to the deeds for my remaining properties, including the house, but I wanted to give this to you now. Even if we don't work out, I want you to have your own property, and... Aza's treehouse."

An ugly sob escaped me. I couldn't even shake my head. I wanted the treehouse too much.

"Think of this as Aza's gift to you, Grant. For the life I believe you could have helped him keep, and for the lives of the children you'll play with and heal." Oliver ran the backs of his hands down my cheeks to wipe at the wetness. "I have no doubt you'll care for your property very well."

I hugged the deeds to my chest and bent to press my forehead to Oliver's knees. *I have a clubhouse.*

I'd always wanted a clubhouse.

For the longest time, I hugged the deeds and blinked away tears, my mind a jumble of blankness, birdsong, and random thoughts. Oliver swept his hands over the back of my head and neck, ran fingers through my hair. I felt like I'd stumbled into one of his fantasies and gotten stuck there.

Clover's clear laugh rang out from the house, brought my attention to a point. Her parents had declined our invitation to the party.

I thought of Clover's sweet, round face. I thought of the long years of my lonely childhood. I thought of Oliver as a little boy abandoned in different ways by his parents, and I thought of our decision to tell the kids they would always have a home with us, if ever they needed it, for as long as we lived. Maybe even after we'd gone. The deeds turned my promises to them into a mission. In my mind's eye, I lifted an infinity symbol to my face like a pair of glasses and saw our rose-colored future, mine and Oliver's and the people we pulled in to journey with us around the loops. *Magic and miracles and love under all our reluctant skins.*

When I could, I gave my face a rub against Oliver's shorts and sat up. "Thank you seems too small a thing to say," I croaked.

Oliver winked. "Give it time. It'll sink in at some point."

"Are you *sure* you don't want to reconsider? Maybe wait a year or two to see what happens with us first?"

"Fuck, no. You need a home base, no matter what, and I have loads more property. What am I going to do with it all anyway?" Oliver stood and reached out a hand to pull me up.

We'll love it together.

I risked a one-handed grip on my precious deeds to take Oliver's hand, breathed through the dizzy moment, and stood, recalibrated to a new order.

As we strolled toward the house, a devious thought slithered through my mind.

Tit for tat.

Chapter 89

OLIVER

Two days after our party, Grant plucked me out of bed much too early, wrangled my legs into my pajama bottoms, and pulled my arms through the sleeves of one of his XXXL sweatshirts. He was back to his normal size, due to all the food I'd been stuffing into him.

"Mmm," I murmured, warm and cozy enough to fall back to sleep.

Grant didn't let me. He slid sneakers onto my feet and led me out the back door. My shoes soaked with dew after a few steps. Sunlight slanted over the yard from behind us. The novelty of being outside at a time of day I rarely saw made me wake up a little more. "Time is it?" I asked Grant.

"Seven."

I let my eyes half-close, hypnotized by the *swish swish* of grass as we walked. Grant led me past the toolshed, down the trail to the throne. When we got there, he sat and took my hands to pull me in and straddle his lap. I squeezed my thighs against his. Grant's wide shoulders bowed toward me in the confines of the curved space. *Face to face with The Wolf Emperor on his throne.*

Grant and I had pored over animal books and scoured the internet until he'd decided on *wolf.* It suited him, and made me feel even more like family. I thought of myself as Coyote-Fox Wolf. *First name, last name.*

Under my left thigh, I felt the tight cylinder of the June Zodiac scroll in Grant's pocket. I'd brought him the August Cancer scroll, assuming he was into astrology, but when I'd given it to him, he'd laughed and chucked it unopened into the kitchen trash with a terse, "Unnecessary." Then he'd mauled me until I came with a startled squeal all over the tile of the kitchen floor. He'd zipped his pants with a leer and ambled out the back door to do something in the tool-shed. I knew he'd gone to the toolshed because I was still sprawled on the cool floor on my stomach—panting, stunned, and sticky—when I heard the power saw start up.

I leaned into the shadow of the throne and licked my lips to tease Grant into getting busy.

"Oliver?" Grant said, caution in his voice.

I gave him a quick peck on the lips and pulled back. "Yes, Grant."

"Have you tried looking for her?"

"Oh." *Topic shift.* I put my sexy daydreams on hold and shook my head. "No. Not... yet. I checked Dad's papers, but there wasn't anything there about her, not after she left."

"Any digital messages from her that you maybe didn't delete?"

"Um... no. And she... stopped trying after a while."

"You haven't looked for her online?"

The frayed collar of Grant's old T-shirt caught my attention. *We need to go clothes shopping again.* I pressed the loose threads with my fingers and shook my head. "She might have moved from... Geneva by now. Or maybe she..." I hadn't done an online search because I didn't want to risk a funeral notice popping up. "She'd be fifty-six now. If she's, you know... alive."

The injustice of what my father and I had done to her brought up a sigh. I bowed my head onto Grant's shoulder. I *did* want to talk about her. I knew I needed to look for her, even if it was difficult. *Because* it was difficult. "Even if she's alive, even if I could find her, it's..." I shrugged against the weight of guilt. "Dad rejected her so completely. And then so did I. She probably doesn't even want—"

"You were wounded, Oliver. I understand why you locked yourself away after Aza and your dad died. It would have been hard to risk more hurt by recon-necting with her."

I turned my face into Grant's neck. "Don't you think I'm too... broken? I mean, even if I found her, I really don't think she'd want—"

"No. I don't think you're broken at all."

I shrugged again, not believing him.

"Hey." Grant gave me a little shake. "Listen up, buddy. When all the people you'd been closest to were gone, like *dead* gone, you did what you had to do to take care of yourself. Coyote-Fox bundled you up to keep you safe. You stayed on your property, secure in your bandages, put up the red flag, pared down to a few friends, and focused on your art—all so you wouldn't break any more than you already had."

I barely breathed, watched Grant's throat as he spoke in his deep voice.

"Those bandages kept you whole," he said.

I felt the truth of what he'd said, how I'd made a life for myself down inside the pain of the lives I'd lost. Grant's version of my life almost turned me into a hero.

"It didn't have to be me who unwrapped you," Grant said. "Any number of people or situations might have done it less annoyingly than I did. Eventually. Maybe even Freddie."

"You don't believe that."

"Nah. You're right. It had to be me."

I chuckled and slumped into Grant's chest, grateful for his warmth.

After a few minutes, I felt Grant move his hands behind my back. It took a moment to realize he was doing something on his phone.

"Let's do this," Grant muttered.

"Okay," I said, too content to need to know what he meant.

"I found her yesterday."

In the middle of an exhale, my lungs failed. "You... What?" My voice degraded to a whisper. "Oh, shit. Is she dead?"

"Madeleine Rossi, Professor of Banking and Finance at a fancy London university," Grant said, "plus about a hundred other titles below that one. I'm looking at her photo right now on the university website. She looks like you, Oliver. Gorgeous, pointy-faced, and foxy. Thick, red-gold hair. Burnished copper eyes."

My face did something it had never done before—pulled in on itself *tight* in a spasm of indecision.

Grant moved his arms against my back again, and I heard a sequence of tones, like he was—"*Stop.*" I jerked back, tried to break free. "I'm not ready."

He held me close. "Shh. Be still."

I went cold and inert, nose pressed to the back of the throne. *Flash freeze.*

The faint sound of a voice from the phone hummed into the shadowed air of the throne. A man's voice, but I couldn't make out his words.

"Good afternoon to you too," Grant said with a lilt. "I'm calling on behalf of Madeleine Rossi's son, Oliver. Is there any chance I could talk with her, or make a phone appointment to talk with her?"

My burst of breath ricocheted back to me off the wood. I stared at a carved mouse on a tree branch. I *waited*.

"Well, when are her official office hours? I can call back when she's—" Grant stopped as if he'd been interrupted. He put a hand up between us to try to push me back, but I held tight to his shoulders.

"It's *her*," Grant said against my ear. He unwrapped my arms from around his neck and tapped the speaker button on the phone.

"Please don't hang up," Grant said. "He's right here."

I couldn't make my arms move, but I lifted my eyes to the infinity symbol I'd carved to hover above Grant's head. *Time to peel.* When I met Grant's amused eyes, he put his mouth against my lips, smiled, and said, "Ollie, Ollie oxen free."

"Hello?" An exhale from the phone, that's all it was, but I recognized it.

I remembered I wasn't broken and found a breath. "It's... it's me."

"Oliver?"

"Hi, Mom."

Isn't that what creativity is—
the natural desire to transcend the
known and become greater than
the sum of our parts?

Deb Norton
Part Wild

Join for
A FREE STORY

Join Alice's reader list and get the free story *Executive Decision*.

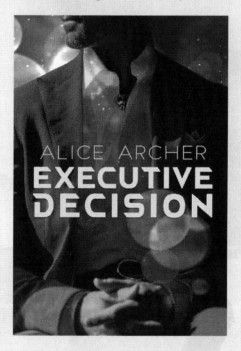

*Dar loved his career...
until he did his job too well.*

The stranger in the electric blue suit who compliments Dar's work is Pierre Catalan, owner of a multi-planet transportation empire—a polished, powerful man Dar considers way out of his league.

Alice Archer's reader list members get this free story, peeks behind the scenes, and unique items to accompany the books. Members are always the first to hear about Alice's new books and giveaways.

Get your free story at
ALICEARCHER.INFO/TIOEDPR

Please Leave
A REVIEW

Thank you for reading! Please consider leaving a review of *The Infinite Onion* on your preferred platform. Honest reviews increase visibility and bring stories to the attention of other readers who may enjoy them. Your thoughts are appreciated and welcome.

A Note
FROM ALICE

I took quite a few liberties when describing the area of Vashon Island, Washington, where Oliver lives. I added and subtracted roads, land features, and buildings to support the tale I wanted to tell.

The town of Vashon underwent a few small revisions in the story.

The route Oliver chose at the end of the story follows actual roads. Take a jaunt to Vashon in high summer and drive or bike it yourself. You'll be charmed.

ACKNOWLEDGMENTS

During the creation of this story, wonderful people and things aided and inspired me.

I offer deep bows of reverence to INFJ writing coach Lauren Sapala and life coach Maggie Huffman. They ripped off the roof, over and over, to reveal views of clear sky.

Amari Ice, Lukas Egetmeyer, and Heather Mae Russell provide bestie juju of the most nourishing variety. I'm thrilled every day by what and how we create together. Suanne Laqueur graces me with her humor, smarts, talent, and friendship (lucky me).

All hail to beta readers Lauren Sapala, Chris E. Saros, Kelly Jensen, C.C., A.B., and K.G. for thoughtful feedback and encouragement.

Christa Désir brought her prodigious editing skills to the final stage of the manuscript. She also brought in Manuela Velasco, who has prodigious editing skills of her own, as a sensitivity reader and additional editor. Christa founded the mentorship and services organization Tessera Editorial, whose members provide editing and diverse perspectives to publishers and authors.

Cover designer Tracy Kopsachilis and formatter Colleen Sheehan again lavished me with artistry and patience, a combination that keeps me going back for more.

Kelly Jensen, Jude Lucens, and Suanne Laqueur shored me up with direction and recommendations regarding independent publishing. I'm very grateful for the guidance and reassurance Mark Dawson and his team deliver in the superb Self-Publishing Formula 101 training course. Judith Utz of A Novel Take PR and her team handle publicity for me and my books with fortifying care, creativity, and professionalism.

Special thanks to *Sex, Lies and Creativity* author Julia Roberts and *Part Wild* author Deb Norton for granting permission to quote from their interesting books. And a tender call-out to Daniel Mathews, author of *Cascade-Olympic Natural History*, for writing about nature as if every sentence and word were the most important he'd ever written.

The glorious paintings of Ophelia by John Everett Millais and John William Waterhouse inspired me to the point of writing them into the story (when I wasn't busy staring at the paintings, lost in the scenes). I also offer nods of acknowledgment to Sharpie and Cadillac. This would have been a different story without their products.

Oliver would like to thank Les Charbonniers de l'enfer for their music, particularly their *Chansons a cappella* album.

My musical accompaniment for *The Infinite Onion* was the a cappella group Pentatonix, which I listened to exclusively as I wrote. They provided harmony and sustenance.

Also by
ALICE ARCHER

*If you woo, win, and walk away,
a second chance is going to cost you.*

Headstrong Ruben Harper has yet to meet an obstacle he can't convert to a speed bump. He's used to getting what he wants from girls, but when he develops a fascination for a man, his wooing skills require an upgrade. After months of persuasion, he scores a dinner date with Henry Normand that morphs into an intense weekend. The unexpected depth of their connection scares Ruben into fleeing.

Shy, cautious Henry, Ruben's former high school history teacher, suspects he needs a wake-up call, and Ruben appears to be his siren. When Ruben bolts,

Henry is left struggling to find closure. Inspired by his conversations with Ruben, Henry begins to write articles about the memories stored in everyday objects. The articles seduce Ruben, even as Henry's snowballing fame takes him out of town and farther out of reach.

Everyday History, a romance told with Alice Archer's unique style and lush prose, was named a Top Book of 2016 in the *HEA USA Today* column *Rainbow Trends*.

Find *Everyday History* order links at
ALICEARCHER.INFO/TIOEHPR

About
ALICE ARCHER

Alice Archer has questions. Lots of questions. Scheming to put fictional characters through the muck so they can get to a better place helps her heal and find answers. She shares her stories with the hope that others might find some healing too.

Archer's first novel, *Everyday History*, was named a Top Book of 2016 in the *HEA USA Today* column *Rainbow Trends*.

For decades, Alice has messed about with words professionally, as an editor and writing coach. She also travels a bunch. Her home base is Eugene, Oregon.

To find out more, visit
ALICEARCHER.COM

Made in the USA
Columbia, SC
01 April 2020